"It's too late, Hope. There's no going back."

Alexei continued heavily. "Can you honestly say that all your time with me has been...unpleasant?"

"No." Hope was surprised at how firmly she was able to speak. "But that doesn't alter the fact that it wasn't by my choice."

"You have the rest of your life to make a free choice—if such a thing exists," Alexei replied sardonically. "Only the very young think that anything in life is free. Take what you want, say the gods," he breathed softly. "Take it— and pay for it."

Hope shivered suddenly, despite the heat of the afternoon. What was the price she would have to pay for loving Alexei, or did she already know?

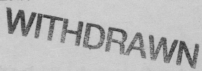

Books by Penny Jordan

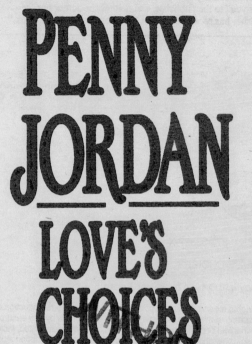

PENNY JORDAN

JORDAN

LOVE'S CHOICES

Harlequin Books

TORONTO • NEW YORK • LONDON
AMSTERDAM • PARIS • SYDNEY • HAMBURG
STOCKHOLM • ATHENS • TOKYO • MILAN
MADRID • WARSAW • BUDAPEST • AUCKLAND

ISBN 0-373-83327-X

LOVE'S CHOICES

Copyright © 1984 by Penny Jordan

CHAPTER ONE

IF ONLY something would happen, Hope wished rebelliously, dragging the toes of already grubby tennis shoes along the dusty earth. If Sister Maria knew of her thoughts she would give her a penance for their wickedness, but as she had undoubtedly already earned herself a scolding by skipping tennis, she might as well compound her sin.

Although hidden from her by the high hedge surrounding them, Hope could hear the sounds from the tennis courts; the almost soporific springy thud of the ball against the racket, which came with such regularity that she knew without going to see that Charlotte Howell was playing. Charlotte was by far and away the convent's best player—way, way out of her class, Hope thought dreamily, bending her head to study the ambling flight of a bee, tennis and her other sins forgotten as she watched the small creature entranced, the silky silver-blonde weight of her hair sliding from its clasp.

Her hair was just another grievance. She hated its long straightness, but whenever she pleaded to have it cut, Sister Maria told her that her father had refused his permission. The nuns knew a good deal more about her father's wishes than she did herself, Hope reflected a little bitterly. She hadn't even seen him in years. Sometimes the panicky feeling that he intended to leave her in the convent for the rest of her life, swept over her, almost drowning her. Already several of the girls in her class had left, swept away by parents and family, some going on to exclusive finishing schools, others disappearing into carefully arranged marriages.

Hope shivered a little, glancing apprehensively over her shoulder, but no one had come to disturb the calm peace of the cloister gardens—her secret retreat for those times when living constantly surrounded by other people swamped her spirit.

What must it be like to have a home and family of one's own, Hope wondered enviously. As a younger girl she had fantasised frequently on this subject, imagining that her father would arrive, a laughing, warm-hearted woman at his side, who would tell her that a daughter was the very thing she had always wanted. Only her father had never married again, and her own mother, who had died when Hope was two, was only a vague memory.

The intensity of the Spanish sun beating down out of the cobalt sky warned Hope that her peace would soon be at an end. The lesson would shortly come to a close and then she would have to join the others for lunch—a frugal but meticulously served meal in the large refectory, as the school dining room was called.

The convent wasn't simply a school in the ordinary sense—even Hope with her limited knowledge of the world knew that. The majority of the girls came from wealthy and titled families who had sent their daughters to St Cecilia's knowing that the nuns' strictly enforced regime and very stern moral attitudes would produce young women of a type the French described approvingly as *bien élevée*.

Even in her innocence Hope was aware that a far different world existed outside the convent walls from that she knew. Although she had no one special friend at school, she was a popular if somewhat aloof girl and knew from the chatter of the others—girls whose parents were not quite as elusive as her own father, and who

spent holidays at home and abroad—that the ways of the
world were not entirely as portrayed to them by the nuns.

Only at Easter—six short weeks ago—Leonor de Silva,
one of her closest acquaintances, a South American girl
of lush, dark beauty, had returned to the convent, her
eyes sparkling, her mouth soft and warm with an emotion which caused a curious pang to quiver through
Hope's own inexperienced flesh, as the girl described her
feelings for the young man she had met while at home.

'Of course, Rodrigo is not "suitable",' she had added
in an unhappy voice. 'My parents have told me this, and
I know that it is so—there has been a marriage arranged
for many years with my cousin...'

That was Leonor's fate, but what was her own? Hope
brooded. She had been eighteen two weeks ago—the
event totally ignored by her father—and she could not
remain at the convent for ever. At least the majority of
the other girls knew what their families had in mind for
them. She was unusual in that she was the only English
girl at the school. Most of the others were Spanish, or
Latin American, with the odd French and Italian pupil,
but she was the sole representative of her own country,
and sometimes that made her feel very alien, despite the
fact that the convent had been her home since she was
eight years old.

As the bell rang for lunch, Hope sighed and slowly
uncurled herself, stretching as she stood up, examining
her uniform for grass stains and dust. Cleanliness *was*
next to Godliness as far as the nuns were concerned, and
Hope, with her long swathe of pale blonde hair and her
coltish, almost gawky limbs, often earned the Sisters'
disapproval for her ungainliness.

Recently, though, her body had started to change—her
legs still seemed as awkwardly long as ever, but she was
no longer as terribly thin as she had been; in fact it made
her blush a little to realise how provocatively full her

breasts had become, her waist so narrow that her uniform, now straining across her breasts, hung like a sack on the rest of her body.

Bianca Vincella, an Italian girl who had befriended Hope when she was a shy young junior, had remarked only days before her scandalous expulsion that Hope was starting to look incredibly sexy, but then Bianca had always enjoyed teasing her. Besides, Hope was not so naïve that she didn't know that 'incredibly sexy' was the last thing the convent wanted its pupils to be.

As she made her way to the refectory, Hope shivered a little, her eyes, a soft dove-grey, pensive. Sex was something only to be discussed in hushed, excited whispers in the dormitories at night, and Hope, who had not spent so much as a few days outside the convent walls since she had entered them, had no knowledge of this activity bar that passed on by the Sisters during biology lessons, and what she had gathered from the other girls' whispered confidences.

From her reading she knew of the ecstasy two people could experience together, but how this ecstasy was to be equated with the dismal facts of procreation described by the nuns, and the fumbling intimacies of her friends, she did not know.

Today was a 'French' day, which meant that only French conversation was allowed, but Hope was fluent enough in this language not to mind. Indeed, she was fluent in most languages, and not simply the regulation French, Spanish and Italian taught at the school. German was another of her languages, and she had started to learn Russian. At the back of her mind was the idea that once she left the convent she would like to have a job—to train as a secretary perhaps, and use her languages in that capacity. Hope always did well at her lessons, but the convent set no conventional examinations for its pupils, so she had no real way of judging her ability.

Lunch was frugal as always, but the food was well prepared and attractively served. Any girl returning from her holidays spotty and plump soon found both spots and extra weight disappearing under the convent's strict regime.

'Summer holidays soon, what bliss,' the girl on Hope's right said dreamily. 'My parents have a villa on Capri and we're going there.' She was a kind girl, who had known Hope since they were both fourteen, and she bit her lip self-consciously, not wanting to hurt Hope's feelings. Many of the girls had invited Hope to share their holidays, but Hope's father had always refused permission.

'It is almost as though he wants to keep you locked up behind these walls for ever,' one friend had remarked rebelliously when yet another refusal had been received, and although she had smiled the comment aside, a tiny sliver of fear had lodged deep in Hope's heart.

But now she was eighteen and surely her own mistress? In law perhaps, she admitted inwardly, but although she was equipped to choose menus for fifty guests and upwards without blinking an eye; although she knew exactly what vintage wine to serve with what dish, and how to cope with staff, she had very little idea of how to take care of herself in a world which she sensed she might find alarming and even hostile after the cushioned protection of the convent.

Hope might be naïve, but she was no fool. The convent had an excellent library and Hope had made good use of it, but all her knowledge of the past could not compensate for her lack of knowledge about the present. Newspapers, other than those permitted by the Church, were not allowed. The convent possessed no television and the girls were not permitted to have radios. In the past this had not bothered Hope unduly, but lately... She frowned as she tried to analyse the cause for her recent discontent, the strange restlessness that pursued and possessed her.

'Hope? Hope, you are daydreaming again!' The exasperated tones of Sister Catherine's voice penetrated her thoughts and Hope flushed guiltily.

'The Reverend Mother wishes to see you,' Sister Catherine told her, watching not unkindly as the colour came and went in Hope's face. 'Run along child—you must not keep her waiting.'

Keep the Reverend Mother waiting? It was unthinkable! Hope didn't believe she had been summoned to the lady's room on more than half a dozen occasions during her school life and her heart started to thud as she wondered why she had been sent for now. It couldn't have been because her father had refused her permission to spend her holidays with yet another schoolfriend—this year she had known better than to ask.

The Reverend Mother had a suite of rooms separated from the main school building by a long cloistered walk, and normally Hope would have enjoyed admiring the enclosed garden the Reverend Mother's rooms looked out on, but today she felt inexplicably nervous, searching her conscience for any sin which might have merited this summons. Skipping tennis hardly seemed worthy of the Reverend Mother's intervention—and surely, omnipotent though she was, she had not read her charge's rebellious and resentful thoughts, Hope wondered nervously.

Outside the study door she knocked and waited to be told to enter. The Reverend Mother was only small, barely five foot two to Hope's five foot seven, but possessed of such a presence, such an aura of calm peacefulness, that it was Hope who felt dwarfed.

'Sit down, child,' the Reverend Mother commanded with a smile. She had been the head of the Convent

School for nearly thirty years, and she knew her charges better than they knew themselves.

Hope was her only English pupil and the Reverend Mother had been startled at first when the child's father had told her his wishes. Hope was to be kept cloistered in a way she herself would not even have recommended for a proposed novice. The Reverend Mother was no romantic—those who wished to forsake the world must first experience it. But while she might deplore what she secretly thought of as Sir Henry's lack of feeling for his only child, with one or two exceptions Hope had been brought up largely as he had wished.

In these enlightened times it was neither wise nor practical to keep young girls ignorant of sexual matters. The Reverend Mother had been of a generation where in Spain this ignorance had been the norm, but it was like trying to hold back the tide to keep mentally innocent, young girls whose families were as wealthy and powerful as those to whom her pupils belonged. Indeed, she herself had had to fight against considerable opposition to have sex education included in the curriculum, and what she knew of Sir Henry made her wonder rather cynically at the double-standards operated by the world. Which made her all the more relieved about today's turn of events.

Sir Henry had not been in touch with her before Hope's eighteenth birthday, as she had expected. Most of her pupils left at seventeen, and it grieved her that Hope, who was one of her brightest pupils, would never go on to university. Indeed, it was her own personal view that Hope would fare better in the life she suspected Sir Henry planned for her, if her intelligence was less, and she eyed her sympathetically. In a school comprised of mainly Latin races, Hope's silvery blondeness was unique. Her bone-structure differed from the other girls, too; like her body it was far more fragile and delicate, betraying her Anglo-Saxon ancestry.

'Don't look so worried, Hope. I've got some good news for you. You are to leave us and join your father, who apparently is in France at the moment. A friend of your father's, the Comte de Serivace, is calling to collect you tomorrow and he will escort you to your father.'

She busied herself kindly with some papers on her desk, well aware of the changing emotions and turmoils churning Hope's stomach and mind. If anything, she wished that Hope was less vulnerable, more equipped to deal with the vagaries of life outside the convent, but it was not up to her to question the dictates of her pupils' families. Sir Henry had been most adamant that Hope was not to be 'contaminated' by any contact with the outside world. A strange desire for a man who... Sternly the Reverend Mother suppressed the uncharitable thought, turning her attention to the girl standing before her.

'I know this has come as something of a shock, Hope. Indeed, we could have wished for your father to give us more notice, but you are eighteen and it is time that you took your place in the world. Remember, child, we will always be here if you should need us.' It was something she said to all the girls when they left, but some deep instinct told her that Hope was more likely to stand in need of the shelter offered by the convent than any other pupil.

Like someone in a dream Hope made her way back to her room. At sixteen, girls were promoted from sleeping in a dormitory to sharing a room with three other girls. The girls who shared with Hope had all left at Christmas and she had been alone ever since. Not that she minded. Solitude was something one came to appreciate, living in such a busy community. But it had happened at last—her father had sent for her!

In her room, Hope sank down on the narrow bed, staring unseeingly through the window down into the convent grounds. Strange how, after she had longed for something like this to happen so much, she should feel so curiously empty; frightened almost. Although never of a particularly religious turn of mind, Hope found herself praying silently, suddenly terrified of the world she would find outside the convent.

After dinner Sister Teresa sent her to pack her things. Her father had sent her an expensive case, no doubt realising that the one she had taken with her to the convent ten years previously was rather the worse for wear. It was a pity he had not realised the same thing about her clothes, Hope thought unhappily. Apart from her uniform, she had nothing!

After dinner the girls were allowed a free period when they could chat, but Hope found herself strangely reluctant to announce her departure. She was intelligent enough to know how much some of the other girls pitied her, and she had no wish to let them know that after ten years her father was not coming to collect her himself, but had sent someone else.

Daddy was probably too busy, she told herself loyally.

Her father had many business interests, but the most important was his small share in Montrachet's, the worldwide merchant bankers, whose headquarters were in Paris. Her father had often written to her about the Montrachet family; their wealth and their pride, and once again she shivered, dreading facing the outside world. How contrary she was. Only this morning she had been longing to escape the convent and now...now she was hanging back nervously, confused and alarmed by her own reactions.

IT WASN'T UNTIL after breakfast that the Reverend Mother sent for Hope. Breakfast was eaten early at the convent, although this morning Hope hadn't been able to touch hers, and she had had nothing to do for several hours afterwards, other than walk in the gardens, trying to suppress her nervousness. No doubt the Comte, who would probably be staying in Seville, the nearest town to the convent, would have breakfast at leisure, perhaps in his room, unaware and uncaring of her growing tension. For some reason she didn't like the Comte, which was surely ridiculous as she hadn't met him. Deep down inside her Hope acknowledged that her resentment probably sprang from the fact that she would have preferred her father to come for her, and that she was transferring her resentment, because he had not, from her father to the Comte—but knowing this still did not change her feelings.

She was walking slowly through the gardens for the third time when Sister Teresa came hurrying towards her, breathless and hot, her brown eyes sparkling with excitement.

'Hope, *mon petit*…the Reverend Mother wishes to see you.' Sister Teresa was the youngest and friendliest of the Sisters. She taught French and often lapsed into this language, forgetting the rules. Today, by rights, was Italian day, but Hope answered her in French automatically, aware that her cheeks were suddenly burning with a colour that had nothing to do with the heat of the sun, as she followed Sister Teresa back to the cloisters.

As before, she paused and knocked outside the Reverend Mother's door, catching the soft murmur of the Reverend Mother's voice and the deeper, masculine tones of her companion. When she entered the room the Reverend Mother smiled reassuringly at her. 'Ah, Hope, my child, let me introduce you to Monsieur le Comte, who has come on behalf of your Papa.'

Stubbornly, Hope refused to look in the direction of the Comte until the last moment, her eyes widening in

stunned astonishment when she finally did so. This man
was not at all as she had imagined a friend of her father's to be. For one thing, he was so much younger.
Thirty, or thirty-five at the most; considerably older than
her, but far, far younger than her father, and for another...

Feeling like someone who has suddenly been deprived
of breath, Hope forced herself to glance a second time
into the face of the man watching her. Was it because she
was used to seeing only softer female features that the
harsh masculinity of high, sharply defined cheekbones
and a dark, taut jaw had such an impact on her?

Hope's eyes returned almost dazedly to the angles and
planes of a face so totally male that she felt the shock
waves of seeing it reverberating strongly through her.
Green eyes, dangerous, predatory eyes, half concealed by
thick black lashes, studied her coolly for several achingly long seconds, before subjecting her to an assess-
ingly keen stare, holding her gaze deliberately until Hope
felt she was drowning in emerald seas.

Tearing her gaze from the Comte's eyes, Hope made
an effort to study him as objectively as he had done her,
her cheeks still hot with colour from the knowledge that
he had deliberately and quite cynically stripped her of
every article of clothing when he studied her—and in the
Reverend Mother's presence! She could not match his
savoir-faire, but she did make a valiant attempt to study
the sharply defined bone-structure of his face, wondering why it should be vaguely familiar and yet so different from what she had imagined. His mouth curled
sardonically as though he was aware of her mental rejection of him, this thick, black hair brushing the collar of
his shirt as he lazily flicked back his cuff to study a pale
gold watch.

Taking the hint, the Reverend Mother came forward,
kissing Hope gently on each cheek. 'Remember, my dear,

we are always here if you want us.' She spoke in Italian and Hope responded in the same language, startled when the tall, dark man at her side drawled cynically in perfect Italian:

'We must hope that life treats her too kindly for her to need a refuge, Reverend Mother,' and then he was opening the door, one dark, long-fingered hand on Hope's shoulder, her fragile bones feeling as though they were burning beneath his touch as he pushed her gently through the open door.

Outside in the front courtyard of the convent, a long, squat car glinted darkly in the sunlight, a fitting means of transport for this dark, almost menacing man, Hope thought, shivering a little as she recognised instinctively the power and threat of two such masculine objects.

Her case was placed in the boot, and the passenger door opened for her, dark eyebrows rising in a sardonic appraisal which hinted that he was not entirely surprised as he drawled, 'Surely you have something else to wear? Or does the good Reverend Mother seek to remind me of what you are?'

Not entirely understanding the reason for his comment, Hope told him coolly that she had no other clothes.

'None? Your father is not a poor man.'

'My father... My father is not a wasteful man,' she managed primly at last, trying not to notice the way in which the fine fabric of his dark pants stretched over his thighs as he slid into the driving seat, and her hands folded tensely in her lap.

'You think it wasteful, to spend money on clothes? But you cannot spend the rest of your life in garments which, rather than reinforcing your schoolgirl status, draw attention to the fact that it is past time for you to change them for something a little more... womanly.' His eyes rested meaningfully on the taut fabric stretching across her breasts and Hope blushed fiery red, hating the way he was looking at her, and yet curiously excited in some strange way.

'You must fasten your seat-belt,' the Comte told her coolly. 'Like this.' He reached across her, the dark fabric of his suited arm brushing the fullness on which his eyes had so recently rested. Something like an electric current shot through Hope making her stiffen automatically, shrinking into her seat as he secured the belt around her, apparently unaware of the effect of their momentary physical contact.

Having fastened his own belt, he started the car, the powerful roar of the engine drowning out the hurried thud of Hope's heartbeat as she tried not to give in to the desolation gripping her as the car swept along the drive and out of the convent gates.

'I cannot drive you all the way to France wearing those garments,' the Comte told her when they had gone several miles. 'I have no wish to be arrested for attempting to kidnap a child.'

'I expect my father has forgotten that I have grown,' Hope offered unhappily, feeling that some explanation was needed. 'I haven't required any other clothes as . . .'

'As your father has never permitted you to leave the convent,' her companion finished for her. 'Yes, I am aware of that.' His attention momentarily diverted from the road to her, and Hope felt herself flushing again under his thoughtful scrutiny. 'However, you have left it now, and your father's past deficiencies will soon be remedied.'

Hope looked into the man's face as he spoke, surprised to see the grim coldness in his eyes, tiny feathers of alarm curling along her spine, and a tension she couldn't understand infiltrating the atmosphere in the car until every muscle in her body was taut in response to it.

After that her companion didn't speak, and although there was a good deal she wanted to ask him, his silence prevented her from speaking, instinct telling her that he had no wish to engage in conversation, and she made use of the silence to study him covertly; the arrogant aquiline profile, the power of the lean fingers holding the steering wheel, sinewy and brown.

Would his skin be that dark mahogany all over? The intimacy of her thoughts shocked Hope into further flushes, hastily averting her eyes from the muscles of his thighs as the Comte changed gear and the fabric pulled tautly, reminding her of drawings she had seen, books she had studied in the convent library, knowing suddenly and overwhelmingly that the old masters had not, as she had childishly imagined, overemphasised the masculine frame, and that this man seated at her side could easily have modelled for them. And yet there was an elusive, alien look about him that suggested another culture, not entirely Latin—something about his face that tormented her memory.

Within half an hour they were in Seville. The city was not entirely unfamiliar to Hope as she had visited it with the school on several occasions, but the narrow street of fashionable shops where the Comte parked the car was somewhere she had not seen before. Her fingers fumbled with the seat-belt as she tried to release it, and this time when the Comte leaned impatiently across she withdrew so that he would not touch her, flinching beneath the sardonic mockery in his eyes as he released the belt and then turned to look at her, green eyes on a level with grey as he drawled softly, 'So, even innocence has some awareness. Was it from the good nuns that you learned to shrink from anyone male, *mon petit,* or is it an instinct that goes far beyond any teaching?'

'I...' Torn between embarrassment and the angry feeling that he should not be talking to her in this fash-

ion, mocking her naïvety with one breath and yet somehow, she sensed, deliberately making her aware of his
maleness all the same. Hope reached for the door, shaky
with relief when it opened and the Comte moved back to
his own seat.

Several curious glances came their way as the Comte
guided Hope along the pavement, and when she caught
sight of herself in a shop window, she shrank from the
image she presented in her too-tight uniform, her hair
dragged back off her face.

The shop he took her to was small and yet somehow
overpowering, so imbued with an atmosphere of money
and elegance that Hope felt ill at ease.

The woman who emerged to serve them surveyed Hope
with raised eyebrows, her demeanour only altering when
she saw the Comte, changing from haughty disdain to
almost fawning complaisance within the space of a few
seconds.

The Comte spoke to her in Spanish, as flawless as his
Italian, but when Hope heard the word for trousseau she
frowned and opened her mouth, only to be silenced by
the Comte who turned to her and said in French, 'I am
only fulfilling your father's wishes, so please oblige me
by keeping silent.'

Having given the saleswoman his instructions, the
Comte turned to Hope and told her that he had business
of his own to transact and that he would return for her in
two hours. 'Your hair needs attention,' he added, studying it. 'I shall ask *Madame* if she can recommend a good
stylist.'

'I have wanted to have it cut for ages,' Hope offered,
'but...'

'Cut! *Mon Dieu!* Are you mad! To do so would be
sacrilege,' he told her unequivocally, adding softly, 'Has
no one told you, you little innocent, that on your wedding night your husband will want to see you covered in

nothing other than this silver veil?' He flicked her hair as he spoke, apparently unconcerned by the hot colour beating up under her pale skin.

Her wedding night! Hope was still turning the words over in her mind when he left the shop. Strangely enough she had not thought much about marriage. She would like to have children and them she could visualise quite easily, plump and dark—but a husband? She shivered suddenly. Why had her father sent this disturbing stranger to collect her? Why hadn't he come himself?

Two hours later she was staring round-eyed at the pile of garments *Madame* had put on one side; separates in cool, soft silk in misty pastel lilacs and greys to tone with her eyes; dresses; underwear in the finest crêpe de Chine, embroidered in silver and grey with butterflies, so fine and sheer that Hope blushed to see herself in it, imagining the disapproval of the nuns.

Madame's grimace over her plain, serviceable underwear and shabby uniform had forstalled Hope's intentions of dressing again in her own clothes. Something inside her shrank from wearing clothes provided by anyone other than her father—especially another man—but common sense told her that eventually Sir Henry would undoubtedly meet the bill, and so Hope allowed herself to be persuaded into the whispers of silk, so smooth against her skin, so shockingly and sensuously clinging to her body, her breasts curving softly above the brevity of a bra so delicate it seemed more seductive than nothing at all.

Hope was tempted to protest against the brief suspender belt and silk stockings proffered calmly by *Madame,* but the thought of having her recalcitrance reported and no doubt mocked by the man who her father seemed to have appointed as her temporary guardian, caused the protests to die unspoken.

Without consulting her, once the girl had donned the underwear, *Madame* handed Hope a three-piece in pale grey silk with undertones of lilac, the skirt hem and jacket reveres in contrasting off white. A brief camisole top buttoned up the back with a multitude of small buttons, and the straight skirt emphasised Hope's narrow hips and long, slender legs. Carefully putting on the jacket, she surveyed herself in the mirror, stunned by the reflection staring wide-eyed back at her.

Of the Hope she knew, all she recognised was the small triangular face. Gone were the awkward coltish limbs, the girl's body; the reflection staring back at her showed her a tall slim creature, far too elegant to bear any relation to the person she knew herself to be, her eyes a smoky lilac, reflecting the undertones of the grey silk.

Madame, however, was not as awed by the transformation as Hope herself. 'And now,' she said ominously, 'the hair and the face. There is a salon several doors down. My assistant will take you there. I shall tell her to wait for you and return with you when Rafael has finished!'

Rafael and his staff were every bit as alarming as Hope had dreaded, although a little to her surprise he echoed the Comte's decree that to cut her hair would be a crime.

'It is untidy at the ends, *si,*' he agreed, examining it closely, 'but wait until they are trimmed and your hair has been conditioned. Tying it back as you do is not good for the texture,' he disapproved, frowning over the thick barrette Hope used to secure her hair out of the way, 'and your skin! Do you never use moisturiser?' he demanded with further disapproval.

Hope felt disinclined to tell him that the nuns favoured soap and water and that the girls were not allowed to use make-up at the convent, although many of the girls did experiment in secret with cosmetics purchased when they were at home on holiday.

Her hair was shampooed and conditioned and then trimmed before Rafael pronounced himself satisfied and handed Hope over to the ministrations of a pretty dark-haired girl, her still-wet hair wrapped in a towel.

The girl introduced herself as Ana, and although Hope sensed her curiosity when her client admitted to having no knowledge at all about applying cosmetics, she did not ask any questions, simply showing Hope patiently and carefully how she could make the best of her features, telling her that she was lucky in her bone-structure which would outlive mere youthful prettiness, and adding that Hope's eyes were especially beautiful.

Having feared from the length of time Ana took over cleansing and then painting her skin, that she would end up looking like a china doll, Hope was astonished when Ana finally swung her round in her chair to face the mirror. A subtle rose glow shone against her cheekbones, highlighting their shape, her eyes mysteriously darker and larger than she remembered, her mouth tremulous and curving warmly pink against the paleness of her skin.

While Hope came to terms with her new image, Ana wrote out a chart showing what colours and cosmetics she had used, which she passed to Hope along with an ornate box filled with cosmetics, all of which Ana assured her she would need to use.

Then it was back to Rafael for her hair to be blown dry, Hope openly astonished by the shining waves he coaxed from what she had always been convinced was perfectly straight hair, now subtly shaped to frame her face and cascade over her shoulders.

Ten minutes later, standing in *Madame*'s shop, her new clothes stored in the shiny black boxes with gold lettering on them, Hope felt her nervousness increase, her fingers itching to touch the silken fineness of her hair. But the habits instilled at the convent went too deep to permit her to fidget or in any way betray her inner anxiety.

Outwardly she looked so calm and composed that *Madame*, who had been apt to dismiss her as a naïve, rather stupid child, revised her opinion. Telling herself that she recognised a well-brought-up young girl when she saw one, she unbent enough to assure Hope that the Comte would not keep her waiting very long.

Almost before she had finished speaking the door opened and the Comte paused, framed there, nowhere near as out of place in the essentially female surroundings as Hope would have imagined. No doubt he was perfectly accustomed to buying his women-friends clothes, Hope thought distastefully. Although in many ways naïve, she was by no means unaware of the relationships entered into by men like the Comte; rich worldly men who could afford to pay for their pleasure and then discard their playthings when they grew bored, with scant regard for any pain they might cause.

The Reverend Mother would have been shocked had she known of the dislike for the Comte which had already taken deep root in her heart, Hope acknowledged, unaware of the picture she made as she waited, unmoving and hesitant, a pale silver girl whose fragility made the man watching her feel that she might break between his hands if he attempted to touch her.

She would serve his purpose even better than he supposed. Sir Henry was a very clever man. With such tempting bait, no wonder he was so sure of persuading Alain Montrachet to take it. An innocent bride for the white hope of the house of Montrachet; a bride to bear the sons who would one day inherit the Montrachet name; a child untouched by man or the corruption of what he had made of his world—a beautiful innocent.

He looked at her, knowing all that he planned for her, untouched by compassion or second thoughts, and Hope, watching him, suddenly realised where she had seen such a face before; an illustration of the young men of Tsar

Alexander's Imperial Guard at the time of the Napo-
leonic Wars. Among them had been men with just such
bone-structures, proudly arrogant, haughtily disdain-
ful, dangerously wild for all their veneer of sophistication.

'Well, Hope, if you're ready?' His tone was so calm
and mundane that Hope thought for a moment that
someone else spoke, but no, the Comte was holding the
door open politely for her, and outside the snarling Ferrari awaited them, while *Madame* smiled obsequiously as
they made their goodbyes.

On the pavement, Hope hesitated. The Comte opened
the car door for her, letting her get settled as he put the
boxes in the boot, and then went round to his own door.
When he was inside, and she had safely managed to secure her seat-belt, she blurted out impulsively, 'Do
you . . . do you have Russian blood in you, Comte?'

For a moment she thought he wasn't going to reply.
Her comment was impolite. The nuns had taught her
never to ask personal questions, but somehow the question asked itself.

'Some,' he agreed, watching her, making her wonder
what thoughts went on behind those green eyes. 'Why do
you ask?'

Haltingly, she told him about the illustrations.
'So . . . you are learning Russian? You obviously have a
talent for languages. My mother was Russian,' he explained. 'Her parents left Russia during the Revolution.
Fortunately they were among the lucky ones. My grandfather had investments in Paris and they were able to live
comfortably, if not in the same style they had known in
St Petersburg; and certainly well enough for my mother
to be considered a more than adequate match for my father, and the Serivace title.

'The Serivace name is an old one,' he further explained when he saw that she was frowning. 'It goes back

to before the French Revolution, but then I suppose the good sisters have taught you that pride is a sin, as indeed is vanity,' he added half mockingly, making Hope wonder if he had guessed how bemused she was by her altered appearance and was simply changing the subject.

'You would be well advised to try and get some sleep, *mon petit,*' he added. 'We have a long drive ahead of us. I do not want to stop until we reach Serivace.'

'Serivace?'

'My estate.' He glanced at her, and then smiled. 'It is very beautiful. You will like it.' But he made no mention of her father and when she could expect to be reunited with him, and all at once Hope sensed that to ask this man any questions he did not want to answer would be a foolish and pointless exercise.

'All in good time, *mon petit,*' she heard him murmur as she obediently tried to relax and closed her eyes, giving the disconcerting impression that he had seen into her mind and read the thoughts imprinted there as clearly as though her forehead were a sheet of glass.

CHAPTER TWO

HOPE WOKE several hours later, stiff and uncomfortable, despite the fact that the Comte had reclined her seat for her. He seemed to know by some sixth sense that she was awake and she felt the decrease in speed of the powerful car as he turned to her. 'Do you feel better for your sleep?'

Hope managed a smile. In point of fact she felt terrible—her head ached and she felt vaguely nauseous, her body stiff from lying too long in the same position.

'You are not well?' The Comte frowned as he looked into her pale face. 'What is it?'

'A headache,' Hope told him, 'but it is nothing. It will soon go.'

'It's probably the result of too much excitement,' the Comte said wryly. 'I forget that your convent life has not prepared you for the hurly-burly of real life.' He glanced at his watch. 'I think we had better find somewhere to stay tonight and then continue our journey tomorrow. When I said we would drive straight to Serivace I had forgotten that you are not as used to travelling as I am myself.'

Hope wanted to protest. She didn't want to spend any more time with the Comte then she needed to.

'I shall not eat you, *mon petit*,' she heard the Comte drawl mockingly above her. 'The good Sisters should have taught you that it is not always wise to look at a man the way you are looking at me. Your eyes have all the dread and fear of the persecuted for the persecutor, and who would blame me, if, when I look into them, I am tempted to make your fears reality.' He saw her flinch and smiled. 'You shrink from shadows, Hope. Do you really fear me so much?'

His mockery brought a flash of rebellion to Hope's eyes. She was not so foolish that she didn't know when she was being deliberately baited. The nuns had taught their pupils from an early age to give respect and obedience to their elders, and the fact that the Comte was her father's friend, coupled with his manner towards her, had made Hope defer to him. Now she faced him with stormy eyes, her slender body braced against retaliation as she said defiantly, 'I am not afraid of you, Monsieur le Comte.'

'Just as cautious as a gazelle penned up with a leopard,' the Comte added wryly. 'Tell me, how long is it since you last saw your father?'

Not sure what had prompted the change of conversation, but nonetheless grateful for it, Hope told him.

'Two years?' His eyebrows drew together, darkly.

'My father has many business interests, it is not always possible for him to visit me, and . . . and during the holidays there is not always someone to accompany me . . .'

'But now you are no longer a schoolgirl, but a young woman. Have you any plans for your future?' He was talking to her now more in the manner she would expect a man of his years and sophistication to address her, and Hope did her best to respond, explaining that the training at the convent did not really equip its pupils for careers.

'Other than the time-honoured one of marriage,' the Comte agreed dryly. 'Is that what you want, *mon petit*? To go from the schoolroom to the bedroom?' He saw that he had shocked her, watching the colour come and go in her face.

'Come,' he murmured, glancing sardonically at her. 'You are not going to tell me that the nuns kept you in complete ignorance of the "facts of life"? There must have been holidays, encounters with attractive young men who were only too willing to add practical knowledge to theory.'

'No!' Hope's shocked denial silenced him for several seconds, while she sat bolt upright in her seat, her body trembling with rejection of his suggestion, her mind unable to analyse why it should have provoked such a strong response. After all, many of her fellow pupils had indulged in just the sort of experimentation the Comte had so mockingly described, and although she had never been included in the excited midnight discussions about them, she was not so naïve that she didn't know that there was far more to human relationships than the cold, dry facts presented to them during their lectures.

'No?' The Comte pulled off the main road, bringing the car to a halt beside a field. They were in the middle of the country and Hope noticed absently that the crop was growing, green-gold fields stretching into the distance, an ancient stone castle perched precariously among the foothills which marked the beginning of the *sierras*.

Her profile averted from her companion, she tensed when his fingers cupped her jaw, forcing her to face his enigmatic green gaze.

'No?' he repeated queryingly. 'Not even so much as a stolen kiss, *ma jolie?*'

Sensing the mockery behind the question, Hope blushed hotly, hating the way he was exposing her life, her inadequacies, because hadn't she secretly wondered what it would be like to share the giggled confidences of the others? Hadn't she secretly lain awake in her bed wondering why she felt none of their desire?

'There is no one to steal kisses from behind the walls of the convent,' she retorted bravely at last, 'except for Father Ignacio who comes to hear our confessions. My father wouldn't let me spend my holidays with my friends and...' She broke off, hating herself for confiding so much to him. Now, doubtless, he would tell her father what she had said and she burned with embarrassment and humiliation. How gauche and disloyal her father would think her.

'So!' His gaze rested disturbingly on her lips, and Hope could almost feel the soft flesh burn from the contact. She longed for him to look away, but his fingers still cupped her jaw, curling against her skin, his thumb gently stroking along the bone, quivers of sensation spreading from the point where his flesh touched hers. Her mouth had gone dry, her lips parting on a small sound of protest, turning to a shocked gasp when the Comte rubbed his thumb over the fullness of her bottom lip, his free hand grasping her wrists as though he sensed her intention to thrust him away. His dark head descended, and the brush of his mouth against hers caused Hope to tense and stiffen, confused by her conflicting emotions. On the one hand was shock, outrage that he should trespass on his friendship with her father, on the other was this curious, languorous sensation that the brush of his lips against hers evoked, making her want to slide her hands over his dark-suited shoulders, explore the shape and feel of him, while his mouth continued to...

With a horrified cry, Hope tore herself out of his grasp, her eyes huge and deeply violet in her small face, her fingers fluttering betrayingly to touch the quivering softness of her lips. Was that compassion she read in the darkness of his eyes? Or was it scorn for her lack of expertise, her inexperience?

'Well, *mon petit?* Is your curiosity now satisfied? Do you no longer envy your schoolfriends their little experiments?'

Hope sat immobile with despair and hatred in her heart. Not even her most secret thoughts were safe from this man. Had he known also that she had looked at his mouth and wondered what it would be like to have it touch her own? She had quenched the thought almost at birth, shocked and disturbed by it, but somehow he had known.

'What's the matter? Did the good Sisters tell you that such intimacies should only be shared with your husband, that no one should touch those soft lips but him?'

'I am not quite a fool, *monsieur,*' Hope managed stiffly. 'I am well aware that it amused you to... to torment me.'

She heard him laugh soundlessly as he re-started the car, and turned back to the main road. Was he married, she wondered curiously. Did he have a family of his own?

'There is a small town a few miles away, where we can spend the night,' she was informed as the Ferrari ate up the miles. 'The hotel was once the home of a local family, but it has now been taken over by the government and opened as an exclusive *hostería.*'

Several miles on they came to the town. The road had started to climb into the foothills, and to Hope's surprise, their destination turned out to be the castle she had noticed before.

'A fitting setting for you, Hope,' the Comte murmured lazily as he stopped the car. 'We shall have to ask them if they can find a turret room for you. You have all the inviolate innocence of a fairy princess.'

She wasn't given a turret room, but the room she was given was far more luxurious than anything she was used to, Hope admitted, smoothing the heavy bedspread over the carved four-poster which dominated the room. Her room had an adjoining bathroom, and she secured her hair on top of her head, almost filling the bath with hot water, indulging in the pleasure of soaking her aching limbs in the scented water. Outside, dusk had fallen. The Comte had suggested that she should eat in her room, and she wasn't disposed to argue with him. She didn't feel hungry, and all she wanted to do was to sleep. Tomorrow, she hoped, she would see her father. Why didn't she feel more excited at the thought? Perhaps her senses had been blunted by too much excitement, after being starved of it, Hope thought wryly, stepping out of the bath and drying herself, studying her reflection wonderingly in the full-length mirror, her eyes drawn to the pointed thrust of her breasts, taut and firm, the skin silky-smooth. A strange sensation curled through the pit of her stomach, her eyes darkening as she remembered how the Comte had kissed her. She must not think about it! Shivering with reaction, Hope looked for her robe, remembering that she had left it in her room.

When she opened her bedroom door she realised someone had been in her room. The lamps had been switched on, her nightdress lay across the bed, and a small enclosed electric trolley was pulled up against a small table. Her supper, no doubt. She walked towards the bed, stiffening with shock as something moved in the shadows beyond the lamps, and the Comte's lean figure detached itself from the darkness.

Every instinct screamed for her to cover her nakedness from him, but strangely she could not move, her muscles locked in paralysing terror as she stared up at him as he studied her body with a clinical detachment that broke through her fear, freeing her to reach shakily for her robe, wishing it was her old school one and not this flimsy fine silk which merely clothed her body rather than concealed it.

'I'm sorry, Hope, I didn't realise you hadn't heard me.'
It was the first time he had apologised to her, and Hope
sensed that it was genuinely meant. 'I did knock,' he
continued, 'but you obviously didn't hear me. They have
brought our dinner—come and sit down.'

For the first time Hope noticed that he, too, had
changed. His darkly formal suit had given way to a thin
silk shirt that made her disturbingly aware of the male
body beneath it, with dark, thigh-hugging pants moulding his legs.

When they were both seated, the Comte indicated the
trolley and smiled, asking Hope if she would like to serve
them or if she would prefer him to do it.

This, at least, was an area in which she was proficient,
Hope thought, approaching the trolley. All the girls at the
convent were taught how to be perfect hostesses, and
even with the Comte's eyes on her, she managed to serve
their soup dexterously and properly.

'It seems to me that your convent teaches the more old-
fashioned virtues; the womanly arts rather than commercial ones,' the Comte murmured when Hope removed the soup bowls and served the main course, a rich
chicken paella.

'Many of the pupils come from the Latin American
countries,' Hope told him. 'Their parents normally arrange their marriages for them, and as they are invari-
ably wealthy and socially prominent, it is important that
they are able to conduct themselves properly.'

'But you are the exception to the rule?' the Comte
prodded. 'No marriage has been arranged for you?'

Hope's revolted expression gave her away. 'So what are
your plans for your life? Do you expect to act as your
father's hostess?'

Hope did have some hazy idea that this was what might
happen to her. Her own feeling was that, having placed
her in the convent, her father had turned his mind to

other matters. As an English girl, the thought of an arranged marriage was totally abhorrent to her, and she had often wished rebelliously that her father had allowed her to have a more normal upbringing. Perhaps now she would be able to persuade him to let her go to college, to gain some commercial skills.

'What do you do, Comte?' Hope questioned politely, remembering the Sisters' lectures on conversation. A smile tugged at the corners of his mouth and Hope hated him for laughing at her.

'That is very good, *mon petit,*' he mocked, watching her fingers tighten on her knife and fork. 'But it is customary to show a little more enthusiasm. Your stilted enquiry reminds me of a child reciting its lessons. However, I shall answer you, since conversation, like any other skill, only comes with practice.'

For some reason his words made Hope remember how he had kissed her. Was that another field in which he found her lamentably lacking? What did it matter if he did? she asked herself crossly.

'As I have already told you, my mother was Russian. My father's family owned vineyards near Beaune. Some of the wines we produce are what is known as Premier Cru.' He saw Hope's expression and smiled. 'Ah, so the Sisters have taught you something about the world, *mon petit?*'

'I know of the great vintages, the classifications for wine.'

'So! You will understand then when I tell you that Serivace wines are Premier Cru wines. This was so in my grandfather's time, as it is during mine. I have other estates, near Nice, which I visit during the summer; during the winter I stay in Paris where I have an apartment. I am considered a moderately wealthy man, not perhaps wealthy enough to merit one of the docile doves of your convent as a bride, *mon petit,* but certainly no pauper.'

'You aren't married, then?'

When he shook his head, Hope asked hesitantly, 'Do you have any family?'

Was it her imagination or did he pause fractionally before answering? Whatever the case, there was certainly no trace of hesitation in his voice when he responded firmly, 'None. One day I shall marry—I owe it to my name to ensure that there will be someone to follow me, but that day has not arrived yet.

'It is a tradition in our family that the men do not marry early. My father was forty when he married my mother.' Just for a moment, with the lamplight casting shadows along the high cheekbones, he looked sinister and withdrawn, more Russian than French, and Hope's heart beat fiercely as she acknowledged that no matter how sophisticated he appeared, somewhere inside that sleekly suave covering was hidden all the ruthless passion of his Russian ancestry. 'What is the matter, *ma jolie?*'

Hope hadn't realised that he was watching her, studying the pensive thoughtfulness of her eyes and the vulnerability of her mouth.

'Nothing—I was just wondering about my father,' she told him huskily. 'It is so long since I have seen him.'

'And you fear that you will meet as strangers?' he asked perceptively. 'Do not. I am sure you are all that your papa hopes you will be—and more,' he added almost beneath his breath, 'much, much more,' leaving Hope to puzzle over what he had said as she picked at her vanilla dessert and watched him eat cheese and biscuits, fascinated against her will by the lean masculine fingers; the taut planes of his shadowed face.

'It is time you were in bed,' he announced eventually. 'You are falling asleep in your seat. Such a baby still— would you like me to carry you to bed and kiss you goodnight?' He caught the tiny fluttering movement of

rejection she made and laughed softly. 'How very con-
fusing it is, isn't it, little one? The good Sisters tell you
one thing and your body tells you another.' He stood up
and came round to stand beside her, bending to take her
in his arms as though she weighed no more than a child,
carrying her to her bed, her face pressed into the curve of
his shoulder, her senses absorbing the scent and feel of
him as he pulled back the covers and placed her carefully on the bed. He folded the covers back over her, the
lean fingers of one hand resting briefly on the pale flesh
of her shoulder before they were withdrawn and he was
gone.

After the door had closed behind him, Hope didn't
know whether it was relief or disappointment that
touched her body so achingly. But surely it must be relief? She couldn't have wanted him to kiss her again!

'IF YOU ARE now ready, I suggest we continue our journey.' They had breakfasted on soft, warm rolls and fresh
apricot jam, and Hope felt as though she could never eat
another thing. Today she was wearing a pleated skirt with
a toning blouson top in soft green silk. Her hair had retained its new style and she had found it easier to apply
her new make-up than she had anticipated, any nervous
trembling of her fingers surely more due to the thought
of coming face to face with the Comte again rather than
anything else.

In the event she need not have worried, the half-
frightening, taunting man she remembered from the
evening had been banished and in his place was a smiling, almost avuncular man she couldn't recognise at all.

They drove all through the morning, the tapes the
Comte inserted into the machine on the dashboard ob-
viating the need for any conversation, allowing Hope to
concentrate on the scenery, lulled by the music.

At lunchtime the Comte pulled off the main road and drove into a small, French market town, parking the car on the forecourt of what he told her had once been a famous coaching inn.

The building was old, wreathed in wisteria, heavy racemes of violet-purple flowers hanging from its branches. The owner led them to their table himself, hovering solicitously to proffer advice on the menu. At first Hope supposed this was because the Comte was known to him, but when he had disappeared to greet some other diners, the Comte explained to her that lunch was often the main meal of the day in French households and that this particular *auberge* had a particularly good reputation.

'Since we are travelling again this afternoon and cannot drowse off the effects of a heavy meal, I suggest we confine ourselves to three courses,' he added with a humorous smile. 'Would you like me to choose for you?'

Shaking her head, Hope reached for the menu. The Sisters had taught their pupils well, and when she had made her choice and conveyed it to the waiter in correct and fluent French she had the gratification of knowing she had not let them down.

The food was everything Hope had expected it would be and she had not made the mistake of ordering anything too rich or heavy. Meals at the convent were always light, but carefully balanced, and Hope found that she had automatically chosen with the same careful precision. When she shook her head over a sweet the Comte raised his eyebrows a little. Hope had been surprised to see that he too was equally selective and that his plate, while it held more food than hers, showed a healthy regard for the nutritional value of food rather than simply its taste.

'You surprise me, *mon petit,*' he commented when the waiter had withdrawn. 'I thought a sweet tooth was the prerogative of the very young.'

'Ice-cream and sticky cakes, *monsieur?*' Hope queried with a smile, shaking her head as she explained the lectures all the students were given by the convent's dietician.

'So, what you are saying is that we are what we eat?' he asked when she had finished. 'That is true to a large extent, but one must make allowances for other...desires. One is not simply a machine functioning on fuel, one must allow for the needs of the senses.'

'You didn't drink any wine with your meal,' Hope pointed out. 'Nor did you have any rich sauces.'

'The fact that I am driving precludes me from enjoying a good wine as it should be enjoyed, and as to my food—' He looked at her, and Hope found herself trembling a little beneath the look in his eyes. 'Make no mistake, *mon petit,* no matter how nutritious or excellent the food, were it not attractively served, and presented, as tempting to the palate as to the eyes, I should not touch it. We are given our senses so that we may enjoy our environment through them whether it be the sense of taste, or the sense of touch.' As he spoke his eyes rested on her body and Hope felt almost as though he had touched her. What would it be like to be made love to by a man like him, Hope wondered, so startled by the way the thought had crept unbidden into her mind that she wasn't aware of the way her eyes mirrored her thoughts, or of how she was observed by the man seated opposite her.

It was late afternoon before they entered what the Comte told her was the Burgundy region of France. His own estate lay to the north-east, he added. The scenery of the Côte-d'Or as they drove through made Hope catch her breath, her eyes rounding in awe, forgetting her tiredness as she saw the vineyards, interspersed with tantalising glimpses of *châteaux* and weathered farmhouses, with the word *clos* constantly appearing on signboards. It referred to enclosed vineyards, the Comte

explained to her; vineyards which had once belonged to
large convents or monasteries, and which still retained
their enclosing walls.

'Are your vineyards like that?' Hope asked him, suddenly curious to know more about his home.

'No. The Serivace lands are too extensive to be enclosed, although there is one small *clos* not far from
the... house.'

He didn't seem disposed to talk any more, and Hope
lapsed into silence, tension knotting her stomach, although she was at a loss to understand why.

At last they turned off the main road, taking a narrow, badly tarmacked track, barely wide enough for the
Ferrari, and open to acres of vines on either side.

'The Serivace vines,' the Comte told her laconically,
adding, 'Serivace is one of the largest vineyards in the
area. The ancestor of mine who first settled here said he
would own land in every direction from his home as far
as the eye could see. Despite the many vicissitudes the
family has passed through, that still holds true today.' He
paused and pointed out a long, low collection of buildings in the distance. 'That is our bottling plant. Jules
Duval, my manager, lives there with his family. There are
many small growers in the locality who also make use of
the plant.'

A large copse suddenly loomed up ahead of them, so
alien in the vine-covered countryside that it took Hope
completely by surprise. The sun, which had been sulking
behind dull cloud, suddenly broke through, glinting on
something behind the trees, and then they were among
them, and the Comte was telling her that many of the
trees were rare and valuable specimens, planted by one of
his ancestors to provide parkland, 'in the English fashion'. Beyond the belt of trees were formal gardens, and
at the end of the drive... Hope's eyes rounded as she saw
the lake with the *château* rising from it, a fairy-tale in

spun white resting on the silver water like a mirage. An ancient, wooden 'drawbridge' spanned the lake at its narrowest part, the Ferrari wheels reverberating noisily as they crossed it, driving under the stone archway and through into the courtyard beyond, the Ferrari coming to rest beside an arched and studded wooden door.

'It's...it's like something out of a fairy-tale,' she stammered, bemused by the total unexpectedness of her surroundings. A 'house' the Comte had said and she, foolishly, had expected a large and rambling farmhouse, not this airy turreted *château* with its peaceful lake and formal parterred gardens.

'*Sleeping Beauty,* perhaps?' the Comte suggested, unfastening his seat-belt and opening his door. 'Rest assured there is no captive princess here, *mon petit,*' he told her dryly, adding, 'Come, I shall collect our cases later.' He saw her confusion and smiled. 'You were perhaps expecting an army of retainers.' He shook his head. 'Those days are gone. The *château* consists mainly of unused rooms. I have a small suite in the main building, which is maintained by Pierre my...general factotum, I suppose is the best description. A word of warning, by the way, before you meet him. He worked for my father and was badly injured in the same car explosion which killed my parents. My father had a minor post in the government at the time of the Algerian troubles. A bomb was thrown into the car. He and my mother were killed outright, but Pierre who was driving was thrown free. However, he was badly burned, and since the accident he has never spoken. He has also lost the ability to hear.'

'Oh, poor man!' The shocked exclamation left Hope's lips before she could silence it. The Comte glanced at her sardonically as he helped her from the car. 'You would do well not to let Pierre become aware of such sentiments. He is not a man who cares for...pity... I was fourteen when it happened,' he added, as though anticipating her next question. 'At an age to feel very bitter, but, as all things must, it passed, and of course I had ...'

'Pierre?' Hope offered, torn by compassion for the pain she had glimpsed in his eyes.

'Pierre?' The glance he shot her was sharply piercing. 'Oh, yes, I had Pierre.' He crossed the courtyard, leaving Hope to follow, and pushed open the heavy door. Standing inside it, surveying the vastness of the hall, Hope shivered, wondering if the chill was the effect of so much marble. It covered the floor in a black and white lozenge design echoed by the stairs, supported gracefully by marble columns, with polished mahogany doors set at pairing intervals along the walls.

'This way.' The Comte touched her arm, indicating one of the doors. 'This central part of the *château* is all that we use now. This is the library. Later I shall show you the remainder of the rooms.'

The library was heavily panelled with an enormous marble fireplace and a carpet which Hope suspected was Aubusson, the colours faded to muted creams, pinks and greens. Pale green velvet curtains hung at the windows, a large partners' desk placed where it would obtain maximum benefit from the daylight.

'This room doubles as my office,' the Comte explained. 'It's where I keep all the vineyard records and data, but I shall now show you the rest and then Pierre can prepare dinner for us.'

Hope's thoughts as the Comte showed her from room to room were that the as yet unseen Pierre must have his work cut out looking after such huge apartments, but the Comte told her that they received help from the village when it was needed. 'After the vintage comes the time when we entertain the buyers, and then the *château* comes into its own. You look tired,' he added. 'I'll take you to your room.'

The marble stairs struck a chill through the thin soles of her sandals, the last rays of sunlight turning the chandelier hanging from the ceiling into prisms of rainbow light, almost dazzling her in their brilliance. The landing was galleried, the walls covered in soft pale green silk, and Hope wondered who had chosen the décor which was obviously fairly recent, and who acted as the Comte's hostess when he entertained his buyers. He indicated one of the doors off the landing, thrusting it open for her, watching her face as she stepped through it and started into the room.

It was huge, almost dwarfing the Empire-style bed with its tented silk hangings, the fabric drawn back to reveal the intricate pleating and the gold and enamel rose set in the ceiling which supported it. A chaise-longue covered in the same cream and rose brocade was placed at the foot of the bed, with two Bergère chairs in front of the fire, and the delicate white and gold Empire furniture made Hope catch her breath in awe.

'The bathroom and dressing room are through here,' the Comte told her, indicating another door. 'I'll leave you to freshen up while I go and find Pierre. He'll bring your cases up for you.'

When he had gone Hope wandered over to the window. It was already growing dark outside and she could just about make out the shimmer that was the lake below her window—perhaps originally it had been the *château* moat—and beyond it the formal parterred gardens, before the ring of trees closed round the landscape obliterating everything else.

While she was investigating the bathroom, Hope heard the bedroom door open and then close again and guessed it must be Pierre with her cases and boxes. The bathroom was obviously a modern addition and rather breathtaking. The walls, floor and sanitary ware were all made from creamy white marble, the huge bath sunk into the floor, and one entire wall mirrored. Hope wasn't entirely sure that she cared for it. It rather reminded her of something she had once seen in a film the nuns had taken them to see in Seville.

The dressing room which she had to pass through to reach the bathroom was lined with wardrobes and cupboards, all of which were mirrored, and thinking that she could hardly expect Pierre to unpack for her, Hope returned to her cases and started to remove the clothes she would need for the morning. She didn't plan to change for dinner—she would simply wash and re-do her makeup.

Just when would her father arrive? She quelled a feeling of disappointment that he hadn't been there to meet them, but then she had guessed that this would be the case, for if he hadn't been busy, surely he wouldn't have sent the Comte to collect her. Rather like an unwanted parcel, she thought wryly as she stripped off her suit and returned to the bathroom to wash.

Half an hour later, her hair brushed and her make-up fresh, she opened the bedroom door and walked across the landing. Her shoes seemed to clatter loudly on the marble stairs. As she reached the hall a door underneath the stairs opened and a man walked through. Hope guessed immediately that he must be Pierre. His face bore several livid scars, his dark hair streaked with grey, but there was more curiosity than embarrassment in the look he gave her, and trying not to feel too self-conscious, Hope said warmly:

'You must be Pierre. I am Hope Stanford and...' Her voice faded away as she remembered that the Comte had told her that Pierre had been rendered both deaf and dumb by the bomb blast and, suddenly feeling awkward, she was relieved to see the Comte coming downstairs.

Unlike her, he had changed and her eyes widened a little as she took in the thick silk shirt and tightly-fitting dark trousers. Gold cuff-links glittered at his wrists, and she was suddenly and overpoweringly aware of him—not as her father's friend, but as a man. Her heart started to thud with heavy, suffocating strokes, her body turned to marble, as stiff and unresponsive as the stairs, as she stared at him, barely noticing the signs he made to Pierre, or the comprehension burning to life in the servant's dark eyes as he turned back to the door.

'Dinner is almost ready. You need not look like that,' he assured her, obviously misunderstanding the reason for her shocked expression. 'Pierre is an excellent chef.' He opened the door that Hope vaguely remembered belonged to the dining room, her eyes dazzled by the sea of polished wood and glittering glass and silver that swam before her, mentally contrasting the magnificence of the *château* to the refectory at the convent.

Two courses were served and eaten in silence, Hope merely sipping the wine the Comte had poured for her. She refused any sweet, watching instead while the Comte helped himself to some cheese—a local cheese called Chaource, he told her, offering her some. Again Hope shook her head. The long journey had tired her, her mind exhausted by so many new impressions.

A portrait on the wall behind the Comte caught her eye and she studied it. It looked relatively modern and depicted a dark-haired woman, proud and faintly arrogant so that Hope sensed a wildness beneath the conventionally elegant mask.

'Is that...was that your mother?' she asked hesitantly.

The Comte turned his head and studied the portrait for a while in silence, his voice harsh as he said, 'No. My sister, Tanya. She is dead now, she committed suicide.'

For a moment Hope thought she must have misheard him, the words seemed to hover between them, and Hope looked again at the portrait. What could have driven a woman as beautiful and proud as she was to take her own life? She hadn't realised she had spoken the words out loud until the Comte said bitterly, 'A man, of course, *mon petit;* a man, and the shame of knowing herself discarded.'

Hope shivered, unable to tear her eyes from the portrait. 'It happened six months ago,' the Comte continued. 'I was in Paris at the time, Tanya was in the Caribbean with her lover. I suspect she had hoped that in the end he would marry her, but I knew he never would. I had warned her, but she would not listen. In the end, she preferred to take her life rather than face his dismissal of her.'

'Had he...had he fallen in love with someone else?' Hope asked huskily, hardly knowing why she asked the question.

The Comte's mouth tightened. 'Hardly. No. Tanya was simply a diversion who no longer fitted into his plans, and so she had to go. She, poor girl, went on deluding herself up to the last that he genuinely cared for her. However, her death will be avenged. He shall not be allowed to shame our family unpunished.' He said the words so quietly that Hope barely caught them.

'Tanya,' she pronounced wonderingly. 'It is surely a Russian name?'

'As is my own,' the Comte confirmed. 'My mother insisted upon it. She could not hand down to her children her own birthright—she was a Princess; Princess Tatiana Vassiliky—but she gave us her family names. Mine is Alexei, after her father.'

It was his Russian blood that demanded reparation for what had happened to his sister, Hope guessed intuitively, sensing as she had done before the savagery and

pride that lay so close to the surface of his French sophistication—a sophistication which was barely more
than a cloak.

'Tanya's lover?' she pressed, scarcely knowing why she
asked the question and yet somehow compelled to do so.

'I think you can guess,' the Comte said slowly, forcing
her to meet his eyes and holding her gaze as he stood up
and came to stand beside her. 'Your father was Tanya's
lover, Hope,' he told her softly, so softly that for a moment she didn't sense the danger surrounding her.

'My father?' She stared up at him in bewilderment.
'My father... but... You and he are friends... Why did
you come for me when ... ?'

'How naïve you are, little one. Your father knows
nothing of me apart from the fact that I am Tanya's
brother, but I know a great deal about him. I made it my
business to know. I discovered, for one thing, that he had
a daughter—a pious, innocent child, who was kept se-
cluded from the world, brought up to be innocent in
mind and body; a child who he intended to use as a pawn
to secure for himself the power he has always wanted.
You are that pawn, Hope,' he told her softly. In the half-
light his eyes glittered dangerously, hard and green as
emeralds, and fear choked Hope of breath as she fought
to take in what he was saying.

'I swore when my sister killed herself that she would be
avenged,' he told her slowly. 'The Russian blood in me
demands that she is, even while the French mocks me for
my passion, but on this occasion the Russian wins out,
although I must admit that the French side of me has
helped me to plan my campaign with care and thought.
My first instinct was to deprive your father of life as he
had deprived Tanya of hers.'

Hope, listening, shivered. She could well imagine this
man killing her father, the lean fingers fastening round

his throat, demanding that he suffer as Tanya had suffered.

'But, on reflection, I decided that that was not enough. Besides, I have no wish to spend the rest of my own life languishing in prison. No, there had to be a better way. A way in which your father was vulnerable, and then, quite by chance, at a dinner in Paris, I found it. You will be surprised to know, *mon petit*, that you were the subject of the dinner-table conversation on that occasion.

'My female companion, I shall not bore you with her name, was telling me of the marriage your father had planned between the Montrachet heir and his carefully reared daughter. It seems your father has been foolish enough to borrow money on his expectations of becoming the grandfather of the new heir-to-be. The Montrachet name is an old and powerful one, and Montrachet brides are always carefully chosen and vetted. Normally, they are also rich, but the numbers of rich young women who are also virginal in body and character are quickly dwindling.

'However, your father has taken care to make sure that you fulfil both those latter two requirements. His name is also an old one—you have no fortune, of course, but Isabelle Montrachet, Alain's mother, prefers a bride for her son who is easily moulded and taught. A healthy young bride, moreover, who will provide her son with children; a bride whose virtue is unimpeachable—and who better than her business partner's daughter; a girl who can bring as her dowry, all these things. In return for your innocence, your father will receive an increased share in the Montrachet business, provided it and his own share is willed to you, and your children after you, upon his death.

'As I have just said, he has already gambled heavily on his expectations, investing in a holiday complex in the Caribbean, which is not paying off as it ought. Before the summer is out, Sir Henry intends to capitalise on his only remaining investment—you—or at least he did.'

The Comte walked away, standing by the fire with his back to her while Hope watched him in stunned and appalled silence. Was it true? Had her father intended such a marriage for her? She supposed she ought not to be shocked, after all she knew that was what many of the girls were at the convent for; to be prepared for such marriages but, somehow, she had never imagined it happening to her—and to suggest that her father was responsible for his sister's death! It was preposterous! Struggling with her feelings, all she could manage was a husky, 'I don't believe you, my father would never...'

'Make love to my sister? Discard her like an unwanted toy? Destroy and humiliate her publicly by telling her he no longer wanted her, so that she was forced to take her own life. I assure you that he did. The newspapers were full of the story—I haven't kept the cuttings, but I could obtain them for you, I'm sure.'

'No!' Hope rejected the suggestion immediately, nausea building up inside her. Could her father have behaved so callously? Hadn't he in many ways behaved callously to her? an inner voice asked. Hadn't he left her at the convent, more or less ignoring her? He hadn't told her anything about his plans for her.

She shivered suddenly, wondering if that was why she had never been allowed to holiday with her friends, in case she became involved with someone; a boy to whom she might have given her body and thus de-valued herself in the eyes of the Montrachets. It seemed incredible, and yet Hope sensed that what the Comte said was true.

'I don't understand,' she managed huskily at last. 'If you are my father's enemy why did you...'

'Take you from the convent?' he supplied for her, turning round to study her pale face and enormous eyes, her expression fearful and yet resolute as she tried to understand what was happening to her.

'You must understand that I mean you no personal harm,' he told her quietly. 'But it is only through you that I can harm your father as much as he harmed Tanya. Oh, I don't mean to kill him,' he assured her, seeing her pale. 'Nor will he end his own life as my poor sister did—he is not that kind of a man. But if this marriage does not go ahead, he will be ruined financially. He will not be able to live the jet-set life to which he has grown accustomed. He will no longer be the darling of the Côte d'Azur; permitted entry into every Casino, the escort of models and actresses, and that will destroy him as effectively as he destroyed Tanya. To see his world turn its back on him— as it surely will—will be all the revenge I need.'

'But how are you hoping to accomplish this?' Hope protested. 'You cannot keep me here for ever, and once I leave...'

'Your marriage can take place.' He shook his head and the look in his eyes sent a chill curling icily all the way down Hope's spine. 'You haven't been listening to me, Hope,' he chided almost softly. 'I have already told you what Isabelle Montrachet looks for in a bride for her son, and she will accept no less. Alain is a young man who has sown more than his fair share of wild oats, and it is rumoured he is looking forward to the piquancy of a virgin bride. My dear, no matter how lovely you are, without your virginity all you can ever be to Alain is simply another pretty diversion.'

As Hope stared up at him, the implications of his words finally struck home, her eyes widening with shocked comprehension, her husky, 'No!' trembling on the air between them.

'I'm afraid "yes",' the Comte corrected gently. 'And that is not the worst of it. You see, I never liked your father, Hope, and I hated him for what he did to Tanya.

She was twenty-one when she met him, young and full of hope. She thought he would marry her and gave herself to him willingly, but once she had done so he let her know that the only place he had for her in his life was as his mistress, and loving him as she did, she accepted it. I had to watch as her pride and respect were slowly stripped from her as he paraded her before the world as his whore. I think it a fitting punishment for him that I do the same to his daughter, don't you?'

She was going to faint, Hope thought hysterically. She couldn't really be hearing this; she couldn't really be listening to the Comte telling her calmly and emotionlessly that he intended first to rape her and then to flaunt her publicly as his mistress. For a moment she contemplated telling him that he was too late and that she had already given herself to someone else, but his voice forstalled her.

'It's no use, Hope,' he told her calmly. 'You have already betrayed to me in a thousand ways that you are an innocent. You cannot leave the *château*—Pierre will not help you—and by morning...' He shrugged, and her appalled senses struggled with the knowledge that he intended to start taking his revenge that night. 'You need not fear that I shall hurt or abuse you—it is not my intention to punish you personally, and indeed in many ways I am sorry that it has to be accomplished through you. Certainly you will suffer no worse at my hands than you would at Alain's...'

'Except for the fact that I would be his wife,' Hope reminded him bitterly. All her life she had heard the Sisters telling her that sex outside marriage was a sin and never for a moment had she contemplated indulging in it with anyone other than her husband. Even if she was married and in love she would still be dreading what now lay ahead of her, she acknowledged inwardly, but to contemplate the Comte's hands on her flesh, his body...

She shuddered deeply, her panicky 'No!' bringing a brief grimace of understanding to the Comte's mouth.

'I'm afraid your protests only make it all the more difficult for you, *mon petit*. Here, in this *château,* it is my will which prevails. We shall stay here for a week,' he told her, as though they were discussing something mundane. 'By that time it is my hope that you will have lost that look of undeniable innocence.' His eyes mocked her pale face and bruised expression. 'Then we shall fly out to the Caribbean. I have a villa there, and the crowd your father mixes with will be at his hotel at this time of year. No doubt your father will be in a benign mood, contemplating the wedding he believes is to take place later in the summer. Your appearance at my side, so incontestably mine, will surprise him.'

'I shall tell him what you have done,' Hope cried out. 'You can't force me to stay with you then, I shall leave you...'

'And your father will take you in?' He shook his head. 'Oh, no, *mon petit,* he won't.'

'How long... how long will I have to stay with you?'

'As long as it takes.'

'And afterwards?' Hope shivered again. The nuns had always stressed to their pupils that once a girl sinned, once she lost her innocence, the downward path was a very steep and slippery one indeed, and a hundred lurid pictures tortured Hope's mind. 'After you have... finished with me, what becomes of me? No man will want me as his wife...'

'I did not say that, nor is it true. You cannot really believe that all men marry virgins—or indeed want to. You are a beautiful girl, Hope, many men will be attracted to you. You have intelligence, and depending on how much you use it, you can be happy and content in your life or not.'

'Would you marry a girl who has...has had other lovers?' Hope flung at him bitterly.

'I would—if I loved her; if she had other assets that I wanted. The confines of your upbringing have been very narrow, Hope. If the Montrachets were not as they are, if your father had not callously traded in your innocence for their wealth, my plans could not come to fruition. In many ways you are an artificial product. Had you been left to grow and develop naturally I doubt you would be a virgin. It is as acceptable for girls to experiment these days as it is for boys.'

'But you intend to...to ravish me because...'

'It will not be a ravishment in the terms that you are thinking of,' he told her calmly. 'I have no desire to inflict pain or degradation on you. On the contrary, I want your father to see that you come to me willingly.' He smiled at the expression in Hope's eyes, and her bitter:

'Never—I could not. I do not love you!'

'How little you know,' he mocked her softly. 'But you will see. Love is not always necessary for pleasure, Hope.'

She closed her eyes in mute agony, unable to understand what was happening to her. Could she really believe that this cool, sardonic man, talking reasonably, almost lightly to her, actually meant to despoil her body, to deprive her of her virginity?

She saw him glance at his watch. 'It is getting late, and you must be tired. Why don't you go to bed?'

Her eyes flew to his face, but he wasn't looking at her. 'I have some work I have to attend to. Don't even think of trying to escape, Hope. The doors are all bolted, the drawbridge raised, and Pierre will not aid you—he was fanatically devoted to my sister. Would you like something to help you sleep?'

For a moment Hope was tempted. Perhaps if he came upstairs and found her sleeping he would...what? Change his mind? Hardly, having gone to so much trouble to bring her here. This wasn't something done in the heat of the moment; his anger had cooled and hardened, and he wouldn't be turned aside from what he intended.

'No, thank you,' she responded formally, wondering if it was admiration she had seen flicker briefly in his eyes, or if she had imagined it.

CHAPTER THREE

IN THE END she was not left alone with the torment of her thoughts for long. A warm bath had done little to soothe her jangling nerves, her various plans for escape all dismissed as wildly impossible as she went through them; there wasn't even a telephone anywhere in sight she could use to contact her father. If she was the heroine of a novel no doubt she would have a knife or a gun to hand with which to defend herself, she thought painfully as she pulled on the old enveloping cotton nightdress she had brought with her from the convent. Not for the world, would she wear the fine, silk garments she had bought in Seville. She was glad that the room was in darkness—she didn't think she could bear to look at the Comte, it would be bad enough to have to endure his touch.

Her fingernails were digging into her palms when she heard the door open. The light was clicked on and the Comte surveyed her, a small smile touching the corner of his mouth as he studied her nightdress, but he made no comment, simply locking the door and pocketing the key, before walking past her into the dressing room.

When he was gone Hope found that she was trembling. She heard the sound of running water, muted by the closed doors, and tried to stop her fevered imagination relaying pictures to her as she visualised the Comte's body, his undeniable strength and her own weakness. A thousand primitive, feminine terrors tormented her, until she had virtually forgotten what little knowledge she

had, her fear reducing her body to a trembling mass of
nerves and muscles.

When the Comte came back he was wearing a dark
towelling robe, his hair damp and curling slightly into his
neck, the sight of the dark hair on his chest and legs
making Hope's stomach clench protestingly in shock at
the intimacy he was forcing on her. She had seen photo-
graphs of men on the beach, pictures in magazines, of
course, but they had not prepared her for the actual
physical reality, the raw maleness that emanated from
masculine muscle and bone.

'*Monsieur*,' her intention to plead with him, to change
his mind, was silenced when he laughed, his teeth gleaming whitely against the tan of his skin. It was the first time
she had heard him laugh and Hope coloured angrily,
wondering what she had done to make herself the object
of his mirth.

'The good Sisters have certainly taught you to be polite, *mon petit*,' he told her, 'but in view of our...
proposed intimacy, I suggest that you use my name instead of calling me *Monsieur*. Say it, Hope,' he demanded softly, watching her with eyes that now held no
trace of humour. 'Say it...'

She pressed her lips together firmly, fingers curled into
small fists, mutely defying him. If he wanted to hear his
name on her lips he would have to beat her first. She
couldn't deny him her body, but this small defiance she
could and would make.

'No matter. You will say it, either tonight or some
other night.' He shrugged off his robe, not heeding her
shocked gasp, and Hope comprehended that this might
be a subtle form of punishment for her defiance. The
sight of his body awed and terrified her, but she couldn't
drag her gaze from the silken ripples of muscles under his
skin as he bent to throw back the covers on the bed.

Her immediate urge was to run, but there was nowhere to run to, and she wasn't going to humiliate herself further. No doubt her panic would only amuse him.

'So...we are ready.' He turned to face her, his eyes
narrowed as he added, 'Apart from this.' His fingers
flicked disdainfully at the shabby nightdress. 'You chose
to wear it as a tactical move to deflect me from my purpose, I imagine?' His eyebrows rose queryingly, but Hope
gave no confirmation. 'Umm...' He studied her for a
moment, his fingers curling smoothly round the neck
fastening. 'I regret the necessity for this, little one, but I
do not propose to lose my dignity and possibly my temper in trying to extricate you from it.'

His fingers tightened and Hope tensed, her eyes
rounding in stunned horror as he ripped the thin fabric
from neck to hem, the violence of his action catching her
off balance and propelling her against him, her hands
immediately raised to fend him off, her palms resting
against his chest for the briefest moment before she
withdrew them as quickly as though she had been
scorched, barely able to comprehend what had happened until she saw the remnants of her clothing lying on
the floor. The knowledge of her nakedness brought her
arms to her body in an age-old gesture of protection, and
her agonised, 'the lights!' brought a glimmer of understanding to the green eyes and a hesitation which made
her suspect that he meant to torment her still further by
leaving them on. He had said he didn't want to hurt her,
but Hope wondered wildly if that was true—he certainly
hadn't shown her any compassion up until now.

He didn't turn the lights off, but he did dim them. 'It
will be less frightening than the dark,' he told her, coming back to the bed, adding emotionlessly, 'there is really nothing to fear, Hope. A moment's pain, which you
will have to endure only once. The nuns did tell you...'

'Yes, yes,' she agreed in an agonised whisper, longing now only for all of it to be over and done with. There was no escape and therefore she must bear the inevitable with what fortitude she could. That was what the nuns had taught her.

'You are cold.' He was standing in front of her, his hands on her shoulders, sliding them downwards over her skin until they reached her waist—it was a slow, gradual exploration during which Hope hadn't breathed at all. When he lifted her on to the bed she held herself as immobile as a statue, refusing to look at him as he pushed back the covers and joined her, his hands gliding slowly over her skin, exploring every shivering inch.

She made no attempt to repulse him, forcing her mind into numb acceptance, expending all her energy in trying to keep still, trying not to cry out a protest or give in to the instincts urging her to move away. The shock of his mouth against her skin, exploring the curve of her throat and shoulder, was like fire against ice. She shuddered deeply, tensing as his hand moved from her arm to her breast, her mind cringing away from the implications of his assured touch. She began to shiver uncontrollably, tremors of fear and shock gripping her body, the Comte's voice reaching her from a distance, the tone low and soothing, although she couldn't understand what he said, only she wasn't to call him 'Comte' or 'Monsieur', but 'Alexei'.

The touch of his hands on her body wasn't painful or unkind in any physical way, but her mental anguish blocked out the knowledge that he wasn't hurting her. He had no right to be touching her like this, to be looking at her and watching her, and she told herself that the strange feelings she could sense stirring within her body came from fear, unable to comprehend why her breasts should swell and harden when they touched his chest, or why she should experience a strange melting sensation in the pit of her stomach when he touched her, as though her bones and muscles had turned completely fluid.

Her mind and body fighting a battle that exhausted her fragile defences, Hope was torn between yielding to the instincts of her body and the knowledge that the man touching her was neither her husband nor someone she loved, but a stranger who was using her as he would doubtless have used anything else that had come to hand in his war against her father. In the end, her mind won, subduing the strange sensations of her body, commanding her to tense every muscle and nerve against the intrusive heat and weight of Alexei's alien body which was forcing her against the bed as he parted her thighs remorselessly, and her body stiffened in real terror, panic washing over her in ever-increasing waves.

She fought against him in mind and body until she was numb with exhaustion, hysteria edging under the control she had let go when his body covered her, and the cry of pain she had sworn he would never hear was followed by tears that welled from her eyes and shook her slender frame. Her agony of mind was more potent than the ache of her body as he withdrew, and she turned from him curling up into a small foetal ball.

She had known what would happen, but the lectures she had heard, the whispered gossip of the other girls, had not prepared her for the trauma of having her body invaded, violated by this stranger. In some ways she could have born it more if he had deliberately tried to hurt her, but there hadn't even been that much emotion in what he had done and her mind cringed from what had happened as much as her body had done earlier.

'Hope.' She felt his hand on her shoulder and tensed. 'It's all right, I'm not going to touch you.' She didn't move, terrified into immobility, not even relaxing when he cursed and withdrew. She felt him leave the bed and walk round it to the window. He didn't bother to pull on

his robe, and Hope's eyes, unable to blot out the shape
and power of his body, watched him look into the darkness.

'I'm sorry it had to be like that, but you were so tense
and terrified it couldn't have been any different. But next
time...' She must have made some small sound that
alerted him because he swung round, catching her anguished, bitter expression. 'Try to get some sleep. Things
will seem different in the morning.' He came and sat
down beside her, watching her shrink back. 'You were
fighting yourself as well as me, Hope. The Sisters have
doubtless taught you that sex is a duty you owe your
husband, a means to an end—children—but it is also a
rare and lovely pleasure. If you listen to your body and
not your mind you will discover that for yourself.'

She saw him get up and expected him to go away, but
to her dismay he walked back to the other side of the bed
and climbed in beside her, pulling the covers over them
both, but not touching her. As she lay tense beside him,
Hope heard his breathing deepen into sleep, her body
gradually relaxing a little, her breathing still shallow.

Had what happened between them brought him any
physical satisfaction? It seemed impossible to believe it
could, but the Sisters had said that male needs were different from female. Hope sighed. She was not completely ignorant—she knew from her reading that there
were women who enjoyed the sexual act, but felt that she
was never destined to be one of them. Her mind and body
both felt bruised and sore, her skin defiled, and she felt
an overwhelming need to soak her body in water, to scrub
away all memories of Alexei's touch.

Slowly, Hope slid out of the bed, taking care not to
disturb the sleeping figure behind her. The carpet felt soft
to her bare feet, but she felt oddly dizzy and breathless.
She reached the bottom of the bed before she felt her
knees start to buckle under her, her body floating,

weightless almost. She heard a sound behind her, barely
registered what it was, uncomprehending even when
Alexei caught her, swinging her up against his chest as the
room whirled unpleasantly round her.

'I wanted to wash,' she told him scarcely aware of what
she was saying. 'I want...'

'Yes, *mon petit*, I know.' The words floated around
her, her head dropping on to Alexei's shoulder, her mind
and body too drained to respond. She was distantly aware
of being carried into the marble grandeur of the bathroom, of being wrapped in a huge warm towel as water
gushed into the bath, but it was too much of an effort to
pay much attention. She didn't *want* to think or remember, this floating, hazy feeling was so much pleasanter.

The water was warm and scented and she wanted to lie
in it for ever, but someone kept talking to her, gently
sponging her skin, the touch soothing, reminding her of
her childhood and the nanny she had had before she was
sent to school. But she had left school now and... Her
mind veered away from the pain she could sense waiting
for her. She was being lifted out of the bath and rubbed
dry, her skin glowing and warm, a brisk command to
open her mouth instantly obeyed, the tablet she was given
making her pull a face and gratefully accept a glass of
water. Almost within seconds she seemed to be pulled
down into an abyss of darkness, fighting against it instinctively, terrified by dim memories of unperceived
horrors waiting for her in the Stygian darkness, until a
cool voice murmured her name, a hand lifting the heavy
weight of her damp hair, her face pillowed against something warm and somehow vaguely comforting.

'Hope.' The sound of her name penetrated the thick
mists. She opened her eyes—she was in Alexei's arms, her
face resting against the curve of his throat.

'You hurt me.' She said it sorrowfully, as though she
were still a child, wondering at the way he tensed, and

then the sleeping pill he had given her did its work and she was sucked back down into the blackness, unaware that when he returned her to the bed, it was to Alexei that she turned, curling into his body in an instinctive search for comfort, or that he watched her long after she had fallen asleep, something very like pain darkening his eyes. It wasn't his way to deviate from any path he had decided upon. Tanya's suicide had to be avenged and this was undoubtedly the best way.

Muttering something under his breath he looked down at the silver head pillowed against him, tear tracks faintly discernible on the pale skin.

HOPE OPENED her eyes, awareness immediately flooding over her, her movements jerky as she turned her head, relief invading her tense body as she saw that she was alone. Shakily she threw back the bedclothes, moving gingerly towards the edge of the bed. She had a dim memory of getting out of bed last night after... She frowned, checking as she fought to remember exactly what had happened, her eyes widening as tiny scraps of memory floated to the surface of her consciousness.

'Ah, you're awake.'

She froze as the door opened and Alexei walked in, tall and lithe in a cotton shirt and jeans. 'Breakfast,' he told her, indicating the tray he was carrying. When she averted her face he put the tray down on a small table and she felt the bed depress as he came and sat beside her.

'There's no point in sulking, Hope,' he told her, not unkindly. 'It won't always be as it was last night. What you suffered was no worse than you would have endured at the hands of Montrachet, probably less, although you probably can't believe that now.'

'Except that he would have married me,' Hope pointed out, ignoring the last part of his sentence. How could he talk so calmly about what had happened between them?

The invasion of her privacy as much as the violation of her body had shocked her. She couldn't accept the unwanted intimacy of their situation; she couldn't endure knowing that this man had not only possessed her body, but also seemed to know, to the last degree, her every feeling and emotion. She felt as though there was nothing left she could call her own, no corner of her soul in which she could hide from him, and the knowledge frightened her.

'Hope.' His hands grasped her shoulders, and he frowned when she tensed, obviously guessing one of the causes of her concern when he saw the sunlight dance on the exposed curve of her shoulder. He got up and walked over to the dressing room, returning with a flimsy, silk robe. 'Sit up and turn round,' he told her, sitting on the bed behind her, and sliding the robe over her arms when she reluctantly did as he instructed.

'Now,' he said, when he had firmly tied a bow in the ribbon that secured the front. 'Try to understand,' he said slowly. 'In the eyes of people whose opinion your intelligence tells you matter, the fact that we have been lovers will mean nothing. They will judge you as the person you are, Hope. Your virginity or lack of it matters only to your father because he regards you as a commodity, as something he can sell,' he told her brutally. 'Women don't barter innocence for marriage these days, little one. Strange though you may find it now...one day you will perhaps thank me for this.'

'Don't lie to me.' Angrily, Hope pushed him away. 'You told me yourself last night that my father made your sister his mistress, that he wouldn't marry her...'

'He wouldn't marry her because of her lack of wealth, not her lack of virtue,' she was told grimly. 'And it was not because my sister chose to give herself to your father that I have brought you here, but because of his treatment of her once she had. Now, I suggest you have your breakfast and then get dressed.'

'What in?' Hope demanded childishly. 'I don't have anything in scarlet...' He laughed, further infuriating her, seeming more amused than annoyed by her comment, saying wickedly:

'Even dressed in the garments of a *putain*, you would still look exactly what you are, *mon petit*—an innocent bearing the outward and inward bruises of her ravishment.'

'When do we leave for the Caribbean?' Hope asked him, trying to subdue the high colour his words brought storming to her face.

'When you have ceased to look like a ravished child and have become a woman.'

'That will never be,' Hope promised him rashly, hating him when he laughed again, curling a strand of her hair round his finger until she jerked away.

'Au contraire, ma jolie,' he mocked her. 'I would hazard a guess it will be sooner than you think—much sooner.' He leaned forward, his fingers sliding along her throat to her jaw, holding her prisoner while he stroked his tongue against her lips and then kissed her, withdrawing to study her flushed cheeks and tumbled hair with a thoughtful expression. Just for a moment, Hope thought that he would touch her again, but to her relief he made no move to do so, simply saying, 'Now, I have to go and inspect the vineyards. You are at liberty to explore the house and inner courtyard, but I'm afraid you cannot wander any further. The drawbridge will remain up, and remember Pierre cannot help you. Take my advice and accept the inevitable, Hope,' he finished quietly. 'There is no shame in finding pleasure in the sexuality of your body, you know, despite what the Sisters may have taught you.'

'How can I find pleasure, as you call it, when I hate you,' Hope flung at him, watching the smile crease his skin, tiny lines fanning outwards from his eyes.

'You will see,' he promised softly, heading for the door. 'Eat your breakfast. I shall see you tonight.'

He was gone before she could think of a suitably cutting retort, leaving her alone with her thoughts. What a complex man he was, one side of his nature passionately Russian, thirsting for the revenge his pride demanded and determined to have it no matter what the cost to anyone else, and yet there was another side to him almost completely opposite, and that had been the side she had experienced this morning. But she wasn't going to make the mistake of underestimating either, Hope decided with a shiver. She couldn't escape, he had told her, but even if she could it was too late, if what he had said about her father's plans were true, and somehow she sensed it was. He would do with her what he had said and nothing would swerve him from his purpose, but one day he would no longer have any use for her, there was nothing to hold them together, no emotion on either side bar his thirst for revenge, and once that was satisfied . . .

Hope's skin chilled and goose-fleshed, and she shivered, struggling to come to terms with what had happened and what her life would now be. Life in the convent had been ordered and peaceful, not requiring any effort upon her part other than obedience, but she wasn't a child any longer and somehow she was going to have to find a way to make her own life. Alexei's plans for her were something she would have to endure until she could escape from him, but once she did . . . gnawing her bottom lip, she wondered what was going to become of her, jolted out of the passive acceptance that had become second nature to her. She would have to find a job; thousands of other girls her age survived on their own. Thousands of other girls had affairs with men outside

marriage; thousands of girls learned to cope as she was
going to have to learn, and feeling sorry for herself would
achieve nothing.

Her coffee was cold by the time she had washed and
dressed. She found the kitchen eventually, and saw Pierre
standing over the sink peeling some potatoes. He raised
his head warily and Hope guessed that Alexei had warned
him about her. A coffee percolator stood on a table next
to the sink and she picked it up miming a pouring action. Nodding his head, he took it from her and Hope
watched him fill it with fresh coffee and water. While it
was perking, he opened the fridge door and indicated the
contents. Guessing that he thought she might want some
breakfast, Hope shook her head, unable to face the
thought of food, although the hot strong coffee was
blissfully reviving.

When she had finished it she went outside into the
courtyard, and walked aimlessly around it. Stables bor-
dered it on one side, but the stalls were empty. When she
peered over the wall Hope saw the water of the moat
glistening below, some ducks diving for food. It was
warm enough for her to be tempted to sit in the sun, but
she felt too restless, too keyed up to relax.

Unwillingly, she returned to the *château*, wandering
from room to room, studying the portrait of Tanya for
several minutes before going into the library and searching the shelves for something to read.

Eventually, she picked out a volume of Tolstoy's *War
and Peace*, something she had not read, hoping she could
lose herself and her fears inside its pages.

At one o'clock, Pierre brought her some lunch—a
light, fluffy omelette and a pot of fresh coffee with some
fruit to eat afterwards. The smell of the omelette made
her realise that she was hungry, and when she took a
forkful, she found that it tasted as delicious as it looked.

When she returned the tray to the kitchen, Pierre eyed the clean plate with a glimmer of approval.

Hope read well into the afternoon, tension curling through her body as the afternoon wore on until she was no longer able to deceive herself that the novel was holding her attention. Closing it, she wandered to the window, looking out on to the lake. The ducks were diving industriously in the pale green water, and suddenly restless she went to the kitchen looking for some bread to feed them, thinking the activity might distract her mind, if only momentarily.

There was no sign of Pierre, but she found a loaf and cut off a small chunk, going outside and walking through the courtyard until she came to the small gap in the wall she had noticed that morning, leaning out from it so that she was directly over the water, breaking the bread into crumbs and calling to the ducks. For several minutes their antics amused her, the inept attempts of the small ducklings to get their share making her smile.

The heavy sound of wood and moving machinery drew her attention, and frowning, she turned, just in time to see Alexei's car drive into the courtyard. He climbed out, hesitating when he saw her, calling her name sharply, his forehead creased in what looked like anger.

Automatically, Hope panicked, retreating into the embrasure as he strode towards her, shrinking away instinctively, not realising how tenuous her foothold was until her shoe slipped and she overbalanced, the water of the moat rushing up to meet her, engulfing her, silencing her choking cry as her mouth and nose filled with the cold water. She could swim, but the shock of falling made her panic and struggle instinctively as she felt something clasp her arm, Alexei's angry features swimming in front of her eyes.

Later, she remembered thinking in a confused way that Alexei was trying to drown her, before she realized that

that couldn't be true. He couldn't flaunt her in front of her father if he drowned her, but at the time the thought made her fight against his constraining arms, consciousness ebbing and flowing until she was suddenly aware of sun-warmed stone beneath her body, and the cold darkness of wet clothes. Alexei was standing over her, water dripping from his lean body, his mouth a grim line that made her shudder.

He muttered something in Russian as he bent to pick her up, and Hope realised that Pierre was standing beside him. Alexei must have indicated something to him, she realised, because the other man hurried into the house.

'Mon Dieu!' Alexei swore as he carried Hope inside. 'Is that how your mind works, you little fool—death before dishonour?'

Hope struggled to tell him that her fall had been an accident, that his sudden grim-faced appearance had frightened her, but the words wouldn't come.

'This is the second occasion on which I have had to bathe you, mon petit,' she heard him say seconds later as he set her on her feet in the bathroom. 'I confess the role of nursemaid is not entirely an unappealing one, although on this occasion...' Hope shivered as full consciousness returned and she realised how easily she could have been drowned.

'I didn't jump.' Alexei had his back to her, his wet jeans clinging to his body as he bent over the bath running the water. She bit her lip—now what had made her say that? A desire to show him that she wasn't quite the weak, childish fool he had thought her? 'It was an accident,' she added huskily. 'I was feeding the ducks, you startled me and...'

'And you fell into the moat rather than endure my company?' he offered grimly. 'God, you are such a child... determined to cast me in the role of villain. Has it not occurred to you yet that once you are free of me you may choose what to do with your life, Hope, instead of having someone else's will imposed upon you— and do not make any mistake, as the bride of Montrachet you would have no choice. Have you no ambitions? No desires of your own? Nothing you want from life?' His voice was edged with impatience, and he gave a muffled curse before straightening up and looking at her. 'You are a person, Hope, a reasoning, intelligent human being. Can you honestly tell me that you would be happy with the life Montrachet would offer you?'

He sighed, suddenly looking tired, and Hope reflected wryly that it must have been a shock to him when she fell—her death would have deprived him of any chance of obtaining his revenge. No wonder he had fought so strongly to save her.

'Get out of those wet things,' he instructed curtly. 'Pierre is making you a *tisane*. I thought we'd dine out tonight, but perhaps in the circumstances...' He looked at her doubtfully, but Hope seized on his words as though they were a life-line. Dining out would be infinitely preferable to remaining here alone with him, dreading the time when she must eventually go to bed.

'No... please, I should like to go out.'

Alexei studied her for a moment, shrugged and then glanced distastefully at the jeans plastered to his legs. Against her will Hope's glance followed his, the taut pull of the fabric against the hard muscles mesmerising her.

'Get in the bath, Hope,' she heard him say in a suddenly hard voice, 'and don't stay there too long—I might be tempted to join you, and something tells me you're far from ready for water sports—yet.'

Her face flaming, Hope glanced mutely at the door, shivering under the impact of raw sensuality she caught behind the words. For a moment she thought he meant to stay, but after a glance at the water, he moved to-

wards the door saying wryly, 'I doubt that it's deep
enough for you to drown in, but I'll be back in ten minutes to check—so I wouldn't linger if I were you, unless
you *want* me to join you?'

When he came back, dressed in a brief towelling robe,
rubbing his damp hair, Hope was seated in one of the
chairs, wrapped in a towel, drinking the *tisane* Pierre had
brought. There was coffee on the tray as well, and Alexei
poured himself a cup as he watched her. Watching him,
Hope felt a strange tendril of sensation curl upwards
from her stomach; a curling, hesitant feeling that made
her pulse race and heat flood her body, the sensation so
unexpected she replaced her cup and stared sightlessly in
front of her.

'Hope? Hope, are you all right?' Alexei's voice, sharp
with impatience, cut through her thoughts. She looked
up, her eyes skimming the length of his legs, darkly
tanned and sprinkled with dark hairs. She had an inex-
plicable desire to reach out and touch him, to discover if
the dark hair felt as rough to her fingertips as it had
against her thighs last night. Hard on the heels of the
desire came realisation of what she was thinking, her
breath expelled on a stifled gasp, her fingers whitening as
they tensed on the cup. She forced herself to look into
Alexei's face to see if he was aware of her reaction. He
was looking down at her through half-closed eyes, smiling faintly, and Hope's skin burned painfully.

'Poor little one,' he said softly. 'It is all very confus-
ing and painful, hmm? But it will not always be so. Drink
your *tisane* and then try and rest for an hour.' He saw her
glance at the bed and sighed, removing the cup from her
tense fingers. 'What an ogre you make me feel, child, but
there is no need to look at the bed as though it is a place
of torture. Can you not try to believe me when I assure
you that one day not too far distant you will find it a
place of considerable pleasure.' He was laughing at her,

Hope was sure of it, and all at once the emotions she had held at bay rioted angrily through her, all the years of convent training overwhelmed in a flash-flood of rage that would have reminded her father of his mother, a red-headed McDonald from the Islands whose temper matched her hair.

Hope's grey eyes as stormy as gale-blown skies, she turned her face to her tormentor, a high flush of colour burning along her cheekbones. 'I will never find any pleasure with you,' she hurled at him, held fast in the grip of a fury that made her long to rake her fingernails along the smooth brown skin to draw blood, anything to make that cool, knowing smile disappear. 'You think you know everything,' she panted. 'But you don't. Whatever you do to me, whatever response you get from my body, my mind will always hate you. You talk about my father using me as a commodity, but that's just what you're doing.'

'You're becoming hysterical,' he told her coldly. 'If you don't stop this tantrum right now I'll...'

'Slap my face?' she taunted bitterly, eyes glittering with rage and pain.

Alexei shook his head, the anger suddenly leaving him, a smile curving his mouth. 'No, it would be a different part of your anatomy to which I would apply the weight of my hand, *mon petit,* but of course I would always be willing to kiss it better—if you asked me.' Her shocked eyes told him that he had won the battle, and Hope was left to acknowledge painfully that in any war against him he would always have the advantage. She put her hands to her burning face, her skin still betraying her shocked reaction to his teasing comment, and the glinting amusement in his eyes when he made it. He was a devil, a cold, hateful devil, and she loathed him!

'ARE YOU SURE you want to go out for dinner?' Alexei
was standing in the dressing room door, fastening gold
links in the cuffs of his white shirt. Hope nodded her
head. She was already dressed, and had just finished applying her make-up. Alexei's shirt was unbuttoned to the
waist, and Hope was sure he knew how much the sight of
his naked chest alarmed her. Again she felt the same
wrenching sensation in her stomach. Alexei was button-
ing up his shirt, tucking the tails into his trousers with a
carelessness that said more loudly than any words that *he*
did not find it strange that someone else should witness
such intimacies.

Some of her feelings must have shown in her face because he paused in the act of fastening his shirt to eye her
thoughtfully, before abandoning his task to stroll across
the room. He stood behind her, and Hope shivered when
he picked up her hairbrush, startled grey eyes meeting
unreadable green ones in the mirror as he drew the brush
smoothly through her hair, repeating the movement until Hope felt herself relax beneath the soothing strokes.

'I appreciate that what has happened to you has come
as a shock, *ma jolie.*' In the mirror the green eyes still
held her own and even though she wanted to look away,
Hope found it impossible to break the contact. 'But you
are an intelligent child, who must realise by now that I
mean what I say. That being the case, there is nothing to
be gained from pointless defiance—you will hurt yourself far more than you will hurt me. Try to look upon this
as another period of learning, after which you will be free
to make your own life.'

'Free to be some other man's plaything,' Hope stormed
back at him. 'The things I shall learn from you are things
I should only have learned from my husband.' Tears
quivered on her eyelashes, a feeling of complete desolation surging over her as she remembered the Sisters' stern
warnings about the fate of girls who were foolish enough

to 'misbehave'. And now this man who had calmly taken her away from the sanctuary of the convent was equally calmly telling her that what he had done would benefit her.

'You're exaggerating like a child,' he told her coolly. 'Life is not all black and white, there are many, many shades of grey, and the days are long gone when a young woman assessed her value in terms of her virginity. In fact, you demean yourself by doing so. In the modern world a woman is assessed as she assesses herself, physical beauty without intelligence, compassion and humour is nothing. No one will judge you unfavourably because you've been my mistress, Hope. It's only in your own juvenile imagination that "fallen women" exist.'

'If that was true you wouldn't be planning to get back at my father the way you are doing,' Hope told him scornfully. Did he think she was completely without intelligence?

The brushing stopped. He bent down until his head was level with her own, grasping her chin and turning her to face him. 'My dear child.' His voice was dangerously cool. 'Your father is far too much a man of the world to give a damn about your virginity, other than as a saleable commodity.'

'I hate you,' Hope told him pathetically, wishing she had the conviction to deny his allegation. 'I can't understand how the Reverend Mother allowed me to leave with you.'

'Quite simple. I forged your father's signature, and anyway, the Sisters were growing concerned about you. They were too relieved to discover that, after all, your father was not the uncaring parent they had believed to question my authority too deeply. And by the way,' he added, reading her mind with an ease that shocked her, 'don't even think about trying to run away. I have your passport and I intend to keep it. You have no money, no friends here, and this part of France is still feudal in many ways. My family have been here for centuries, the same tenants living always on the land. Unless you give me your word that you will not try to escape, I shall let it be known that you are suffering with a mental disorder which makes you think you are the victim of a kidnap plot...'

He was still watching her, and Hope knew with a sickening sense of certainty that he meant every word he said. Dear God, how she longed to be able to do something...anything to break through that implacable mask, to hurt and destroy him as he had done her.

'I've changed my mind,' she said bitterly, 'I don't want to go out to dinner after all.' She turned away, refusing to look at him although she was aware that he was standing up and then walking towards the dressing room.

'Very well,' he said from the door. 'I shall instruct Pierre to prepare something for you.' He went on fastening his shirt, and it was several seconds before the implications of his words sank in. *He* would still be dining out, she would be eating alone. Hard on the heels of the knowledge came a sense of... disappointment? No, simply one of anticlimax, Hope assured herself, anticlimax because her opponent had removed himself from the ring. The action of someone who knows he cannot win, she told herself, but somehow the thought was not convincing. If ever a man knew exactly how to win, it was Alexei.

Pierre brought her meal into the library, placing the tray on a small table in front of the fire. It was some kind of casserole, and Hope saw that he had also opened a bottle of wine and set the tray with a glass. The wine bore the crest of an eagle and Alexei's name and she sipped it cautiously. Although they had been taught to recognize all the great vintages, and how to select the correct wine to serve with a meal, Hope had seldom tasted any.

The liquid she had poured into her glass was pale gold, sharp and clean to the palate, bringing out the flavour of the chicken in its delicate sauce. The world, which had seemed a grey hopeless place when she first came down to the library, suddenly seemed less oppressive. In fact, she could well understand why people drank, Hope decided owlishly as she poured herself a second glass.

She was halfway through her third when Pierre came to remove the tray and replace it with a pot of coffee, and Hope felt that the warm, slightly hazy cloud enveloping her was a definite improvement on the terrifying misery that had gripped her ever since Alexei had told her of his plans. Recognising that she was probably a little drunk, she contemplated the coffee pensively and then decided that her present delightfully relaxed state was infinitely preferable to sobriety.

The Sisters would be shocked if they could see her! For some reason the thought of the convent was so upsetting that Hope took another few gulps from her glass, dismayed to discover how the room whirled colourfully round her when she tried to stand up. Her only clear thought as she walked unsteadily upstairs was that at least she was spared the ordeal of having Alexei witness her foolishness. Deep down inside herself she knew that there could be no escape, and the rosy glow of good-feeling fostered by the wine started to fade as she opened the bedroom door and stared at the bed. There was no key in the door and somehow she knew that if she found another bedroom Alexei would only seek her out and bring her back. A small sob-turned-hiccup broke the silence of the darkened room.

It was only ten o'clock, but suddenly she felt very tired, so tired that she almost fell asleep in the bath, but at last she was dry and wearing one of the thin silk nightgowns she felt she hated, her body a tiny bump in the vastness of a bed plainly meant for dual occupation. Just as her eyes closed, for a brief heartbeat her mind cleared and Hope had a vivid impression of how her life would now be, her soul in perpetual torment, unless, as Alexei had suggested, she found a way to live with what had happened, to build on it and grow from it... Could he be right? Was the world not as clearly divided into black and white, good and evil as the Sisters had taught her? She couldn't withstand him physically, but her mind was still her own, still inviolate, and she could keep it that way...

CHAPTER FOUR

HOPE WAS DREAMING. It was an intensely pleasurable dream. She was lying on a warm beach, the heat of the sun caressing every part of her body, its touch so relaxing that she felt as though her flesh and bones were dissolving, becoming part of the sun's warmth, fluid and formless. But all the time at the back of her mind was the fear that something would take the sun away from her and that without it she would no longer be able to enjoy the languorous pleasure its touch brought.

Even as she enjoyed its caress her fears grew bigger, growing from a small cloud to a large one, a shadow stalking across the sand, obliterating the heat of the sun, depriving her of its touch. The shadow took on human form. Her heart started to pound, her mouth dry with fear as she struggled to recognize the formless person standing over her, knowing that she could recognise the features while struggling to put a name to them, until it swirled from the depths of her subconsciousness, forcing its way past her lips, breaking and shattering her dream, bringing her shiveringly awake, suddenly conscious of her whereabouts and Alexei's arm curving her possessively against his body.

'Hope? Are you all right?' Any hopes she had had that her dream had been pure imagination were shattered as Hope recognised the impatience edging his voice.

'I was having a dream,' she muttered, suddenly conscious of the spread of his hand against her midriff, and the pleasurable heat of his body against her back, the same heat she had been dreaming about when . . .

'You called for your father. Why? Were you dreaming about him rescuing you?'

The warmth of his hand seemed to radiate right through her body, and Hope had to restrain a small murmur of protest when it lifted, both hands going to her her shoulders and turning her so that they were face to face.

'I can't remember what I was dreaming about,' she lied huskily, 'but isn't it only natural that I should want my father, that I should dream that he is helping me . . .'

'Quite natural, but you cried his name in pain and rejection, Hope, and the tears came afterwards, not before. In short, you were crying because of your father and not for him.'

She wanted to deny it, but all her energy was absorbed in trying to understand her own emotions. When the dark head bent towards her she made no move to avoid it, lying boneless and unresisting as Alexei's mouth brushed her lips.

'Pierre has been giving you the Serivace wine, I can taste it on your mouth.' His tongue licked along the outline of her lips and something seemed to quiver into life inside her, fragile and trembling. She must still be suffering from the after-effects of the alcohol she had consumed, Hope thought dizzily as she lay motionless while Alexei removed her nightgown. She knew she ought to resist, yet she was too curiously weak to do any more than simply follow the movements of the lean brown hands as they dispensed with the fine silk, the moonlight revealing the hard contours of Alexei's body to her as he thrust back the covers, propping himself up on one elbow to study her silvered curves in silence.

As he watched her Hope felt something happening inside her. It was the same sensation she had experienced during her dream, only this time the heat seemed to come from within herself, spreading languorously through her body, the alcohol relaxing her mind and undermining her defences, so that although she could register the slow movement of Alexei's hand as it drifted over her body, it was with curiosity rather than tense panic. Her skin relayed the fact that the hardness of his palm and fingertips against her was pleasurable rather than painful, and her mind noted hazily that he was touching her rather as one might stroke a cat, and she felt the same urge to stretch and luxuriate beneath the slow caress.

If she closed her eyes the urge became even stronger, her senses oddly sharpened so that she was acutely aware of the differing textures of their skins. Her breath suddenly caught as Alexei's hand reached her breasts, his palm cupping one gently until she felt weak with the surging sensation of her own flesh, the need to press herself into his hand, a tugging, aching sensation beginning somewhere deep inside her so intense that in ordinary circumstances it would have sent alarm signals racing to her brain. But now it only made her open her eyes in hazy surprise—not even the suddenly brilliant green of Alexei's gaze alerting her to impending danger.

It was only when Alexei removed his hand and she glanced down and saw the unfamiliar burgeoning of her breasts, her nipples swollen and aching, that awareness finally pierced through her sleep and alcohol-induced haze, her mind shrinking in panic from the knowledge that she was exposing herself to Alexei like a...like a slave girl bent on teasing and arousing her master.

Instinctively, she knew that the languorous curves of her body *were* provocative, deliberately enticing the smooth brush of his hand against her, and the knowledge shocked her into panic, her body tensing, the fierce intensity of Alexei's gaze shifting from her body to her face, his hands clamping on her shoulders forcing her back against the bed, stroking and soothing until panic gave way to a return of her earlier languor. This time it was very much against her will, her mind revolting against the weakness of her body, even while she admitted her inability to do anything about it.

By the time Alexei's mouth touched the pulsing nerve at the base of her throat, her body was already a quivering mass of responsiveness. She should never have drunk all that wine, she thought weakly, subduing a small moan of pleasure as Alexei's lips teased the smooth skin of her throat, tracing a line of tiny kisses from her ear to her lips. His breath was warm against her face as his tongue drew the shape of her mouth, his voice husky as he instructed her to part the lips she had tightened against him, teasing her with light kisses until she did so, her body's involuntary response to the warm possession of his mouth making her tremble convulsively as he held her against him, deepening and intensifying the kiss until nothing else existed.

Vaguely, Hope was aware of Alexei's hand resting at the top of her thigh, her lungs drawing in deep breaths of air, her body still trembling from the impact of his kiss. His teeth nibbled gently on her ear-lobe, waves of sensation exploding inside her as he explored the shape and curves of her ear, one hand holding her securely against him, the other...

She gasped and tensed, trying to pull away, trying to stop his hand from parting her legs, her small fists making no impression against the breadth of his shoulders, shock and outrage rapidly overtaken by sensations she tried to deny. Her eyes widened in stunned reaction, and she looked straight into Alexei's face, hard-boned and watchful, something fierce and elemental glittering behind the impassive shadows in his eyes. The touch of his fingers made her writhe and gasp, hating him for touching her so intimately—what he was doing to her was worse, far worse than what he had done last night—and yet unable to prevent her body from responding almost deliriously to him.

'Stop it. Stop it,' she panted unsteadily, fingers curling into her palms as she tried to move away, but his free hand merely curled round her throat, tilting her head back until the pale skin was fully exposed. His lips moving lingeringly along it, his kisses punctuated with softly murmured sounds of pleasure, and a furious desperation was building up inside her. Barely aware of what she was doing, Hope uncurled her fingers from her palms, transferring them to Alexei's shoulders, small whimpers of pleasure forced past her tightly-closed lips, her body abandoning her, seduced by Alexei's touch, the aching urgency below her stomach increasing in time with the waves of sensation burning through her, her body trembling violently.

Gradually, the touch of Alexei's hand became soothing rather than arousing, comforting her for the vague sensation of disappointment that somehow lingered, her mind too confused and bewildered by the reactions of her body to martial what was left of its defences. When Alexei's mouth left her throat to explore the slope of her shoulder she was too exhausted to protest, too drained to even move when his hands cupped her breasts, his lips exploring their curves.

It wasn't until she felt the rasp of his tongue against her nipple, that Hope felt a resurgence of that earlier sensation, a tensing in the pit of her stomach, and then the slow uncoiling of tense muscles, the heady, liquid warmth that spread right through her urging her shamelessly to abandon herself both to the feeling and to the man arousing it.

She heard Alexei's hoarse murmur of satisfaction as she stretched against him, but it was lost in her own sharp cry of pleasure as his mouth closed once again over her tautly erect nipple, his eyes closing and the moonlight revealing the dark surge of colour to his face as his body responded to the taste and feel of her, the ache inside her still unappeased when he eventually released her swollen flesh.

Hope shivered in rejection as she felt him move away, her mind telling her that what he was doing was wrong, but her body wantonly aching for closer contact with his maleness.

'Hope, open your eyes.'

Unwilling, she did as she was bid, conscious of Alexei's hands on her shoulders, his chest hard against the softness of hers.

'I had no idea our wine would have such an effect on you, little one, or else I might have thought to give you some last night.' There was humour in his eyes and something else too, that brought her to shivering awareness of where she was and what she was doing.

'Don't touch me,' she stammered bitterly. 'I hate you... I hate what you've done to me... I...'

'You hate yourself for responding to me?' he suggested dryly, shaking her gently. '*Ma belle, that* was almost inevitable. Your body is ready for maturity even if your mind is not. Beneath the conventions taught to you by the Sisters, you have a very sensual nature.' He saw her colour, anger darkening her eyes, and laughed softly, 'You don't want to believe me, but I assure you it is true. Tonight, when I came home, you curled into my arms as naturally as though you had always slept there. It was all I could do not to wake you up there and then... Even now, while you are glowering at me, your body craves physical satisfaction, as does mine,' he added softly, his eyes on her breasts as he held her a little away from him, Hope's own eyes widening and hurriedly averting from the evidence of his physical arousal.

She tried to tense her body against him, and for a moment her muscles did lock in fear at the remembered pain of his possession, but other alien sensations spread through her as Alexei looked down at her, and when his body moved over hers, he parted her thighs easily, the weight of his body strangely pleasurable, reminding her of the sensation his fingers had induced earlier—an aching, wanting sensation building up inside her, her breathing ragged and unsteady as she felt him move against her and tensed herself for the expected pain.

'Relax...there's nothing to be frightened of.' He seemed to be breathing the words into her, parting her closed lips with the tip of his tongue, coaxing her to relax and share the pleasure of his mouth against hers, his hand touching her as it had done before, bringing back the same sensation of pleasure, only this time increased to such a pitch that she ached for something more, for... As though she had spoken her need out loud, she felt the pulsating hardness of his body against her, within her, but this time without pain, this time bringing only wave after wave of mindless pleasure, until Alexei muttered something against her mouth and the world seemed to shatter into a million brilliant crystals around her, tears cascading down her face as her body trembled in the aftermath of satisfaction.

She came back to earth to find that she was still in Alexei's arms and that strangely she wanted to remain there. Her lips were pressed against his throat, his skin warm and salty, her body entwined with his, her mind trying to comprehend what had happened. When the Sisters had discussed the sexual act they never mentioned this. The pleasure was a man's; a woman found hers in the children she would ultimately bear.

Hard on the heels of pleasure came pain and self-disgust, how could she have behaved so wantonly, so abandonedly? She tensed and tried to pull away, but Alexei's arms merely tightened.

How triumphant he must be, probably laughing at her naïvety and surrender! Tears stung her eyes and she raised her hand to brush them away, tensing when she felt Alexei's mouth against her lashes, his tongue delicately licking away the salt moisture.

'I hate you for what you've done to me,' she told him in a low voice that trembled.

His mouth stilled, and then placed a light kiss against her skin, his hands framing her face as he tilted it upwards.

'No, little one,' he said softly. 'You hate yourself for responding to me. That is only natural, but it will pass. There is no shame in finding pleasure in someone's caresses. I am not ashamed of telling you that I look forward to the day when your hands and lips explore my body with as much pleasure as I have explored yours.' He felt her tense and pull away and laughed. 'It is all so very shocking, is it not, but I promise you that will soon pass, and there will come a day when you cease to be embarrassed or humiliated by your body's sensuality, and instead find pleasure in knowing yourself so responsive to the caresses of a lover.'

'You are not my lover,' Hope threw back at him. 'You are simply a man who has taken me because he wants to be revenged on my father.'

'And that is why you are so angry, isn't it?' he said, watching her. 'Because there is no love between us? Sometimes two people love each other very much and yet are unable to find the physical pleasure together we have just experienced. Love and sexual satisfaction do not always go together, *mon petit*, and of the two, I'm afraid I much prefer the latter.'

Cynical, loathsome creature, Hope thought bitterly. Her skin burned when she thought of how he had touched her, and how she had responded. She wanted to pull out of his arms, but he wouldn't let her, and her body traitorously wanted to remain entwined with his. She felt physically sick whenever she thought of what had happened—of how he had touched her and how she had felt. It must have been the wine, she would never have allowed him to touch her like that if she hadn't drunk it. He had talked about them sharing 'pleasure', but at least then she had retained her self-respect and her pride, now... Shivering, she told herself she must try and get some sleep, although how she was supposed to do that when every breath from the man lying against her brought his body into contact with hers, she didn't know.

'WAKE UP, sleepyhead, I've brought you your breakfast, and the morning papers. Sorry to wake you up so early, but I have to leave in an hour.'

Groggily, Hope opened her eyes and struggled to sit up, realising too late that she was completely naked, her eyes angrily daring Alexei to look at her as she reached for the protection of the covers.

How long had he been awake? He was wearing a formal business suit, and an immaculate white shirt, the suit emphasising the lean, powerful lines of his body. Against her will, Hope found herself remembering things from the night, a dark painful tide of colour sweeping over her body.

'Hope, you must learn that there was nothing to be ashamed of in what happened between us last night. The fault is perhaps mine in that I didn't fully realise how uninformed the Sisters had kept you, and that it had never occurred to you that you might feel as you did. Am I right?'

Wishing him a thousand miles away, Hope could only wonder at his ability to remain so clinically detached when he asked such intimate questions, the mere sound of which was enough to subject her to another wave of burning heat.

'The Sisters said that it was men who...who experienced...pleasure,' she managed at last, knowing that he wouldn't go until he had received his answer.

'And you believed them?' He had come to sit beside her. She felt the bed depress under his weight and tried to move away, but his hands were on her shoulders, pulling her into a sitting position, her arms folding instinctively over the sheet she had tucked around her body.

'I...I don't know...'

'Umm. What I think you mean is that you had perhaps read that it wasn't always so, but never expected to experience it for yourself. Only a certain kind of women experience sexual pleasure, that's what you thought, I suspect?'

He had gauged her thoughts so accurately that Hope could only nod dumbly. 'I should have talked to you more, prepared you for what you would experience, although something tells me that you would not have believed me, so perhaps after all... Try not to hate yourself too much, Hope. I shall be away for several days, and although I have given instructions to Pierre that you are not to leave the *château*, my library is at your disposal. Every day I receive several journals and papers from Paris. You might find it educational to read them and discover more about the world you are shortly to enter. That way it may not come as such a culture shock.'

'You are going away?' Hope was appalled by the sense of panic that gripped her, the longing to clutch hold of his immaculate jacket and beg him to stay. To punish herself for such a stupid weakness, she added bitterly, 'I should have thought you would lose no time in whisking me off to the Caribbean to flaunt me before my father, or do you want to savour your vengeance?'

'Revenge, like a fine wine, matures with keeping,' he agreed, smiling at her. 'But you are far from ready to be "flaunted", as you put it, before your father yet. Only when you are ready to welcome my caresses will we seek out your father. I want him to know that you come to me willingly.'

'Never!'

He laughed softly, getting up from the bed.

'Most assuredly you will, and I confess that when you do, my pleasure will not come completely from the fact that I have accomplished another step on the road to fulfilment of my vow to avenge Tanya. You yourself are proving an unexpected bonus, *mon petit,*' he informed her lazily. 'I confess last night, hearing the cries of pleasure on your lips, made me forget why you were in my arms and think only of the pleasure of having you there. Go and shower, and I will pour our coffee.' He looked up at her and laughed at her expression. 'Ah, no, you are quite safe this morning, I have no intention of following you there, but perhaps on another occasion...if you were to ask me nicely...'

His laughter followed her into the bathroom, reinforcing her bitter anger. He had humiliated her by subjecting her body to physical need, by kidnapping her and holding her prisoner, and all he could do was laugh. Well, she would show him. Somehow, during the time he was away, she would find a defence against him. What happened last night was not going to happen again!

When she returned from the bathroom he glanced up at her, indicating the chair opposite him. Feeling at a disadvantage wrapped in a towelling robe when he was formally dressed, Hope sat down, picking up the cup of coffee he had poured, inhaling the rich fragrance, studying him over the rim as he read his paper.

'Taking an inventory?' His lazy amusement unnerved her, her hands shaking as she gripped her coffee cup.

'I was just thinking,' she lied, hastily looking away, flushing when he laughed, and said softly:

'Liar.'

Before she could repudiate his comment, he passed her one of the papers, her eyes automatically scanning the headlines as she took it from him. Current affairs were included in the school curriculum, but they had been taught as dry, dusty facts, and Hope found her interest growing as she read the front-page stories.

'You have a keen brain, Hope,' Alexei remarked as he poured them both a second cup of coffee. 'Use it and you will find it a constant source of compensation.' The look in his eyes rather than his words made Hope aware of a streak of cynicism in his nature underlined by the mockery in his smile. The blend of Russian and French blood couldn't be one it was easy to live with, she reflected thoughtfully, there must be times when war broke out between French hardheaded cynicism and Russian hot-blooded passion. She didn't need to ask which side of him had prompted his need for revenge against her father, but it was the French blood in him that had carefully thought out the nature of that revenge, not the Russian.

'I must leave now.' She saw him glance at his watch and then frown. 'I'm taking your passport with me, Hope, and I'm not leaving the car. Remember, you gave me your word that you wouldn't attempt to leave.'

'It would be too late if I did, wouldn't it?' Hope asked dully. 'My father can't marry me to Alain Montrachet now, although if I did leave, at least I would spare him the humiliation of having me paraded in front of his friends as your mistress.'

'You have two choices, Hope,' Alexei told her evenly. 'Either you stay here as my . . . guest . . . with the freedom of my home, or I shall instruct Pierre that you are to be locked in these rooms until I return—the choice is yours. You can be treated as an adult or as a child.'

'You accept my word?' Hope asked him half scornfully and half curiously.

'I believe that I can do so,' Alexei said quietly. 'Am I wrong?' What could she say? That he couldn't trust her to keep her word. Biting her lip, Hope looked away. 'Am I wrong, Hope?' Alexei repeated.

'No, damn you,' she flung at him. 'You needn't tell Pierre to lock me in. After all, I've nowhere to go, have I? According to you, my father won't even give me house room now, and I don't suppose they'd take me back at the convent.'

'Poor little unwanted girl,' Alexei mocked. 'You will always be wanted . . . by someone, Hope, but first you would be wise to learn to want yourself, to accept yourself as a human being.' He got up, stooping swiftly to drop a kiss on her unguarded lips, straightening with a smile to tousle her hair and open the door. 'Think of me tonight, little one,' he drawled as he paused by it, 'sleeping alone without the tempting distraction of your body in my arms.'

He was gone before she could think of a fitting retort, and although she heard the car engine fire a little later in the courtyard, she didn't leave her seat, instead forcing herself to finish her cup of coffee.

An hour later she was dressed, and she had stripped and remade the bed, gathering up the breakfast things automatically. Pierre turned round as she walked into the kitchen and Hope ventured a tentative smile, feeling unreasonably pleased when it was returned.

The day stretched emptily in front of her and she frowned, impatient at her own boredom. She was intelligent, Alexei had said, and that intelligence told her that the blame for her boredom and its relief lay within herself. One day she would be free of Alexei, free of the nightmare that had darkened her life since Alexei arrived in it, but what was she going to do? She chewed her lip as she walked towards the library, remembering her wistful ambition to make a career for herself using her languages. She would do what they had done at school, she decided impulsively. She would make herself think, speak and read in a different language each day, starting today with Russian—the most difficult and least fluent of her languages.

As she had expected, she managed to find some Russian books in the library, and settling down with a selection of short stories by Chekhov, Hope forced herself to concentrate on the written words.

When Pierre came in at lunchtime he found her engrossed, and mimed to her that he had prepared some food. Unwilling to eat alone, Hope followed him to the kitchen, wondering if it would be possible for her to see the wine cellars and the bottling plant Alexei had pointed out to her. It would be pleasant to go out for a good long walk, but Pierre might mistake her motives and she decided she would have to content herself with exploring the gardens, irritated with herself for her self-imposed imprisonment.

If she had not given Alexei her word... If she had not he would undoubtedly have instructed Pierre to stand guard over her night and day, Hope thought wryly. He was unswervingly determined to have his revenge on her father.

What had Tanya been like, she wondered idly. Her portrait showed a startling similarity to her brother, although in Tanya, the harshly masculine features were softened into feminine lines. There was a vulnerability about her, too, that Alexei didn't possess, and Hope shivered, remembering that she had taken her own life. She must have loved her father very deeply, and he...hadn't he guessed how she would react when he ended their relationship?

In many ways her father was more of a stranger to her than Alexei. It was a disquieting thought, but one which Hope found recurring as the days passed.

The fourth morning of Alexei's absence found Hope reading Claire Bretécher's cartoon in *Le Nouvel Observateur*, when she heard the sound of a car outside. Immediately her body tensed, but she forced herself to keep on reading, picking up her coffee cup and drinking a little unsteadily from it, not because she was thirsty, but because the action prevented her from jumping up and running to the window overlooking the courtyard.

Masculine footsteps and the deep timbre of Alexei's voice warned her of his arrival before the kitchen door opened, and Hope was amazed at the wealth of information her senses relayed to her about him long before she lifted her eyes from the papers.

'*Bonjour, mon petit.* Have you missed me?'

His tan had deepened while he was away, and Hope felt her stomach clench disturbingly as she looked into his face. Had he been to the Caribbean? Making sure perhaps that the scene was set for his big dénouement. She responded coolly to his greeting, seeing his smile widen, his teeth white against the darkness of his skin, as he bent towards her and murmured against her ear. 'I have driven at a speed well in excess of the limit all the way from the airport, hoping to find you still in bed, but Pierre tells me you have become an early riser during my absence. Dare I hope it is because you find our bed lonely without me beside you in it?'

'It is not "our" bed—it is yours—and if I rise early perhaps it is because I have no wish to linger somewhere that holds unpleasant memories for me.'

She had had three days in which to martial her defences against him and Hope had the satisfaction of seeing his mouth tighten, the smile disappearing. The sensual response of her body to his lovemaking was something that still had the power to shock and disturb her and her own intelligence conveyed to her the knowledge that she could not depend on herself to resist him physically. For the sake of her pride and her sanity she had to find some other way to erect a barrier between them and she had come to the conclusion that while she could not resist him physically, she must do so mentally, so that no matter how many times he tortured her with the vulnerability of her body, her mind remained aloof and antagonistic.

Pierre came in with fresh coffee and warm croissants and Hope watched as Alexei poured himself a cup and bit into the flaky, sweet roll. He looked well-pleased with life, a warm smile curling his mouth, faintly reminiscent as though he were remembering something—or someone—with whom he had shared pleasure. What did he do when he wasn't pursuing his vengeance against her father, Hope wondered sharply. He was a sophisticated man, who had already shown her by his tastes and conversation that he did not remain on his estate all year round, merely tending his vines, and yet he had mentioned his sister's lack of wealth which seemed to suggest that he himself was far from being a wealthy dilettante, free to pursue a life of pleasure and idleness. No, that was definitely not Alexei, she thought intuitively, his mind was too keen and sharp to be that of a man who did not use it. The papers which were delivered daily to the *château* covered a diverse number of subjects.

'You're looking very thoughtful.'

Hope raised her head, her eyes clashing bitterly with his. 'And you find that surprising?' Her temper rose when she saw the indulgent amusement her anger brought to his eyes. 'Your absence seems to have improved your mood in addition to your tan,' she said heatedly. 'What did you find in the Caribbean? That my father is in even greater financial difficulties than you thought?'

'The Caribbean? What makes you think I have been there?' The good humour fled from his eyes and he said curtly, 'You are behaving like a child, Hope. If it has not yet occurred to you that I have a life apart from that which contains my feelings towards your father, perhaps it ought to. I have been to the Napa Valley where I own a vineyard. It is a new venture for me, and one in which I have sunk a large amount of capital. If my "mood", as you call it, strikes you as "good", you can put that down to the fact that I now believe my investment will pay off. I am not a wealthy man in the terms that your father and his crowd define "wealth" . . .'

'And you envy those who are?' Hope demanded scornfully. His face tightened and darkened slightly. 'No, Hope, I do not,' he corrected slowly. 'When you have a little more maturity, you will appreciate that men value most that which they earn for themselves. I personally can conceive of nothing worse than inheriting or owning vast wealth. Everyone needs a goal in life, or something to work and aim for. My aim, or one of them, is to restore this *château* to what it once was—that, and to produce a new wine from my Napa Valley vineyards which might one day equal those we produce here in France. My trip to California had already been postponed once, and consequently there is a considerable backlog of work for me to catch up on.'

'Here at the vineyard?' Hope asked the question reluctantly. She didn't want to get involved in Alexei's day to day life. She wanted to hold herself aloof, to remain distant from him, and yet, in spite of her resolutions, she was interested.

'Here, in Beaune, where I serve on the committee which upholds the old traditions of this area, and in Paris, where I have an interest in a wine-broking business.'

'I'm surprised as such a very busy man that you managed to fit in the time to... to kidnap me, and plan your revenge on my father,' Hope said with what she hoped was a commendable degree of sarcasm, but it was her face that was tinged with betraying colour and not her opponent's, his face calmly unimpressed as he poured himself a second cup of coffee.

'You would do well to learn how to wield the rapier correctly, before you attempt to thrust against an expert, *mon petit*,' he mocked her, refilling her own cup. 'Now, have you any more questions for me, anything more you wish to know about my life?'

'Nothing!' Hope told him vehemently, too vehemently she feared if his amused expression was anything to go by. She glanced into his dark face and wondered numbly about the women who shared his life, quickly trying to quell the thought. What were they to do with her? Did they resent his absence while he spent his time with her? What sort of relationships did he have that he was able to do so? Was he as remote and taunting with them as he was with her?

'So many busy thoughts chasing one another through your head.' He picked up his cup and finished his coffee. 'What is it that brings such an arrested expression to your face, I wonder?'

'I was just thinking. You are spending a lot of time with me.' She had blurted out the truth without thinking, and came to an abrupt halt, realising the dangerous ground on which she was treading, but it was too late.

'And...' Alexei pressed softly, the mockery in his eyes daring her to ask the questions she was sure he knew were racing through her mind, prompting her to ignore the warning voice inside her skull and to say instead, her chin lifting firmly:

'I was thinking you must be a very cold, hard man, and one who does not care where he causes pain, just so long as he is able to accomplish what he desires.'

'Meaning?' Now there was an iron hardness beneath the soft tone.

'Meaning, I am not so naïve as to suppose that you live your life as... as a monk,' she managed, hating the colour seeping up under her skin, 'and that it surely must cause your...'

'Lovers?' he put in helpfully, watching her with narrowed eyes, and willing her, Hope was sure, to abandon her probing and be overwhelmed with the embarrassment she was suffering. But she wasn't going to. Her chin lifted higher, and she continued firmly:

'It must cause them considerable pain when you abandon them to pursue... other matters...'

'I daresay it would,' Alexei agreed carelessly, 'if they were the foolish adolescents you seem to imagine. My relationships are always with women sophisticated enough...'

'Not to care how you treat them,' Hope burst in angrily, flinching back as she saw the reflection of her anger mirrored in Alexei's eyes.

'I am no bluebeard, Hope, for all that you seem determined to make me into one. I have never knowingly encouraged any woman to think I have more to offer her than I have said. You still have your foolish romantic illusions; at your age, perhaps I did too, although I suspect I grew up a little faster. With age and experience there comes the ability to detach oneself from one's emotions, to stand aside and remember that there are other things in life.'

Had Alexei ever been anything other than detached? She tried to imagine him as an awkward, uncertain teenager, and abandoned the struggle when it taxed her imagination too much.

'Have you ever loved anyone—besides Tanya?'

'That, I think, is a question I must not answer.' He said it quietly, almost gently, but Hope knew she had strayed on to forbidden ground, and her heart leapt uncomfortably. Strangely, the thought of Alexei actually loving a woman was even more hard to come to terms with than his cool remoteness.

'I think we have discussed this subject for long enough,' Alexei told her firmly, breaking into her thoughts. 'My personal life is not something which need concern you...'

'No, indeed,' Hope agreed, suppressing a breathless sob. 'I wonder what your friends, your "lovers" would think about you if they knew the truth? If they know what you planned to do to my father?'

'Many of them would probably applaud me.' Her shocked expression drew a twisted smile from his mouth. 'Oh yes, I am speaking the truth. Your father is not a popular man, and I am not the only one to have reason to hate him.'

Hope shuddered, recognising the intensity of emotion his cool façade cloaked, shivering with the knowledge that beneath the cool exterior there were emotions which, once out of control, would be very difficult to restrain, and she prayed instinctively that those emotions would never be loosed against her. As though he sensed her fear, Alexei talked for a few minutes about his visit to California, explaining that they were experimenting with a new type of wine, talking to her as though she were someone he had to entertain as a duty, as indeed perhaps she was, she thought bitterly.

When he changed the subject it came as something of a shock, and it was several seconds before she could pick up the threads of what he was saying, until he repeated patiently:

'Pierre informs me you wanted to see over the cellars and the bottling plant?'

'You were the one who reminded me that I had a brain,' Hope countered, meeting his eyes. 'Although we were taught to recognise the great vintages at the convent, I know very little about the actual process of making wine.'

'And even less about the dangers of drinking it,' he agreed sardonically. 'As it happens, I have to go and see Jules this morning. You may accompany me, if you wish.' He looked at her as though waiting for her to make some comment, and Hope replied coolly:

'Thank you, I should like that.' She sensed that her cool manner was not what he anticipated. He had probably expected her to fling herself at him in tears begging to be set free, she thought wryly, but beneath the obedience and dependence the convent had taught was a streak of a strong-minded independence which was beginning to resurface. Alexei had been right about one thing, she had discovered from her daily reading of his papers and journals that there were indeed many shades of grey in the outside world, that men and women lived openly together without the benefit of marriage and no one thought any the worse of them for it. She was beginning to feel that it might be possible for her to make a life for herself after Alexei had finished with her, but an instinct that went deeper than logic and education urged her to protect what she could of herself from him; physically that was impossible, but mentally she would never surrender.

'What are you thinking about, you were miles away?'

'I was wondering how long it will be before I'm free,' she told him quietly. 'When do you intend to leave?'

He glanced at his watch, and for the first time Hope saw lines of tiredness etched against his eyes.

'I need a shower, so say, an hour, unless, of course, you want to join me?' His eyes slid over her body in sexual appraisal, and Hope felt a deeply urgent response surge through her body. She had found it difficult to sleep alone in the large bed, but she had told herself that was because she was a prisoner, held against her will.

'No? Another time, perhaps,' Alexei drawled as he got up. 'I suggest you change into jeans for your visit to the cellars, little one, you will find them dark and dusty.'

In the library, among the other books, Hope had found a history of the Serivace family, with several chapters devoted to their wine which they had started making commercially during the nineteenth century, when the *château* and lands had been returned to them by Napoleon, following the Revolution. But fascinating though the book had been, it was the Russian side of Alexei's ancestry that Hope found more interesting, because she sensed that it held the key to his personality.

When she went upstairs to change into more casual clothes the bathroom door was closed and she could hear the sound of running water. It only took five minutes to change from her silk suit into the emerald green cut-off cotton jeans and matching T-shirt they had bought in Seville. The jeans hugged the narrow bones of her hips and Hope was eyeing her reflection in the mirror when she heard the bathroom door open. Alexei hadn't bothered to dress, and a towel draped round his hips drew her attention to the muscular flatness of his stomach, darkly tanned against the whiteness of the towel, drops of water clinging to the hair on his thighs and chest.

Her jeans were almost the same colour as his eyes, Hope thought dizzily, wishing her senses were less attuned to the physical reality of him. She could smell the clean, fresh scent of his skin, her body pulsing with a breath-stopping excitement; torn between an urge to run, to put as great a distance as she could between herself and the intimacy she knew presaged danger, and the physical temptation of reaching out to touch the sun-bronzed male flesh.

'Hope?' She winced as Alexei's fingers dug into the tender flesh of her upper arms, not sure if it was anger or mockery that darkened his eyes as he bent over her. 'This isn't a Victorian melodrama,' he told her. 'You don't need to look as though you're going to faint every time you set eyes on me. I don't possess any superhuman powers, for all you look at me as though you expect me to change you into a pumpkin. I'm quite human... All too human,' Hope thought she heard him add tautly as his hands slid from her arms to her shoulders and down across her back, bringing her into contact with his still damp body. The heat from his skin burned through her T-shirt as he held her full length against him, muttering something that sounded suspiciously like a curse before his mouth closed over hers, in hard, insistent determination.

It wasn't the same as it had been when he kissed her before, Hope thought numbly, unable to pinpoint the difference between those earlier kisses and this one, except that she suspected this one had a trace of anger in it and it made no allowances for her inexperience. When Alexei released her her lips felt swollen and tender, and for some reason she wanted to cry.

'You'd better wait for me downstairs,' Alexei told her curtly. 'I want to get dressed and I'm not in the mood to pander to the delicate sensibilities of an over-prim adolescent.'

For a moment she was too shaken to move, still trying to recover from the effect of his almost brutal kiss. 'For God's sake, Hope,' she heard him add savagely, 'if you know what's good for you, you won't choose now for

teenage defiance. To put it bluntly, I'm mentally too exhausted to play games, the only thing my body cares
about right now is that you're female, so get out before
it overrules my mind, will you?'

She was still shaking when she got downstairs, disturbed by the unexpectedness of the change in Alexei,
and wondering about the reasons behind it. Had the
Russian side of him taken ascendancy over the French,
and was it growing impatient at the delay in putting into
effect his plan? Half an hour later, when Alexei joined
her in the library, Hope could see no sign of the tense
anger she had sensed in him earlier, and he was once
again the urbane and sophisticated male creature she had
first seen in the Reverend Mother's office.

They drove to the bottling plant and wine cellars,
Alexei pointing to Hope the vines growing alongside the
road, and describing their various stages of development. 'Each one of which is crucial in its own way,' he
said as he turned the car into the lane that led to the collection of buildings he had pointed out to her on her arrival. 'This month we spray against pests, and as with
everything else the timing is all important. Jules's family
have been involved in the making of wine as long as we
have ourselves. Come,' he told her when he stopped the
car in front of the farm buildings, 'Jules is not expecting
us, but we shall probably find him in the cellars.'

Dutifully, Hope followed him, avoiding the hens
scratching in the yard, blinded for a moment by the lack
of sunlight as they stepped inside one of the buildings.
Above the noise of the machinery a tall, brown-haired
young man greeted Alexei, his eyes widening fractionally when he caught sight of Hope herself, although he
kept on talking to Alexei, explaining to him that there
had been some problems with the machinery which was
now solved. 'How was California?' he added. 'Did your
business go well?'

From the conversation which ensued, Hope learned more about the winery in the Napa Valley, and she listened with interest while the two men discussed the various differences in the two wine industries.

'Hope is staying with me for a while,' Alexei said eventually. 'Her father is...a friend of mine.' While he introduced them, Hope struggled to understand why he had lied to Jules. Did he think the younger man might disapprove of what he was doing, or didn't he trust her to keep her word? Did he think she might appeal to Jules to help her and this was his way of stopping her?

Whichever the case, there was no mistaking the frank admiration in the young Frenchman's eyes as he smiled at her, and Hope felt a purely feminine response when she smiled back teasingly at him, until it was checked by the pressure of Alexei's hand on her arm, and the way his brows drew together repressively.

Jules offered to show her round the wine cellars, and although Hope would have liked him to do so, Alexei reminded the younger man that there was work to do and escorted her himself. Hope had learned enough from her reading to be genuinely interested in the cellars. Alexei pointed out to her several dusty racks which he told her held bottles of their very best vintages.

'These,' he told her indicating one row, 'are the bottles my father put down the year I was twenty-one—to celebrate my son's twenty-first. It is the custom to put down wine in the year of one son's birth to be opened at his coming of age, but the first years after the war did not produce a good enough wine and so...'

He was still talking, but Hope wasn't listening. Alexei's son... He talked so naturally of him that Hope wondered if he had plans to marry. Presumably he must, or see the family name die with him. Who would he choose to share his name? One of the elegant worldly women who were no doubt his normal choice of female companionship, or someone innocent...untouched...an arranged marriage like hers would have been? What did it matter? Why concern herself with him when their lives were only going to touch so briefly?

Jules was waiting for them when they returned. His mother had just finished baking, he told them, adding that it was a long time since she had seen Alexei.

Taking the hint, Alexei guided Hope towards the farmhouse. The door opened straight into the kitchen, stone-flagged and huge, dominated by the enormous fireplace and the large scrubbed wooden table. Jules's mother was small and plump, with dark eyes that moved shrewdly over Hope before turning to Alexei. Watching them embrace, Hope was conscious of being an outsider, and as though he sensed her feelings Jules murmured quietly, 'Maman was Alexei's nurse when he was a baby. In many ways she still considers him as much her child as she does me. Are you staying long at the *château?*' he added, and again Hope noticed the warm gleam of appreciation in his eyes as they rested on her.

'I'm not sure,' she told him truthfully.

'Perhaps I might be permitted to call and take you for a drive,' he suggested formally. 'I shall ask Alexei, if you are in agreement?'

'If she is in agreement to what?' Alexei interrupted, obviously catching the last part of their conversation.

'I was asking Hope if I might show her some of our countryside while she was staying at the *château.*'

Alexei's eyebrows rose. 'I thought you were too busy spraying to take any time off, Jules. Your mother has just been telling me that Marie-Claire has been complaining that she never sees you.'

The olive-skinned face coloured faintly, and Jules shrugged uncomfortably. 'I have been busy, it is true,' he agreed, 'but now that the machinery is mended ...'

'You will have time to visit Marie-Claire,' Alexei interposed smoothly. 'When is the wedding to be? After the vintage?'

So Marie-Claire, whoever she was, was engaged to Jules, Hope realised, and Alexei was making sure that she knew it. Did he think she might have some idea of escaping from him by using Jules? She sighed. She would have enjoyed some young companionship.

Madame Duval had cut them all thick wedges of home-made cake, and Hope found she was hungry enough to eat all hers, which drew an approving smile from Jules's mother. Alexei, she noticed, barely touched his, although he did drink two large cups of coffee before saying that it was time for them to leave. On the way back to the *château* he was silent, and some small devil prompted Hope to say casually, 'Jules is very nice. I would have enjoyed going out with him.'

'No doubt,' came the dry response, 'but neither his *maman* nor Marie-Claire would have shared your enjoyment. You are a very beautiful girl, Hope, and Jules, I'm afraid, is extremely susceptible. Marie-Claire is his second cousin, and I suspect this marriage is wanted more by his parents and Marie-Claire herself than by Jules. His mother would not thank me for adding further doubts to his mind by letting him roam around the countryside neglecting his work and his fiancée to be with you.

'I have to go into Beaune this afternoon, would you like to come with me? It is a very old town with much that would interest you; we could dine there this evening if you wish?'

'No, thank you.' Hope sat upright in her seat, ignoring his profile and concentrating on the road ahead.

'Ah.' There was a dangerous softness underlying the word and she tried not to let it affect her. 'But surely I am right in thinking that had Jules been the one to invite you you would have accepted with alacrity. Are you punishing me, little one, for refusing to let you dazzle him?' He sounded more amused than annoyed and Hope was disturbed to discover mingled with her totally justifiable anger, a small flare of disappointment, the reason for which she did not feel inclined to investigate too deeply.

CHAPTER FIVE

ALEXEI WAS NOT disposed to be amused, however, the following day when Jules drove into the courtyard and announced that he had to go into Beaune and he wondered if Hope would care to go with him.

A little to Hope's surprise, Alexei had made no move to touch her or make love to her the night before. She had been in bed when he came up, far from asleep, her body and mind both tensely alert for his slightest move. But none had come and, as she lay, tensely, with her back to him, she had felt the unmistakable relaxation of his body into sleep. This morning she felt unusually edgy, something which she put down to Alexei's presence after several days of her own company, and her anger fanned when Alexei shook his head over Jules's invitation and announced that she would be unable to accompany him as they were going to Paris.

Hope waited until Jules had gone before venting her feelings. 'Why did you lie to Jules?' she demanded angrily. 'You know we're not going to Paris and . . .'

'Oh, but we are,' Alexei corrected calmly. 'We're leaving today.'

'But . . . but why?' Hope had a vague memory of a school-friend reporting gleefully on the jealousy of a boy she had met on holiday.

'The moment Gary saw me with Tom, he couldn't wait to prise us apart and keep us that way,' she had told them. But Alexei couldn't in any way be jealous of any relationship his reluctant guest might build up with Jules, who was in any case apparently involved with another girl, and yet he had quite deliberately and cold-bloodedly deprived her of Jules's companionship.

'Why?' The dark eyebrows rose quellingly. 'Because I deem it necessary, *mon petit,* but if you must have a reason, put it down to the fact that I feel my cause will advance faster in Paris, rather in the way in which a gardener places a plant in a hot-house to force the bloom.'

Hope waited suspiciously, but he said nothing more on the subject, merely suggesting that she might save Pierre the task of packing her case. 'In fact, you might pack for both of us,' he added carelessly. Hope was glad he had already turned away from her and so was unable to see the colour staining her skin. She still found any reference to their intimacy embarrassing, the more so because that intimacy had been forced upon her, and later, in their room, she found it difficult to remain objective and detached as she folded and carefully packed Alexei's clothes in the cases she had found in the wardrobe.

She had nearly finished when he walked in, looking faintly amused as he watched her. 'There's no need to remove the entire contents of my wardrobe,' he assured her. 'I keep some clothes at my Paris apartment—it makes life much easier—so one case will do.'

He had a Paris apartment? Hope didn't know whether to be pleased or sorry that they would not be staying in an hotel. On the one hand it would be embarrassing for her to have it known publicly that they were lovers, but on the other, at least staying in an hotel would be less intimate than sharing an apartment.

'I am not the ogre your eyes would have you believe,' Alexei commented sardonically, watching the differing emotions chasing one another across her face, 'and it is not my lovemaking you object to, is it, Hope?'

'Yes!'

His eyes hardened slightly, his smile derisory. 'If I didn't want to be on the road in half an hour I would take great pleasure in proving that you're lying—to our mutual satisfaction. Be honest with *yourself,* Hope, even if you can't be honest with me. Your body responds very readily to mine—something I doubt you would have experienced with Alain Montrachet.'

'Why shouldn't I have done?' Hope lashed back at him bitterly. 'As you have just pointed out, it is my body that responds—not *me*—so presumably it would have responded just as well to the husband my father had chosen for me.' She didn't know if what she was saying was true, but the fact that it might be had haunted her constantly since the second night Alexei made love to her. Perhaps there was something wrong with her? Perhaps she was the sort of woman who responded to any man; every man.

Alexei's harsh laugh cut across her thoughts, the look in his eyes making her pulse flutter with apprehension. 'You really think so? Then perhaps I'd better tell you a little more about the man your father chose for you.' It struck Hope that he was furiously and dangerously angry, although she couldn't understand why. He hadn't struck her as the sort of man who needed to bolster his ego by bragging about his sexual expertise, so what had she said to anger him?

'Montrachet is twenty-five years old and Tanya told me, although it isn't commonly known, he was expelled from his private school for an incident involving several other pupils and a girl from the local village.' Alexei's mouth twisted as he looked at her. 'Are you so naïve that you don't understand what I'm telling you, Hope?'

'You mean they...he...raped her?'

'That's one way of putting it, although in my view the word "rape" has become cheapened with overusage recently. Destroyed would be a better choice of word, or even "murdered" because the poor girl took her own life later. And it hasn't just been a teenage escapade. Montrachet is well known in certain circles for his . . . tastes, and you may be sure his mother knows it. Why else is she conniving with your father for this marriage? I'm not saying Montrachet couldn't find a woman to marry him, he's rich enough to find himself a dozen, but French parents are careful with their daughters' futures. His reputation has become widespread, and if he is to have the type of bride the Montrachet name demands, the family must lower their sights a little.

'Does that answer your question, or do you still believe you would have found the same pleasure in his arms that you did in mine? I made you a promise when I abducted you that I would not vent my hatred of your father on you, and I have kept that promise, whether you recognise that fact as yet or not.' His fingers curled along her jaw, forcing her to face him. 'Do not doubt for one minute that I could have shown you hell in my arms far more easily than I showed you heaven, and don't make me think you are more your father's daughter than I believed by lying that I didn't.' He saw the tears trembling on her lashes and frowned. 'I'm sorry if I was hard on you, but I will not be compared to an animal like Montrachet.'

Hope shook her head. 'It wasn't that.'

'No?' His eyebrows drew together. 'Then what was it? You are still annoyed with me because I refused to let you go out with Jules?'

Again Hope shook her head, too relieved by the horror and revulsion she had felt at his disclosures about Alain Montrachet to prevaricate. 'I thought I must be a . . . I thought my body would respond to anyone no matter whether I hated them or loved them.'

She stiffened as she felt him tense, wondering if he was going to laugh at her, wondering why she had been so stupid as to confide in him. Whenever he was near, her emotions seemed to see-saw wildly out of control, but he wasn't laughing, in fact his expression was unusually grim as he sat down on the edge of the bed, pulling her with him so that she was sitting opposite him.

'Is that honestly what you thought? That you were a potential nymphomaniac? Of course you did,' he added, answering his own question. 'There are times, little one, when you make me feel extremely old—and very guilty. There is no one reason why you responded to me, and it is certainly not because you would respond to any man who touched you, and even while your body responds, your mind fights me, is this so?'

'Then why do I?' Hope ventured, feeling very daring, almost holding her breath as she waited for him to answer.

'Why? Perhaps the main reason is the same reason that a hostage turns to her captor, because to some extent I am in control of your life. Also, I cheated a little, your body is ready for womanhood, even if you are not. Later, when you know more of the world, you will have more discernment, more control over your emotions and physical responses. There is always a special relationship between a woman and her first lover. It was not part of my plan to make the experience an unpleasant one for you, Hope, and by the time one reaches my age one has the knowledge to be able to differentiate.

'However, I confess that even I was surprised by the extent to which our bodies are attuned to one another. That is something which is rare. Try to look upon what you will learn while you are with me as several years of learning compressed into a very short space of time. I cannot turn the clock back, Hope, even if I wanted to. My desire to make your father pay for what he did to

Tanya has burned within me for too long for that. All I can and will do is to reiterate that I shall not knowingly hurt you.'

His words stayed in Hope's mind during the drive to Paris. Strangely, she had believed all that he had said about Alain Montrachet; Alexei wouldn't stoop to lying to her, she knew that instinctively. Their talk emboldened her to put to him a request that had been in her mind for several days; something she had thought about when he was away.

'Alexei?' He turned to look at her when she murmured his name, a disconcerting gleam in otherwise enigmatical eyes. 'I was wondering...while I am...with you, I should like to equip myself for afterwards. I was wondering if I could learn some secretarial skills, something that would help me to get a job when...when it is over.'

As she had half dreaded, her request seemed to anger him. The gleam disappeared to be replaced by hard scrutiny, his voice clipped and faintly edged with impatience as he replied dryly, 'You know, Hope, it is hardly flattering that already you should be thinking of "afterwards". However commendable though your desire to be independent is, I am not about to abandon you—an orphan to the storm, as it were—and we shall not be staying in Paris long enough for you to attend college, if that is what is in your mind, and certainly when we are in the Caribbean it will not be possible. When "afterwards", as you put it, comes, we shall talk again of this matter, and you shall have a training in whatever field you desire, after which I shall do my best to ensure that you find a suitable job.'

'No!' Hope was surprised at her own vehemence, at a loss to understand why she should feel this revulsion against Alexei paying for her education, perhaps asking one of his friends to employ her. 'I don't want your charity, Alexei,' she told him. 'I have some money of my own.' This was a lie, but he wasn't to know it. 'I just thought if I had any spare time...'

'You won't have,' he assured her inexorably.

'Meaning, I suppose, that it wouldn't be the "done thing" for your mistress to attend college?' Why was it that every time she felt that she could almost like him, something happened to bring back all her animosity and disturb her peace of mind?

'None of them has done before,' Alexei agreed suavely, 'they haven't needed to—and while we're on the subject, I don't care for the word "mistress". We're lovers, Hope, equal partners in a mutually pleasurable occupation.'

His words alone were enough to make the dark colour burn up under her skin, without the look which accompanied them. Yes, they were 'lovers' as he chose to term it, and there was nothing she could do to wipe out the memories imprinted so vividly on her mind and body, memories of her heated, undeniable responses to him; of the feel of his body against hers; of the way he touched and aroused her. And of course none of his other women would need to go to college. No doubt they already knew all there was to know—about life; about men; about everything—while she...

Hope bit her lip in an agony of mortification. No wonder she sometimes felt he was laughing at her, and the knowledge hurt, fresh colour searing her pale skin as she wondered if he made comparisons... if he wished when he held her in his arms that she was one of the older, experienced women he so obviously favoured.

'I didn't ask to be taken to your bed, Alexei,' she reminded him bitterly, a little shocked to hear herself saying the words.

'No, and believe me had you done so, you wouldn't have been there.' He saw her face and added dryly, 'Girls of your age tend to have too many romantic daydreams;

had you invited yourself into my bed it would most probably have been because you imagined yourself in love with me, a complication which...'

'Is never likely to happen with the sophisticated, worldly women you prefer,' Hope shot back. 'I feel sorry for you, Alexei. You're so cynical...so...clinical and detached.'

'While you, my little hot-head, are far from being either, but you will see, they will come with time.'

Hope fell silent, acknowledging that she wasn't going to get the better of him, but she found her thoughts drifting, as they tended to do more and more lately, to what she privately termed as Alexei's 'real' life; the life he lived when he was not pursuing vengeance against her father. His ability to remain detached from her and what he was doing to her sometimes appalled her. Was he always like this? Did the other women in his life share her feeling that there was always some part of himself he held aloof? And did they, like her, experience a faint pang of pain that this should be so? Unaware of the dangerous ground her thoughts were treading, Hope continued to muse.

Wasn't Alexei worried that his business interests would suffer because he was spending so much time on her? He had already told her that he had two vineyards to run and other business dealings, or had he allowed for them in his calculations? Sometimes his attention to detail, his fanaticism where her father was concerned, frightened her. This, she suspected, was not a side of him which was commonly known to his friends. Indeed, she guessed that the Russian side of his nature—the side brought into prominence by her father's rejection of Tanya—was something deeply secret and hidden, revealed to very few. It would be possible to know Alexei for many years and yet know nothing of what lurked behind the urbane mask—but she knew. He had revealed to her how deeply

Tanya's death tormented and tortured him, and intuitively Hope sensed that that knowledge created a bond between them which would run deeply and potentially dangerously.

She shuddered, despite feeling quite warm, acknowledging that there was no reason for her to feel personally fearful of Alexei, he had already shown her that. No, what she felt was fear *for him*. Her thoughts skidded to an abrupt halt. Why on earth should she feel that? Her mouth went dry as she tried to analyse her complicated thoughts. The very intensity with which Alexei was pursuing his revenge betrayed a compulsion that dangerously weakened him. If somehow her father should escape his vengeance... She shivered again, without knowing why. Surely this wasn't pity she was feeling for Alexei? After what he had done to her, how could she pity him? And yet she did. He had loved Tanya, very deeply.

'You are frowning—why?'

She hadn't realised he had been watching her, and she gave a small start. 'I was thinking about Tanya,' she admitted, blurting out the words without thinking, 'about how much you loved her...'

'And?'

She glanced at him sideways and, taking her courage in both hands, said nervously, 'And I wondered why, when you loved her so much, you seem only to feel contempt for... for the rest of the female sex.'

'Contempt?' His eyebrows lifted. 'What gives you that idea?'

'You do,' Hope told him heatedly, not liking the amusement she could see in his eyes. 'You use them,' she continued indignantly, 'and then when you're no longer interested in them you just... just throw them aside...'

'Very dramatic and not precisely true. Your sex is as guilty of using mine as you claim I am of using yours,

Hope.' He reached out and grasped her chin so that she
was forced to look at him. 'You are still very much a
child, *mon petit,* but it will not hurt you to learn young,
as I did, the dangers of placing too much reliance on the
existence and constancy of such ephemeral emotions as
"love". It's a word we use when very often we simply
mean physical desire,' he told her calmly. 'Oh, yes, you
may look at me as though you do not believe I speak the
truth. When I was your age, I suppose I was equally naïve.' A brief smile touched his mouth. 'You once asked
me if I had been in love, little one.'

'And you refused to tell me,' Hope reminded him,
wondering why she should feel this plummeting sensation in the pit of her stomach.

'And that still holds good, but what I will tell you is
that there comes a time when we must all put aside our
romantic daydreams, our idealism, and accept life as it
actually is. Because of my Russian blood I learned quite
young that I was not entirely acceptable to my peers, and
it isn't always a bad thing to have a shield behind which
one can conceal one's true thoughts and feelings. Being
too open with others leads to vulnerability.'

Vulnerable, Alexei? Hope found it hard to believe and
yet there had been a quiet sincerity in his voice when he
talked about his Russian blood, and hadn't she, too, experienced a little of what he meant at school herself, the
only English girl among so many Latins? A sensation
sometimes of being something of a freak? A curiosity?

They arrived in Paris just after five. Alexei's apartment was on the elegant Avenue Foch, one of several in
a building which had once belonged to a Prince, Alexei
told her as they were borne upwards in the lift. They
stepped out into a square hallway, decorated with a good
deal of rococo and ornate plasterwork, various figures
from the Muses gazing down at them from a painted
ceiling.

The door opened as they reached it, and they were ushered inside by a dapper manservant—very different from Pierre—and apparently used to women sharing his master's apartment, because he made no comment on Hope's presence.

A little to her astonishment, she was given her own bedroom with its accompanying bathroom, and although the rococo effect had been somewhat muted, she still felt as though she had stepped backwards in time. Alexei had told her that they would dine in the apartment as it was their first night in Paris.

André had prepared a meal for them and Hope was a little surprised to discover, in place of the French cuisine she had expected, blinis served piping hot and absolutely delicious, followed by chicken in a sour-cream sauce.

'My mother always favoured Russian cooking,' Alexei told her. 'André, like my mother, has Russian ancestry.'

Declining a sweet, Hope sipped her wine and watched Alexei from beneath her lashes. He was a man with formidable will-power, all the more formidable because it was kept so tightly under control. Only very rarely, she sensed, did the Russian side of his nature get the upper hand, as it had done over his sister's death. There was a portrait of Tanya hanging in the dining room and Hope studied it covertly. What would her reaction be to Alexei's means of avenging her? Would she applaud him or would her sympathies lie with her, Hope wondered; would she have understood her fears?

'Tanya often talked to me about you,' Alexei told her, shocking her once again with his ability to follow the course of her thoughts. 'She thought it was unkind of your father to leave you alone at school, never visiting you. I think she never gave up hoping that he would marry her. When she discovered she was pregnant I sus-

pect she thought he would want their child as much as she
did herself. She told me she wanted to give him a son...'

'She was going to have a child?' Hope blenched, staring at him. He hadn't mentioned this before.

'Yes.' His expression grew brooding. 'So your father
didn't merely rob me of a sister, Hope, he robbed me of
a niece or nephew, as well. Poor Tanya, she didn't realise that men do not feel the same attachment for the
children they father while they are still in the womb that
women do. Your father told her to get rid of it. I think
that, as much as his rejection of her, prompted her to end
her life. She had hoped that the thought of a child would
bind them closer together. She often used to tell me how
she longed for you all to be together as a family. She
begged him many times to allow her to visit you. Tanya
had a thwarted maternal instinct, and longed to make
you as much her child as you were your father's.'

Tears stung Hope's eyes. How she wished she had met
Tanya. She had a feeling that they would have liked one
another. No wonder Alexei felt so bitter. In fact, if he
hadn't been using her as the means of gaining his revenge she would have sympathised with him more. As it
was... 'Why have you given me my own room?' she
blurted out unthinkingly.

'Because we are now in Paris, and Paris loves an in-
trigue. Had I brought you here simply as my lover it
would occasion no comment, but when Paris learns that
I have a young and very lovely girl living under my roof,
ostensibly in my care, Paris will delight in the piquancy
of the situation and will start to talk.'

Afterwards, Hope looked back on those days in Paris
as being the time she started to grow towards maturity.
Alexei was, in a way, her Svengali, taking her and
moulding her, and as the days flew past she began to understand what he meant about the 'hot-house' atmosphere forcing her development.

To begin with, he took her to several of the famous couturiers, ordering her clothes, ignoring her own choice in favour of far more sophisticated garments, but never clothes that by their very sophistication would only emphasise her immaturity. There was underwear quite different from the underwear they had bought in Seville; still made of the finest silks and satins, but the underwear a woman would choose to wear for her lover rather than that worn by a girl on the threshold of womanhood.

They were invited out, to parties, to the ballet, to dinner at the American Embassy where Hope learned more of Alexei's involvement with the growing Californian wine industry, and all the time she was aware of being assessed and discussed. At one party she had slipped upstairs to escape from the constant barrage of curious eyes and was sitting in a darkened bedroom among the coats when she heard two women discussing her outside.

'She is so very young,' one of them said, and Hope recognised the voice of Madame Latour, Alexei's lawyer's wife. 'So very young, like a bud in bloom. I wonder if Alexei quite knows what he is doing.'

'If you mean is she under age, I shouldn't think so,' came the amused response, the smoky voice that of a woman who Alexei had introduced to her as the widow of an old friend, but Hope had picked up the unspoken messages passing between them and had guessed that at one time the relationship between them had been a more intimate one than mere friendship.

'You are too cynical, Élise,' Madame Latour responded. 'That was not what I meant at all. The child has a vulnerability that concerns me. Alexei says she is the daughter of a friend, and yet they are staying alone in his apartment, one wonders...'

'If she has shared his bed? I do not believe there can be many women who could resist Alexei when he sets himself out to charm them, and he is an excellent lover.'

There was a wealth of reminiscent satisfaction in the
husky voice and Hope shivered, tremulous and uncertain, troubled by the sharp pain stabbing through her.
Alexei had made no move to touch her since they had
come to Paris. At first she had been glad, but lately...
They had been in Paris five days and her initial relief was
giving way to another emotion.

'Alexei has changed since Tanya's death,' Madame
Latour murmured. 'He has hardened and seldom seems
to laugh. He should marry, Élise, if only because of the
title.'

'We have discussed it, but if I remarry I lose my inheritance, Georges stipulated that in his will.' Hope could
almost see her shrugging. 'I did not marry him to lose all
that I have gained, and Alexei says he will not marry
where he does not love. The Russian in him, one must
suppose.'

'His parents were very deeply in love, and I did hope
when I saw Alexei with Hope that...'

'That he had fallen in love with that *bébé*?' Hope
heard Élise laugh. 'My poor Hélène, Alexei is a man not
a boy, the woman who shares his life must be a woman,
not a half-grown child. Have you talked to her? She has
no conversation, no charm...'

'But presumably she still shares his bed?'

'Have I not just said that he is a man? But come, we
must get back, Carlo will be missing me.'

'Carlo? He is your latest?'

'And very Italian,' Hope heard Élise agree as they
headed for the stairs.

Long after they had gone she remained in the darkened room, struggling to come to terms with the change
in direction of her life, and the news that Alexei had
been, and possibly still was, in love with Élise. Who could
blame him? The Frenchwoman was everything that she
was not; elegant, dark-haired with incomparable chic,

and a subtle sensuality which pervaded everything she said and did. Poor Alexei, it must have come as a blow to him to learn that Élise refused to give up her fortune for him. Her husband had been Greek, or so she had heard someone say, and fabulously wealthy, although considerably older than she was; with a son and daughter by an earlier marriage. She couldn't imagine Alexei in love; his mental and physical control overborne by the intensity of his emotions, and she shivered suddenly, feeling very much alone.

When she returned to the party Alexei seemed barely aware that she had been absent. He was talking to three other men, fellow vintners Hope learned as she picked up the threads of their conversation, and when Alexei's fingers curled round her wrist she knew the other men were aware of it, and had put their own interpretation on his action. For one wild moment she thought of going to Madame Latour and telling her everything, pleading with her for help, but Alexei still held her passport, and no doubt he would think of some plausible reason for her behaviour. Madame Latour would obviously be far more inclined to believe a man she knew and who probably was an important client of her husband's rather than a strange young girl.

On their last evening in Paris, Alexei took her to dinner at Maxim's. Élise and Carlo joined them, and Hope felt very much at a disadvantage with the other woman, who was wearing a flamboyant, red silk dress—a perfect foil for her colouring.

Despite the fact that Élise was partnered by Carlo, Hope was acutely conscious during the meal of the fact that there was an unmistakable sexual awareness between Élise and Alexei, to such an extent that she felt sure it was only Alexei's pride and his love for the other woman that prevented them from recommencing their affair. Hope felt she had come to know Alexei a little

better and could perfectly well appreciate that his was a
temperament that would not allow him to settle for anything less than what he wanted. In Élise's case, he had
wanted her as his wife; that much had been obvious to
Hope from the conversation she had overheard between
Élise and Madame Latour, and since Élise was obviously not intending to give up her fortune and marry him,
it seemed that Alexei had decreed that their affair was
over.

Did he think of Élise when he made love to other
women, Hope wondered. When he made love to her?
Somehow she doubted it. Alexei was not a man to com-
promise or practise self-deceit, his pride would not allow
him to do so. He had told her that being in love did not
always automatically lead to sexual harmony, but looking at the seductive curves of Élise's body in their covering of red silk, Hope suspected he had been speaking
more in warning to her than in memory of some lack in
his own love-life.

Despite the excellence of the food, she found she
wasn't able to do it justice. Just before she went to change
Alexei had told her that they were flying to the Caribbean in the morning; their destination the small French
Caribbean island of St Marguerite. Perhaps it was the
thought of the coming dénouement; the thought of facing her father as Alexei's lover that robbed her of her
appetite, but as Hope lifted her fork to her mouth and
saw the look Élise slanted to Alexei, she knew the reason
for her malaise was much closer to home. She was jealous; jealous of the relationship they shared—but why?
Was it because of her own lack of emotional commit-
ments; no one in her life with whom she could exchange
just such a look? She didn't know. She only knew that to
see Élise smile at Alexei and to see that smile returned
caused a pain inside her the like of which she had never
known before.

It was Élise who suggested they went on to a night-club. Hope would much rather have gone straight back to the apartment. Carlo was doing his best to entertain her and, although he had been pleased to discover how well she spoke his language, Hope was conscious that his attention wandered to Élise and Alexei as nearly as much as her own did.

To Hope's dismay, Alexei agreed instantly, suggesting a nightclub he knew. All four of them travelled in Alexei's car, Carlo and Élise having come to the restaurant by taxi. The doorman greeted Alexei by name and they were shown to a table close enough to the dance floor to be able to have an uninterrupted view of the small stage and yet far enough away for them to have some privacy.

'I see Lisa Bouchard is on tonight,' Élise commented as the waiter brought their drinks.

'Lisa sings *chansons*,' Alexei told Hope, 'a sort of story set to music—the French are very fond of them.'

'Yes, so I was taught in school,' Hope agreed freezingly. How dare he patronise her in front of Élise. Did he think she knew nothing? She could tell from his tight-lipped expression that she had annoyed him. Élise merely looked amused.

'So your little kitten has claws, Alexei. You must be careful not to get too close to her, *mon ami.*'

The singer finished her act and the lights were dimmed. Couples started to fill the small dance floor, swaying in time to the music, the seductive and haunting tunes playing on the emotions until it seemed to Hope that the very air tightened about them. Élise turned to Alexei with a smile. 'Are you going to dance with me, Alexei, *mon coeur?*' she asked softly.

'If Carlo has no objections?' Carlo shrugged and smiled, and Hope sat as frozen as a small statue as Alexei led Élise on to the crowded floor, wondering why she should feel so much pain, and wondering acidly if it was necessary for Élise to press herself so close to Alexei while they danced, or for Alexei to so obviously enjoy it. They made a striking couple, their steps matching so that they seemed to move effortlessly together, and Hope wondered how Carlo felt about Élise's obvious preference for Alexei's company.

The minutes seemed to crawl past, although they remained on the floor for only two dances. If there was such a thing as making love to music, she had just seen it, Hope thought miserably when they returned, Élise alive and glowing, Alexei watching her indulgently.

'Carlo, you should have asked *la petite* to dance,' Élise chided her boy-friend, her careless comment starting a slow burning fuse inside Hope's body, accelerated by the look Élise gave her, and the blow to her pride.

'Hope shall dance with *me*,' Alexei pronounced, apparently oblivious to the rage glittering in Hope's eyes as he grasped her wrist and she was obliged to stand up beside him. She was wearing one of her new dresses, silver-grey and extremely simple, covering her from neck to knees at the front, with long sleeves cut into points that ended on the backs of her hands, but dipping down almost to the point of indecency at the back, revealing the pure line of her spine. A provocative dress which she would never have chosen for herself, but which Alexei had insisted upon.

It was a nerve-racking sensation, feeling his fingers and palm against her bare back, pressing her far closer to him than she would have wished as they moved in time to the music. Hope had a natural sense of rhythm and in other circumstances would have enjoyed dancing. However, she was too conscious of Alexei to relax; too aware of the hand spread across her back and the frisson of pleasure touching her body when it came into contact with his.

Her hands were resting on his shoulders—not looped round his neck as Élise's had been—but the two of them were still close enough for Hope to feel the warmth of his breath against her skin. It must be the music that was making her feel so strangely breathless, her body suddenly fluid and weak. She glanced at Alexei and wished she hadn't as her eyes were drawn to the contours of his mouth, her own softening and parting in a response she wasn't prepared to admit, much less name.

She trembled and felt Alexei tense, his expression altering. Hope missed a step, glad of the darkness to conceal her flush. Had he guessed what she had been thinking? Or was he simply bored, wishing he could exchange the hostage he had in his arms for the woman he loved? Hope wasn't surprised when he suggested abruptly that they return to their table, nor was she entirely surprised when, half an hour later, he said that it was time for them to leave.

'We have an early flight in the morning,' he told Élise when she pouted.

When they got outside Élise suggested that since Alexei had his car he should drive Carlo to his hotel and then drop her off at her apartment which wasn't far from Alexei's own. A little to Hope's dismay, Carlo did not protest, and somehow Hope found herself seated in the back with him, while Élise occupied the front passenger seat next to Alexei.

It wasn't very far to Carlo's hotel, and after the Italian had left, Alexei glanced into the mirror and said to Hope, 'You're half asleep already, *mon petit*. Since my apartment is the nearer, I shall drop you off first and then return when I have taken Élise home.'

She ought to have been glad, Hope knew, but for some reason another emotion took supremacy as she listened, and she wondered if Alexei and Élise had planned this when they were dancing. Perhaps Alexei was not as strong-willed as she had suspected, or was it simply that his love for Élise gave her the means to penetrate his armour?

Hope had been in bed for well over an hour when she finally heard him return to the apartment. She had been reading, knowing that she could not sleep, buoyed up with nervous dread about their trip to the Caribbean and racked by the savage pain she had experienced when she saw Élise in Alexei's arms, and her bedroom light was still on. She heard Alexei pause outside her room, and when he called her name she made no move to answer. The door opened and Alexei reached for the light switch, pausing when he realised that she was still awake.

'I thought you had fallen asleep with the light on.' He looked tired, his silk shirt unbuttoned at the throat, or was it simply that he hadn't bothered to fasten it after leaving Élise? It was a physical effort not to think of him in Élise's arms, not to let the rage, and, yes, jealousy she felt building up inside her to some huge, primaeval force, burst out and pour itself over him in a torrent.

How could she be jealous of Élise? She ought to be grateful for her; grateful, because surely Alexei would never come from Élise's bed to hers, and he didn't actually desire his reluctant captive, anyway. Hadn't his attitude towards her while they were in Paris shown her that?

'What's the matter? Can't you sleep?' His expression and the smile which accompanied the words seemed to imply that he knew quite well that she couldn't, and why, and they destroyed the last ounce of Hope's self-control. Her eyes darkened to amethyst, and her mouth tightened as she looked at him, standing there so... so arrogant and sure of himself.

She had meant to sound cool and scathing, but somehow her, 'Get out of my room,' only sounded childishly defiant. Certainly Alexei wasn't impressed by it.

'Well, well,' he drawled. 'What's brought that on?' Far from leaving her room, he came farther into it, arms folded across his chest as he surveyed her laconically from the end of the bed.

'I just don't want you in here.' Hope's chin tilted as she tried not to sound defensive. 'I don't want you coming from Élise's bed to mine,' she added. She had expected her words to surprise him. He would surely never expect her to be so outspoken, but far from being surprised he merely seemed angry—angrier than Hope had ever seen him before.

'Don't you now.' His voice grated against her ears. 'Since when did you lay the law down between us? What you want or don't want doesn't come into it. Or is there another reason for that little outburst?' His eyes sharpened and he came towards her, scrutinising her until Hope felt that he must be able to see every thought in her head. 'And why all the violence?'

'You were the one who brought me to Paris so that I would grow up,' Hope reminded him doggedly. 'Surely you didn't expect me not to realise the relationship between you and Élise?'

'Because I took her home, that means I must have made love to her as well?'

'I don't care whether you've made love to her or not,' Hope lied wildly. The conversation was getting out of control and all she wanted now was for Alexei to leave her room. 'All I want is for you to leave me in peace. I hate you!' she flung at him childishly. 'I hate and loathe you!'

He moved so quickly that she didn't have an opportunity to escape. One moment he was standing over her, the next she was lying flat against the bed, her arms pinned at her sides, the weight of his torso restricting her breathing. 'Hate...you don't even begin to know the meaning of the word,' Alexei told her thickly. 'But you've challenged me once too often, *ma belle*. Tomorrow I shall be a step nearer achieving my ambition to destroy your father—as he destroyed my sister—and tonight I'm in the mood to celebrate that victory…with you,' he added cruelly.

'No!' Hope could feel the heat coming off his body, his eyes dark and cloudy with what she sensed was anger-fuelled desire. But surely Élise had . . . But what if Alexei had denied himself, knowing that Élise was not prepared to give up her inheritance for him? Was it rage and frustration that motivated him now, that burned in the jade depths of his eyes as they searched her pale face without mercy or compassion?

He was looking at her mouth and she knew he intended to kiss her. Angry with herself for the weakening sensation she could feel spreading through her, she turned her head into the pillow, tensing as she felt Alexei move, pulling aside the bedclothes with one hand while the other held her against the bed, unfastening the bows that formed the shoulder-straps of her nightdress, his mouth exploring the exposed column of her throat.

She tried to twist out of the way, to avoid the lips exploring her skin, and just for a moment thought she had succeeded when Alexei released her arms. But to her horror, instead of getting up, his hands went to the covers, which he wrenched off the bed, and her thrashing attempts to evade him only had the humiliating result of revealing more of her body to him as the top of her nightdress slid down her body. Alexei foiled her hurried attempt to retrieve it by pinning her wrists together above her head, slowly surveying the hurried rise and fall of her breasts.

Élise had a much fuller figure than her own and, as she tried to squirm out of his grasp, Hope wondered if he was comparing them. She deliberately whipped up her anger against him, knowing with some deep-seated instinct that anger was her best defence against the weakening sensation flooding her body, urging her to stop fighting.

'I'm not Élise, Alexei,' she threw bitterly at him, 'and if you touch me, all you'll do is make me loathe you even more. It makes me sick to think of you making love to me.'

'Does it now?' The moment she saw his eyes, Hope knew she had gone too far. He had been angry enough before, but that anger was nothing when compared to the rage she could now see glittering in his eyes, scorching a trail along her body as it moved downwards, his free hand wrenching her nightgown away until she felt there was no part of her body on which his burning angry gaze had not rested.

'I think it's high time someone taught you not to make claims you can't fulfil, Hope,' she heard him say tautly, watching in dread fascination as his free hand moved to his shirt, pulling open the buttons, more in anger than in impatience, every movement motivated by an icy implacability that sent twin messages of panic and fear coursing to every nerve ending. He paused with his hands on his belt buckle, and for one relieved moment Hope thought he must have changed his mind. Her relief changed to disbelief when he said calmly. 'You do it for me, Hope. It's quite acceptable these days for a woman to take the initiative. In fact it can be quite a turn-on to know a woman wants you enough to make the moves.'

'But I *don't* want you,' Hope choked back at him. 'I wouldn't touch you voluntarily, of my own free will if...' She stopped, warned by the look in his eyes and the colour seeping darkly under his skin, that she had gone too far.

'Oh yes, you will, and not just touch me, Hope,' she heard him say through gritted teeth. 'You're going to tell me how much you want to touch me, you're going to beg me to let you touch me...'

What had happened to the cool, urbane man who had told her he had no wish to hurt her? Was she responsible for the unleashing of this anger, this rage that threatened to destroy her? Was this the side of Alexei that had prompted him to swear revenge against her father?

She tensed as she felt him lower his body to hers, his tongue exploring the delicate shape of her ear, then moving across her face. She bit her lip, keeping her face averted. She wasn't going to let him kiss her—if he kissed her she didn't know if she could withstand him.

His free hand rested against her thigh, the lean tanned fingers splayed out across her much paler flesh, and something seemed to twist and churn inside her, her body going hot with remembered shame and delight as she thought of how he had touched her, bringing her body to such a shuddering peak of delight that everything else had been forgotten. Was that what he had meant? His mouth was moving slowly over her throat and without looking down Hope knew that her breasts were swelling and peaking in response to his languorous caress.

She felt weak with relief when Alexei's hand moved from her thigh to her waist, but her relief was short-lived, her body tensing as he moved, bringing her arms down to her sides, and keeping them fastened there, the full weight of his thighs pinning her against the bed as he kissed the sensitive curve of her shoulders. Pleasure shivered through her, followed by an overwhelming urge to reach out and touch him with her fingertips, to breathe in the scent of his body and explore it with her lips.

How she had changed, she thought wryly. Less than three weeks ago the direction of her thoughts would have appalled her, but at this particular moment she could think of nothing more pleasurable than abandoning her pride and telling Alexei that he had won. But she could not do that.

She moved, resisting the sweet persuasion of his lips, trying to pull away from him and finding that her urgent movements did nothing more than allow her a few inches' purchase; enough to bring his head level with her breasts, she realised, acknowledging that she had been outmanoeuvred, and that she was still trapped beneath him while he was free to explore her soft curves with a leisurely appreciation that seemed to rocket her pulse-rate and threaten her hardly-won self-control.

When his tongue touched the hard peak of one breast she was more than ready to abandon the fight and admit defeat, but when she protested thickly, 'Alexei, please...' he only mocked:

'Please what? Please this?' Shock and pleasure met in equal engulfing waves when his hand cupped her breast and his mouth closed over it. 'Or this?' Her heart seemed to stop beating as his hand touched her thigh, anticipation shivering through her, her small moan of pleasure turning to a heated plea as her hands went of their own volition to his shoulders, touching the brown flesh.

'Alexei...'

'Beg me, Hope,' she heard him mutter hoarsely. 'Beg me...' His head was still against her breast, but his words destroyed her pleasure and reminded her instead that this was punishment and not pleasure. As though he sensed her withdrawal, Hope heard him curse, his eyes almost black as he lifted his head and stared up at her, his body lifting away from hers so that for one brief moment she actually thought she was free and she started to roll away. He caught her before she reached the edge of the bed, imprisoning her hips with his hands, the black head against the quivering softness of her stomach, the fingers tugging at his hair ignored as he feathered soft kisses against her skin, his hands sliding down to her thighs. All the twistings and turnings of her upper body could not remove him. Hope felt her legs go numb from the weight of him and still his mouth moved over her, exploring the curve of her hip, the smoothly taut line of her thigh, his hand forcing her legs apart, her resistance completely overturned as his tongue stroked along her thigh.

She wanted him and she knew she wasn't going to be able to prevent herself from telling him so. In fact, the words were already trembling on her lips when he moved and pleasure gave way to shocked disbelief—a high, strained cry of protest wrung from her throat as she twisted and fought to escape an intimacy she had never in a thousand years dreamed existed. Her mind revolted against the sensual contact of his tongue against such an intimate part of her body, while that same body seemed powerless to prevent the waves of pleasure coursing through her. Hope alternated between sobbed protests and fevered struggles, but Alexei wouldn't let her go, and she knew suddenly that this was what he had meant when he had said she would plead to be allowed to touch him. She felt her body contract on a shameful surge of pleasure, knowing Alexei must have felt it too, and completely unable to bring herself to look at him when he shifted his weight and looked up at her. Pleasure faded in the tidal wave of shame that flooded her.

Her voice was totally devoid of emotion when she spoke, barely discernible as she admitted her defeat. 'If you want me to plead to be allowed to touch you, Alexei, I will,' she told him huskily, 'anything... anything, but don't—' she shuddered deeply, turning her head away so that she wouldn't have to look at him '—don't touch me like that again.' She knew she was crying, she felt as though every pore in her body was weeping with shame, and couldn't understand the expression on Alexei's face as he moved and came and sat down beside her. She had expected triumph, but instead he looked...tired: that was the best way she could describe his expression.

'Hope...' When she wouldn't look at him he sighed and picked her up as easily as though she were a child, tucking his shirt round her as he pulled her on to his lap. 'I'm sorry. I lost my temper with you, my Russian temper,' he admitted wryly. 'It doesn't happen very often, and if you knew me better you wouldn't have exacerbated the situation by deliberately provoking me. I'm sorry if what I did... upset you. In my anger I had forgotten how...'

'Naïve I am?' Hope supplied for him.

'Inexperienced, shall we say. It won't happen again, unless you specially want it to,' he added wryly. His hand was against her cheek and Hope knew he must have felt the burn of colour washing through her skin.

'Poor Hope.' She suspected he was smiling, but the smile faded from his voice as he added, 'Perhaps now that this *has* happened we had better talk about it. What upset you the most, Hope? What I was doing? Or how you felt about it?'

Another wave of colour seared her. How could he expect her to talk about how she had felt? 'It was... it was...'

'Loathsome?' he suggested, again with a smile.

It was the smile that made her give a heated, 'Yes.' But Hope knew she hadn't been entirely truthful; what he had done had been shocking, but although her mind had been shocked, her body had found his touch pleasurable.

'What we were doing was perfectly natural.'

What *we* were doing? 'Perhaps it is,' she told him, trying to fight down her embarrassment and appear calm, 'but you were doing it to... to punish me...' She dared a glance upwards and saw that he was frowning. 'You wanted to shock me because I'd defied you.'

'You're partially right, but that wasn't my sole motivation, nor even my main one. You'd better try and get some sleep,' he told her abruptly. 'We have an early flight

in the morning.' He deposited her in the bed and Hope
had an illogical urge to beg him to keep on holding her,
to stay with her. Her body still ached tormentingly and
she knew if he were to turn to her she wouldn't deny him,
but he didn't, getting up instead and walking over to the
door. Obviously he realised as much as she did the futil-
ity of trying to substitute her for Élise, but she couldn't
help wishing that he had wanted her for herself, and she
had fallen asleep before the full import of that thought
had sunk into her mind.

CHAPTER SIX

HOPE WOKE UP early, hunching her body as she clasped her hands round her knees, listening to the silence of the apartment and watching the false dawn break over the rooftops of Paris. She glanced at her watch and shivered. In four hours they would be leaving for the airport. Her cases were packed, full of the new clothes Alexei had bought for her; clothes that would reflect the person she now was, the person he had made her, she thought bitterly.

She wasn't going to think about last night ever again, she had made herself that promise before she fell asleep and yet images, sensations crept into her mind with vivid clarity, ignoring all her efforts to hold them at bay, until a husky, 'No,' was wrenched from her throat, her body quivering in rejection.

She couldn't go to the Caribbean with Alexei, she couldn't remain in this apartment with him a minute longer. Feverishly showering and dressing, Hope tried to still the tiny voice in her brain that asked if she was running from Alexei or from herself. She had hated what he had done to her last night... hated and loathed it. But had she? With cruel objectivity her brain reminded her of the intense pleasure she had experienced.

'No!' Again the anguished sound echoed in the silence of her room. She could not stay here to face Alexei, to be further tormented by him, to face her father as Alexei's mistress. But where could she go? She had no money to speak of, no passport... She bit her lip, wondering wildly if she could go to the British Embassy, but if she did what could she tell them? That Alexei had taken her by force? Even to her own ears her story sounded far-fetched. But surely there must be someone who would believe it? And then it occurred to her. Of course! The Montrachet family had a house in Paris, she could remember Alexei telling her so. Paris was the headquarters of their vast merchant-banking empire. The fighting spirit the nuns had taught her to restrain and control surged into life inside her.

Picking up the suede coat Alexei had bought her, and snatching up her bag, Hope tiptoed past his door. The apartment was practically in darkness, no sign of André as she opened the front door, but it was only when she reached the street that Hope expelled her pent-up breath.

However, now that she was free, what was she going to do? She had no idea of the Montrachets' address. Nibbling her lip, she tried to marshal her thoughts, the sight of a cruising taxi sharpening her fuddled wits. Of course! The Montrachet name was a famous one, she would hail a cab and ask her driver.

The results of her resourcefulness were extremely rewarding. Her driver apparently did know their address, and after a rather careful scrutiny of her person, agreed to take her there. Half an hour later, Hope found herself standing outside an imposing and rather off-putting mansion, which her driver told her had once been part of a wealthy aristocrat's *hôtel*. 'Lost his head and his *hôtel* during the revolution,' he added with very evident satisfaction, as Hope paid him off, a little alarmed to see how few francs she had left. Although she hadn't wanted for anything, Alexei had never given her more than a few francs at a time and she had been too proud and too conscious of the fact that he was supporting her to ask for more.

As she stepped forward to ring the bell another taxi pulled up outside the house, disgorging three young men, obviously all the worse for drink.

'Hey, Alain,' one of them called out. 'Here is one of your lady-friends come to pay an early-morning call. What a pity she has not brought a couple of friends with her. No wonder you were so anxious to return home, my friend.' He added something under his breath that made Hope colour brightly in mingled shame and fear, her head held high as she realised the interpretation he had put on her appearance outside the house.

He had called one of his companions 'Alain' which must mean that here was Alain Montrachet, the man her father had intended her to marry.

Covertly, Hope studied him. Medium height, pale blue eyes, an olive complexion and brown hair, but his features had a coarseness, his eyes a cold cynicism that warned her that Alexei had not lied to her. Now those pale blue eyes were turned in her direction, studying her with unfeigned sexual explicitness, his breath sour with wine as he took a few paces towards her.

'Goodnight, my friends,' he said softly to his two companions, without lifting his eyes from Hope. 'It seems I have other business to attend to here.'

Hope felt a frisson of fear when neither of his companions objected, and began to turn away. It was stupid to feel alarmed—all she had to do was simply knock on the door and ask to see Madame Montrachet, but she began to shiver as she saw the way Alain was watching her.

'I do not know what brings you to my door at this hour, *ma chérie,*' he drawled stretching out a hand to touch the soft fairness of her hair where it lay against her cheek, watching Hope quiver in rejection with an unpleasant smile. 'Who sent you?' he asked. 'Sophie? How well she knows my tastes, although I must admit you are something of a novelty...'

'*Monsieur,*' Hope began hesitantly, 'I'm afraid you don't understand. I have come to see your mother.'

'My mother.' He threw back his head and laughed. 'That's a good one. My mother, my little one, is at this moment at our *château* in the Loire, as all the world knows. What's the matter? Got cold feet?' His hand was already on the door, and he turned, circling Hope's wrist with his fingers.

'Please... Please let me go,' Hope pleaded, tears suddenly stinging her eyes. It appeared that in her haste to escape she had well and truly leapt from the frying-pan into the fire, and she already knew which was the lesser of the two evils.

Too late now to long for the warmth and comfort of her room in Alexei's apartment. At least Alexei had been honest with her and—most of the time—treated her politely. This man... Her heart thumped heavily as she looked up at him. Even without Alexei's graphic description of his nature, she would have guessed instinctively what kind of a man Alain Montrachet was. It showed in the weak sensuality of his features, and she shuddered, knowing that she had to get away from him. Her chance came as he raised his hand to rap on the door, his loosened grip of her wrist enabling her to tug away and run down the street, without pausing to turn to see if he was pursuing her. Panic aided her headlong flight, her lungs gasping in air until they and her side ached with pain.

In the distance she was aware of a car suddenly screeching to a halt and a door slamming, but it wasn't until she heard Alexei call her name that she came to an abrupt halt, turning to see him crossing the road and hurrying towards her. Her relief at seeing him overwhelmed every other emotion and she turned and ran blindly towards him, sobbing his name, and seeking a comfort that was denied her when, instead of opening to hold her, his arms were merely raised so that his hands could grip her shoulders and administer an angry shake.

'Hope, *mon Dieu!* What's the matter?' he demanded curtly, adding in a sardonic undertone, 'You ran to me like a child to its father... not at all the reaction I expected when I awoke to discover you had fled from my apartment during the night. Little fool,' he added roughly, 'there are far worse things in life than what you believe you were forced to endure last night. Where were you going? Montrachet's?'

Hope's faint gasp betrayed her. 'How... how did you know?'

His mouth was wry. 'It didn't take much deduction, *mon petit*. It was either there or the British Embassy. What happened?'

Hope shuddered. 'Alain Montrachet arrived with some friends just after my taxi left. He thought... I... he... I tried to tell him that I had come to see his mother, but...'

'He told you that she was in the Loire?' Alexei added grimly for her. 'You look as pale as death; remember, little one, he is the man your father wished you to marry.'

'Yes.' Hope shuddered again, suddenly desperately cold and tired. 'You were right in everything you said about him,' she admitted in a voice drained of all emotion. 'I managed to escape from him while he was waiting for someone to open the door.' Alexei had taken her arm and was leading her across the road, now busier with traffic than it had been when she arrived, to the Ferrari, which she now realised had been the reason for the screeching tyres and brakes she had heard earlier.

'Alexei.' He opened the passenger door for her and she climbed in feeling like a naughty child being punished by adult disapproval of actions she knew were foolish. 'Alexei.' He paused to glance at her before quickly se-

curing her seat-belt. 'I'm sorry...' The moment the
apology was out she wished it unspoken. What cause had
she to apologise to him? Wasn't he the one who had
snatched her away from the nuns, who had deliberately
seduced her and who last night...

When he eventually swung into the car beside her, his
face was unexpectedly grim. He fastened his own seat-
belt and then said in a voice that Hope barely recog-
nized, 'So am I, *mon petit.*' His thumb stroked caressingly along her jaw, making her quiver with strange
sensations which she told herself must be relief at having
escaped Alain Montrachet. 'We must share the penance
of our mutual remorse—perhaps it will serve as a timely
reminder to both of us.'

'Alexei—' Hope moistened suddenly dry lips as she
tried not to admit the fear that had possessed her from
the moment she realised what Alain Montrachet intended. 'If I hadn't been able to get away...if Alain...'

'Had succeeded in raping you?' Alexei continued her
train of thought calmly, inclining his head slightly towards her, his eyes and face grave. 'If that had been the
case I'm afraid I should have had to have married you.'
He saw her expression and explained emotionlessly,
'With me you will learn the pleasure of becoming a
woman; as I have told you before I have no intention of
hurting or scarring you, but you have not yet come far
enough along that road to be able to endure mentally or
physically the Montrachets of this world, and because the
blame for your going to him is mine, it is only just that I
should be the one to make reparation.'

Hope was too stunned to speak. Alexei would have
married her? It took several seconds of thought for her
to understand why. 'There is cruelty in caging the bird
that can fly whole and unharmed, but when that bird is
injured, crippled, it needs the protection of its cage.'

Hope shivered as she listened to him. This was the Russian side of him, the side that dealt in strong emotions and a code of ethics that she already knew demanded an eye for an eye. This morning had shown her that she wasn't yet equipped to leave the cage Alexei had fashioned for her, and Alexei, for all his faults and the fear he sometimes engendered in her, was far, far preferable to Alain Montrachet.

'What about our flight?' she asked Alexei half an hour later as he opened the door to his apartment.

'We'll go tomorrow. Another day matters little.'

'Alexei.' A new and sudden thought struck her. 'What if my father chooses not to believe that... that we are lovers and...'

He shook his head, dismissing her hesitant words. 'A woman who has been made love to, who knows the secrets and pleasures of the flesh, has a certain air about her, a certain bloom which perhaps you do not yet have in total, and which has nothing to do with age. But before you come face to face with your Papa, you will have it, *mon petit*. When he sees you at my side he will know just as surely as though he had seen you that you have shared my bed.' He laughed softly when he saw her expression. 'You have had a busy morning, little one, and perhaps an even busier night, with shock upon shock, all of which are written on that pale face and in those bruised eyes. I suggest you go back to bed and rest. Your Papa will not give you to Alain now, I promise you that. And perhaps, after all, you can now believe that what you have endured with me is not the very worst terror that this world holds, hmm?'

Hope could not deny it. She watched Alexei walk away, consumed by an exhaustion which was both physical and mental. At dawn she had fled this apartment and this man because she believed she could not endure another moment in his company, but when she had turned in the

street and seen him, her reactions had been automatic and all she had wanted had been the haven of his arms. She was still trying to digest the import of that admission when sleep suddenly claimed her, and she was lying fully dressed on her bed an hour later when Alexei opened the door and studied her, his eyes bleak as they surveyed the pale face and shadowed skin. His resolve didn't often fail him, but there had been a moment this morning when he had woken up and found her gone...
He walked over to the bed, deftly removing the quilt without disturbing her and carefully wrapping it round her, watching the frown that marred her forehead at his touch, and smoothing it away with gentle fingers until Hope relaxed back into deep sleep.

When she woke up again Hope discovered that it was nearly lunchtime. Her sleep had refreshed her, a new reckless need to live only from day to day, from hour to hour, driving out her old cautiousness. Alexei was taking her to the Caribbean, a place of languor and enchantment; an opportunity which might not come her way ever again. Since she could not alter the terms of their relationship and neither could she escape it, she must just learn to endure and grow, to find the courage to build on what she had.

That mood helped her get through the day. Over lunch Alexei was pleasant, making no reference to the events of the morning. Hope had been reading a book on viticulture and Alexei answered her questions easily, diverting the conversation into other channels, talking so knowledgeably that Hope couldn't help feeling aware of her own ignorance.

'You've got a lot of catching up to do,' Alexei agreed when she commented on it, 'but the intelligence is there to do it, and the time.' What he said next surprised her so much that she couldn't respond to it, merely staring at him, wondering if she had misheard. 'You have all the qualities that make a woman constantly alluring, Hope, perhaps it is true that some of them need refining, but ten years from now you will be a woman few men can resist and I will doubtless consider myself privileged to have known you. Already today you have learned one valuable lesson. You have courage, *mon petit,* and pride.'

During the afternoon Alexei worked, and Hope entertained herself with some guidebooks he had bought her on the Caribbean.

It was one of the most restful days she had ever spent in Alexei's company, and she was at a loss to understand the restlessness that possessed her when he excused himself after dinner, explaining that he wanted to finish an article he had begun after lunch for a viticulture magazine. Left to her own devices, Hope passed the elegant drawing room, eventually going to study the books filling the shelves which lined the alcoves either side of the fire.

A book of poetry caught her eye, and she extracted it, wondering idly why it was always men who wrote the most evocative and emotive love poetry. These were verses translated from the original Persian and the words drew her like a magnet, the sentiments they expressed awing her with their breadth and depth, their grasp of emotions as age-old as the human race. With a faint sigh, Hope started to replace the booklet, pausing as it fell open at the front and saw Alexei's name written there. Had someone given it to him as a gift? Élise perhaps? Somehow Hope couldn't imagine the Frenchwoman being the donor of such a present; it was out of character.

As she replaced the volume on the shelves, the same sense of restlessness which had pursued her all evening returned. It was gone ten, and she might as well go to bed, and yet she felt curiously reluctant to do so without seeing Alexei... which was surely ridiculous. It was as though what had happened this morning had somehow fostered inside her a dependence on him, an emotional link she felt powerless to sever.

Sighing faintly, Hope made her way to her own room where she showered and prepared for bed. This time tomorrow they would be in the Caribbean, and she would be experiencing something thousands of girls her age would give their eye-teeth to share. But the confrontation with her father loomed large in her mind, and when she slept Hope found herself dreaming once again of that dark shadow coming between herself and the perfect bliss she had been experiencing, but this time there were two shadows, her father's and Alain Montrachet's. The shadows pursued her along the smooth pale beach. Somehow she knew if she could just outpace them there was sanctuary, but no matter how fast she ran the shadows grew larger, and she started to cry out to the one person she knew could help her.

'Hope... Hope...' She came to, to find Alexei shaking her gently, his hand on her shoulder, the bedroom shrouded in darkness, his face dimly visible as he sat on the edge of the bed.

'You called out to me,' he told her. 'I was just on my way to bed...'

Just on his way to bed? Hope frowned, glancing at her watch. It was gone two o'clock. And he looked tired, she realised as her eyes accustomed themselves to the darkness. 'Did you finish your article?' she asked him, adding, 'Couldn't you have finished it on the plane?'

'I could have,' Alexei agreed dryly, 'but working can sometimes be... therapeutic. It keeps the mind off other things,' he added, and Hope wondered if he meant Élise; if he was cursing the fact that Élise's husband had left her a wealthy woman, because surely otherwise she would have married him.

Her hand reached towards him and her small instinctive gesture of comfort seemed to startle him, his mus-

cles tensing beneath the fingers she placed on his arm.
She could feel the hardness of his sinews beneath the fine
silk, bunched as though in repudiation of her touch.

'Why did you call out?' Alexei asked her tersely.

'I was having a bad dream.' Hope frowned as she remembered vivid snatches of her dream; of her flight
across the sand; of her certainty that sanctuary lay ahead,
Alexei's name leaving her lips.

'And I was the cause of it?' He swore harshly, withdrawing from her. 'Even in your dreams you cannot escape me, is that it? I am a monster who destroyed your
innocence and who inflicted upon you the brunt of a
temper I should long ago have learned to control.'

Something in his eyes made her correct his statement,
an honesty she couldn't abandon. 'No, it wasn't you who
frightened me,' she admitted. 'I called your name because...'

'Because? He prodded, watching her closely.

'Because I wanted you to help me,' Hope admitted
honestly, shivering suddenly as she realised the strange-
ness of her dream. Why should she run from her father
to Alexei?

'I'm all right now,' she assured him huskily. 'I'm sorry
if I disturbed you.'

'Are you? Most women are only too pleased to have
that effect on my sex.'

Hope frowned up at him, her cheeks flushing faintly
as she realised what he meant. 'I... I didn't mean that
kind of disturb,' she told him.

'But perhaps I did,' Alexei murmured. His watchful
gaze passed over her flushed cheeks and lingered on the
outline of her lips until Hope moistened them nervously
with the tip of her tongue, her throat suddenly tense and
dry.

'Have you any idea what I experienced this morning
when I awoke to find you gone? When I knew what had

driven you to flight and where you would probably try to take refuge?'

Hope shivered and then trembled as she felt his hands brush against her skin, exploring the fragile bones of her shoulders. 'Are you cold?'

'No...yes...I...' Her thoughts whirled in chaotic confusion as he bent his head and started to explore the skin stroked by his fingers with the warmth of his lips, delicate butterfly caresses that touched lightly against her skin and left her aching for something more. She lifted her face automatically towards his when he raised his head, the tantalising kisses he brushed against her closed eyelids making her quiver deep inside, her lips parting instinctively in anticipation of his touch. But it never came.

Instead, his lips continued to torment her with tiny unsatisfying kisses feathered against her skin, dexterously avoiding the closer contact with her mouth that she yearned for. Her mind barely registered the moment when he slid the tiny straps of her nightgown down her shoulders, pulling them free of her arms, his hands cupping her breasts as he continued to let his lips drift lightly across her skin now so acutely sensitised to his touch, that each breath against it seemed to add to her torment.

'Alexei.' Hope was barely aware of murmuring his name, all her senses concentrated on the need to be lost in the hard possession of his mouth, the light stroke of his thumbs circling the tender areolae of her nipples having much the same effect on her body as his lips were having on her mind, tormenting her until Hope felt maddened by the teasing game he was playing with her. Her fingers laced tightly into his hair as she strained towards the source of her torment, letting her tongue stroke moistly against the firm outline of his mouth as she tried to transmit her need. The effect was almost instantaneous and extremely satisfying, her soft moan of pleasure lost beneath the warmth of Alexei's mouth as it opened over hers, his tongue ruthlessly exploiting the advantage she had given him, drawing the sweet moistness from her mouth. His hands slid from her breasts to her shoulders as he pressed her back against the bed without taking his mouth from hers, and then returned to possess and arouse the rose-tipped flesh he had exposed with the same expertise his lips had used to such devastating effect.

Slowly, he released her mouth, her lips clinging wantonly to his as though they never wanted to forget their taste, his eyes studying her desire-flushed face and hazy, clouded expression. All at once, Hope started to tremble, troubled and confused by the enormity of her actions, by the emotions she had experienced. As though he knew exactly what she was feeling, Alexei drew her into his arms, curving her face into his shoulder, his arms locking round her, allowing the hurried, uneven thud of her heart to steady, the light brush of his lips against her head imparting a comfort she hadn't known could exist.

Shyly, impelled by some inner need she couldn't explain, Hope placed her lips against his throat, experiencing an aching sense of wonder as she felt the muscles beneath his skin clench. She kissed him again, lost in the heady discovery of how pleasurable it was to explore his skin with her lips, to breathe in the male scent of him.

'Hope...' His hand grasped her hair, tugging gently so that she was forced to look up at him. 'I appreciate your need to experiment,' he told her huskily, 'but unless you're prepared to accept the consequences, now really isn't the time to do so...'

Later, Hope couldn't understand why she had not heeded his warning and responded to it, but the restlessness she had experienced earlier had been transformed to a dull ache that seemed to spread through her body, melting only when he touched and kissed her. So, instead, she watched him mutely as she slid nervous fingers into the gap between his shirt buttons, wondering a little at the silken feel of his skin beneath its fine covering of dark hairs, feeling his muscles clench in the same way they had done when she kissed him.

It was the first time she had touched him of her own free will, and the 'Hope,' he growled warningly against her ear barely impinged upon her consciousness. She let her lips drift leisurely against his skin, tugging impatiently at the buttons that impeded her progress, giving a small satisfied murmur when she was free to smooth the soft silk of his shirt away from his body and enjoy the tactile voyage of discovery that followed.

Half bemused, she registered Alexei's reaction to her touch, the suddenly increased thud of his heart when she smoothed the dark arrowing of hair downwards along his body to his trousers. The pressure of his arms tightened and she made the intoxicating discovery that the rough scrape of his body hair against the aroused softness of her breasts was infinitely pleasurable, her brain registering the message that there was nothing alarming in the light pressure of Alexei's lips against her skin, exploring her shoulder, finding the spot against her throat where they could wreak sensual havoc on her senses, inciting her to do the same, until he groaned huskily, 'I'm a man not a boy, Hope, long past the stage of playing these games. If you keep on touching me I'm going to make love to you...'

It was the first time he had given her a choice, and in giving it he had awoken her to what she was doing. She withdrew from his body as though she had been scorched, flushing beneath the sardonically grim amusement darkening his eyes as he looked down at her. 'I've a good mind to take you, anyway,' he told her softly, 'and this time you wouldn't be unwilling. Well, Hope, have you got the courage to admit that it's true?'

If he hadn't put it into words she would have let him make love to her, Hope acknowledged achingly. She had wanted him to, but when he spoke he spoiled it, forcing her into a realisation of what she was doing.

'Well?'

Numbly she shook her head, still hoping with one half of her that he would overrule her decision and take her back in his arms, but instead he simply touched her mouth with his thumb, rubbing the soft flesh caressingly until her lips parted and her tongue touched automatically against the hard pad of flesh. Almost immediately it was withdrawn, and Alexei sat up, watching her with narrowed eyes for a second before standing up. 'Goodnight, little one,' he drawled as he towered over her, his mouth twisted as he added softly, 'sweet dreams, and remember, if you call out for me in the night again I shall take it that it is because you have had a change of heart, and not simply because you are running from some unnamed terror. You know very well what manner of man I am, Hope, and if nothing else, you are infinitely desirable.'

'Desirable enough to make you forget why you brought me here?' Hope asked bitterly, not needing to look into his face to know the answer. Of course she wasn't. And she was a fool if she let herself believe otherwise. She was here simply as an instrument of revenge. His company was something she was forced to endure, so why did she feel this acute sense of loss when the door closed quietly, but firmly behind him?

'DON'T BE NERVOUS, there is really no need, I promise you.' Hope hadn't realised her feelings were so apparent, and she gave Alexei a slightly forced smile. She had flown before as a child, but then she had never felt the anxiety she could sense creeping through her body now. Alexei indicated a plane similar to the one they would be flying in, as it stood outside on the tarmac apron. His hand rested lightly on her shoulder as he indicated which plane he meant, his dark head bent slightly towards her, the gesture fraternal rather than amorous, but Hope was aware of him with every nerve ending in her body.

Dutifully concentrating on the scene outside the departure lounge windows, she tried to banish from her mind the memory of dark silk skin beneath her fingers and warm male flesh against her lips, willing herself not to blush. Her first thought when she woke this morning was that she didn't know how she was going to face Alexei, but he had been so coolly polite that she had managed to put out of her mind her memories of how she had caressed and responded to his body, and of how long she had lain awake once he had gone, yearning for something with a restless ache she didn't want to name.

'That's us, Hope. They're boarding our flight,' Alexei told her. 'As I just said, there's no need to be nervous.'

Hope smiled wanly, wondering how much of her unease was ascribable to the coming flight and how much to the confrontation she knew awaited her in the Caribbean.

They were travelling first class and the stewardess smiled warmly at Alexei as she showed them to their seats. Hope had grown accustomed to the way women regarded him and his own careless acceptance of their interest. A woman would need more than looks and sensuality to keep a man like Alexei. Now why had she thought that? Annoyed with herself, Hope ignored Alexei's offer to help with her seat-belt, struggling with it by herself, while he looked on with eyes the colour of grey slate.

'I would hardly ravish you here, Hope,' he remarked in cool tones, loud enough only to reach her ears, 'so you need not react like a Victorian heroine at the thought of my touch, a pose we both know to be assumed. You were ready enough to welcome it last night.'

Infuriated and embarrassed by the reminder of events she only wanted to forget, Hope said bitterly, 'Like an addict dependent on his next fix.' She had read about the problems of drug abuse sweeping the Western world in the newspapers and felt rather proud of this simile, invoking a picture of Alexei as a man on a par with those who sought cynically to destroy young lives simply to satisfy their greed, but to her chagrin he laughed softly, his fingers curling round her upper arm as he leaned forward to murmur:

'Are you trying to tell me you have become addicted to my touch, little one, craving it until your body shakes with sickness. You draw a very illuminating parallel and I suspect that you intend me to know—and to punish me with the knowledge—that it is only by force that I can possess your body, but we both know that that is not true. It is hard for you, I know,' he added, as the seat-belt warning light flashed and the jet engines started to whine, and Hope, who had been gripping the arms of her seat with whitened fingers relaxed enough to listen to what he was saying, the build-up to their take-off momentarily forgotten as he continued, 'Had you been more worldly and less intelligent you would have found it easier, but you have spent most of your formative years in what is virtually an enclosed society, where girls are taught that their first duty is to God and their second to their husband, and I suspect you are finding it hard to forgive yourself because your body is rebellious enough to respond to mine. But, as I have told you before, that is not something for which you should feel shame.'

Hope gave a faint gasp as she felt the plane lift, and then they were airborne. 'No?' she countered quickly, fighting down her apprehension. 'And what of the man who I will eventually love? Will he be equally understanding and philanthropic when I explain to him that it was only my "body" that responded to you?'

'I sincerely hope that by the time you do anything so foolish as falling in love, my name will be one you have long forgotten.'

'But you told me a woman never forgets her first lover,' Hope reminded him bitterly. His smile was wry. 'You are learning too fast, *mon petit*, and I think I begin to understand a little the alarms that beset fathers when they see their daughters growing to womanhood. One day you will be *très formidable*, and some man...'

'Some man who does not mind taking your leavings,' Hope spat at him, not knowing why she was talking to him like this. After all, it was a subject they had already discussed and he, no doubt, thought suitably disposed of.

'Mon Dieu,' he swore, suddenly angry. 'Will you cease talking in terms more suited to some cheap novelette. You will only be my "leavings", as you so unpleasantly put it, if you consider yourself to be an object instead of a human being. It is you who sets your worth, not I, Hope. You are a person in your own right.'

He paused as the stewardess approached with a well-laden drinks trolley, ordering for them both without consulting Hope. She was surprised to be handed a glass of Perrier water, and when she raised her eyebrows, Alexei said calmly, 'Alcohol has a dehydrating effect which adds to and sometimes is the cause of what is commonly described as "jet lag", but if you prefer something else...?' Hope shook her head, sipping the water, and wondering why these verbal exchanges with Alexei should leave her feeling as though she had been mentally charged. He ran rings round her with his cool logic which she wasn't yet knowledgeable enough to refute, but whatever he might say to the contrary, she knew deep down inside her that she would want the man she loved to be her first lover. But yet she would want him to be as skilled and appreciative of her body as...as Alexei.

'I do not know what it is you are thinking about,' she heard him say dryly, 'but it looks very much as though you believe you have just discovered a profound truth.'

Perhaps she had, Hope admitted mentally, still trying to come to terms with the mental image she had just had of Alexei as her true lover, suddenly pierced by the knowledge of how much she wanted him in that way; of how jealous she was of Élise who was able to meet him on his own ground. She didn't want to be treated as the weapon he would use to wreak revenge on her father; she wanted him to desire her purely as a woman. Hope had never thought of herself as particularly brave, but as she struggled to come to terms with the enormity of her private thoughts, she refused to give into the temptation to bury them away, instead forcing herself to examine and study them as clinically as she could. One part of her brain acknowledged sardonically as she did so that already Alexei's lessons were having their effect, and that already she was seeking to reason rather than to simply ignore or accept.

Lunch was served to them after they had been airborne for three hours, and delicious though it was, Hope could barely touch hers. Alexei, too, ate sparingly, and during the afternoon when they were shown a modern comedy film, Hope noticed that Alexei seemed to be asleep, thick dark crescents of lashes lying across his cheeks, making him look almost vulnerable. Her heart turned over with a sudden bitter-sweet pain, and unbidden the thought 'so this is love' floated from her subconscious. She was being ridiculous, she thought, face flaming as she tried to give her attention to the film. In love with Alexei! All right, she admitted daringly, so she was attracted to him sexually, but that didn't mean she loved him. But mere sexual chemistry did not account for

her sudden desire to smooth the small lines away from the
corners of his mouth, or to cradle him in her arms.

It was just proximity, Hope thought wildly; the fact
that she was so constantly in his company. How vividly
she could still remember the first moment she saw him,
and her fear. Had she sensed even then the devastating
effect he was going to have on her life?

DUSK WAS almost falling when they landed in Martinique. St Marguerite did not as yet have an international
airport, Alexei explained to her as they waited to claim
their luggage in an arrivals hall, clammy with heat. 'And
that is one of the reasons why your father's hotel has not
been as successful as he and his partners hoped. They are
presently trying to get permission to build an international airport on the island. However, the islanders prefer to remain as they are, as do the many wealthy people
who have bought villas there, for the simple reason that
St Marguerite should not become infested with tourists.'

'But surely my father knew this when he invested in the
hotel?' Hope asked.

Alexei turned to her, his mouth wry. 'Oh yes, he knew,
but you see, Hope, your father's a gambler—he thought
he held the winning ace, and that he would be able to
persuade the island's governor to give his permission.'

'And?' Hope asked, her mouth dry with apprehension, sensing that what she was about to learn would be
detrimental to her father.

'Oh, nothing unusual,' Alexei told her, shrugging his
shoulders. 'There was a change of government and the
incoming governor was not as amenable, shall we say, to
your father's proposals as his predecessor. He is also a
man who, it is known, does not take kindly to any attempts to corrupt government officials. In fact, had the
hotel not already been complete, I doubt your father and
his friends would have got permission to build at all. As

it is, they have a huge hotel, capable of housing nearly eight hundred people, and virtually no means of transporting those people to St Marguerite. Ah . . . here is our luggage.' A smiling porter collected it for them and Alexei said something to him in a sing-song mixture of French and Creole, then told Hope that the inter-island flight would leave in half an hour.

'You will find that here in the Caribbean, time does not have the same meaning as we understand it, but for many, and I'm afraid I must include myself among them, this is only an added attraction, although I can appreciate that it must be infuriating in a business sense.'

Hope quailed a little at her first glimpse of the small plane which was to transport them to St Marguerite, but Alexei seemed so relaxed and composed that she refused to show her apprehension in front of him. The flight took a little over forty minutes, and Alexei told her that had it been daylight they would have been afforded a magnificent view of the Caribbean and its islands, but Hope was rather grateful that she hadn't been called upon to glance out of the window and down at the sea.

If she had thought the airport terminal on Martinique a little primitive it was nothing to that on St Marguerite. A long corrugated iron shack best described the airport building, and the arrivals lounge, without the benefit of air-conditioning, made Hope long for a cool shower to wash the sticky perspiration from her skin. At Passport Control, Alexei was recognised, and Hope tried not to colour under the frankly appreciative look the official gave her as he examined her passport, making a comment to Alexei that made them both laugh.

'He said that from the looks of you, you will give me much pleasure,' Alexei translated mockingly for her, once they were through the barrier, 'or at least that's the polite translation. Come . . .'

He led her to a bright yellow jeep, grinning when he
saw her expression. 'These are the most popular form of
transport on the islands. Neither ourselves nor the British have left roads suitable for modern cars—the jungle
eats into them almost as soon as they are laid, and St
Marguerite is so small that one can circumnavigate it in
a day in one of these.'

He took their cases and put them in the back, the
muscles beneath his shirt taut. It was only as he stood up
that Hope realised that she had been holding her breath
and that her body ached in a way that had nothing to do
with their long flight.

They didn't talk on the drive to Alexei's villa. The road
was bumpy and unilluminated, and Hope left Alexei to
concentrate on his driving while she tried to come to
terms with her feelings.

'The main town is on the opposite side of the island—
the Atlantic side,' Alexei drawled, when he had finished
negotiating a particularly hazardous bend. 'The planta-
tion owners favoured that side of the island because it is
cooler, more healthy. It is only during the last century
that Europeans have come to appreciate the benefits of
the sun.'

In the glare of the headlights Hope could see the thick
vegetation on both sides of the road, and Alexei explained that they were driving through a small pass in the
ridged backbone of the island which was clothed in
tropical forest.

'Lower down are the banana plantations and the villages,' Alexei told her, as he turned off the main road—
if such a bumpy and ill-maintained piece of tarmac could
merit such a grand title—and they bumped down what
Hope suspected was more of a track than a proper road,
coming to rest eventually on some hard-packed earth, the
lights of the jeep illuminating the soft peach-washed side
wall of a villa.

As her eyes and ears accustomed themselves to the dark silence, Hope realised that the soft sound she could hear must be the sea. Stars, far brighter than any she had ever seen at home, shone on a scene straight out of a travel brochure of the most glossy and expensive kind. To her left, through the scattered palms, she could just about make out the silver smoothness of a beach, surf curling along it with a platinum glitter. To her right, all she could make out was more of the thick vegetation they had passed through on their drive.

'Do you intend to stay there all night?' She hadn't realised that Alexei had climbed out of the jeep, and reached awkwardly for the handle of her door, surprised to discover how stiff she felt. Alexei caught her as she stumbled, the hard warmth of his arms closing round her and Hope closed her eyes knowing how much she longed to remain within their protective circle, but Alexei was already setting her on her feet, and motioning towards the peach villa.

It was all in darkness.

As Alexei opened the door he switched on the lights, making Hope blink a little in the unfamiliar brilliance. The door opened directly off a creeper-clad verandah into a large square room with a floor tiled in the Spanish style, cool and austere, brilliant patches of colour provided by the scattering of rugs against the dark tiles. The walls were painted white, the furniture mainly cane.

'Anything left alone in this climate for any length of time rots,' Alexei told her, as he opened another door which Hope discovered led to a cool inner hallway with several doors leading off it.

'The villa has four bedrooms,' Alexei told her, 'but on this occasion, I regret, little one, that you must share mine. Berthe, who comes in to cook and clean for me, is an inveterate gossip and I should hate it to reach your father's ears that we are sleeping apart.'

He took her upstairs, indicating a room which was decorated in cool blues and greens, a surprisingly luxurious bathroom off it. 'I asked Berthe to leave us something cold in the fridge. I'm sure you want to shower and change. For tonight I'll use the other bathroom,' Alexei added, smiling sardonically when he saw her expression. 'I am only human, *mon petit*,' he told her dryly. 'Long flights are notoriously draining, and I have neither the desire nor the stamina to indulge you in sulks and tussles tonight.'

Wondering why she should feel so aggrieved by his comment, Hope showered quickly, changing into fresh cotton underwear and a simple, cool cotton dress with a blouson top and a slim skirt, grimacing a little over the paleness of her skin.

Alexei was just on the point of replacing the telephone receiver when she walked into the salon. His eyebrows rose as he looked at her.

'That was quick. Did you fear I might change my mind?' He laughed softly when she coloured, and added succinctly, 'Or did you hurry to punish yourself for hoping I would? I have just telephoned the hotel and it seems that your Papa is presently in Martinique—trying to raise more capital for his venture, no doubt—but he should be back by the end of the week.'

'Three days away...' Hope wasn't aware of murmuring the words until Alexei said softly:

'Yes, and I mean to make the most of them. By the time he returns, it will be obvious beyond any doubt that you are mine.'

Which was surely an odd remark from a man who had earlier claimed that women were people and not objects, Hope thought crossly later on as she lay in bed, desperately trying to court sleep and wondering how long it would be before Alexei stopped whatever it was he was doing downstairs and came to join her.

CHAPTER SEVEN

FOR A MOMENT, when Hope opened her eyes, she felt totally disorientated—the result of so many changes in her surroundings in a relatively short space of time, she decided, when her brain finally disentangled itself from the cloaking mists of sleep and she remembered their arrival at the villa the previous evening.

Even without turning her head to look, she knew she was alone in the double bed—that was something no amount of jet lag could conceal from her. Her awareness of Alexei was something that seemed to have imprinted itself on to her bones.

She got out of bed, stopping when she glimpsed the dizzying view from the window. An unending vista of blue-green water hypnotised her, her dazzled glance sliding eventually to the silver-gold stretch of sand and then the sparse 'grass' immediately below the window, and the palms edging what was a perfect and obviously private half-moon of a beach. The bedroom windows opened on to a verandah and, contemplating the bliss of enjoying breakfast on it with its panoramic view of the Caribbean, Hope headed for the bathroom.

She had no idea where Alexei was, but she didn't want him returning to find her standing by the window wearing only a flimsy cotton nightdress. Her cheeks flushed as she remembered his mocking laughter of the night before when he had slid into bed beside her and discovered what she was wearing, adding that the fragile garment

would have been no deterrent against him had he wanted
her to sleep naked as he did. But although he had known
that she was awake, he hadn't touched her, and Hope
knew her frown and the disquietude which accompanied
it sprang not so much from a fear that his restraint would
not be repeated tonight, but from a disappointment that
it might. She actually wanted his lovemaking. Uneasy
with her thoughts, she turned on the shower, hoping the
needle-sharp sting of the cold spray would banish the
disturbing images conjured up by her brain; images of
Alexei sharing the cool caress of the water with her,
smiling as his hands moved sleekly over her damp body.

'No!' Hope said vehemently as she stepped out of the
shower and wrapped a towel round her body sarong-wise.
A walk on the beach might calm her restive thoughts, and
give her the equanimity to face Alexei without betraying
her feelings. Did he know how she felt? She bit her lip,
feeling tired of the constant battle going on inside her, the
incessant see-sawing of her emotions and thoughts, suddenly wanting desperately to escape from them, and perhaps the hypnotic lull of the surf against the shore would
help her achieve the sense of peace and calm she had always envied the nuns at the convent.

Even with the breeze blowing inland off the sea, Hope
was conscious of the heat of the sun. Now she knew
where Alexei got his deep, almost ingrained tan, and she
wondered how long it would be before her own skin
started to take colour. She was wearing a minuscule pair
of shorts in pink and white striped seersucker, her white
T-shirt banded with the same fabric.

Alexei had bought her the outfit in Paris before they
left, and although at first she had felt absurdly self-
conscious because of the brevity of her shorts, there was
no one to see her on the beach and it was undeniably
pleasant to feel the warmth of the sun against her skin.

Even better, she was able to take off her shoes and paddle in the surf as it creamed over the sand.

A dog appeared almost out of nowhere, taking Hope off guard for a moment as it rushed towards her over the sand, barking hysterically at the waves. It was thin with a plumy tail and a dark brown coat, the mournful eyes fixed pleadingly on Hope as it brought her a piece of driftwood.

Pets had never been allowed at the convent, but Hope liked animals, and when she had conquered her initial caution she began to enjoy their game, throwing the stick for the dog as it accompanied her in a companionable way along the beach. She remembered Alexei telling her that there was a village not far away from the villa and she wondered if the dog belonged there. It certainly seemed to have a good deal of energy despite its extreme thinness and rather shabby appearance. It brought her the stick, dropping it at her feet, and when she picked it up to throw it, the animal grabbed hold of the opposite end, tugging frantically, the plumy tail sending up a spray of sand as the dog tried to retrieve its prize.

Almost helpless with laughter, Hope was just about to give in when she heard Alexei call her name, his voice deep and sharp with command. She dropped the stick immediately, turning in the direction of his voice to see him swimming towards her.

The dog had heard him too and slunk off, its tail between its legs, never hesitating although Hope called after it. Alexei was in shallower water now, his torso slick with moisture, the heat of the sun already powdering his shoulders with salt where they had dried. As she waited for him to join her, Hope tried not to react to his masculinity, wondering what power he possessed that enabled him to make her aware of everything about him in such a small space of time.

She gasped when she realised he had been swimming in the nude, but he seemed too angry to be aware of her embarrassment as she averted her eyes from his tanned physique.

'You little fool,' he berated her as he stepped on to the warm sand, 'this isn't England—or even Spain. That animal could have been rabid!'

'It was quite friendly,' Hope retorted, resenting his ability to talk to her as though he were fully dressed in a crisp white shirt and a business suit, instead of standing at her side, six foot odd of magnificent maleness, and all of it unashamedly on view to anyone who cared to look.

'It didn't bite me,' she added huskily, refusing to turn and look at him, even though she knew he was standing at her shoulder. 'We were just playing...'

'Playing is for children,' Alexei told her curtly. 'And for your information, you don't need to be bitten, a lick can be enough. Let me look at your hands.'

She wanted to refuse, and was halfway to whipping them behind her back when Alexei stepped in front of her and lifted them palms upwards, inspecting the soft skin and slenderly tapering fingers thoroughly before he turned them over and did the same to the backs.

'Umm...no cuts. Just as well, if that damned cur had licked you and you had had a cut...' He had gone slightly pale beneath his tan and Hope felt the blood drain from her own face as she contemplated the meaning behind his words. Developments in modern medicine mean that contracting rabies doesn't necessarily lead to death, but the thought of dying, raving mad, must surely be every human being's worst nightmare. The sun seemed to dim, the landscape darkening as the sound of the surf increased, obliterating everything but Alexei's shape.

'Hope!' But even his calling her name couldn't blot out the darkness for very long and from a distance she heard Alexei exclaim sharply in Russian something she couldn't understand, and the next thing she knew she was seated on the sand, her head bent forward against her knees, Alexei instructing her to breathe slowly and deeply. His voice came from somewhere far off and it wasn't until she straightened up that Hope realised he was behind her. She could feel the warmth coming off his body and wanted nothing more than to simply lean back and be enveloped by the vitality of his life-force.

'All right now? You were about to faint,' he told her. 'I over-reacted a little, *ma belle,* and I'm sorry for frightening you. It could easily be that the cur is not infected at all, but with rabies one cannot take chances.'

'I was just playing with him.' It hurt her to talk, her throat swollen and sore. 'It reminded me of when I was little. We used to have a dog, but...'

'Yes, yes, I know,' the rich voice soothed, lean fingers smoothing the bumpy goose-flesh from arms suddenly cold, pulling her back so that her head nestled against his shoulder.

'You frightened me,' she added half drowsily, 'appearing like that...'

'Like that?' He sounded amused. 'Do you mean because I choose to swim as nature intended? This is a private beach, but I confess that even had I known you would decide to stroll down here while I enjoyed my customary morning swim, I would not have denied myself its pleasure. You should have joined me—the water feels like warm, liquid silk. In such a sea it is a crime not to feel its caress against every part of one's body.'

'No...no, I meant the way you suddenly appeared, when I wasn't expecting to see you,' Hope tried to explain, unwilling to admit just how much she had been affected by the sight of him emerging from the sea like some Greek god of old. Not Neptune; perhaps golden Apollo, taking human form as in the best of Greek myths.

'If you're feeling better we'd better get back to the villa. Berthe will be arriving soon to cook breakfast. Are you hungry? You should be, you barely ate a thing yesterday, or are you planning to starve yourself to death before we confront your father?'

'Like you, my father obviously sees me as a tool he can use to further his own cause,' Hope said quietly, glad that she had her back to him and he couldn't see the pain in her eyes. 'I am not completely stupid, Alexei. If I've learned nothing else from you, I have learned to rely only on myself. It's much safer that way.' She got up before he could speak and walked quickly away from him.

'Hope!' She tensed as he caught up with her, grasping her wrist and deftly turning her to face him. His skin was scented with the sea and fresh air, mingling with the unique scent that was his alone and which she suspected was imprinted on her senses for all time.

'It would be a poor thing if you settled for safety at your time of life, scuttling for the sanctuary of your convent and all that the good Sisters taught you the moment you feel sightly threatened. Forget what the future holds, Hope, live for the present, like this.'

She could feel the strength and warmth in the fingers splayed across her back, moving up from her waist to tangle in her hair, tugging gently until her body arched, and Alexei used his free hand to mould her to his body, his lips cool and salty against hers. He made an explosive sound in the back of his throat and raised his head slightly, green eyes meeting grey. 'I was frightened for you,' he said softly, 'frightened that that damned mongrel...'

'Might damage your valuable pawn,' Hope supplied with fine irony. How quickly she was learning, how easily she was sliding into the habit of dissecting every word to seek out its true meaning.

'No, damn you!' Alexei swore, his fingers digging painfully into her waist. 'With you everything must be black or white, mustn't it, Hope. Good or evil—there is no grey area between. Can you not accept that I would not wish any hurt to come to you?'

'Actions speak louder than words,' Hope told him slowly, when she had sustained the fiery blaze of anger in his eyes for what seemed more like hours than seconds.

'Damn you, Hope,' he swore thickly again, 'and damn that high-minded Jesuit upbringing of yours. Perhaps it's time I reminded you of your very human frailty. It's a sin to lie, Hope, a sin for which you could burn in purgatory for a thousand lifetimes.'

His mouth came down on hers, hard and purposeful, bruising the vulnerability of her lips, forcing them to part beneath the savage pain of teeth that nipped painfully to gain what she tried to withhold. The storm of feeling that swept her when Alexei got his way and overcame her resistance, obliterated the steps which had led to this place of desire and need she now found herself in. Her hands gloried in their freedom to touch and caress Alexei without the barrier of clothes, her impatience until Alexei pushed aside her T-shirt and cupped his fingers round the soft wantonness of her breasts, barely concealed.

Past, future—both ceased to exist. There was only now, and the hurried thud of both their heartbeats echoing the pounding of the surf, and her body's primitive response to the proximity of Alexei's. His fingers slid from her breast to her jaw, holding her mouth locked to his, devouring its moist sweetness, and then they were lying together on the warm sand, Alexei removing her T-shirt, leaning over her to study the pale curves of her breasts. And she felt no shame beneath his scrutiny, her nipples flowering into hard buds of desire as he watched her.

Suddenly, some instinct warned her that he was going to withdraw from her and, without stopping to rationalise her actions, Hope reached out to him, pressing her lips to the warm curve of his shoulder, feeling his body's instantaneous response as her fingernails raked lazily across the taut flatness of his belly.

'Hope!' What he had begun as a lesson she no longer wanted him to end. If what she was doing did lead to endless purgatory, it would be worth it, her body breathed, its cry for fulfilment drowning out any other voice raised against it. Alexei's hands were on her shoulders, and Hope heard him mutter, 'Now tell me, if you can, that you don't want me.' She had known all along that he was punishing her, but the punishment lay, not in forcing her to admit that she wanted him, but in being denied the ending for which he had so thoroughly prepared her body.

She locked her hands behind his neck, raising her head until their eyes were level. 'I want you, Alexei,' she admitted huskily. Her tongue touched the dry skin of her lips, Alexei's glance fixing on the small movement. Like someone in a trance, Hope leaned forward, touching her tongue to Alexei's lips. He was as still as a statue. Goaded on by his indifference, she closed her eyes to blot out the coolness of green eyes that seemed to mock her in her inability to arouse him as he could so easily arouse her. Her fingers explored the silky thickness of his hair and the bones that lay beneath with avid need, her tongue licking moistly against his lips until Alexei tensed, muttering her name thickly as he wrenched her hands away and then pushed her back on to the sand, the pressure of his thigh imprisoning her there, his mouth fastening on hers, releasing her only briefly to mutter:

'*Ma belle,* you push me too far, you played with fire and we're both going to burn for it. Kiss me, Hope,' he groaned huskily against her mouth, his lips coaxing hers into hungry impatience as his hand slid down her body to unfasten and push aside the barrier of her shorts.

Hope's fingers clutched at his hips, her breathing suddenly accelerated, small moans of pleasure stifled in her throat as Alexei refused to release her mouth.

When he did, she gasped in air, too bemused to even think of protesting when he removed her shorts completely and then bent his head to her breasts, checking as he said thickly, 'I think I must be the one who's mad,' and Hope shuddered deeply, arching towards him as his thumb stroked over her nipple, her feelings rioting out of control, all thoughts of shyness or reserve forgotten as her body gave in to passions as old as Eve. She felt Alexei's instinctive response to her arched invitation, the teasing pressure of his thumb replaced with what Hope recognised shudderingly as a deep male hunger when his mouth moved compulsively over the heart of her breast, his lashes fanning darkly against his face as his hands slid to her hips, holding her tightly against him. The feelings she experienced as she looked down at him, the fierce pangs of pleasure engendered as he sucked her breast, made Hope wonder half-lightheadedly if such wanton desires were quite normal.

'*Mon Dieu,* I shouldn't be doing this,' Alexei muttered harshly as his tongue explored the sheltered valley between her breasts, his hands tilting her sideways so that she was pressed into his body.

'Why not?' Hope was amazed that she had the courage to make the whispered demand. 'It's no different from what . . . what you've done before . . .'

Alexei's smile was without mirth. 'That you should think that, *mon petit,* is one very good reason why I should stop right now, but we have come too far along the road for me to turn back now.'

'And it's hardly convenient now for you to go to Élise to find the satisfaction you obviously can't experience with me,' Hope flung at him, heartsick to think that it was only the appeasement of a physical need that made him touch her. First she was an instrument of revenge, and then she was someone to be used in place of the woman he really wanted.

'Élise...?' Hope felt him tense. 'What has she to do with this?'

'You love her, don't you?' she flung recklessly at him. 'She's the one you want...'

'But you're the one in my arms,' Alexei told her cruelly, 'you're the one who has aroused my body to a pitch that admits no withdrawal. And this time, *ma belle,* if I hurt you I will make no apologies, neither for that, nor for the bruises of passion which I suspect will mark this pale skin of yours by morning.'

Now, when it was too late, Hope regretted what she had started, but Alexei was already rolling her back on to the sand, pillowing her head with his hands, and the aroused weight of his body re-lit the fires he had kindled earlier. Her body arched to meet him, wanting his intimate invasion of her femininity.

This time he made no allowances for her inexperience, but it was fierce pleasure she felt, and not pain, beneath the fevered stroke of his body, and it freed her to respond half-deliriously to the desire she could feel pounding through him, sharing with him a culmination which vied with the explosion of a shooting star in intensity, the satisfaction she felt when she looked down at the sleek male body covering hers, sated and relaxed, making her feel as old as Eve herself.

'Another lesson you would do well to remember,' Alexei told her grimly, when his heart had stopped thudding against her breast. 'When a man is aroused he is apt to forget to be a gentleman. I never intended that to happen, Hope. Next time you feel like experimenting, you might give me ample warning.'

'You were the one who started it,' Hope began childishly. Why did he have to spoil what had happened by analysing it?

'Yes.' Alexei was standing up, and this time Hope didn't avert her eyes in shyness from his body. 'And my control wasn't all that it should have been, I admit, but you deliberately enticed me.' His fingers curled along her jaw, forcing her to look at him, 'Didn't you?'

'Yes.' There was a curious pleasure in making the admission, an elation that sang recklessly through her veins, and as she stood looking up at him, it came to Hope on a blinding flash of insight that she loved him, and that no matter what the rest of her life held, there would never be another man to match this one.

'Now,' Alexei said huskily. 'Now I could take you to your father and say "this woman is mine", and *no man* would even think of denying it.'

He released her and walked away, heading for the villa, and Hope wondered if she had imagined the faintly bitter expression in his eyes. For a moment she had almost thought he disliked himself. Perhaps because he had made love to her, a girl he neither desired nor wanted, someone who was just a pawn in a game of vengeance his honour demanded he play. Shivering, she turned and followed him, wondering why life seemed to hand out its moments of greatest pleasure at the same time as it gave those of intense pain.

Alexei spent the afternoon scuba diving. He had asked Hope if she wanted to go with him, but being close to him physically and so far apart mentally was almost a physical pain. Even his most impartial touch made her feel as vulnerable as though she had lost a layer of skin, and so, instead, she chose to sunbathe.

Berthe had left them a cold meal—a native of the island, she had chatted cheerfully to Hope when she insisted on helping her after breakfast. Her approval of

Alexei was patent and extremely verbal and Hope had blushed on more than one occasion when Berthe had announced that Alexei would give some woman very fine sons. Berthe had six children, Hope learned, and like most of the native population they had different fathers. Monogamy was not practised on the islands, and girls became sexually mature very young, often having three or four children before they left their teens. Berthe had three by her first 'husband' and three by the man she was now living with. 'Him one fine fella,' she told Hope with a beaming smile. 'Plenty loving...'

Something she was hardly likely to find with Alexei, Hope thought sadly as she tried to concentrate on the paperback she had bought at the airport, and constantly finding that her attention wavered from the characters to Alexei, a far more powerful character than any she would ever find in a book.

After dinner, Hope found the effects of their long flight had caught up with her. Alexei made no demur when she said that she wanted to go to bed. 'I've brought some work with me,' he told her. 'St Marguerite is the only place I ever get time to concentrate.'

Hope was at the door when she blurted out painfully, 'Élise... did she...'

'Élise is a Parisienne,' Alexei told her, watching her with green eyes suddenly extremely alert and knowing. 'She would find St Marguerite intensely boring, but why this sudden interest? This is the second time today you have mentioned her.' He put down the papers he had been extracting from his desk and studied her intently. Another minute and he would guess the truth.

Hope's throat closed on a tight knot of pain. That final humiliation was something she really could not bear. 'Surely it's only natural that I should be interested in Élise—a woman beautiful and intelligent enough to hold a man like you. Perhaps I could learn more from watching her than I can from living with you.'

'You could never be like Élise.' The cruelty of his words robbed her of breath, and with a swiftly stifled indrawn breath she flung open the door and ran, too hurt to care what interpretation Alexei put on her behaviour.

She was still awake when eventually he came to bed. She was acutely conscious of him moving about the bedroom, her body tense as she heard the bathroom door close behind him, willing sleep to come before he returned, but when he got into bed beside her she was still painfully awake. The fact that he found it easy to go to sleep was no compensation, and it seemed hours before she finally succumbed to the exhaustion of her body. Her sleep was troubled with nightmares, and the restless movements of her body finally woke her.

'What is the matter, little one?' Alexei asked, adding wryly, 'It is like trying to sleep with a restless colt, you are all arms and legs, all movement.'

Just in time, Hope bit back a scathing comment to the effect that she had no doubt that she was an unsatisfactory substitute for Élise. Alexei was no fool, and unless she wanted him to guess how she felt, she would be well advised to think before she rushed into hasty speech.

'How painful this transition from child to woman is,' Alexei murmured. 'One moment all wanton, the next a child, badly in need of the comfort of its mother. I regret that is something I cannot supply, but perhaps this will offer some measure of comfort.' He reached out, taking her in his arms, and for once making no comment about the fine cotton nightdress she was wearing. 'Now, go to sleep,' he instructed, when she was curled against his body. 'I believe that households taking possession of a new puppy are often advised to wrap a ticking clock in the animal's bedding. The sound is like the beating of its mama's heart and so, then, it does not render the night hideous with its plaintive howls. You might not howl, *mon petit,* but nevertheless you are rendering my night sufficiently uncomfortable for me to hope that the beating of my heart has much the same effect. You were crying while you slept . . . why?'

What could she tell him? That she cried because she now knew that she would never have the one thing in life that mattered, and because he had taught her that life would go on and that somehow she would have to find the strength to live with that knowledge and build her life without him?

'Don't you think I have anything to cry for?' she countered, wondering a little as she felt him tense, his harsh:

'Ah, yes, my villainy in taking your innocence. Shall I spoil your role-casting by telling you that it was an act from which I derived scant pleasure?'

Now it was Hope's turn to stiffen, regretting her own foolhardiness of opening herself to further pain. But Alexei was right about one thing, she did find the even beat of his heart soothing and she did fall asleep, sleeping so heavily that when she woke later in the night, she was still lying in his arms, his hand curving possessively against her breast.

His eyes opened as though he sensed that she was awake, instantly alert. 'Shall we have peace?' he asked lazily, reaching for her hand and conveying it to his lips, turning it palm upwards, his teeth nibbling softly at her fingers. He laughed as she tried to draw away, the warm satisfied laugh of the hunter, devilry gleaming in the slitted darkness of his eyes, as he drawled, 'Of course, we could always engage in further...hostilities...' He moved purposefully, and remembering how completely she had abandoned herself to him the previous day on the beach, Hope said quickly:

'No... No... peace...'

'At any price?' His lips feathered across her face, his tongue lazily exploring the shell-like curls of the ear closest to him. 'Be still,' he commanded when she tried to pull away. 'We still have to seal the treaty.'

Hope tried to resist him, but with his lips coaxing hers to respond, his tongue teasing their firm lines, it was hopeless right from the start.

Every one movement a languorous incitement of her senses, Hope was aching for his possession long before it came. This man knew all there was to know about female sexuality, she admitted painfully, as he slowly aroused her to a pitch where need became a molten frenzy, and the intimate touch of his hands and lips no longer a shocking act of sensuality but a powerful stimulant that swept aside her inhibitions so that the only cries that left her swollen lips were the sweet ones of desire. Only when she begged him incoherently did he end her torment, and it was only as he cried her name at the final moment of pleasure that Hope guessed that his fine control had splintered.

Afterwards she fell asleep, waking to find Alexei shaking her gently. 'I've brought you some breakfast.' He had been swimming and grains of salt clung to his body. Without pausing to think, Hope leaned forward to lick them off his skin, revelling in the shudder she felt pulse through him.

'When I made my plans, I miscalculated,' Alexei groaned into her hair as he took her into his arms, her naked breasts stimulated by the abrasion of his still-damp body-hair. 'You're going to wear me out. I'm thirty-four, not seventeen, Hope, and right now I need a shower. When did it happen?' he asked gently, standing up and taking her with him, slowly sliding her down his body until her feet touched the floor, but still maintaining the sensual contact between their bodies. 'When did you abandon all those black and white ethics and opt instead for pleasure?'

His hand smoothed the tangled hair back off her face. 'You're such a little sensualist, and you don't even know it yet. Your skin glows like a peach and tastes of warm honey. When I came out of the sea, I remembered yesterday, and I couldn't wait to get back here and...'

'I thought you wanted a shower,' Hope said breathlessly, unable to believe that she was hearing correctly and that he had virtually admitted that he wanted her.

'I do...' Alexei agreed, burying his face in the sleep-warm curve of her shoulder, his teeth tracing its sensitive chord, gentleness turning fiercely to passion as she responded with blind instinct.

Much later he did shower, taking Hope with him, slowly arousing her body with his lightly delicate touch, studying her aroused and flushed face with faintly amused eyes as he carried her back to bed. 'So perfectly responsive,' he murmured, watching her. '*Mon Dieu*, how you would have been wasted on Montrachet.'

'But not, of course, on a connoisseur like yourself?' Hope suggested with dangerous sweetness. He was studying her like something beneath a microscope, and she hated his detachment. 'Well, it might please you to treat me like some...some houri...but right now I'm hungry and I want my lunch.' She made to get up, but Alexei wouldn't let her.

'As my houri it's your duty to please your master and satisfy his desires,' he told her softly, watching the angry colour come and go in her face. 'It was you who chose the simile, not me, *ma belle*,' he pointed out as she gritted angrily:

'You...you sexist beast!' He easily fended off the blow she aimed at his chest, letting her think she might escape him as she struggled in his arms.

Softly he whispered:

'You don't want to escape me any more than I want to let you go.' And Hope knew it was true, as her stomach muscles clenched in mute pleasure as he suddenly tired of the game, and anger turned to molten passion beneath his touch.

FOR THREE DAYS, apart from Berthe, they were completely alone, isolated from the rest of the world, and during those three days Hope told herself that she wasn't being greedy, she was simply trying to take enough to help her endure the lonely years to come. Alexei was a skilled and imaginative lover, and Hope suspected he was right when he told her she was a sensualist.

When she looked back she was amazed how far she had come from the shy, embarrassed girl who had cried in shame and anguish at his touch. Now she knew Alexei's body as intimately as he knew hers. He had taught her to enjoy the maleness of it, to entice and arouse him almost as skilfully as he could arouse her.

They swam together off the small beach, and although Alexei soon divested her of her bikini, he preferred her to wear it when she sunbathed. At first she had thought it was because of Berthe, but she realised how mistaken she was when her skin began to turn golden, and in the coolness of their bedroom in the heat of the day, Alexei showed her with his lips and hands exactly how erotic he found those paler bands of flesh that said the secrets of her body were reserved for his eyes only.

On the third day everything changed. Hope overslept and, when she did wake, there was no Alexei with breakfast and a promise in his eyes that it would be some time before either of them left their room. Instead, she found him downstairs in his study, dressed in a shirt, and dark tailored trousers, suddenly a stranger, his frown preoccupied.

'Your father's back,' he told her curtly. 'This afternoon we're going to the hotel. I've booked us a room
there. We'll have dinner tonight, and then...'

'And then you're going to flaunt me in front of him.
Oh God...'

'Why the histrionics? You knew what I intended—it's
never been any secret...'

No, but her feelings were, and so was the hope that had
been growing inside her that somehow he would change
his mind, that he might come to care enough for her to
change his mind. Or didn't he realise the ordeal he was
about to inflict upon her? Apparently not. Anguish made
her retaliate, her anger a wall towering between them as
she bit out acidly, 'I'm surprised you don't invite him up
to our room so that he can see with his own eyes...'

'That remark was crude and uncalled for,' he told her
icily. 'Perhaps I was wrong about you, Hope—perhaps
you don't have the character I once thought...'

'How easy it is for you to sneer,' Hope cried wildly,
'but, after all, that is what you are doing—oh, you might
not want my father to witness your actual possession of
me in the physical sense, but you want him to know what
you have done. You are sick!' she flung at him. 'Sick and
depraved.'

But she was the one who was sick, and a phrase from
the Bible came back to her, 'comfort me with apples: for
I am sick of love...' It was from the *Song of Solomon*,
wasn't it? And with nothing else to do she went to
Alexei's study and removed a copy of the Bible, flicking
through until she found what she wanted. The words
drew her, as fresh and emotive now as the day they had
been written, surely one of the greatest tributes to love
there has ever been. She was engrossed in it when Alexei
walked in and for a moment Hope's eyes mirrored her
pain. He took the book from her and studied it carefully
before saying quietly, 'One day there will be a man for

you, Hope, about whom all these words will have a true meaning.'

'Has there been a woman like that for you?' Hope asked miserably, knowing the answer in her heart—Élise was that woman.

'Perhaps,' he closed the Bible decisively and quoted softly, '"My beloved is unto me as a cluster of camphire in the vineyards of Engedi . . ." We leave after lunch,' he added coolly. 'You will want to shower and change.' And then he left, leaving Hope to wonder why he had chosen that passage.

Élise was undoubtedly his beloved and Hope experienced bitter anguish at the thought. And yet in many ways she was glad she loved him; glad she had had the experience of loving and giving even though she knew her life was unlikely to hold anything that would come close to touching it again.

Later, Hope traced the change in his manner to her to that day. When they set out for the hotel he was once again the cool stranger who had come to the convent, offering her no comfort or reassurance on the ordeal that was to come.

It crossed Hope's mind that she might be able to find her father and explain just what Alexei had in mind.

CHAPTER EIGHT

THE HOTEL WAS something of a shock. Later, Hope suspected that she ought to have been prepared from what Alexei had said, but the sudden emergence of the vast, raw, concrete collection of buildings among the green vegetation was unpleasantly incongruous.

'Unlike the other islands, St Marguerite has no restriction on the height of new buildings. Most of the islands engaged in tourism have seen what's happened in Europe and Florida, and have a law that no building can exceed two storeys in height, which is why most of the holiday complexes consist of chalets dotted in informal gardens, or small blocks of rooms separate from the main hotel complex. Your father managed to persuade the island's previous hierarchy that more money could be made from a European-type hotel, and this is the result. That hierarchy is now gone and, although the new officials cannot undo the harm perpetrated before their time, they are, as I said, refusing to allow a new airport to be built to service your father's hotel.

'I've heard that the other investors he persuaded to join him are none too pleased with the way matters have fallen out. That pile of concrete represents several million pounds, and with only approximately a third of the rooms occupied—most of them by your father's friends and the world's gossip press on "freebies" it won't be long before the jungle invades.

'Mould is the destroyer in this climate. The moist heat encourages growth, and as you've already seen with the roads, nothing can stand in the jungle's way if it isn't properly maintained.'

As Alexei finished speaking they arrived at the entrance to the hotel. An electronic barrier and two "sentry-box"-type buildings guarded it, and Alexei explained tersely that with half the population of the island barely existing, expensive hotels and rich tourists had to be protected.

'These islands have been deprived of proper investment for years, they've been the victim of a system similar to that which operated prior to the revolution. Men came here to make money, using the fertile climate and the cheap labour, and then once they'd made their money, they went home, taking it with them. I'm sure I don't need to tell you of the abuses that went on. There are no more slaves as such these days, but the people are still enslaved by poverty, and the whole of the Caribbean is a spawning ground for communism.'

An unsmiling black guard raised the barrier for them, and Alexei said dryly as they drove through, 'He's probably earning the equivalent of forty francs or less for a month's work, and your father and his co-investors are probably congratulating themselves on how cheap they got their labour. A pity they haven't the eyes to see how costly that labour could be in the long term.'

The drive swept round to the front of the hotel, its entrance impressively enclosed in bronzed glass that concealed the interior.

A porter rushed forward to take the one case Alexei had told her to pack, and then they were in the foyer, blissfully cool from the air-conditioning after the heat outside. A uniformed receptionist smiled welcoming at Alexei as he gave her his name. Women would always smile at Alexei, no matter what their race or colour, Hope thought, watching them.

He returned with a key and a glossy brochure. 'A plan of the hotel—according to its publicity it possesses every luxury known to man. We're on the second floor.'

When Alexei unlocked their door, Hope thought at first he had made a mistake. They were in a lavishly furnished sitting room, decorated in soft shades of rose and green. Cane furniture was stained to match the colour scheme, and the cushions were made out of the same rose and green fabric as the curtains. Underfoot, the soft rose carpet was inches thick, and Alexei grimaced wryly. 'They'll find this a costly mistake. No one has carpets in this climate. If the damp doesn't get it, the termites will.' He saw Hope shudder and laughed. 'Don't worry, it's the dry season at the moment, so you're perfectly safe.'

'This isn't a bedroom,' Hope pointed out, wondering nervously if Alexei had brought her to her father's private rooms.

'No, but it is part of our suit. The bedroom is through there.' He indicated a door Hope hadn't noticed, and she opened it, her eyes widening at the luxury of their bedroom. The colour scheme of the sitting room was repeated—the same rose and green fabric draping the bed as it fell from a circlet set in the ceiling, the same rose-coloured carpet covering the floor, the furniture once again cane, and stained soft rose.

Beyond the bedroom was a bathroom, its walls mirrored to make the most of the small space, the fittings obviously expensive. 'For another thousand francs we could have had a "jacuzzi",' Alexei drawled as he followed her through the suite, explaining dryly what it was. 'Umm, hardly necessary in the circumstances.'

Hope found it hard to visualise any circumstances where Alexei would need sexual stimulation, and she tried not to wonder how many other women had found the same pleasure she had known in his arms, and what it was about Élise that made him love her.

A knock on the door startled her. Alexei went through to the sitting room to open it, and she heard him say, 'Yes, put it down there,' and then the door closed.

She walked into the sitting room. A bottle of champagne in an ice-bucket sat on the cane table, two fluted wineglasses beside it.

'Well, *mon petit,*' Alexei murmured as he removed the cork, and poured the chilled effervescing liquid into the glasses. 'The game, I believe, is on. Will you drink to its success, or am I to celebrate its commencement alone.'

Trying not to tremble as she picked up the glass, Hope said softly, 'I won't drink to that Alexei, but I will drink to Tanya, and to your finding peace of mind.'

For a moment a dark, terrible shadow seemed to cloud his eyes and then Alexei said quietly, 'Yes...to Tanya, my beautiful and foolish sister.'

As she sipped the cold liquid, Hope wondered when the confrontation would come. Alexei had told her nothing of his plans. Like any commander he would probably use his advantage of surprise, after all her father knew nothing of what had happened. As far as he was concerned, she was still at the convent. Term didn't end until July which was still weeks away. Alexei had planned his campaign well; the Frenchman in him, Hope decided as she tried to focus her attention on the brochure Alexei had picked up in reception.

As Alexei had said, the hotel possessed every luxury known to man. There was a beach with every kind of sail and jet-powered craft; there was para-sailing, windsurfing, hang-gliding, surf-boards, and even a gleaming yacht for champagne tours of the island, with a stop at a local beach, then dinner on board. The hotel had two swimming pools, a number of tennis courts and a golf course, as well as a sophisticated indoor gymnasium and cinema. There were half a dozen bars, three luxury dining restaurants, and even a small casino.

'Do you feel like a walk?'

Hope nodded her head nervously. Already she could feel the tension building in the sitting room, and walking through what the brochure described as 'beautifully landscaped gardens' might help her to relax.

The brochure hadn't lied, the gardens were beautiful, ablaze with oleander and hibiscus, bougainvillaea blossom trailing everywhere, and an artfully contrived stream complete with waterfall and pool wended its way through the grounds. Huge carp basked in a more formal pool, the iridescent colour of their scales glowing luminously beneath the surface of the water.

'Paradise on earth,' Alexei remarked sardonically as Hope bent to study the fish more closely.

'With my father cast as the serpent,' she said lightly getting to her feet. 'If this is Eden and my father is the serpent, I feel as though I must be the apple—essential to the plot, but not allowed the luxury of any feelings on the subject.' She said it without rancour, glancing up towards Alexei to see what sort of response her comment got. He was studying a hibiscus bloom, a look which was almost pain in his eyes. What was he thinking about? Tanya? His parents? Élise?

'It is too late, Hope,' he said heavily at last. 'There is no going back. Can you honestly say that all your time with me has been . . . unpleasant?'

'No.' She was surprised at how firmly she was able to speak. 'But that doesn't alter the fact that it wasn't by my own choice.'

'You have the rest of your life to make a free choice— if such a thing exists,' Alexei replied sardonically. 'Only the very young think that anything in life is free. Take what you want, say the Gods,' he breathed softly. 'Take it—and pay for it.'

Hope shivered suddenly, despite the heat of the afternoon. What was the price she would have to pay for loving Alexei, or did she already know?

When they had finished their walk Alexei asked if Hope wanted to go down to the beach, or swim in the pool, but she shook her head. She had enjoyed those activities too much on the small private beach outside his villa to want to spoil her memories. The attractions of the hotel beach held no allure—not when she could almost still feel the fine grains of sand against her skin when Alexei had made love to her.

'We're dining in the Tobago Restaurant,' Alexei informed her as they returned to their suite. 'Your father always dines there, and our table is close enough to his for him to see us.'

Hope tried not to shiver. 'You *have* laid your plans carefully, haven't you. Do they extend to include what I am to wear?'

'Meaning that your choice would be sackcloth and ashes? No, Hope, I am not going to instruct you. Your father will draw the correct conclusion no matter what you wear.'

And that being the case she owed it to herself to dress as proudly as she could, Hope decided as she walked into their room. Everyone might know that she was Alexei's mistress, but everyone was also going to know that she wasn't ashamed of that fact!

She spent a good deal of time getting ready, soaking in a bath scented with Balmain's, *Ivoire,* and then smoothing the perfumed body cream into her skin. The dress she had decided to wear was a simple black sheath of supple jersey, clinging to her skin, and under it she could wear virtually nothing apart from a silk and lace teddy, through which her skin gleamed lustrous as a pearl. She came out of the bathroom wearing it and found Alexei lying on the bed fully dressed, hands linked behind his head. He turned as she walked in, his eyes slowly darkening as he scrutinised her.

'I hope you're planning to wear something more than that,' he said at last. 'What are you trying to do, Hope, make me feel ashamed of what I've done to you?'

'Could I?' she asked flippantly, adding, 'Anyway, martyrs don't normally dress in silk and lace. I'm wearing this dress,' she told him, indicating the black gown hanging on the wardrobe door, 'and I can't wear very much underneath it. The saleswoman recommended this when I bought it.'

'Dressed like that you're probably the epitome of seventy-five per cent of the world's male population's favourite fantasy. Innocence dressed as a whore in a garment that reveals tantalisingly more of her body than it conceals. And who's responsible for this delectable sight?' He bit out the words, getting up to stand in front of her. 'We both know the answer to that, don't we, Hope? Take the damned thing off,' he grated at her, 'before I or someone else tears it off you. For Christ's sake, Hope,' he swore when she didn't move, too shocked at his words to do so. 'Do you honestly think I can do what I have to do tonight with you sitting beside me wearing that? What did the woman who sold it to you think you were?'

The savagery was still in his voice, and through her pain Hope heard herself saying, 'She knew what I was, Alexei—she knew I was your mistress...'

'And so she dressed you like that... in scraps of black lace and a few inches of silk; a statement that you're sexually available? Are you, Hope? Is that what you're trying to tell me?'

His anger overwhelmed her. 'I came here to get my dress. I didn't even know you were here...'

'But you've scented your skin with perfume, and it gleams like honey beneath that... that...'

'Teddy,' Hope supplied feverishly. 'It's called a teddy...and...' How could she explain to him that the perfume was her armour, and that she had wanted to do everything she could to bolster her courage, and maintain her pride. 'If I take it off I haven't anything else to wear under my dress.' To her horror she knew she was on the verge of tears. She tried to blink them away, but one fell and then another and then her whole body was shaking with sobs.

She heard Alexei swear violently in French before he switched to what she presumed to be equally vitriolic expressions in Russian, and then his hands were on her shoulders, pressing her head against his chest. She felt like a child secure again after an adult storm of anger she couldn't understand.

'Hope, I'm sorry, I shouldn't have said any of that. You go ahead and wear it.' He pushed her slightly away from him and studied the warm curve of her body beneath the spotted net. Hope saw their reflections in the mirrored doors of the wardrobe—Alexei could crush her in his hands if he chose and she shivered, frightened of the anger she had unleashed.

'I didn't put it on to...to...'

'Seduce me,' Alexei supplied dryly, as he released her and stepped back. 'No, I know.' He turned away and Hope thought she heard him mutter under his breath, 'and the damnable thing is, I almost wish you had,' but it was so indistinct and so unlike Alexei to express such a sentiment that she suspected her ears were deceiving her.

If her underwear hadn't gained Alexei's approval, her dress definitely did. She saw him almost do a double take when she emerged into their sitting room fully dressed, the high-heeled sandals she was wearing emphasising the sophistication of her outfit. The black jersey clung lovingly to every curve, and her hair was swept up in one of the styles the Parisian stylist had shown her, her make-up applied with skill and subtlety to highlight her eyes, making them glow amethyst in the lamplit room. Soft pink polish gleamed on her fingernails, and pearl ear-studs were fastened in her small ears.

Alexei was dressed impeccably in a white dinner jacket over his silk shirt, with narrow dark trousers emphasising the muscled length of his legs. He got up from the chair he had been seated in when Hope walked in, studying her for a second before taking hold of her hand gently and raising it to his lips. The kiss he placed against her palm triggered off the emotion she had fought hard to keep at bay all day and Hope was terrified that she was going to cry again.

'My apologies and congratulations,' Alexei murmured softly. 'I should have ordered a second bottle of champagne. We have more than my cause to toast. Tonight, Hope, you have become a woman. A woman of great beauty and, I suspect, of great courage. Are you still very angry with me for criticising your "teddy"? I confess the look you gave me when you walked through that door put me very much in mind of my mama at her most princessly.'

'Why were you so angry?' Hope asked him, relieved to see that his earlier anger had gone.

'Because I thought you were wearing it to underline to me how you thought of yourself and our relationship. An act of defiance if you like, a reminder that I had stolen from the cloister and turned innocence into sensuality.'

'When really the reason was much more mundane,' Hope said mildly. 'It's normally women who look for deeper motives. Men are normally content to accept life at face value.'

'Some women, and some men,' Alexei corrected. 'Tonight, Hope, you are very much a woman, proud and not ashamed. Quite a transformation...'

'You're a good teacher,' Hope replied coolly. 'As you said, what I make of my life is up to me, if I start being ashamed now, I will go on being ashamed for the rest of my life, and after all—'

There is nothing to be ashamed of in feeling as I do, she had been about to say, but Alexei forestalled her, interrupting almost curtly '—after all, you have nothing to blame yourself for, have you, *mon petit*. The blame and the contrition are both mine.'

The restaurant was as expensively decorated as their suite; several of the tables were occupied when Alexei and Hope walked in. The Head Waiter was at Alexei's side immediately, deferring to him in the manner Hope had noticed people always deferred to Alexei. They were shown to their table and handed menus. Alexei's fingers, fillibert-nailed, lean and brown, brushed hers as he leaned forward to ask Hope what she wanted, and she had a momentary vision of those hands against her body, stroking and caressing it into willing ardour.

'Alexei . . . *Mon Dieu*, I didn't know you were here.'

Both of them turned, Hope's heart thudding heavily as the short, dapper man at the next table stood up and came over. 'Alexei, *mon ami* . . . and who is this so charming lady you have with you?' He had a cheerful round face, and snapping black eyes, French obviously, and just as obviously very keen to know who she was, Hope realised as the Frenchman subjected her to a thorough scrutiny.

'Hope is—' Alexei smiled lazily at her, and then addressed his friend '—mine.'

'Ah yes.' The Frenchman laughed. 'I thought it must be so, and you have chosen well my friend. Will you not introduce us, though. You are quite safe from any competition,' he added roguishly. 'I am here with Isabelle.' He looked across to his table where an elegant Frenchwoman sat, studying the wine menu.

'Hope, meet an old acquaintance of mine, Philippe Montrachet. Philippe, Hope.'

Montrachet—that meant he must be some relation of Alain, and then when she looked at his wife, Hope knew they were Alain's parents. Had Alexei known they would be here? Alain had told her his parents were in the Loire valley, at their *château* . . .

'What brings you here, *mon vieux?*' Philippe Montrachet asked Alexei curiously. 'Apart, of course, from the so beautiful, Hope,' he added gallantly.

'Business . . . and I have a villa here. And you?'

The Frenchman shrugged. 'It was Isabelle's idea. We are the guests of Sir Henry Stanford.' He coloured suddenly, the sallow skin faintly tinged with pink, and Hope wondered if he had suddenly remembered how her father was connected with Alexei.

'Yes, I know Sir Henry,' Alexei said, smoothing over the awkward moment.

'Perhaps later on I might be allowed the privilege of dancing with Hope?'

The question was addressed to Alexei who smiled and said dryly, 'Perhaps . . . if we are still here—'

Philippe looked from Alexei's amused face to Hope's flushed one and said smilingly, 'Of course . . . I quite understand my friend.'

And so did she, Hope thought tiredly as she waited for Alexei to order their food. The gauge had been cast; the Montrachets knew she was Alexei's mistress, irrefutably.

'Did you know they would be here?' Hope asked quietly when they had been served with their seafood cocktail.

'No, it was as much a surprise to me as it was to you.'

'But a good omen for your cause,' Hope pressed. 'Now my father cannot hope to convince the Montrachets that I am innocent. They *are* Alain's parents, I take it?'

Alexei nodded his head. 'How did you guess?'

'From your description of Madame Montrachet, and the obvious disapproval on her face when she looked at us. Alain's father seems very pleasant.'

'Very,' agreed Alexei in clipped tones, 'but do not look at Philippe for succour, *ma belle*. He is a Frenchman first and foremost. Oh, he will offer it to you and most charmingly, but it will have a price-tag and it will not be marriage to his son. I believe he has a charming apartment off the Avenue Niel which he maintains for the use of his...friends. Madame is the ruler of their household and...'

'She knows now that we are lovers.'

The waiter brought their wine, pouring Alexei a glass which he didn't bother tasting, simply instructing him to fill both their glasses. 'Tasting in a restaurant can sometimes be a pretentious procedure. Any wine waiter worth his salt does it himself by sniffing the cork. A well-known vintage should not need checking in any other way and they are too well-listed for anyone to mistake their taste.' He lifted his glass, and out of the corner of her eye Hope found Philippe Montrachet studying her. Remembering Alexei's caution, she raised her own glass, silently saluting him, bravely defying her fear to let Philippe Montrachet know that she belonged to Alexei.

'What was that for?' Alexei asked when they had replaced their glasses.

'I don't want to end up on Avenue Niel.'

He smiled at her wry remark, and began, 'You know, Hope...' only to break off and glance at the entrance to the restaurant. Hope had her back to it, but she knew without turning, by the prickling of the hairs at the back of her neck, that her father had just entered. Her hands started to shake and she folded them on her lap under the table, composing her features into the serenity taught by the nuns.

'Isabelle, Philippe...' Her father was greeting the Montrachets, all unctuous charm. Hope writhed in mental humiliation, wondering why she had never noticed his tendency to grovel before. Probably because she had been too young. He had changed since she had last seen him, too, Hope decided, his hair was greyer, thinner, and he had developed a slight stoop. Despite the *bonhomie* and exaggerated heartiness he looked a worried man—a very worried man. Beneath the table Hope tensed her fingers, interlocking them until they were almost numb. Any moment he was going to turn and see her. What would he do?

When he did turn, he stiffened slightly as he saw Alexei, bristling almost like a dog sensing an adversary.

'Sir Henry...' The briefest of smiles—a polite formality, no more—accompanied Alexei's cool greeting. He had to acknowledge Alexei, Hope knew that, but it was obvious to her that he didn't want to, and she felt sick when she saw the fear lying behind the bravado he was using to hide it. If she had doubted Alexei's word at all about what had happened to Tanya, she no longer did so. All she could feel was a vast empty sense of let-down as she faced her father for the first time in two years, and a vague feeling of surprise that Tanya could have loved him.

'Comte.' The acknowledgment was curt, without the addition of Alexei's title, and then the light blue eyes turned to her, studying her absently, the forehead creasing in a frown that brought hysteria bubbling up inside her. Her father didn't recognise her, he had no idea who she was. But then, she supposed, she had changed from the gauche teenager of sixteen he had last seen in the care of the nuns. She could sense Alexei's frustration and knew the same thought must be going through his mind. Poor Alexei, to have come so far and expended so much only to have victory snatched from him at the last mo-

ment. She looked across at him and saw the brief stark-
ness of defeat and pain in his eyes, caught the muttered
'Tanya...forgive me...' and knew what she had to do.
Just as her father was about to turn away, she said coolly:

'Hello, Daddy, aren't you going to speak to me? I told
Alexei that you wouldn't, but he said he was sure you'd
have forgiven me for being a bad girl by now.' She pulled
a wry face, her lips forming a soft moue, sophistication
in the mocking glance she darted into her father's
stunned face. 'After all...like father, like daughter...
and I haven't done anything worse than you, have
I? Alexei, darling, I suspect you were right,' she continued, disengaging her eyes from her father and smiling
warmly across the table at Alexei. She knew without
bothering to look that the attention of most of the restaurant was riveted upon them, especially that of the
Montrachets. She could almost feel Isabelle Montrachet's glance piercing her skull. 'Daddy is going to dis-
own me. Let's go to our room, shall we, and have our
dinner sent up there.'

There, it was done, let her father try now to tell the
Montrachets she was still an innocent, convent-reared
virgin. She looked at Alexei, unable to read the expression in eyes which were suddenly hooded and reserved.
He looked angry, and she wondered how that could be
and why. This was what he wanted, wasn't it?

'Bitch!' The imprecation came thick and slurred from
her father's throat, the muscles working convulsively as
he spat the word at her. 'Just like your damned mother.
She was a whore too...marrying me when she was carrying another man's child. Her lover's child... My
brother... Only he was dead, killed in Malaysia—my
heroic elder brother—before he could marry her, and so
my father ordered me to take his place because my
brother's whore might be carrying his heir. But she
wasn't, was she, Hope. She was carrying you. A deceit-

ful slut not fit to bear our name! Take care you don't end up in the same condition as your precious mother. He won't marry you if you do.'

Sickened by the vicious outpourings, and conscious of the avid interest of everyone who had heard them, Hope wanted only to run. This was something she hadn't thought of, not even in her worst nightmares, but it explained so much. Her father's detachment, the pale sorrow of her mother. And suddenly she was fiercely glad that he wasn't her father. Knowing severed the last strand of guilt, releasing her from the duty of a loyalty she had not been able to feel.

'As you refused to marry Tanya,' she heard herself saying evenly. 'Yes, I know all about that... and about your plans for me...' She allowed herself to look at Isabelle Montrachet, and saw from the writhing fury on the older woman's face that Alexei had been right. While she had her virtue and innocence she would have tolerated her as a bride for her son, but now...

'I've met Alain Montrachet,' she told her father quietly, 'and marriage to him would have been the very worst sort of prostitution. When Alexei first told me what you intended I thought it was simply greed that motivated you, and I tried to understand, but Alexei didn't know it all, did he. It wasn't just greed, but hatred as well. Hatred of me because of my mother...'

'You little bitch—when I think of the money it cost me sending you to that damn school, having you brought up as...'

'As strictly as a novice,' she smiled humourlessly at him. 'I'm sure Alexei appreciated it, but as for what it cost you—' She stood up, facing him, a slender girl in a black dress that made her look heart-breakingly fragile, her hair spun gold in the flickering glow of the lamplit restaurant, her eyes dark amethyst against the soft peach of her skin '—I shall repay every penny you ever spent on me.'

'In the same way as you earned that dress you're wearing, the pearls in your ears and the soft sheets you sleep in at night? Like I said,' he sneered, 'you're just like your damned mother...'

Hope wasn't aware of Alexei moving, but one moment her father was facing her, the next he was lying at her feet, glaring furiously at Alexei as he tested the bone in his jaw. 'I could have you thrown in gaol for this,' he threatened thickly.

'I'm sure you could,' Alexei agreed curtly, 'but can you afford it? Come on,' he added to Hope, 'we're leaving. You can have our things sent on—they've got my address in reception,' he addressed her father.

He walked so fast Hope practically had to run to catch up with him. When she had faced the man she had always thought of as her father, something had died inside her, the tiny hope she had cherished that he would open his arms to her, and tell her it didn't matter what she had become, that no matter what Alexei had made of her, she was still his beloved daughter. But life wasn't like that, she thought hardily, and tonight she had learned a lesson that would stay with her for the rest of her life. Within the matter of an hour she had changed from a child to an adult, from a romantic to a cynic.

'Why are we leaving?' she asked the question breathlessly, causing Alexei to pause and stare down at her, his expression only partially illuminated by the flickering lamps in the reception area. The shadows added to the austerity of his features, lending them a cruel cast that she recognised with a shiver of apprehension as his Russian face.

'Do you want to stay? Do you want to go back in there and listen to more? Did you know? About your mother, I mean.'

Hope shook her head. 'No, but I suspect it was true. He was too bitterly vitriolic for it not to be. I'm almost glad—glad that he isn't my father. It was almost funny—his face, the Montrachets...'

'It wasn't funny,' Alexei interrupted harshly as he took her arm and led her through the door. 'It was damnable.' Outside, the night was almost stiflingly hot, the noise of crickets and other nocturnal creatures filling the soft moist air. 'Why did you do it, Hope?'

She didn't pretend not to understand. 'Why?' Her voice sounded brittle and she knew she had reached the edge of her control. 'If you want to give it a name, call it *noblesse oblige*...or perhaps I was foolish enough to think that, after all, blood might have meant more than money. You must find it richly satisfying to have your cynical view of life reinforced Alexei; an added bonus to knowing that you have done what you set out to do. I hope now your spirit will find peace.'

'Isn't it Tanya's spirit you should wish that for?'

In the darkness Hope smiled bleakly. 'Tanya wouldn't have found any satisfaction in what you did. God knows why, but she loved my father...'

'And because of that you would have forgiven him for destroying her? What do you know of the kind of love that is a torment to those who suffer from it?'

'Nothing,' Hope lied. 'What do you know of it, Alexei?'

She hadn't expected him to answer, and when he paused by their jeep and said huskily, 'Too much, our family is plagued by it, and I'm no exception,' she felt as though ice had encased her heart. He was talking about Élise. Élise who loved him, but who loved her husband's wealth more.

All the way back to the villa Hope kept up a flow of small talk, the polite, chic conversation she had learned to mimic in the salons of Paris. Alexei replied in monosyllables. One would almost have thought he had been more affected by the scene in the restaurant than she was herself, but Hope knew her bright chatter was only a wall behind which she was hiding. She wanted to cry, but she knew there would be no tears, no tears ever now, she promised herself fiercely. It was over. Alexei had gained what he wanted. Soon he would tell her that she was free. Free! She choked back a sob.

'What's wrong?' In the darkness Alexei's profile turned towards her.

'Nothing,' she responded coolly. 'Should there be?' They were fencing like enemies, dislike and suspicion arming the silences between their conversation, enemies and lovers . . . A dangerous combination.

'I'd prefer to sleep alone tonight, Alexei,' she said tightly as the villa came into view. 'It can scarcely matter what Berthe thinks now. The Montrachets know quite well what I am . . .'

'As you wish.' She might have been talking to a stone.

He stopped the jeep and she got out, walking towards the villa, her back a taut straight line of courage and pain. She heard Alexei follow her and then pause, and because she didn't turn round, she never heard his breathed, 'Dear God, what have I done . . . ?' nor see the expression mirrored in his eyes before he followed her.

She hadn't expected to sleep but she did. The moment she woke up she remembered, and she felt as though she were constructed of fragile glass, so fragile that she couldn't even bear the breath never mind the touch of another human being, so painful would such a contact be. If anyone touched her she would break into a thousand million pieces, and somewhere deep inside her she acknowledged that what she really wanted to do was to run, to find a place where she could hide from everyone, but if she did that they would know how much she had been hurt, and that was something she didn't intend anyone to know. If there was pleasure in knowing that Sir Henry was not her father, there was also pain in knowing that he had never loved her, that she had no one, that she was as every human being must be, alone.

She got up, feeling faintly nauseous, but not totally surprised. Her sickness must be a reaction to the scene in the restaurant. Every second of it was imprinted with vivid clarity against her brain, and while she would not take back a word of what she had said, given the chance, she knew it had been the death scene of any hopes she might have nurtured that either her father or Alexei cared enough for her to put her before their hatred of one another.

She was the victim and she had been sacrificed, but she had survived the flames to rise again, and in so doing, like the phoenix, had become impervious to fire, to the weakness of love. She loved Alexei, but never again would she be foolish to dream that he, or any man, could match that love. Whoever had said that love was of man's life a thing apart had spoken truly. Who had it been? Byron? She couldn't remember, but it seemed a cynically Byronic comment, made perhaps in the ashes of his affair with Lady Caroline Lamb. Poor Caroline, she had risked all and lost all, whereas he had risked nothing and lost nothing—a warning the female sex would do well to heed.

She didn't go down to the beach—she didn't want to see Alexei. The jeep was outside, but she ignored it, walking determinedly along the path which led, so Alexei had told her, to the next bay. It took her an hour to reach it. Larger than theirs, it boasted a small village, a collection of wooden huts with a jetty, off which half a dozen raggedly dressed urchins fished. Villas, similar to Alexei's, were dotted on the hillside rising from the bay, and Hope studied them absently from her vantage point above them.

'Hello, where have you sprung from?' She whirled round, and found herself confronted by a lean, sun-bronzed young man, about her own age, with a shock of salt-coated blond hair. He was grinning at her as he appraised the bare length of her legs in her brief shorts. 'You're not from the village, are you? I haven't seen you around.'

'I'm staying in one of the other bays,' Hope told him coolly. 'Not that it's any of your business.'

'No... but I'd like to make it mine. Blonde sea nymphs with long legs and amethyst eyes aren't exactly common around here. I'm Hal George, by the way,' he offered, holding out his hand. 'My folks own the villa over there.' He indicated vaguely in the direction behind him. 'I'm just on my way down to the harbour. See that boat out there—' he pointed to a white-hulled craft, riding lazily at anchor '—she's mine.' There was pride in his voice, and Hope thought dully, once I was like that... young... unknowing... and suddenly she felt a fierce sense of injustice. They had robbed her of that, Alexei and her father. They had taken her youth and destroyed it to fuel their mutual hatred. 'My dad runs the local marina. We get all types of craft coming in here. Fantastic million-aire-style yachts... smaller craft. Dad bought me the *Seabell* for my eighteenth birthday. How old are you?'

'Eighteen,' Hope told him expressionlessly. He reminded her of a huge puppy, all enthusiasm and gam-bolling playfulness, unaware of his own strength. 'Where is the marina?'

'Round the next bay? Want to take a look? We could go round in *Seabell*. Wait until I tell Lucy about you. She's my sister,' he added with a grin, 'and she keeps telling me no pretty girl is going to look twice at me. How about proving her wrong? She'll be down at the marina now with Dad. You could stay and have lunch with us?'

'I'm sorry, I can't,' Hope apologised.

'Maybe tomorrow then, we could go out for the day, take some lunch with us. There's a small island not too far out. When we were kids Lucy and I used to play at Robinson Crusoe there.'

Suddenly Hope was overwhelmed by a longing to share his uncomplicated youthful thirst for life. She should have been like him... but she felt immeasurably older. Why shouldn't she go with them? Why shouldn't she be young and free for once? Alexei wouldn't care. No one would care.

'All right,' she agreed rashly, taking a deep breath. 'I'll meet you here tomorrow!'

'Great... what's your name again?' he asked her admiringly.

'Hope...' She took another deep breath and said firmly, 'Hope Stanford.' After all, it was true. Her father had been Sir Henry's older brother... she was his daughter... nothing could change that.

'Okay, Hope Stanford, you've got yourself a date,' Hal told her smugly. 'I suppose I'll have to bring along the small-fry just to prove to her that you exist. Bring your swimming gear, by the way. The island has a perfect beach for surfing. It's right out beyond the lagoon. I promise you're going to love it.'

'WHERE THE HELL have you been?' Alexei looked white and strained, temper flaring in his eyes as Hope mocked:

'I went for a walk. What did you think I'd done? Thrown myself from the nearest cliff?' She shook her head mirthlessly. 'You taught me better than that, Alexei. You taught me to be a survivor—remember? Anyway, why should I want to follow Tanya's example, or my mother's come to that? I'm never going to love another human being so much that they have the power to hurt me. Never...' But even as she brushed past him and went into the villa Hope knew she had lied. It wasn't true. She already loved like that. That was the way she loved Alexei.

She toyed with the food when they sat down to eat, unable to take more than a few mouthfuls.

'When are we leaving?' The question had to be asked, even though she was dreading the answer. She had had her brief idyll, the lull before the storm, and now it was over, just as her relationship with Alexei would be over once they returned to France.

'So anxious to leave?'

'What is there to stay for? You've achieved your purpose.' Heavens, how calm she sounded. Alexei looked furious, almost as though he resented her calm. She wondered why. She was, after all, what he had made her, she thought bitterly, pushing away her plate with her food virtually untouched.

She was just on the point of going to bed when Alexei said brusquely, 'You might as well stay in that room...' And because his face was in the shadows, Hope had no way of knowing what he was feeling, whether it was relief, or merely indifference. What had she expected? He had desired her, briefly, but his desires had been fuelled by his thirst for revenge, by the fact that he was using her as Sir Henry's pawn... Now, with that thirst assuaged, wasn't it only natural that his desire should be assuaged as well?

CHAPTER NINE

THERE WAS no sign of Alexei when Hope got up the following morning, which made it easier for her to leave for her rendezvous with Hal George without telling him about it. Her confrontation with the man she had thought of so long as her father still lay across her mind like a bruise and seeing Alexei reminded her painfully of what had happened.

Hal was waiting for her alone on the quay. 'Lucy couldn't make it,' he told her cheerfully, 'so it's just the two of us, is that okay? Look, I promise you there are no strings,' he added when he saw her expression. 'I'm lonely, you're lonely, why shouldn't we be friends?'

'No reason,' Hope agreed, 'as long as you understand that's all we can be, just friends.'

'You're very cagey about yourself,' he teased her ten minutes later as they chugged out to his boat. 'You haven't told me what you're doing on the island, or whom you're staying with.' He eyed her curiously and Hope felt her stomach sink. She didn't want to lie to him, but she couldn't tell him the truth. She had agreed to this outing because she had wanted a day of uncomplicated companionship, someone to take her mind off her problems without intruding on her life, and now Hal was questioning her.

'I'm here on holiday,' she told him carelessly. How could she tell him about Alexei? If she did he would immediately leap to the wrong conclusion, and she didn't

want to see the guileless friendship in his eyes change to
the same knowing contempt she had seen in her father's.
Alexei had said that to a man who loved her, his relationship with her wouldn't matter, but what about all the
other people she would come into contact with? She
loved Alexei and always would, but she couldn't bear to
expose the fragility of that love for the contempt and
mockery of outsiders.

'Here we are.' Hal secured the small craft before
scrambling agilely on to the deck of his yacht, leaning
down to give Hope a helping hand as she followed more
gingerly.

'Isn't she fantastic?' he demanded half an hour later
when he had shown Hope over the elegant craft. As well
as the salon there were two small bedrooms, with their
own showers, and a well-equipped galley. 'I'd love to sail
her over to Florida, but Dad won't let me—at least, not
alone,' Hal complained, 'and he's too busy to take time
off to come with me at the moment. He's promised to
crew for me though, the first moment he gets.'

The yacht was an expensive toy for a boy Hal's age, but
Hope guessed that Hal was to follow his father into the
family business and had probably done half his growing
up on board various crafts. He certainly seemed to handle the controls of the yacht with assurance.

'What I'd really like to do is to enter one of the famous sail-boat races—now there's a real test of nautical
skill. All you need to have to sail this thing is a knowledge of mechanics and an ability to read sea-charts.' In
spite of his disparaging comment, Hope could tell that he
was extremely proud of his yacht, and he also proved an
interesting companion, telling her various stories about
the first French settlers on the islands, as he headed for
a gap in the coral reef and the small island that was just
a dot beyond it. 'Most of them were fleeing from France
for one reason or another—adventurers, aristocrats who

had fallen foul of their king. They made a rich living on these islands.'

Once they were beyond the reef the colour of the sea deepened in intensity, the brilliance of the sunlight dancing on the peacock waves, making Hope wish that she had had the foresight to bring sunglasses and a hat. Over her bikini she was wearing a pink knit top and toning, deeper pink cut-off cotton jeans. The slight swell made her feel distinctly queasy, and she remembered uneasily how nauseous she had felt when she had got up that morning. Perhaps she had eaten something that disagreed with her—or perhaps her nerves were still overwrought from the confrontation with her father.

'You okay?' Hal frowned, confirming her fears that her queasiness was more than simply imaginary. 'You look very pale? Not feeling sick are you? You shouldn't be.' He frowned again. 'The sea's like a mirror. No one could feel sick in these conditions.'

But she had done, Hope admitted wretchedly, when the sickness thankfully passed, her skin cold and damp with perspiration where previously it had been over-hot.

'Perhaps I've eaten something that disagreed with me,' she suggested lightly, 'but I'm feeling fine now.' She crossed her fingers behind her back, hoping that she was speaking the truth.

'Good. The last time I saw someone looking as green as that on a sea as calm as this was last year when the wife of one of our clients was pregnant.' He laughed and then flushed almost crimson. 'Oh . . . you're . . .'

'No, I'm not pregnant,' Hope assured him coolly, wishing she could convince herself as easily as she had apparently convinced Hal.

'No, of course not,' he agreed with a relieved smile. 'Like you said, it's probably something you've eaten. Why don't you go below and lie down for a while?'

'No thanks, I'm fine now,' Hope lied. It was true that she wasn't feeling nauseous any longer, but something far worse than mere sickness had taken its place. Pregnant! Her hands clutched instinctively at the reassuringly flat planes of her stomach. Of course she couldn't be... Why not? a cold little voice prompted. There was just as much chance of her conceiving as there was of her not doing so; more so. The nuns had been quite explicit about that! But there were ways and means... Hope thought feverishly, trying to remember the gossip she had picked up from the other girls. Surely Alexei...

Dear God, what if she was pregnant? What would she do? She could feel hysteria storming through her veins, tears pricking at the back of her eyes. For heaven's sake, she wasn't a child...she couldn't simply give way to tears, and besides, what good would crying do? If she was expecting Alexei's child tears wouldn't wash it away, she thought with grim bitterness. When she had made her plans for life without Alexei they had never included a child. She suddenly went very cold. Had Alexei deliberately planned this? Was it another part of his revenge? Her body shivered, encased in icy fear. She wasn't to worry about the future he had told her, he wasn't going to abandon her completely. But a child...

Somehow Hope knew it couldn't have been deliberate—Alexei was too proud to ever tolerate a child of his being born without his name. She was letting her imagination run away with her, Hope told herself chidingly. She probably wasn't pregnant at all. Alexei would never... She bit her lip. She was eighteen—a woman—and it was time she started to rely on herself to take charge of her life, not other people. She had to get away from Alexei, she decided feverishly. He had gained his objective, and no longer wanted her company—he had made that obvious. But where would she go, and how?

She had no money to speak of and Alexei still had her passport.

Thoughts twisted and turned in her brain, pulling her this way and that so that she was barely aware of the passage of time until Hal commented, 'We're about an hour from the island. If you like we can weigh anchor now and eat here, or if you can wait...'

'We might as well wait,' Hope told him, feeling even more nauseous at the thought of food. Dear God, if she was carrying Alexei's child, what would she do? Her mind went blank. What could she do? Dramatic passages from books she had read sprang vividly to mind. Wasn't it at this point that the poor heroine decided to end it all. But she didn't want to die, she wanted to live, Hope thought vehemently. She wouldn't be the first girl to give birth to an illegitimate child.

Perhaps she ought to follow the example of her mother and... A small sob tore at her throat, but she suppressed it. No—not that way. She remembered once when she was at the convent that one morning the Sisters had found a baby outside the convent doors in a basket. The school had buzzed with excitement over it, and Hope remembered one of the older girls saying the child had been born outside marriage to one of the village girls and that it had been left with the Sisters so that they could find a home for it. But she couldn't give her child up for adoption, Hope knew. Her child, if indeed she was to have one, would remain with her. Somehow she would find a way... Somehow...

And yet, despite her resolve, there was pain in the knowledge that she couldn't turn to Alexei; that she couldn't confide in him, or ask his advice; somehow she knew that although both of them were responsible for its being, the child was hers, and suddenly Hope felt a decade older than the carefree boy sitting opposite her.

The island was little more than a patch of sand and grass topped by half a dozen palms. The yacht would have to be anchored on the far side, Hal explained to her, because the water was deep enough there to take the draught. 'We can swim to the island, or use the inflatable raft if you prefer?'

Hope opted for the raft, not sure of her ability to swim the two hundred yards to the island, and Hal grinned good-naturedly. 'Okay, let's pack our lunch into it and then we'll go play Robinson Crusoe.'

Hal's mother obviously knew her son's appetite, Hope reflected sleepily an hour later when they had devoured what seemed to her to be an enormous quantity of salad and fruit, washed down by a light white wine.

'If it had been left to Mama, we'd have got orange juice,' Hal grinned. 'She still seems to think I'm her little boy. Do you get that from your parents?'

He asked the question quite casually, but Hope stiffened. 'Umm. I don't know about you, but I'm going to sleep for an hour now, and then I'm going to take you fishing. How do you fancy barbecued fish for your supper tonight?'

She was sleepy, Hope acknowledged, as she followed Hal's example and settled herself on her towel beneath the shade of one of the palms. Her queasiness had disappeared and she had almost convinced herself that her earlier fears were nothing more than frightened imaginings. She must have slept for some time because when she woke the sun was dipping down towards the horizon and there was no sign of Hal, although the yacht still rode lazily at anchor in the small bay.

'Great, you've woken up. Do you realise you've been asleep for three hours?' Hal reproved her, as he emerged from a cluster of palms. 'Are you ready to come fishing now?'

'Oughtn't we to be getting back?' Hope glanced at her watch, dismayed to see that it was after four. It would be several hours before they got back to St Marguerite and there was a strong possibility that she would be late for dinner. What would Alexei say when she didn't appear?

'Umm, I suppose you're right,' Hal agreed. 'Come on, then, back to the boat.'

Half an hour later he emerged from the engine room looking disheartened and worried. 'We've got a problem,' he told Hope heavily. 'She won't start, and the radio is out as well. I can't understand it!'

'You mean we're stuck here?' Hope stared at him in dismay.

'Until someone comes to find us. I didn't tell my folks where I was going, that's the only thing, and I doubt they'll start to panic until after dinner. I often take *Seabell* out for a day.' He saw the expression on Hope's face and said rather unconvincingly, 'Look, it will be okay, I promise you. Lucy knows I intended coming out here. She'll tell the parents, and Dad will guess what's happened. We've had one or two problems with *Seabell* before, but I thought we'd got them all ironed out. What about you? Will your folks . . . ?'

'No one knows I'm here,' Hope said bleakly, adding mentally, and no one would care if they did.

Without the power, nothing on board the yacht would work and it was an unpleasant sensation sitting in the small cabin watching the sun set, knowing they were marooned until someone came to find them.

'It could be worse,' Hal offered apologetically when darkness finally fell. 'At least we've got somewhere to sleep, and there's still some food left. Dad should be here by morning at the very latest.'

'Are you sure you can't find the fault?' Hope asked him, her mouth dry with tension. What was Alexei going to think when he found she was missing. He wouldn't have any idea where she was, and she knew enough about him to know that he would be concerned—if only because he considered her still to be his responsibility. Perhaps he would think she had gone to her father. Her mouth compressed. No, he was hardly likely to think that.

'It's a pity you didn't think to tell anyone where you were going.' Hal's voice reached her in the darkness, and she suppressed a sigh at the faintly accusatory tone of it.

'If I'd known this was going to happen I might have,' she replied dryly. 'We can't even read ... or play cards,' she added, sensing from his silence that she had offended him.

'I know one way we could pass the time.' Hope tensed, her mind racing, instantly alert as she sensed the innuendo behind the words.

'We're just friends, remember?' she said as lightly as she could, glad that the darkness hid from Hal the nervousness in her eyes. What on earth could she do if he refused to accept her words?

'C'mon, Hope,' he wheedled. 'You know the score. What harm is there? I can't be the first guy who's wanted you?'

Her heart thumping, Hope thought quickly. How could she handle this without antagonising Hal, or making herself vulnerable. 'I'm sorry, Hal,' she said firmly at last, 'I like you very much, but—'

'But there's someone else?' he suggested. Hope pounced on his words gratefully. 'Yes ... yes ... there's someone else.'

'Just my luck. I get stuck on a desert island with a beautiful girl and she's involved with someone else. What's he like?' Sensing that the danger point had passed, Hope searched wildly for a description that would satisfy Hal's curiosity, only realising as she drew a word picture for him that the man she was describing was Alexei.

'How old is this guy?' Hal interrupted at one point, 'he doesn't sound like anyone I know? Or do you go for the more mature type?'

'He's...' Not sure of how she should continue, Hope fell silent when Hal commanded swiftly:

'Shush! I think I hear something.'

They both listened, and sure enough the sound of another yacht was carried faintly to them, the sound gradually increasing as they held their breaths.

'Looks like we're going to be rescued, willing or not,' Hal said laconically, adding, 'after all the trouble I went to, too, to make sure we were stuck here...' He saw Hope's expression and laughed, acidly. 'Looks like my kid sister has done me a favour for once. She was as mad as hell when I refused to bring her with us, and no doubt she's blabbed all to my folks.'

Hope stared at him. 'You mean all this...we aren't...'

'We're out of gas, that's all,' Hal told her. 'I left instructions at the marina that they were to bring some out to us in the morning. I'm surprised you didn't guess—it's the oldest trick in the book. Oh, come on,' he expostulated angrily when Hope remained silent. 'Surely you didn't think I brought you here simply for a picnic? That's kids' stuff!'

'You should have told me what you had in mind,' Hope told him through almost numb lips, 'then you'd have been saved a wasted journey.'

Quite what else she might have said she didn't know, because at that moment they were hailed by the approaching yacht, piloted, as Hal had anticipated, by his father.

That Mr George was angry was quite evident from the thin-lipped glare he gave them both when they were instructed to board his craft.

'You fool,' he growled at Hal. 'Your mother is clean out of her mind with worry. If it hadn't been for Lucy.'

'Tell-tale,' Hal muttered, flushing a little under his father's keen surveillance. 'What did she have to go telling for, anyway?'

'And as for you, young lady.' Now it was Hope's turn to be subjected to his angry scrutiny. 'Your father was extremely shocked to learn where you were.'

'My father?' Hope's mind reeled. How had Hal's father known about hers.

'Lucy told her mother who you were with,' Mr. George continued, addressing his son, 'and naturally we got in touch with him, thinking that he would be as concerned as we were when you didn't come back by dark.'

'And?' Hal demanded truculently.

Hope's body went tense as a dark shadow suddenly emerged from the companionway. 'And—' she heard Alexei say tautly, his dark features materialising as he emerged from the shadows '—Sir Henry advised him to see me.'

'Alexei!' Hope was barely aware of gasping his name, but she did see the look of contempt Mr George gave her, his eyes hard as he looked first at Hope and then at his son. 'You've been poaching in mighty deep waters, Hal,' he told him curtly, 'a pity you didn't check out your new friend a little more before you decided to take off into the blue with her. And as for you, young lady...' His eyes returned to Hope and she quailed beneath their cold anger.

'I think you can leave Hope safely to me,' Alexei cut in softly. 'No, I don't want to talk about it right now.' He raised his hand to silence her when Hope would have spoken, and out of the corner of his mouth Hal muttered. 'That's him, isn't it? Why the hell did you come with me? Had a lovers' quarrel, did you?'

The rest of the journey back to the island was a night-mare of pain and desolation. For some reason Mr George seemed to blame her for what had happened, and every time he looked at her, Hope could see contempt and dis-like in his eyes. Alexei never spoke a single word to her, simply thanking Mr George when eventually they parted company at the marina, his hand on Hope's shoulder as he marched her towards his jeep.

The journey back to the villa was accomplished in a silence as intense as the tropical darkness around them. Once inside, Alexei motioned Hope into a chair.

'Right,' he said evenly, 'now perhaps you'll favour me with an explanation? Why did you go with him, Hope? To prove that your father was right and that you are like your mother?'

His cruel words bit into her, pain a seething, writhing mass invading her body. Like my mother, like Tanya, like every other woman who has ever loved, she wanted to scream at him, but she kept the words back. 'I just wanted to escape... to get away from everything for a while,' she said tiredly. 'Was that so wrong?'

'If you think you can gain freedom by casual sex, then, yes, it is,' Alexei told her harshly. 'Your young friend's mother already believes that you've seduced her pre-cious son. She went to see Sir Henry, you do realise that, don't you? Apparently young George's sister told her your name—and then she came up here... to tell me that my whore had gone off with her precious son.' He saw Hope wince beneath the blows of his words, pain knif-ing through her as she pictured the scene. No wonder Hal's father had looked so contemptuously at her.

'It wasn't like that.' She was shivering, despite the heat. 'I had no idea... I thought he just wanted to be friendly... I didn't know...' She was crying in earnest, weak tears pouring down her face, Alexei's anger com-

ing on top of the shock of being marooned and then discovering Hal had done it deliberately, too much for her.

'Then you damn well ought to have done,' Alexei
snapped back. 'Where's your sense of self-preservation?
Didn't you guess what he intended? Surely you aren't so
blind that you thought...'

'That Hal simply liked me as a person?' She was practically screaming the words at him, but Hope no longer
cared. 'Yes, I did think that...yes, I did think, stupidly,
that he simply wanted my company, but I should have
known better, shouldn't I? I should have known that all
he wanted was my body? I should have learned that much
from you, shouldn't I?'

'Hope...'

'Don't speak to me,' she stormed. 'Haven't you already done enough?' She tried to push past him, but his
arms stopped her, his fingers curling painfully into her
tender skin as he lifted her and shook her.

'Have you any idea of what might have happened to
you?'

His angry concern was the last straw. Laughing hysterically, Hope flung back her head so that she could look
up into his face. 'What?' she demanded bitterly. 'What
could have happened that hasn't already? What more
could there be?'

'You really want to know?' Green eyes blazed down
into her, threatening to consume her in their flames.
'Fine, I'll show you. Perhaps it's time I did anyway. I'm
tired of being treated like Bluebeard.' His arms tightened round her as he lifted her, and Hope felt too weak
to protest. She had pushed him beyond the edge of his
control, and she shook with the fear of it, too proud to
back down and apologise. Despite the burden of her
weight, Alexei was still breathing evenly when he pushed
open his bedroom door and deposited her on the bed. She

scrambled up and tried to escape, motivated by a primitive fear that blocked out everything else.

'Oh no you don't. You've hurled enough insults at me, *ma belle,* and you've looked once too often at me with those wounded accusing eyes. Perhaps it's time I gave you something to accuse me of, something with which to compare what you choose to think of as my cruelty.'

There was no evading or stopping him. The hands which she had only known as determinedly gentle were almost brutal as they stilled all her attempts to escape, the musky, aroused scent of his body clouding her senses as she struggled, not just against him, but against herself. She knew with a shaming knowledge that she couldn't escape, that even like this she wanted him. The appetites he had tutored and fed burst into a conflagration she could not control and long before Alexei had removed her shirt and jeans she knew she couldn't continue to fight.

He looked down at her as he continued to imprison her, his glance sweeping her body, the curves of her breasts barely covered by the delicate lace of her bra, the briefs that did little to conceal the femininity of her body. She had changed on the yacht after her swim, and her bikini and towel were still there. Not that the loss of mere clothes mattered in the slightest when set against the loss of self-respect she was enduring now.

'Look at me, Hope,' Alexei gritted commandingly. When she obeyed him there was no warmth in the cold green eyes, no heat of desire or wanting, simply an icy determination that pierced her to the heart. 'If it was variety you wanted, you should have told me,' she heard him drawl as he lowered his head. 'I wouldn't have thought young George would have had sufficient experience to...'

'Hal didn't touch me,' Hope told him stiffly, refusing to let her eyes drop from the icy coldness of his.

'No?'

The scorn and contempt in his eyes made her writhe in humiliation, but she refused to give in. 'No,' she whispered dryly. 'I told him ... I told him there was someone else.'

'And that stopped him?' He laughed disbelievingly, covering her body with his, parting her thighs without gentleness, watching her as the hawk watches the dove, but Hope refused to give way to fear or panic. He wanted her to fight him, she could sense it inside him, but she wasn't going to, and she tried not to flinch even when he possessed her body almost brutally, without tenderness or preparation, her tense muscles protesting, part of her crying out against the cruelty of what he was doing, part of her submitting to it in self-administered pain.

When it was over, Alexei jeered coldly, 'No comment?'

'What is there to say?' Hope was glad of the darkness to hide her expression from him. 'Except that you lied. There might be people who will judge me for myself, Alexei, as you once told me, but I haven't met them. Sir Henry, Hal, Hal's parents—all of them judge me in relation to you. What you just did to me was what I deserved. At least, if I tried to take you to court for rape that would be the judgment, wouldn't it?' She laughed bitterly. 'Even you judge me—even knowing the truth. If I hadn't slept with you would you have believed I would permit Hal to make love to me on the strength of two brief meetings? I am what I allowed you to make me, and I can't defend myself. I was taught by the Sisters that we must all pay for our crimes, our omissions and sins, but women pay a greater price than men ...'

'Hope.'

'Don't they say that actions speak louder than words, Alexei?' she interrupted bitterly. 'Despite everything that you have said to me, what you've just done proves that

the Sisters were right—that there are two kinds of
women: those who men respect and those who they
don't.'

'Hope—'

'Oh, I'm not arguing with you,' she went on bitterly,
'I deserved what you did, I deserved to be punished . . . I'm glad you showed me how contemptible you
think I am.' In the darkness he moved towards her, and
Hope froze. 'No! No, don't touch me any more. I'm going to my own room . . . I don't want to talk about it any
more, Alexei.'

He didn't try and stop her, but Hope knew that he
wouldn't. What had happened between them had opened
her eyes to the truth. Despite all his protests and grand
words, he was no different from Hal or Hal's parents, or
even Sir Henry. How could he be, when he actually
thought that she might have deliberately encouraged Hal?
She wouldn't think about his cold possession of her, his
usage of her body as so much feelingless flesh, but with
a wisdom beyond her years Hope knew instinctively that
if she stayed, if she allowed herself to be weak, to remain with Alexei after what had happened, they would
destroy one another.

Already she had seen the contempt half hidden in his
eyes, both of her and of himself. He had gained his revenge, and if she stayed all she would be would be a reminder of the past and all the pain it held for him. Real
love, adult love meant putting the object of one's love
before oneself. She wanted to stay with him, she wanted
to cry out, to plead with him to keep her, to accept whatever crumbs guilt and remorse caused him to throw down
to her, but how long could she live with herself if she did?
She had to leave. She must leave, for Alexei's sake if not
her own. It was over. Surely now he had achieved some
measure of release? Surely now he could let Tanya rest
peacefully and take up the reins of his own life again?

If she stayed all she would be doing would be keeping the past alive. He loved Élise and not her. She knew that what had happened—what they had shared together—had forged deep links between them, and she also knew that Alexei would never let her go while he thought she might have need of him. That meant that it was up to her to find the strength, somehow, to leave.

If she stayed, how long would it be before he came to resent and despise her? How long before she ceased to be a responsibility and became a burden? No, far better a clean break now, an opportunity for Alexei to sever himself from the past. He had done what he set out to do, and in her love she wanted to make him whole again, to free him from the chains that bound him to her, chains forged in bitterness and hatred, but chains which his conscience would not allow him to loose for himself. He had taught her so much. Here was her opportunity to show him how well she had learned the lessons of self-reliance; of self-respect; of pride... and of love... that most powerful of all human emotions. Alexei had never intended her to fall in love with him, she could not accuse him of that, and nor could she burden him with her unwanted emotions.

Before it was too late and Alexei guessed the truth, she would have to find a way to leave the island. She didn't know how yet, but she would find a way—and it would be a way that didn't involve bartering her body or her self-respect.

She was awake early, emerging from a nightmare-strewn sleep feeling unrefreshed. The moment she got out of bed a curious weakness overcame her, a faintness, coupled with a return of the previous day's nausea. She had almost forgotten... How could she find out if she was carrying Alexei's child? The simplest way would be to see a doctor. There must be one somewhere in the main town.

Early as she was, Alexei had beaten her. An empty glass stood beside the fridge, the remains of his orange juice in the bottom. The jeep was outside, which meant that Alexei had probably gone for his morning swim. Hope wandered into his study, gnawing at her bottom lip as she remembered her passport. If she was to leave the island she would have to find it.

Trying not to feel too guilty, she opened his desk, and saw her passport almost straight away. The keys to the jeep were on the table and she picked them up. The convent had owned a small van which had often been run on errands of mercy to the poorer villages. Hope had learned on this old vehicle and was now able to drive with some confidence. If she travelled to the main town she could see a doctor and find out the best way to leave St Marguerite. At the back of her mind, but not as yet admitted, was the thought that she might approach Sir Henry. Any interview with him would be humiliating, but she was still his niece, his heir and, as such, Broadvale, and all its lands, would one day be hers. Her chin lifted proudly. If she was to have Alexei's child it would need some degree of security, and she was prepared to fight for her baby's rights if she couldn't fight for her own. After all the years of misery she had endured, Sir Henry owed her something.

A quick glance through the telephone book gave her the names and addresses of three doctors, and quickly noting them down, Hope walked out to the jeep, holding her breath as she ran the risk of coming face to face with Alexei. Fortunately he was nowhere in sight. She couldn't have endured meeting him—not after last night. Her body ached slightly, there were bruises on her upper arms, but the physical signs of his possession were nothing when compared to the mental torment.

Although the doctor couldn't confirm her pregnancy absolutely, it came as no surprise to be told that he was more or less convinced that she was to have a child. He surveyed her pale face with a certain degree of sympathy, having already noted the lack of a wedding ring, and he cleared his throat as he looked at the downbent blonde head. Such a pretty girl, barely more than a child... In his day... He sighed. 'If you do not want to have the child, we could perhaps...'

Hope listened in growing shock as he told her that he might be able to arrange for her to have an abortion. What he described was a sin, or so the Sisters would have said, and while Hope could see that there might be circumstances when such a course of action was necessary, she wanted to keep her child. When she told him so the doctor's brow cleared. 'Well, you must come back and see me again. You're too thin and this climate isn't a good one for Europeans.'

'I probably won't be staying here,' Hope told him, hoping that it was true. Outside his surgery, the sun beat down on her head, making her eyes ache painfully as she made her way back to the jeep. She bumped into someone, and apologised automatically, tensing as she heard a familiar voice exclaim, 'Hope! Hope, it is you, isn't it?'

The woman standing before her was vaguely familiar, and Hope's forehead creased until the girl laughed, and said softly, 'Don't you remember me? Bianca. I was expelled from the convent.'

'Bianca, of course I remember you,' Hope exclaimed, recalling the older girl who had been so kind to her. 'But what are you doing here?'

'Filming,' Bianca told her with a grin that Hope remembered from their schooldays, and which was at odds with her glamorous appearance. 'I've been working in Hollywood for the last couple of years. A soap opera,' she made a face, 'but at least it got my face known— without my having to take off my clothes—and now I'm starring in a full-length film. But what about you?'

Hope tried to smile, suddenly conscious of her pale face and the tears that were threatening. 'Honey—' Bianca exclaimed softly, grasping her wrist. 'Honey, what's wrong? Look, we're on location not far from here—I've finished my work, I'm leaving for the States tomorrow, so let's go somewhere and talk. There's a café right here,' she added, indicating the building behind them.

Weakly Hope allowed herself to be taken charge of, as Bianca marched her into the café and made her sit down while she ordered drinks for them. 'Now...tell me about it.'

'I'm pregnant.' The moment she blurted the words out, Hope regretted them. Bianca was shocked, she could see, and her pale face flamed.

'Oh, honey...I'm so sorry. You of all people.' Bianca covered Hope's hand with her own. 'No, don't look like that—I'm not condemning you. It's just that you were always such a little innocent...so protected. Do you want to tell me about it?'

Hope found that she did. There was a certain sense of release in unburdening herself to the older girl and Bianca listened carefully in silence, without stopping her. 'And you love this Alexei guy, honey, is that it?' she asked softly, when Hope reached the end.

Hope nodded her head. 'I love him, but he doesn't love me, Bianca. I've got to get away from this island and from him.'

'You certainly have, honey,' she agreed warmly. 'The man ought to be shot. What was he about, anyway, giving you a child when...' She bit her lip, an arrested expression on her face as she said excitedly, 'Hope, I have thought of the very thing. I'll tell you what you're going to do, honey, you're going to come to Hollywood with me. No, listen,' she said firmly. 'I need a friend, Hope. Hollywood is a lonely place. I might be a successful actress, but I'm a lonely woman. We need each other. We always got on well at school. You need sanctuary...I need support. We'll help each other... It'll work out, you'll see.'

'But there's the baby,' Hope reminded her, hardly daring to hope that Bianca meant it. 'I'm not going to have an abortion or...'

'Honey, in Hollywood one more love-child isn't going to cause the slightest stir.' She grinned suddenly. 'In fact, you'll probably find that most folks will think the baby's mine. I mean it, Hope,' she added quietly. 'I want you to come back with me. I'd never know a moment's peace if I left you here. When we were at school I always thought you'd be a nice kid to have as a little sister, so how about us making it official. Neither of us has anyone else. You're going to need someone, Hope—and I'd be proud to be that someone. And I promise you it won't be all one-sided.' She grinned again. 'I can't wait to see Dale's face when he discovers I've got me a watch-dog. Dale is my producer,' she explained to Hope. 'He wants to go to bed with me, but that's all he wants, and I'm frightened I might give in. Old lessons die hard, Hope. I love him the way you love your Alexei, too much for a one-night stand. So far my refusals can't have been very convincing. Having you there to prop up my flagging resistance might just convince him that I mean business.'

'But...but won't I be in the way?' Hope protested anxiously. Much as she wanted to accept Bianca's offer she felt reluctant to take advantage of her friend.

'Look, I've just bought a ten-bedroomed mansion—you won't be in the way. In fact you can help me in more ways than one. I need a secretary—someone to keep track of all my business affairs. I have an accountant, but that's not enough. I'm constantly being asked to do endorsements and ads. I've got a film coming up in Italy, I don't speak Italian, but I remember that you do. It won't

just be a casual arrangement, Hope, I'll pay you and give
you room and board, and don't worry about the baby. I
promise you, in Hollywood you won't even get a second
glance.'

Bianca was able to get Hope a seat on her flight. Dale
Lawrence, her producer, wasn't flying back with them,
and Bianca told Hope she wouldn't meet him until he returned to the States in ten days' time. 'Plenty of time for
you to get settled in, honey. Still not sorry you didn't
leave word where you were going?' She looked seriously
into Hope's set face. She had found a boy to drive her
jeep back to Alexei's villa, and had asked him simply to
pass a note over to Alexei saying that she was safe and
well, but that she wouldn't be seeing him again.

'He lied to me,' she said tonelessly, ignoring Bianca's
question. 'He told me that what happened between us
wouldn't matter.' Tears welled and threatened to spill.

'Hope, he was right,' Bianca assured her gently. 'It
doesn't matter. Not to me . . . not to the friends you will
make, nor to the man who eventually falls in love with
you, and from what you've told me about him I don't
think it would have mattered to your Alexei, either.'

'He's not my Alexei—he loves Élise—and it does matter, otherwise, he would never . . . never have done what
he did.'

At her side Bianca sighed. 'Hope, men and women are
motivated by many things to actions they later regret.
Perhaps he was angry because he thought you'd deliberately encouraged Hal, perhaps he felt guilty, perhaps he
even felt jealous. Oh, yes, he could have felt jealous,' she
insisted. 'He obviously desired you.'

'He desired revenge,' Hope said tiredly. 'He didn't
even care enough about me to make sure I didn't have his
child.'

'Yes,' Bianca agreed thoughtfully. 'Do you know I
find that the strangest thing of all. Hope . . .' she glanced

at her companion's face and discovered that Hope was asleep. Best thing for her, she thought compassionately. Poor little Hope, who would have thought of her ever finding herself in such a situation? Thank goodness she had bumped into her. It was true that she had always been fond of her, and she did need someone to help her keep Dale at bay.

Dale was a cynic and made no secret of the fact that he wanted her. She had a reputation she had never made any attempt to refute, but Dale, if he became her lover, would be her first, and she grinned a little to herself. How would he like that, the high and mighty arrogant director who thought he knew all there was to know about her? Telling herself she was being weak-minded to even think of wanting to find out, she tried to follow Hope's peacefully sleeping example, making a mental note to arrange for Hope to see her doctor as soon as they were settled in.

CHAPTER TEN

AT FIRST Hollywood and its environs—Beverly Hills, Los Angeles, and the Pacific Coast—came as something of a culture shock to Hope, but she was young and strong, and Bianca was determined that she wasn't going to brood.

Her friend's first act once they were settled in her comfortable Beverly Hills home was to call her doctor to ask him to recommend an obstetrician to attend Hope, and Hope had found in Dr Friedman, not just a doctor, but another friend.

Paul Friedman was as different from Alexei as chalk from cheese. For a start he had none of Alexei's commanding physical appearance, he was barely five foot ten, with mid-brown hair and a mild manner that did nothing to hide his compassionate nature. In addition to his remunerative Beverly Hills practice, Paul Friedman gave a considerable amount of his time and energy to the immigrant communities along the coast and in him Hope found a man who, as Alexei had predicted, accepted her for herself. Apart from the necessary medical questions, he asked nothing about her past or the father of her baby, and for that, Hope was grateful.

Almost her last act before leaving St Marguerite had been to write Alexei a letter explaining that she was leaving the island with a friend, and telling him that she was absolving him of all responsibility towards her.

Did he ever think about her, she wondered sleepily as she lay beside Bianca's pool, soaking up the sun. Here, in the privacy of Bianca's 'yard', she felt no embarrassment about her pregnancy as she would have done on the beach. Paul still claimed that she was underweight, and it was probably the slenderness of the rest of her body that made her six-month bulge look so large, she reflected as she placed her hand over the spot where the baby kicked restlessly, as though already impatient of his confinement within her body.

'Hiya, Hope.' She straightened up as she heard Dale's voice, reaching for her robe as she did so. Charming though he was, she still hadn't learned to feel completely relaxed when Bianca's producer was around. With work on her film completed, Bianca was once again working on the popular serial in which she starred as one of the main female characters; the rich and beautiful widow, Hilary Dawlish. Much to Bianca's amusement, Hope had become a keen fan of the series, and a large proportion of her time was spent answering the fan correspondence Bianca received as the rich widow.

The month she had spent at a centre, learning to use a typewriter and word processor, and the speed-writing course she had done, had equipped Hope to work as Bianca's secretary and she was forced to admit that the arrangement was working well. Right from the start, she had insisted that publicly at least Bianca was to treat her as an employee, and although Bianca had baulked, Hope had got her way. However, surely no employee ever had such luxurious accommodation, Hope thought wryly. Bianca had insisted on her having her own private suite, and when Bianca wasn't filming or socialising they spent most of their time together.

At first, Bianca had tried to interest Hope in the many social engagements she undertook, but Hope had excused herself. Her pregnancy made her feel self-conscious, even though she was now aware, as she had become aware of so much since coming to California, that her position was by no means unique; scarcely a day passed without some beautiful actress announcing that she was to have her lover's child. She was the one who was out of step, Hope admitted, and although she could not entirely regret the fact that she carried Alexei's child, she often worried about that child's reaction to its single parentage later in life.

'Where's Bianca?' Dale asked as he strolled towards her. He was tall and dazzlingly handsome with wheat-blond hair and silver-grey eyes, and Hope could well understand why her friend found him so attractive. Bianca was playing a dangerous game with him, Hope acknowledged as she studied his tanned features, and she shivered suddenly, frightened for her friend. Bianca loved her producer and, like all women, she was vulnerable through that love. And Dale? What did he feel for her lovely red-headed friend?

Hope stifled a sigh. That Dale desired Bianca she did not doubt—neither did Bianca. She hadn't exaggerated when she had said that she needed Hope as a guard-dog, and it was this that made Hope feel so acutely uncomfortable whenever she saw Dale. He must know what Bianca was doing—he was too intelligent not to—and although he never said, Hope couldn't help feeling that he must find it irksome that Bianca should refuse to allow him to become her lover because of Hope's sensibilities. One look at Hope's bulging stomach was surely enough to totally destroy Bianca's claim that, as a convent-reared girl, Hope would be embarrassed by the knowledge that Bianca and Dale were lovers.

'She's gone into Beverly Hills to have her hair done,' Hope replied, shading her eyes. 'Can I get you a drink?'

'Scotch and soda would be fine,' Dale responded, adding wryly, 'I'm beginning to think Bianca has developed second sight where I'm concerned. Whenever I come round she's never here. I might feel more disheartened,' he added in his slow drawl, 'if I wasn't sure she's running scared.'

Hope couldn't stop herself from flushing guiltily. 'I ... I'm sure she's not deliberately avoiding you, Dale.' She stumbled over the words, knowing them for lies. Bianca was avoiding him. She had told her only that morning that she was beginning to get tired of running.

'I want him, Hope,' she said quietly, 'but I want him too much to be just another girl on a string, and I know that's all he has in mind.'

He waited for her to pour his drink and bring it from the poolside bar, patting the seat beside him when Hope brought it over. 'Sit down, and talk to me,' he told her. 'How do you like the States? You've been here, how long now?'

'Four months,' Hope told him. 'I like it very much.' She wasn't aware of how wistful her voice was until Dale said dryly:

'But you're missing whoever it is who's responsible for junior here like mad, is that it? Look, honey,' he drawled when Hope went pale. 'I'm not about to sit in judgment over you. Bianca's already told me a little of what happened and I know you've had a raw deal. As far as Bianca's concerned, you're going to be a permanent feature in her life from now on, and since I aim to be the same, it's time you learned to quit jumping five miles in the air every time I come near you. For one thing, it can't be good for junior. Whatever Bianca might have told you, I don't eat little girls like you for breakfast.'

'Bianca hasn't suggested that you do,' Hope defended her friend.

'But she has told you something,' he guessed shrewdly.

'She's told me that you want to become her lover,' Hope admitted.

'And?'

The question begged an answer Hope wasn't prepared to give. 'And,' she said firmly, 'if I seem self-conscious when you're about, it's simply because I feel you must be wishing me still on St Marguerite.'

Dale laughed and leaned forward, ruffling her hair with the same sort of affection he might have used on a child. 'So, that's it, and there was I thinking it was my virile machismo. Look, honey, Bianca can surround herself with half a hundred guard-dogs, all of them ten times more effective than a pretty little girl like you, and it still wouldn't stop me. Right now, Bianca's playing games, and I'm willing to let her, but not for ever, Hope, not for ever.' He stood up and Hope was aware that he possessed the same potent masculinity as Alexei. Like Alexei, he was a man who wouldn't be denied what he wanted, nor turned from any path on which he set his feet, and she felt a tiny frisson of fear for her friend, but she didn't have the right to interfere, nor to plead mercy for Bianca's tender feelings.

'When Bianca comes back, ask her to give me a call, will you? Her film is being nominated for inclusion in the Cannes Film Festival. That should soften that ice-cold heart of hers a little. Oh, and I'm taking the both of you to dinner tonight.' He mentioned a restaurant which Hope knew was patronised by the élite of the film world and she blenched, a refusal on the tip of her tongue. 'Don't refuse,' Dale warned her. 'I'm bringing a friend—someone I want you to meet.'

He saw her expression and sighed, squatting down beside her and taking her hand. Silver streaks mingled with the wheat-blond hair, and Hope realised that he was probably speaking the truth—if stretching it somewhat—when he said softly, 'Look, honey, I'm old enough to be your father. I know how badly you've been hurt, and I want you to know that I admire you—for the

way you've coped, for the way you've helped Bianca—
but once junior comes along, you're going to want more
security, a place of your own. It's only natural—the
nesting instinct—and I think I can help you.'

'How?'

He laughed when he saw Hope's incredulous expression. 'A friend of mine does high-class advertising vid-
eos, and he's got a client who wants to promote baby
gear—it's a new shop that's opening in LA and Beverly
Hills. They're from New York and they specialise in
continental stuff. He's looking for someone they can use
in the ads, you'd be a natural, and it will pay very well.
All you'll have to do is to appear in their ads during your
pregnancy, and with junior once he arrives. I'm not saying you'll get the job, but Roy is willing to see you. Like
I say, we're talking about a high-class outlet, and I've told
him he won't find a pregnant lady any classier than you.
Now, will you accept my invitation to dinner?'

'You're very kind,' Hope said shakily. Not even to
Bianca had she admitted how concerned she was about
the future. Her job was very well in its way, but Dale was
right when he said she would want a home of her own,
some stability for the baby.

'Oh, I'm not completely altruistic,' Dale chuckled,
'don't forget part of the deal is that Bianca comes to
dinner, too.'

BIANCA GRIMACED when Hope passed on the invitation,
brightening when she added Dale's message about the
Cannes Film Festival. Hope told her about Dale's friend
and the job he might have for her.

'Roy? Oh, you must mean Roy Grundberg, he and
Dale were at UCLA together. You'll like him, but don't
sell yourself short,' she warned, as she sipped the mar-
tini Felipe, her houseboy, had prepared for her.

Felipe and his parents adored Bianca and Hope knew that she payed them wages that were well above the average, allowing them to live in the garden apartment over the garages. Felipe was their eldest child, and after him were five others, all of whom were at school. Felipe was working his way through medical school, and earned a little extra money by helping his father with the gardens, and generally helping out where he could. The Mexican family were just another example of Bianca's generosity, her compassion for 'lame dogs', Hope reflected, thanking Felipe for the glass of orange juice and lemonade he brought her.

'What else did Dale have to say?' Bianca asked casually, but Hope wasn't deceived. She glanced at her friend, as she lounged on the long green and white covered chair, even in relaxation her body graceful, her flaming red hair curling on to her shoulders, the pale skin she had to protect from the strong Californian sun gleaming like the inside of a seashell.

'He said that he means to have you—by hook or by crook,' Hope told her dryly, watching the expressions chasing one another over Bianca's face. Anger and longing fought together as she gripped her glass, so tight that Hope thought it might crack.

'Oh does he,' she said lightly at last, when anger had won. 'The conceited bastard!' She grimaced and then saw that Hope wasn't shocked. 'You've grown up fast these last few months, little Hope, and I suppose if they could hear me now the Sisters would accuse me of corrupting you. I've brought you something back from Beverly Hills,' she added when Hope denied her assertion. 'I must have been gifted by second sight, you can wear it tonight.'

She tossed a bag across to Hope, smiling when Hope investigated the mass of tissue paper inside and held up the dress of crinkle-cotton she had extracted. Tiny shoestring straps held up the simple round neck, the dress falling in a mass of tiny pleats to a hem scalloped like shells and edged with silver embroidery to match that adorning the bodice of the dress. It was white; two fragile layers of it that moved delicately in the evening breeze and Hope knew it must have cost the earth.

'Oh, Bianca,' she began, but her friend cut her short, saying firmly:

'Hope, I'm not taking it back, and I certainly don't intend wearing it myself. I know you think of yourself as a charity case, but you aren't. My correspondence has never been so in order. I've never had a secretary who has been so conscientious, and your salary, if that worries you, is tax deductible. Jeff, my accountant, tells me that you spotted a very interesting article about tax-free investments which he's pursuing and which could potentially save me ten times the amount your salary costs.

'And it's not just a question of money and hard work, you're my friend, Hope—the only real one I have. Hollywood really deserves the title Tinsel Town, and that's what so many of the friendships that spring up are. Having you here means a lot to me. You know how I feel about Dale—you're the only person who does—that's something I can't share with anyone else, and seeing you, realising that what happened to you could so easily happen to me, has given me the strength to hold him at bay.'

'Perhaps you're wrong,' Hope said softly. 'Perhaps he will marry you.'

Bianca shook her head. 'No. He's been married once and went through a very bitter divorce. It was just when his career had got started. His wife was an actress and she left him for her leading man, taking Dale's little girl with her, and nearly everything Dale had earned. It's left him totally opposed to marriage, or any form of permanent relationship, and his bitterness is intensified by the fact that his wife neglected Debbie, their little girl, and she was killed in a car accident two years after they parted. Dale feels very bad about it. He thinks he should have fought harder for custody. He says he knew that Myra would neglect the child.'

Hope's hand covered her stomach protectively. Her heart ached with pity for Dale and for Bianca. 'I'm not foolish enough to think a marriage license could tie him to me,' Bianca added dryly, 'but at least it would be proof of his intent. Dale wants me, I know, but wanting isn't loving.' Unknowingly she was repeating what Hope had said to herself in Paris and gone on thinking ever since. Wanting was a long way from loving, but it was also a lot, lot more than the nothing she had now.

'Come on,' Bianca instructed, 'we've gloomed enough for one day. Let's go out and put on our glad rags. So Dale reckons he's going to win out in the end, does he?' Her green eyes gleamed and Hope suppressed a smile, knowing that Dale wasn't going to get things all his own way.

Roy turned out to be a pleasant man in his mid-forties, who appraised Hope thoughtfully over their meal. She admitted to a feeling of nervousness, even though she had set out by no means sure that she wanted to go ahead with the ads, even if she was offered the chance.

Over dinner Roy explained what was involved; an entire campaign which would run for twelve months, featuring various aspects of the soon-to-be-opened shops, from maternity clothes from the continent right through to nursery equipment and children's clothes.

'You would be ideal,' he confirmed, when they had reached the coffee stage. 'You've got another three months to go, so Dale tells me, which means we should shoot the film of you for the first set of ads, featuring the maternity clothes and some of the nursery stuff, starting off again once the baby arrives and running them right through until he's twelve months old. This campaign is costing my clients a bomb.' He named the fee that Hope could receive if she was chosen, and it made her gasp in astonishment. 'But they believe they'll more than recoup it if it's successful. There's a baby boom on in Hollywood at the moment, just in case you haven't noticed, and they don't want to use a known name or face, because they want the woman they choose to be associated only with their name and motherhood. You were right,' he added in an aside to Dale, 'she does have an almost madonna-like quality.'

'That's the calm and serenity they tried to instil in us at the convent,' Bianca interrupted, pulling a wry face when Dale drawled:

'Unsuccessfully in your case, my sweet, you are turbulence personified. You need an outlet for all that nervous energy.'

Nothing else was said, but Hope had an acute feeling that the gauge had well and truly been flung down between them, and it came as no surprise to hear Dale suggesting when they had finished their meal that they all returned to his house. 'Roy and Hope can continue their discussion and you and I—' he smiled lazily and trapped Bianca's fingers beneath his, raising them to his lips, kissing them slowly with a panache Hope wouldn't have expected from a man who was so totally American '—can talk about our trip to Cannes next spring.'

Much to Hope's surprise, Dale's home turned out to be not in one of the expensive film-star-thronged suburbs, but out along the coast. A Spanish-style building, simple in design, built round a patio and pool, completely lacking in ostentation and luxury, with even the furnishings slightly austere.

'Dale's hair shirt,' Bianca quipped when Hope looked her surprise. 'At heart I suspect he's not just an aesthetic but a potential martyr as well.'

Dale returned the mocking look she gave him with one of his own, and drawled so softly that Hope suspected the words were meant for Bianca's ears alone. 'Self-sacrifice can sometimes make the ultimate pleasure all the sweeter. You might try it some time.'

Did Dale think that the gossip about Bianca's many lovers was true, Hope wondered as they all went through into the main salon, starkly white with a polished pine floor and a scattering of rich Mexican rugs, the furniture solid and comfortable. It was something that hadn't occurred to her before; she frowned, wondering if Bianca realised what he might be thinking.

When they had finished their coffee and it had been arranged that she would attend Roy's studio for a screen test the following day Roy offered to drive her home. Hope darted a brief glance at Bianca, but she and Dale were arguing about something and Hope hesitated to interrupt. 'Come on, let's leave them to it,' Roy suggested with a smile. 'You needn't worry too much about Bianca. She can hold her own, and Dale isn't the type to force himself on a woman who doesn't want him. He doesn't need to,' he added frankly.

Nevertheless, Hope lay sleepless, listening for Bianca's return, finally falling asleep with the false dawn, concern for her friend pleating her forehead as she slept.

When Francisca brought her breakfast she confirmed that Bianca had not arrived home. The Mexican woman didn't seem overly concerned and Hope thanked her with a smile, gnawing at her bottom lip wondering what she should do. A quick glance in Bianca's diary confirmed that she had no engagements for the morning, and only one in the afternoon—a fitting for some new gowns for the series. Hope herself had an appointment with Paul Friedman. He greeted her with a warm smile when José, Francisca's husband, dropped her off outside his surgery.

'You're looking well,' he told her. 'Let's just see how junior's doing, shall we?' When Hope told him that she might be asked to do some filming and explained what Roy had in mind, Paul checked her over thoroughly. 'Well there's certainly no reason why you shouldn't work from a health point of view.'

'And if I get the contract it will make me independent of Bianca... I'll be able to buy myself a house... somewhere in the country.'

'Try the Napa Valley,' Paul suggested. 'Get Dale to take you out there, he owns a half-share in a winery.'

The Napa Valley, Hope had almost forgotten California's wine-growing district, and suddenly she knew that she wanted to live there, that she wanted Alexei's son to grow up with at least one part of his heritage. She might never be able to tell him about his father, but at least he would have the land, the vines, the French side of his father.

When she left the surgery José drove her straight to Roy's studio. She found she quite enjoyed the small test his crew gave her. They were all very friendly, especially Roy's assistant, Kate Harding. 'You're a natural,' Kate enthused when they had finished. 'And you're the best we've tested so far, but a lot depends on the clients. Roy's going to see them tomorrow, so you shouldn't have too long to wait. When's the baby due?'

Hope told her and she in turn told Hope about her own twins and her husband who was a cameraman with Dale's studio. When Kate suggested they lunch together Hope accepted, thinking how readily Americans made friends, and how she was beginning to adopt their life-style.

She was growing up; more slowly now perhaps, but the complexities of other people's relationships were beginning to teach her that nothing in life was ever simple. From bitterness she was slowly learning fresh acceptance of Alexei, and even of Sir Henry, and she was learning also that Alexei was right and that even if during that last bitter scene she had discovered that he could not judge her as impartially as he had promised her thinking people would judge her, there were those who did.

Her pregnancy had ceased to be something of which she was ashamed, and her life had opened out into a rich new vein. She was her own person, complete within herself, able to support herself—almost—able to rely on her own judgment and assessment of situations and people. She was free... She realised it for the first time as she stepped back into the car, pausing on the sidewalk to savour the knowledge. She was no longer frightened or afraid of life and other people, and if her heart still ached for the impossible, for a love she knew she would never share with Alexei, well at least she had friendship and warmth in her life.

Paul wanted to date her, he had told her so, chiding her gently when she refused, telling her that she couldn't shut the entire male sex out of her life because of one man, and it boosted her ego to know that he found her attractive, even while she knew he could never be anything more than a friend.

In sharp contrast to her own buoyant mood she found Bianca tense and distressed when she returned to the house. She was still wearing the clothes she had worn the previous evening and was pacing the patio with all the angry energy of a restless lioness.

'Bianca... Are you...'

'I'm fine and still *virgo intacta*,' Bianca told her sardonically, ceasing her pacing. 'But I almost wasn't.' She shivered briefly and poured herself a drink. 'God, I never thought I could be such a fool. It must have been the wine we had at dinner. Dale's own wine, you might know. I almost spent the night with him,' she said slowly. 'I wanted to... God knows that... but when he looked at me and said in the slow drawl of his how pleased he was that he was at last about to be admitted to the ranks of my lovers, I knew I couldn't. I knew I couldn't do it and keep my self-respect, so I left, and spent the night driving up and down the coast, hating myself for leaving...'

'And now?' Hope asked quietly. Bianca pulled a face.

'Oh, my body still hates me right enough, but my mind is glad.' She dropped tiredly into a lounger. 'I'm going to my room to rest. If Dale calls...' She grimaced. 'You're right—he won't. Not after last night. I won't tell you what he called me when I left, but he had every reason to say it...'

THREE DAYS LATER Hope had a call from Kate to confirm that she had been chosen for the ads. 'Not that it was really ever in doubt. The owner took one look at your film clip and decided there and then, and I don't blame her. She wants to meet you, by the way, Hope. She's suggested dinner at her hotel tonight. She's staying at the Beverly Wilshire at the moment. Can you make it? Roy will be there, too.'

Hope wanted to refuse, but Bianca wouldn't let her, and when Bianca's limousine with José at the wheel swept her towards the Wilshire just after eight that night, Hope vainly tried to quell the nervous bubbles exploding inside her stomach.

She needn't have worried. Helen Warfman welcomed her warmly, telling her frankly how pleased she was with the screen test she had seen. 'Roy isn't here yet,' she told Hope when the Maitre d' had led them to their table. 'Has he told you much about my stores?'

Hope shook her head. 'Only that you specialise in continental nursery and baby equipment.'

'Mmm. Well that does just about cover it. It's luxury-class stuff and we don't try to pretend otherwise, but I think there's a market for it out here. I go to Europe twice a year on buying trips. Spain and Italy produce the most marvellous stuff.' She glanced curiously at Hope. 'Roy tells me you're English?'

'Yes. Bianca and I were at school together,' Hope told her, adding calmly, 'I don't know if Roy has told you or not, but I'm not married and . . .'

'He has told me, and no, it doesn't matter. If we need to do any ads featuring the traditional family unit Roy will find someone to model the "father". Does it worry you? Not being married I mean?' she asked Hope.

'It does in some ways. More for the baby's sake than my own. Oh, I know it's very fashionable at the moment, but what happens in say ten or fifteen years' time?'

'Well, whatever does happen, your child won't be on its own. There's a positive wave of women in your position at the moment—most of them by choice. Ah, here comes Roy.'

While Roy greeted his client, Hope reflected on what Helen had said to her. She was relieved to know that the New Yorker didn't object to her unmarried status. Bianca had told her there was no need for her to mention it, but Hope had wanted to be honest from the outset. Her thoughts drifted to Alexei. What was he doing right now? Scarcely a day went past without her thinking about him. Was he somewhere with Élise? Did he remember her at all?

'Hope, where are you?' Roy chided gently. 'I was just saying, we can start work right away on the first ads. The baby's due, when? January or thereabouts? That means we can plan the main body of the campaign for the spring. Just right . . .' He sounded so pleased with himself that Hope gurgled with laughter, realising as she did so how long it had been since she last laughed. A curious tight pain settled round her heart as she listened to Helen and Roy discussing the campaign and her baby; the child Alexei would never know he had fathered.

It was late when she got back, but Bianca was still up pacing the room angrily, her cheeks flushed. 'Dale's just left,' she announced abruptly. 'That man really is the limit.'

'What did you quarrel about this time?' Hope was growing used to the arguments between the two of them; Dale was a demanding producer and Bianca's red hair meant that she responded fierily to the least hint of criticism. The sheer professionalism of both of them was something Hope admired tremendously. When they were working Bianca never allowed her love for Dale to cloud her reactions.

'There's a nude love-scene coming up in the serial. I've told Dale I won't do it.' Green sparks flew from her eyes as she turned to glower at Hope. 'I've never done anything like that, and I'm not going to start now, no matter what Dale says.'

'And what does Dale say?' Hope probed gently, sensing that Bianca hadn't disclosed the real core of her anger.

'He says,' Bianca told her tightly, struggling for control, 'that I've played such scenes often enough in my private life not to need to worry about a lack of authenticity...'

Hope expelled a slow breath, her heart aching for her friend as she saw the tears glittering in her eyes. She was just about to join Bianca in condemning Dale when a thought struck her. 'Bianca, do you think Dale could be jealous?'

'Jealous? Huh! To be jealous he'd have to care, and how could he do that when he's telling me I've got to go through some explicit love-scene in front of the cameras.'

'The same way that you constantly goad him about his past,' Hope told her lightly. She had noticed that her friend constantly referred to Dale's reputation; and the fact that he regularly escorted a positive bevy of beautiful women.

'Come on, Hope,' Bianca said tiredly, 'Dale isn't some shy young boy. If he really feels anything for me, all he has to do is say so.'

'But does he know that?' Hope asked reasonably. 'Look, you've told me yourself he wants you; it isn't impossible that he feels something more than mere desire.'

Bianca grimaced. 'There's no point in discussing it any further. Oh,' she turned by the door, 'I've mentioned to Dale that you might be interested in acquiring a property in the Napa Valley. Like I said, he has a part-share in a winery out there. He suggested we all go out there for a weekend, so that you can look around. Not now—it's their busiest time of the year—but later, perhaps, after the baby arrives...'

'WELL, THAT'S one in the can.' Hope relaxed as Roy signalled to the camera crew to stop filming. 'How did it look to you, Kate?' he asked his assistant, rumpling already untidy hair. They had been working on the ad for nearly a month, and Hope held her breath as she waited for the verdict.

'It looked good,' Kate told her. 'If it goes out as we plan, at prime time just before Christmas to catch the opening of the two new stores, I think it will show really good results.'

The first ad in the campaign showed Hope walking through a mock-up of the new Beverly Hills 'store', examining the nursery equipment, and one shot had cleverly included a banked wall of soft toys and dolls as well as other Christmas gifts, including a very special handmade and limited selection of rocking-horses from England.

'The next one runs after Christmas, doesn't it?' Kate asked, checking their list.

'Umm...the first one after Hope has the baby. We start with a shot of her getting out of the car. Did we finally decide on a model to play the father?' he queried. 'We're going to need him for this one. Then we go to the nursery, but we can't pick out the stuff until we find out whether Hope has a boy or girl?'

'Which do you want, Hope?' Kate asked her. 'Or don't you mind?'

Hope didn't, but she was secretly convinced that her child would be a boy. She looked sombre. Would he grow up to hate her for ever giving birth to him? At least this campaign would mean that he had a secure start in life. Dale had told her that she shouldn't have too much trouble finding a small property in the valley, as often larger properties acquired more land which meant that the houses on them were sold off more cheaply than they might otherwise have been.

Concern for the future had occupied much of Hope's thoughts as her pregnancy advanced, mercifully protecting her from the worst of the pain of loving Alexei, although she sensed it would return. She had already decided that if she did manage to find a property she was going to start working as a freelance secretary, possibly finding work in the valley from the various wineries, although she had promised to stay on with Bianca at least until after the Cannes Film Festival.

Christmas was only weeks away and as she left the studio and José drove her back to Bianca's house, Hope tried not to give in to the feeling of loneliness that swept her. Bianca, too, seemed to be adversely affected by the mood of the season. 'Just look at us,' she exclaimed moodily over dinner. 'Christmas always makes me miserable. I'd thought of flying to Switzerland, but somehow I can't summon up the enthusiasm. Christmas is a time for families—something neither of us possesses.' She looked at Hope. 'You still miss him dreadfully, don't you? Oh, I know you try to hide it, but some things can't be hidden. I've watched you these last few months and it terrifies me, Hope, to know that I'm just as vulnerable as you; that Dale could walk out of my life tomorrow and for the rest of my life there'd be an empty space inside me that no one else could fill.'

Hope felt tears prick her eyes. Bianca's words summed up exactly how she felt. But this searing, hopeless pain couldn't last for ever, surely. Some time there must be a respite.

Dale asked them to spend Thanksgiving with him, but Bianca refused. 'I couldn't bear it,' she told Hope simply when he had gone, leaving the house in a blaze of rage. For Christmas she had planned a large party, without inviting Dale, and when he came round to discuss some detail of the script with her, Hope noticed how dangerously close to exploding both of them were.

Before he left, Dale removed a small box from his jacket. 'Here,' he said curtly, tossing it across to Bianca. 'You might as well have this now. I'm spending Christmas and New Year in the Valley, so I won't be seeing you until January.'

He left before Bianca could speak, and Hope felt a tug of sympathy for her when she saw her ashen face. 'I didn't buy him anything,' she said in anguish. 'We've been quarrelling so much lately.'

'He's probably hurt because you refused his invitation for Thanksgiving and you didn't invite him to your party.'

'He has family in the Valley,' Bianca told her. 'He's part Italian.' Which accounted for his hot temper, and perhaps even more, Hope reflected when Bianca had gone to dress for a date she had with her agent.

Left on her own, Hope flipped idly through some of the magazines on the coffee table. A photograph in *Paris Match* caught her eye and she studied it avidly, her heart

thudding, perspiration breaking out across her skin.
Alexei! Greedily she consumed every detail of the grainy
photograph. He was wearing a dinner suit, and the photographer had caught him in profile. A wave of desperate yearning swept over her, tears tasting salty as they ran
down her face. A reception had been held for the Beaune
wine-growers and Alexei was one of the guests. There was
no mention of Élise, and long after she had closed the
magazine Hope lay in bed unable to sleep, tormented by
memories, knowing that as long as she lived she would
still feel the same way, that nothing had changed, time
only increasing the depth of her loneliness.

Christmas came and went. A gentle lethargy seemed to
possess her; a feeling of great calm, which she knew to be
false and yet she lacked the energy to break it.

Dr Friedman told her that he suspected the baby's birth
was imminent. He had booked her a bed at a prestige
Beverly Hills private maternity hospital, which Bianca
had insisted on paying for. 'There's nothing to worry
about,' he assured her when he had finished his examination. 'Junior's fine and healthy. You're still a little
underweight, but nothing that will hurt.'

Three weeks later Hope woke in the night disorientated by the sharp pain which had disturbed her, telling
herself it had been pure imagination until she felt another. There had been none of the back pain she had expected to herald the baby's birth, but she knew
instinctively that her labour had begun.

Bianca insisted on driving her to the hospital herself,
having alerted them to expect them. 'I must ring Dale,'
she added as she hurried Hope out to the car, more nervous than Hope was herself. 'He told me to,' she added
when Hope demurred. 'He wants to be there, Hope—we
both do.'

The hospital was bright and cheery, calm nurses reminding her to do her breathing exercises, the quiet calm

of the restful delivery room a place where they were all a
team working together to bring her child into the world.

Bianca wanted to stay with her, and the doctor gave his
permission. It was comforting to have her there, but it
was Alexei's name Hope cried out in the final struggle to
obey the doctor's exhortations. Alexei who she wanted
with her. Alexei who would never know she had borne
him a son.

'Oh, Hope, he's so beautiful.' Bianca was crying, but
Hope was barely aware of her friend, lost as she was in a
rapt concentration and exploration of the new life she
was holding in her arms. A fluff of dark hair, still damp,
clung to the well-formed skull, deep, dark blue eyes surveying her gravely. Alexei's son . . . She wanted to laugh
and cry at the same time.

'DON'T WAKE HIM UP, Dale—you'll wake poor Hope.'
Bianca's chiding voice reached Hope distantly, and she
opened her eyes, shifting her aching, curiously weightless body, and then she remembered. Her eyes flew open
as she sat up in bed. Her room was full of flowers, the
scent filling the air. At the bottom of her bed was the
small portable cot, but Nikolai Alexander Stanford
wasn't lying in it.

'Dale, put him down,' Bianca pressed, and Hope
glanced anxiously across the bed, but she needn't have
worried—Dale was holding the baby tenderly in his arms,
his expression absorbed as he studied him.

'I hope I'm going to get to be godpapa to him, Hope,'
he said huskily. 'I nearly wore out that carpet outside the
delivery room last night.'

'Huh!' Bianca snorted derisively. 'Men! Hope's the
one who should be exhausted.' Her eyes filled with tears.
'Oh Hope, I've never experienced anything like it in my
life. To see him being born. After they shooed me out,
I . . .'

'Burst into tears and wept all over me,' Dale supplemented, reluctantly placing the baby back in his crib. 'Perhaps you ought to try having one of your own. You're getting broody.'

'Just like that!' Bianca snapped. She heard Hope's faint sigh, and was instantly remorseful. 'Oh, honey, I'm so sorry but it seems Dale and I can't meet these days without quarrelling.'

They left shortly afterwards, and although she had been glad to see them, Hope wasn't sorry. When she had seen Dale holding Nikolai in his arms she had been racked by a pain far fiercer than any she had endured in giving him birth. It should have been Alexei holding their child, watching him with that awed, absorbed tenderness. Alexei—she had cried out his name in the dark of the night, her body aching for his warmth.

Within four days she was allowed to return home. Bianca had organised a nursery suite for her while she had been in hospital and a fresh wave of gratitude swamped Hope as she looked round it.

'All the equipment came from the store,' she told her, 'a present from Helen. She says business was fantastic over Christmas, and she puts it all down to the success of the campaign. With the new ad due in the spring, she expects a real boom, so this is by way of an extra "thankyou".'

Tears misted Hope's eyes as she studied the dainty blue and white colour scheme, the dark wood rocking-cradle with its blue and white hangings, the huge coach-built pram. 'Oh, that's from Dale,' Bianca told her when she saw Hope gazing at it. 'I've never seen him like that before. His Italian heritage, I suppose. That, and losing his own child.'

Hope looked at her friend. 'You'd like to have his child, wouldn't you?' she asked gently.

'So much,' Bianca admitted, 'but not without love. I'll leave you to get settled in. And you can take the rest of the week off,' she grinned as she closed the door behind her.

SHE WAS SO very lucky, Hope reflected a month later. Bianca was more of a friend than an employer; sometimes Hope felt guilty about taking her salary. Nikolai Alexander was thriving, and Dr Friedman said wryly that it was no wonder. 'I've never known a child have so many adults willing to spoil him.'

Dale had become an almost daily visitor at the house, always taking time to visit the nursery, and Bianca teased him that the only reason he had bought the pram was so that he could walk the baby in it. He had offered to take Hope to the Napa Valley for a week at the end of the month so that she could look at several properties. Bianca had been invited to go, but she had refused, claiming that she was too busy. Hope had been with them when Bianca had turned down the invitation, and for a moment she had thought she saw pain in Dale's eyes.

They had filmed the second advertisement in the series; Nikolai had been an instant success, adapting to filming as though to the manner born.

Helen called to say how delighted she was with the results. 'He's gorgeous,' she cooed, bending over the pram. 'And I'm wild about the advert. If that doesn't bring every wealthy mama-to-be in Beverly Hills and LA into our stores I'll be one very surprised lady—and it takes one whole lot to surprise a New Yorker!'

Hope laughed her agreement. 'But your things are so gorgeous I'm sure they'd have been tempted, anyway. Bianca insisted on buying Niko an entire layette from the Beverly Hills stores, and the things are so gorgeous.'

Helen picked him out of the pram. 'Umm. This silk romper-suit is from Paris. Just look at that embroidery.'

The romper-suit was embroidered with butterflies in blue and silver, and Hope had been secretly pleased when Bianca had picked all traditional clothes as her gift. Hope didn't dispute the practicality of modern garments, but she wanted to enjoy Niko as a baby and not rush his growing up. Time enough for sombre, more practical colours when he was toddling.

'You made a terrific hit with Ben Harman, by the way,' Helen added slyly, grinning at her. 'Roy told me Ben asked him where he could get in touch with you. Could it be he doesn't just want to play "daddy" for the cameras?'

Hope smiled. She had quite liked Ben Harman, the darkly attractive actor who played her husband in the new ad, but liking was a very pale thing when compared with the intensity of emotion she still felt towards Alexei.

'Why the Russian names, by the way?' Helen queried casually. 'I know you're English.'

'I liked the sound of them,' Hope responded equally carelessly, hoping that Helen wouldn't probe any further.

'Umm. They do have a certain ring to them. There's quite a contingent of people of Russian descent in Paris. I met quite a few when I was over there. Most of them had families who fled from the Revolution, apparently.'

Hope discovered that she was holding her breath, and in an effort to appear calm, she got up and walked round to the pram, lifting Nikolai out, and cradling him against her shoulder. Already at six weeks he had a marked disinclination to lie still. He preferred to be held upright, the small, chubby legs kicking out quite hard as he fought to establish his independence.

'Oh?' Hope wondered if she succeeded in sounding uninterested.

'Umm.' Helen was playing with the fringed silk sun-canopy attached to the pram. 'You know this has been one of our best sellers. Dale spent hours choosing it.'

Hope caught the inflection and lifted her head. 'Dale isn't Nikolai's father,' she assured her firmly. 'But he has been very good to us. Partially, I suspect, because of the loss of his own child.' Quickly she outlined the story Bianca had told her.

'Umm. He's quite a man—all man,' Helen added with a grin. 'Don't you think so?'

When she had gone Hope wondered if she ought to warn Bianca that she could have a possible rival in the New Yorker. Helen had a certain brashness that sug-gested that she wouldn't be frightened to say what she thought—and felt—and she was attractive enough to ri-val many of the women Dale had taken out.

Nikolai started to protest as she held him too tightly and Hope put him back in his pram, her eyes misting with tears. Alexei would probably never see him; never know she had borne him a child. One day he would surely marry, if only to ensure succession to his name. The woman he loved was lost to him, unless Élise decided to forgo her late husband's fortune, so he would have to marry elsewhere, and Hope felt saddened by the knowl-edge that some other child would follow in his footsteps; that Alexei would never know of the precious gift he had given her, and Nikolai would never have the companion-ship and love of his father.

'HOPE, JUST read this.' The spiralling excitement in Bianca's voice caught Hope's attention and she took the newspaper Bianca was waving in front of her. It was an English paper, one she herself had ordered but hadn't had much time to study since Niko's arrival, and she frowned as Bianca indicated the personal column, her own name leaping at her from the small print. 'Hope

Stanford...that's you,' Bianca exclaimed excitedly. 'I wonder what it's all about?'

Hope read the brief notice twice. It gave the name and address of a firm of solicitors in London and simply requested that she get in touch with them.

'Perhaps Alexei is trying to trace you,' Bianca murmured excitedly. 'Perhaps you were wrong, Hope, and he does love you after all.'

'No.' Her voice was curt and she could see Bianca's face fall. Could it be that Alexei was trying to find her? Against her will she felt the fierce, hungry beat of her heart, the thud of her pulse beneath her skin. How much she yearned for him, even now. She only had to close her eyes and she could see his face, feel the texture of his skin against her hands, her senses overwhelmed by memories time was doing nothing to eradicate.

'You must ring them,' Bianca was urging. 'Now. Just think if I hadn't seen that notice.'

It was one among many, dreary, heart-wrenching pleas for people long-gone and uncaring, and her heart ached with the burden of the miseries of the human race. Why must there be so much pain?

'Come on. I'll get the number for you...' Bianca got up and then paused when she saw Hope's white face. 'Hope, you still love him so much, don't you?' she whispered sympathetically.

'Too much.' Hope acknowledged. She wished Bianca hadn't seen the notice—she didn't want her to make the phone call, but she knew there was no swaying her friend. What if the notice had been inserted on Alexei's instructions? It did seem unlikely that he would use a London-based firm of solicitors, though. What would getting in contact with him achieve now? All it could do was cause her further pain.

Bianca's excited, 'Hope, it's ringing, come on...' impinged on her train of thought and Hope moved auto-

matically towards the phone, taking the receiver, giving
her name to the girl who answered the telephone, telling
her about the notice.

There was a delay of several seconds and then she was
speaking to someone else, a man with a cool, clipped
English voice.

'Miss Stanford? Ah, you saw the notice, excellent. We
are acting for your late, er... uncle, Sir Henry...'

Until that moment Hope hadn't realised how much she
had wanted the notice to be placed by Alexei. She had
been deceiving herself when she thought she had the
strength to remove herself from his life. She wanted to be
with him so much it was an ache inside; a pain of unshed
tears, which she forced herself to keep at bay while she
listened to Mr Swindon explaining to her that her uncle
had died of a heart attack and that they needed to talk to
her about his will.

'Broadvale was heavily mortgaged and must be sold,'
he explained, surprising her, although she ought not to
be surprised after what Alexei had told her about her
uncle's life-style, Hope thought tiredly. 'However, there
is an inheritance due to you from your grandfather, but
I should like to discuss this with you in person. At the
moment it is invested in gilts and brings in a small income. We shall need to talk about how it should be
managed in the future. Is it possible for you to come to
London? The estate will pay all the expenses involved, of
course,' he added tactfully.

Hope asked if she could ring him back. There was no
real reason why she shouldn't fly to London, but the news
of her uncle's death had come completely out of the blue
and she needed time to come to terms both with it, and
with the knowledge of how desperately she had hoped
that Alexei might be trying to find her.

'Of course you must go,' Bianca informed her, when
Hope explained the reason for the notice. 'You've got

Niko to think about now, Hope. You'll have to clothe and educate him, the money will come in useful however little it is, and it's not costing you anything to go and talk to the lawyers.'

Bianca's words only echoed her own thoughts and both of them carefully avoided looking into one another's eyes, neither of them willing to mention Alexei. Time seemed to increase her aching need for him rather than reduce it. Without him her life was incomplete and always would be, she acknowledged, but she was not the sort of person who could accept a substitute—it was either Alexei or no one—and at least she had Niko. Niko, who reminded her more and more of Alexei with every day that passed. Niko, who was so precious to her both on his own account and because he was Alexei's child.

They flew to London at the end of the week. The solicitors had booked her into the Dorchester, and the warmth of its foyer was a welcome relief after the cold stinging rain of Heathrow and the darkness gradually infiltrating the London streets.

Niko was tired and went straight to sleep in the pleasant suite they had been given. The young girl sent up by room service to watch over him while Hope kept her appointment with the solicitors was reassuringly placid and competent, but just to be on the safe side, Hope gave her the solicitors' number where she could be reached if there was any emergency.

It took her less than half an hour to reach the office by taxi and she was shown almost immediately into a comfortable if rather old-fashioned office. Mr Swindon, the man she had spoken to by telephone, rose to greet her. He was about her uncle's age, tall and thin with a slight stoop and a reassuring smile, plus an endless supply of patience, Hope reflected an hour later when he had been over every detail of her uncle's will.

The money that was to come to her came from her grandfather, and during his lifetime her uncle had enjoyed the income from it—an income which the solicitor explained had been used in the main to pay her school fees. Now, both the capital and the income devolved on her, and Hope listened carefully while the solicitor explained the options open to her, thanking him for his advice and assuring him that she would let him have her instructions before she returned to California.

'There is one more thing before you leave...' Hope was already on her feet and she paused, watching him fiddle with his pen, wondering a little at his obvious reluctance to continue. What further revelations about her family was she going to hear?

'We have been approached by—er—the Comte de Serivace, who also saw our notice in the paper. It seems he is very anxious to discover your whereabouts. Indeed, he came to see me personally to ask me to advise him should you get in touch with us.'

Hope sank back into her chair, her face paper-white. 'I... Why... What did you tell him?' she managed in a husky whisper.

'The truth—that at the time we had heard nothing from you and did not know where you might be found. However, he is a very determined gentleman and seems very anxious to contact you.'

'Did he say... did he say why?'

Mr Swindon looked at her uncertainly. 'He seemed to indicate that he felt a certain degree of responsibility towards you. He was a friend of your uncle's at one time, I believe.'

Responsibility! Hope quelled a bitter laugh. Oh yes, Alexei would feel responsibility towards her, just as he had a responsibility to avenge Tanya, but it wasn't responsibility she wanted from him...she didn't want his pity or his protection, she wanted to meet him as an equal, she wanted his love, and she was pitifully equipped to do either.

'Now that you have contacted us...' Mr Swindon's voice trailed away, and Hope said firmly:

'I do not want the Comte to get in touch with me or to know where I am. It is true that he did know my uncle, but there is no need for him to feel responsible for me in any way, and I should prefer it, if he contacts you again, if you do not tell him anything.'

'Of course, if that is your wish.' Mr Swindon did not make any further comments, but Hope could tell that he was curious. She also felt that she could trust him not to betray to Alexei that she had been in contact with him. Only a week ago she had longed to believe that Alexei was trying to find her, and now she knew that he had, she was desperately afraid that he might succeed; that he would see Niko and realise the truth; that that same sense of pride and honour which had driven him in his search for revenge would seize him again and that he would sacrifice them both to a marriage that would give Niko his rightful status in life, but which would deprive Alexei of the woman he really loved, and herself of all hope of pride and self-respect.

When she returned to the hotel she found Niko still asleep. She ordered dinner to be served in her room, and decided to watch one of the video films being run that evening, but it was still early and she had three hours before she could reasonably order dinner.

Waking Niko up, she secured him in the folding pram she had brought with her and wheeled it out to the lift. Outside it was dark and cold, but Niko was well-protected from the elements. The porters smiled warmly at her as she walked past and turned out on to Park Lane.

Walking briskly soothed her turbulent thoughts. She couldn't have remained in her room, not after what she had just learned. Alexei had seen that notice and had

been making enquiries about her. Her heart and body
ached at the knowledge, but she knew she had done the
right thing in telling the solicitor she didn't want Alexei
to know where she could be found. Why should both of
them endure heartache and misery? Because that was
what would happen if he did insist on marrying her because of Niko. There could be no happiness in such a
marriage for him and none for her; she loved him and she
wanted him to love her in return with all the fierce elemental Russian passion she knew he kept hidden because of the suave French mask he adopted in public, but
that love—that passion—belonged to Élise.

She walked for half an hour, past imposing buildings,
and then turned into the park, the wheels of the pram
squeaking slightly as she walked. She was trying to use
the physical motion to ease the pain.

She reached the Dorchester just as a line of expensive
cars was disgorging its passengers, mainly men in dinner
suits, the odd woman, darkly and formally dressed
among the company. One man caught her eye and her
heart lurched spectacularly, the breath leaving her lungs
on a sudden gasp of pain. Alexei! Was she imagining
things? Had she somehow conjured him up by her feverish thoughts, or had she simply mistaken someone else
for him? But no, it was Alexei and she stood in the shadows of the large hotel, watching him greedily as he
strolled up the steps. He looked thinner, his face, carved
more sombre than she remembered it, thrown into relief
by the lights from the foyer. There was a brooding, dark
quality about his looks that wasn't familiar. He paused
in the illumination of the lights, turning to wait for the
man who had followed him from the car, and Hope heard
his companion saying dryly:

'Alexei, my old friend, you seem to have an over-
abundance of physical energy these days, you take life at
far too fast a pace, and it is not doing you any good.'

'One must take life at the pace urged on by one's inner devils,' Hope heard Alexei respond sardonically.

'Then yours must drive you exceedingly hard—too hard, I suggest. Or not hard enough. There is a saying, is there not, that no man is asked to endure what he is not fitted by fate to withstand.'

'Perhaps, but we do not always get the fate we deserve. Tanya's death—' Hope saw Alexei's shoulders rise in a brief shrug. 'Tanya's death was a tragedy, but as to the rest, I think I can safely say that I deserve whatever misfortunes fate may choose to send in my direction... have even actively invited them.'

'You are too hard on yourself,' his companion chided. 'You always have been, Alexei.'

They started to move away, still talking, and Hope watched Alexei go with unwittingly hungry eyes. What was he doing here, of all places? Oh, the awful irony of it. He had been so close that she could simply have reached out and touched him, but had she done so it wouldn't have stopped there; couldn't have stopped until she was in his arms protected by him... loved by him. She drew a deep shuddering breath. She was deceiving herself. Alexei did not love her, he loved Élise, and she must never, never forget that.

She waited until she was sure all the cars were empty and their occupants safely inside before she followed them into the foyer, now thankfully empty.

'You seem very busy tonight.' The porter smiled cheerfully at her comment.

'Yes, it's the annual dinner given by a London-based firm of wine importers.' Which explained what Alexei was doing in London.

She shivered as she took Niko back upstairs, aware that tonight she would find it very hard to sleep knowing Alexei was so near, not just in her thoughts, but in physical reality. Dear God, would this aching inside, this hunger for him, never cease?

ATTENDING THIS dinner had not been a good idea, Alexei reflected, his mind wandering from the speech being made. Never inclined towards self-deception, he had tried, for a time, to convince himself that the malaise he suffered from was a direct and perhaps to be expected result of fulfilling the promise he had made to himself at his sister's grave. But he was too honest to pretend that far from being a dish best-savoured cold, his revenge had tasted like so much dust in his mouth, leaving an after-taste that lingered unpleasantly on his tongue. His mouth compressed and further down the table he caught a glimpse of Montrachet's flushed, plump face. Alexei had bumped into him earlier and the Frenchman had been unusually verbose; a combination of freedom and the excellent wine they had been served over dinner.

The speeches were over and the guests free to mingle. All he really wanted to do was to escape to his room. Escape! His mouth curved wryly as he savoured the word. It seemed to feature strongly in his thoughts these days, but from some things there could be no escape. For someone who prided himself on being an intelligent, rational human being, he had made some glaring errors in his self-judgement. Pain tinged his eyes as he remembered his last meeting with Hope.

What had he expected? That she would be pining away, yearning for him? The thought didn't bear close examination, perhaps because he knew how much he had dreamed of such an impossibility. Dreamed was the right word. There were moments now when he barely recognised himself. His mouth curled sardonically. Had Svengali ever suffered these pangs? It was a novel point of view but scarcely profitable, and, after all, the signs had been there plain enough, but he had chosen to disregard them.

Why else had he changed his plans and taken Hope to Paris if it hadn't been because he had known even then that his feelings towards her were becoming too personal? In Paris he had hoped to set a distance between them; had hoped that seeing her against the sophisticated backdrop of his Parisian friends would destroy the dangerous emotional hold she had on him. It had quite definitely been a case of the biter bit.

He had known that in the Caribbean; had known then that he was ridiculously and quite impossibly in love with her. He had told himself that his feelings were some arrested form of infatuation; had reminded himself that she was the instrument of his revenge not the recipient, but all of it had been in vain.

The day he recovered her from young George's yacht had been one of the worst of his life. Never in his other relationships with women had he suffered so much as a pang of jealousy, but that morning he could willingly have killed them both, preferably after he had made violently possessive love to her.

His face hardened, his thoughts turning inwards, memory unreeling flickering pictures in his mind's eye. For some things there could be no self-forgiveness. He had been brutal that last time; unforgivably so. Was it any wonder she had run from him? It was his own private living hell and torment that she had run straight into the arms of another man, and only now was he prepared to admit to himself that he had never had any intention of letting her go; not from the time he had taken her to Paris, although he had been too blinded by his thirst for revenge to see the danger that lay past it.

He shivered suddenly, despite the warmth of the conference room. Until his dying day he would remember

finding her gone; searching the island, imagining...
imagining that he had driven the woman he loved into
taking her life.

Seeing her that last time he had been to California had
been a shock and not a pleasant one. She had changed;
matured into the woman he had always sensed she would
be, and in maturing, had only increased rather than de-
creased his hunger for her. The part of his mind which
had always stood aside and monitored his reactions
mocked him for the undiluted sexual jealousy he had experienced, for the sheer blind masculine need to stamp his
possession on her—both emotions normally totally for-
eign to him.

Alexei had known the night she defied the man she had
thought of as her father, to save his pride, that he wanted
her as his wife; that he wanted her blood to run in the
veins of his children; hers to be the hand and heart that
guided them towards adulthood, and he had even felt a
certain ungenerous satisfaction in the knowledge that she
had no one in the world but him. Because even then, he
had known that he was cheating her; had known that he
would use the sexual chemistry between them to get her
to marry him.

In saner, more rational moments, he had berated himself for the selfishness of his intentions, knowing that he
was depriving her of the right to make her choice with
free will, but he had still known that he would do it, just
as he had known the first time he saw her at the convent,
that despite everything he was going to tell her, above and
beyond it all, he wanted her for himself.

He had thought that he would have time; time to convince her that marriage to him was what she wanted, but
the gods had decreed otherwise; it was as though they had
looked down from above and decided to punish the

foolish mortal who took it upon himself to usurp their privileges and powers, and he had lost her.

He went up to his room and stood staring out across Park Lane towards Hyde Park, not seeing the street lights or the trees beyond, his eyes picturing other things, other times; Hope lying in his arms, smiling tremulously up at him; facing Sir Henry with all her young pride and a dignity that tore at his heart; and that last time, looking at him with eyes made carefully blank behind which she had escaped from him. He spread his hands in front of him, palms down, noting with ironic mockery the way they trembled. Fifteen years ago he might have cried his anguish out loud, but the habit of years had grown too strong to be broken, and besides his pain went deeper than that.

Was she really happy with her film director; a man who was quoted as having affairs with so many others? And how ridiculous that he should want to protect her; that he should feel such a compulsion to go to this man and tell him of her innocence; her defencelessness; to demand that he cherish and protect her; to ask if he could give her a love to match his own.

Alexei smiled cynically, remembering how tempted he had been in California to simply snatch her up and bring her back to Europe with him; to carry her off to the *château* and keep her there. How surprised they would be, those people who thought they knew him best, if they were privy to these things. But they weren't. No one was. They were his own private agony; his penance; a burden the Russian side of his nature accepted as due punishment, while the French side looked on in sardonic appreciation.

If he had left her innocent and untouched would she be with this American now? If he had not... But he had— he had thought himself invulnerable, and his arrogance had cost them both dear, and yet he knew that if he could turn the clock back, if he could make his decisions all over again, he would find it hard to find the strength to deny himself what he had had of her.

CHAPTER ELEVEN

'ARE YOU SURE you won't change your mind and come with me?' They were in Bianca's pool-room—the glass open-fronted room full of plants and pastel cane furniture which opened out on to the pool area. Bianca looked tired and pale. She was still vehemently opposed to the explicit love-scenes Dale wanted her to play and the atmosphere between them had worsened to such a pitch that Hope lived in fear of an imminent explosion.

'If I see Dale right now, I'm likely to either hit him or fling myself into his arms,' Bianca admitted huskily. 'Oh God, Hope,' she added, 'I just don't know what to do. Part of me simply wants to go to him and say okay I give in, I'll take what's on offer and count the cost later, but another part tells me that I'll never be happy with a brief affair; that it would destroy me only to have so little of him.'

Bianca's words struck a painful echo in Hope's own heart. She couldn't help remembering that brief sight of Alexei in London; an older, tireder Alexei whose drawn features touched her heart. 'Bianca, I'm sure he genuinely cares about you. If he didn't the atmosphere between the two of you wouldn't be so explosive. Come with me to the Valley this weekend. Perhaps when you're both away from Hollywood you might be able to...'

'No!' Bianca's refusal cut sharply across Hope's quiet plea. 'No, Hope, I can't,' Bianca added in a less forceful tone. 'Besides, I wasn't even invited.' A look of pain crossed her face. 'Dale's crazy about Niko. His face when he looks at the two of you...'

'And yours when you look at him,' Hope told her gently. 'You want his baby, don't you, Bianca?'

Her friend nodded her head. 'Yes. Crazy, isn't it? I know damned well that if I allowed myself to get pregnant at this stage, my career as an actress would be virtually over, but it doesn't seem to make any difference. I can't come to the Valley with you, Hope. I'm so afraid that if I do I'll give in and go to Dale. I can't deceive myself that he loves me and I'm not going to try to. Anyway,' she continued on a lighter note, 'if I go with you, who's going to look after Niko?'

'I wish I could take him with me,' Hope admitted, 'but Dale's organised so much house-viewing.'

'You should have flown up with him when he left yesterday. That would have given you much more time.'

Dale kept his own private plane at Santa Monica Airport, and he normally flew himself from Santa Monica to Santa Rosa, completing the rest of the journey by car. But he was planning to spend over a week in the Valley and Hope hadn't wanted to subject him to too much travelling and the upheaval in his routine that the trip would inevitably cause. Because of that she had decided merely to spend the weekend at Dale's home, flying from Los Angeles to San Francisco where a hire-car would be waiting for her.

'I'd better run,' Bianca announced, glancing at her watch. 'We're filming this morning. I should be back in time for supper.' She groaned. 'Anyone who still thinks this life is a glamorous one should try standing around waiting for the directors to call you on set for the best part of ten hours.'

'You love it,' Hope chided her, but her friend's face looked unusually drawn.

'I thought I did,' Bianca admitted, 'but I'm beginning to realise that you can't wipe away ten years of growing up. Deep down inside I guess I'm still a good convent-reared girl looking for a good home!' She laughed, but Hope knew Bianca wasn't happy. And why? Didn't she herself suffer from the same complaint? She was sure that Dale genuinely cared for her friend, and she was tempted to talk to him on Bianca's behalf. But would she be justified in meddling in her friend's life? After all, Bianca knew Dale far better than she did, and just because Dale cared about Bianca did not mean that he would want to marry her. Bianca, Hope knew, was not prepared to settle for anything less. She had a pride that matched her fiery hair, and Hope suppressed a small sigh as she watched her leave.

In the morning she was leaving herself. José drove her to the airport, her overnight bag clutched tightly on her lap, not because she was nervous about flying but because she was leaving Niko behind. It was the first time they had been parted since his birth and it had been a tremendous wrench to leave the sleeping baby, even though she knew he would receive every care while she was gone.

'It's only for two days,' Bianca had told her, 'and besides you can't deprive me of the thrill of playing mama for a while. Have you got the christening all fixed?' she asked. Bianca and Dale were to be Niko's godparents, and Hope had stifled her qualms when she approached her local church, wryly amused to discover that christenings where the child only possessed one parent were the rule rather than the exception in their sophisticated Hollywood suburb.

Her flight was uneventful, although she couldn't help remembering, as she walked down the gangway alone, her flight to the Caribbean, Alexei at her side. Squashing the familiar surge of pain, she forced herself to con-

centrate on other things. It was pointless thinking about
Alexei. Pointless causing herself additional torment, but,
oh, how badly she longed for him, for his love.

As she walked through the arrivals hall a newspaper
and magazine stand caught her eye. One news magazine
in particular seemed to stand out, and Hope felt the colour drain from her face as she recognised Élise's features. The print blurred and swam in front of her as she
approached the stall almost like a sleepwalker. Quite how
the magazine came to be in her hand, bought and paid
for, she couldn't fully remember, but the headlines blazed
across it seemed to be etched on her heart with acid.
'Widowed heiress marries,' they screamed. She found her
way automatically to a seat—the hire-car waiting outside for her—her trip to the Valley and its purpose all
forgotten. Élise had changed her mind and had decided
that she wanted Alexei more than she wanted her late
husband's fortune.

With trembling fingers, Hope flicked over the pages,
finding the relevant ones at last. There was a colour
photograph of Élise looking very unbridal in a Dior suit;
Alexei stood behind her and Hope drank in every familiar feature, unaware of the small moan that escaped her
lips as she studied the leanly athletic figure. His face
seemed thinner, the cheekbones more prominent, in direct contrast to the man standing at Élise's side; small,
rotund, heavily jowled, with dark hair and even darker
eyes.

A name caught Hope's eye. 'Aristotle Nicholaus,
cousin of the bride's first husband, one of the most
wealthy men in the world, celebrates his marriage to
Frenchwoman Élise...' Hope didn't read any more, her
eyes returning hurriedly to the start of the paragraph
checking the photograph and seeing what she had missed
the first time in her avid absorption with Alexei.

Élise and Aristotle were holding hands, a huge diamond ring glittering on the bride's finger. Élise had married Aristotle, not Alexei! And yet she had obviously invited Alexei to the wedding—how could she be so cruel? She glanced again at Aristotle Nicholaus. He didn't look like a man who would countenance his wife having an affair with anyone else. One of the richest men in the world—marriage to him would more than compensate Élise for losing her first husband's fortune. But Alexei, how he must be suffering.

She was halfway towards the Air France desk before the absurdity of her actions struck her. Her first instinct had been to go to Alexei and somehow try to comfort him, but what need did he have of her comfort? They had parted in anger, she still smarting from his punishing invasion of her body, and yet the moment she thought he was hurt she wanted to drop everything to go to him. That was the measure of her love, but she had too much pride to burden him with a love he did not want.

Rolling the magazine up and stuffing it into her bag, Hope walked towards the exit, looking for the car rental firm's offices.

'Yes, we have a car for you,' the receptionist confirmed when Hope gave her name. 'One of our best ones. Mr Lawrence insisted on it.' She glanced rather speculatively at Hope, who prayed that she wasn't flushing. 'Here are the keys, and if you'd just sign here, I'll get someone to take you out to the lot.'

When the youth who accompanied her out to the lot led her to a gleaming red Mercedes convertible, Hope simply stared. When Dale had promised to organise a car she had visualized something less luxurious—never this.

'Oh, I don't think I'm going to be able to drive it,' she protested doubtfully when the boy handed her the keys and some maps.

'Sure you will. It's as easy as pie. She's a real lady to handle. Why don't you take her round the block awhiles while you get the feel of her.'

Sliding in through the door he had opened for her, Hope adjusted the seat and mirrors, starting the engine gingerly. She needn't have worried, by the time she had circled the block twice she felt pretty much at home in the Mercedes. The boy had been right, the car was a pleasure to drive.

Dale had given her detailed instructions before he left Los Angeles, but nevertheless Hope spent fifteen minutes rereading them and checking her maps before she set off. As she headed for Vallejo along the freeway, she gradually felt her tense muscles relaxing, although her thoughts kept returning to Élise's marriage.

It must have been a bitter blow to Alexei to know that the woman he loved valued wealth more than she did him. At Vallejo she turned off for Napa. Dale had told her that the journey from San Francisco to Napa should take just over an hour, and she was well within that time-scale, the Mercedes eating up the miles. It had been raining, heavily, and there were flood warnings posted along the road.

Dale's family's winery was just outside St Helena, but as Hope approached the small town, dusk started to fall. She paused to check her directions, confused when the road ahead had two forks instead of the one she had expected. Both signposts listed several wineries, but Dale's wasn't included.

In the end, Hope decided on the more major of the two roads, telling herself that she could always turn round and come back, but the country road seemed extraordinarily long in the darkness, her progress hindered by the number of times she had to slow down to check on the side-road signs. After over an hour, she was forced to concede defeat. She must have taken the wrong fork.

Backing the Mercedes into one of the drives ready to turn round, she frowned when the engine died on her.

After several abortive attempts to get the car started, her eye was caught by the instrument panel and a small sound of dismay escaped her lips. Oh no, she was out of petrol! How could she have made such an elementary mistake?

What did it matter now? Hope asked herself sardonically. The mistake had been made. Now she would have to find some means of rectifying it, and since there had been no petrol station along the road she had just travelled, her best bet was to walk down the drive she had just turned into and hope that the winery wasn't too far down it. From there she could phone a garage, and get in touch with Dale to let him know why she had been delayed.

She wasn't really dressed for a stroll through dark countryside. Her cotton separates were a pretty cool blue—a matching T-shirt and straight skirt with a small vent at the front. Over them she had a white cotton zipper-jacket to wear which matched the white sandals she slipped on as she climbed out of the car. Carefully locking it, she set off down the drive.

She had just begun to think it would never come to an end when she glimpsed lights up ahead. She turned a corner in the drive and saw the house ahead of her, long and low, creeper-clad and very Italian in conception and Hope almost burst into tears with relief. The cobbled expanse in front of the house was as dangerous as a minefield to Hope in her high-heeled sandals, and when one ankle turned painfully beneath her she slipped them off, wincing with the pain in the ankle she could already feel swelling slightly.

Her knock on the door seemed to elicit no response, and Hope held her breath. Surely there must be someone inside? She could see a light. There must be! She knocked again, more impatiently this time, stifling a small sigh of relief as she heard the sound of movements coming towards the door.

It was the old-fashioned sort, and bolted, to judge by the noises she could hear, but at last the bolt was withdrawn and it was creaking open, darkness yawning up inside.

It was almost like something out of a horror movie, Hope thought, subduing the thought as she cleared her throat and began to speak. 'I'm terribly sorry to disturb you, but my car has run out of gas at the end of your drive. I was wondering if I might use your phone.' It was disconcerting speaking into the darkness like this, knowing that her features must be clearly revealed to whoever had opened the door, as she stood almost immediately beneath the light illuminating the courtyard.

'Of course you may, Hope, please come in.' The familiarity of the drawling, accentless English knocked the breath out of her body. She leaned instinctively against the door-jamb, trying to collect her scattered wits. 'Alexei?'

'Don't sound so disbelieving. I assure you I am no phantom, if that's what's worrying you, although I do accept that meeting like this is stretching the arm of coincidence rather far.'

'But...' A thousand questions trembled on her lips, but Alexei had stepped forward out of the darkness. He was wearing a towelling robe and she had been right when she had seen his photograph, he did look thinner. He reached forward, grasping her arm with a firmness she recognised, just as her body recognised and responded to his touch, her legs practically melting beneath her. 'Come inside, Hope, it's cold out there. Sit down,' he instructed when he had closed the front door behind her and snapped on the light illuminating a pleasant country-style living room.

Alexei stifled a yawn, and Hope noticed for the first time that his hair was ruffled, his legs and feet bare beneath the hem of his robe.

'Jet lag,' he offered wryly. 'I only arrived myself a couple of hours ago. I'd just gone to bed when I heard you knocking.'

'You're here alone?' Now what on earth had made her ask that? Of course he would want to escape France and Élise, and where better to come than to this valley, where she knew he had business connections.

'Yes.' His glance mocked her. 'I normally come here at this time of the year to check on the vines. The winery does have a manager, but he's on holiday at the moment.' His mouth twisted suddenly. 'I must admit that when I heard that knocking the last person I expected to find was you. You covered your tracks very well, Hope, but then I suppose you reasoned that I deserved the torment of not knowing where you were. A little revenge of your own?'

'I sent you a note.' Hope was horrified that he had thought she might have wanted to inflict revenge on him.

'Yes, I know you did.' His expression was sardonic. 'But time doesn't have the same meaning in the Caribbean as it does in Europe, you should have remembered that. It was three days before your messenger decided he was bored enough to bring the jeep back—and with it your note. Three days during which I hadn't had so much as a second's peace of mind...'

'I'm sorry, I didn't think.' She hung her head, feeling very much like a child, too bemused to reflect on the irony of the situation, or the fact that she was the one feeling guilty.

'Sorry!' Alexei's mouth hardened. 'No, I'm the one who's that, Hope. Sorry that I ever contemplated what I did. Sorry that I was crass enough to give you reason to run from me.' Hope watched him close his eyes and swallow, her eyes riveted on the small movement of the muscles in his throat, of her overwhelming need to go up to him and place her lips against his skin. Sexual hunger for him, raw and burning, swept through her, but she fought it back.

Alexei was still speaking, his face shadowed, stubble darkening his jaw. 'I imagined you dead...hurt... alone...a vulnerable child, who I had destroyed.' His fingers found her shoulders, digging into the fragile muscles, tightening over them until she could feel real pain. 'Was it deliberate, Hope, leaving me like that... without a word...?'

'No.' Her throat ached with pain. 'No...I told you. I left you a note.'

'You also told your solicitor not to give me your address.'

She swallowed painfully. So he had gone back to see Mr Swindon. She turned her head, wishing he would release her. Every breath he took increased her physical awareness of him, her desire to abandon all pride and beg him to make love to her. Only the knowledge that afterwards she would have to contend with even more pain stopped her. 'Why Hope...why didn't you want to see me?'

'Can't you guess?' She was playing desperately for time.

'Too many painful memories, is that what you're trying to tell me?'

She seized on the excuse he had given her. 'Yes.' The way he was looking at her disturbed her and she rushed into impulsive speech. 'I saw you in London...at the Dorchester...I...'

'You saw me and you ignored me?' He was shaking her, almost violently, anger blazing in the depths of his eyes.

'You were with someone else, I didn't want to...to intrude.'

'Liar... You didn't want to speak to me for the same reason you left the island, isn't that it?'

It was, but in the sense that he meant from the bitter twist of his lips. 'I frightened you and you ran. Are you sure that all your memories are unpleasant ones, *mon petit?*' He was leaning towards her and panic surged through her veins. If he touched her, kissed her, she wouldn't be able to hold back her love. He had lost the woman he loved and Alexei was cynical and worldly enough to take her in substitution, using her body as a narcotic to dull his pain, if she was stupid enough to let him.

'Alexei, it's over,' she said weakly, adding, as she drew away, 'You must have wanted to wring my neck when you did get my note.'

'Not half as much as I wanted to wring my own. They couldn't remember you at the airport when I eventually went there to check—can you imagine what it felt like, not even knowing where you were or who you were with?'

'I told you in my note that I'd gone with a friend,' Hope interrupted. 'I couldn't stay, Alexei,' she added huskily, turning away from him. 'Not after...'

'Not after I'd raped you,' Alexei submitted in a hard voice. His hands were on her shoulders, swinging her round to face him. 'Well, that is what you were going to say, isn't it? Young George came to see me after you'd gone. He had a fit of conscience and came to tell me the truth; that everything had been quite innocent; that he was the one who was responsible for your staying on the island. I don't think I've ever hated myself as much as I did at that moment, even though I already knew in my heart that he was telling the truth.'

'The Russian side of you again?' Hope said lightly. She tried to move away and winced with pain, glancing down at her ankle. To her horror it was swollen.

'Let me see,' Alexei's head bent, his fingers curling round the aching flesh as she tried to conceal it from him. 'I turned my ankle on the cobbles,' she told him quickly, praying that he would release her. Having him this close was a torment she didn't think she could endure for very long. All she had to do was merely reach down and her fingers would be lost in the soft darkness of his hair, so like Niko's. His fingers felt warm and familiar against her skin, and tiny flames of hunger licked through her veins as she sought to control the swift uprush of desire enfolding her.

'Come and sit down, I'll make a cold compress. That will keep the swelling down.'

'I must phone a garage, and my friend. He'll be wondering where I am.'

'He?'

She was appalled by the cruel contempt she saw lacing the green eyes. 'This same friend who "rescued" you from me I presume?'

'And if he is?' If she had been appalled by Alexei's reaction before, she was even more appalled by her childish response to it. What on earth was she doing intimating that she and Dale were lovers? But it was too late to back down now—Alexei's eyes were glittering with the green fire she remembered from past occasions when she had pushed him close to losing his control, his voice silky as he drawled, 'I trust he found I had schooled you well?'

The cruelty of the blow left her white and speechless. Not five minutes after telling her that he knew he had misjudged her, he was now accusing her of taking another lover. Didn't he know that the only man she wanted in her arms was him? Some desperate need to protect herself made her say tautly, 'You once told me I should use every talent I possessed to its fullest degree. I think he finds me...satisfactory.'

It was a sordid exchange, and every bone in her body seemed to weep her pain, but there was no going back now. Alexei indicated the telephone. 'Make your call,' he told her coldly. 'I'll go and see about getting something for that ankle.'

She rang Dale first, explaining what had happened. His laughter soothed her bruised heart. 'Say, honey, if you've hurt your ankle it might be worth asking if you can stay where you are for tonight. I should hate for you to put any undue strain on it—we've got a pretty full weekend ahead of us, you know.'

'Dale, I can't stay here,' she started to say, when Alexei walked back in, a bowl of ice cubes in his hands. She finished her call quickly, picking up the phone again to ring a garage, then his fingers closed warmly over hers. Even that briefest of impersonal touches was enough to set her pulse racing. Her T-shirt revealed the slender bones of her throat and she knew he could see the pulse beating frantically there, betraying her responsiveness to him.

'What was all that about?' he demanded without preamble. Hope didn't bother hiding anything, there was no point, he would want her in his home as little as she wanted to be there.

'Dale thought it might be as well if I stayed here overnight. We've got a pretty full weekend planned, and he wanted me to rest. I told him it was impossible.'

Alexei's expression was unreadable as he looked down into her pale face. 'On the contrary,' he said at last. 'He sounds a very sensible man. I doubt you'd get any garage to come out here with a can of petrol at this time of night, anyway. You're quite safe, Hope,' he added sardonically, 'if that's what's worrying you.'

'It wasn't,' she told him honestly. 'After all, we both know that your…interest in me wasn't personal. I'm not afraid of you in that way, Alexei. I just wish we need never have met again.' She said the words beneath her breath, but he still caught them, his face whitening, the hard bones standing out in harsh relief. 'I'm sorry about Élise,' she added lamely, 'that must have been a blow to you. I know…I know how much you loved her.' How foolish he would think her if she admitted how close she had come to rushing to France to comfort him. What comfort could she possibly give him?

'Élise?' His voice sounded thick and strange.

'Yes. I read about her marriage.' Hope continued half feverishly. 'I know she wouldn't marry you because it meant she would lose her first husband's fortune. I heard her talking about it when we were in Paris.' She bit her lip, wondering if she had said too much. 'I heard her saying that you loved her. It must be…'

'Yes? Go on, it must be…'

'You must be very hurt,' Hope concluded huskily. She turned away from him, the curtain of her hair shielding her face, hiding from him the tears that filled her eyes. 'To love someone who can't love you in return is…'

'The very worst sort of hell?' Alexei suggested softly. 'You sound as though you speak from experience.' Realising that she was getting into dangerous waters, Hope changed the subject quickly, chattering feverishly about the Napa Valley, asking him questions about how he had come to own the winery, all the time conscious of the deeply-etched pain that shadowed his face, the aloofness that seemed to have dropped on to his shoulders like a cloak, setting a distance between them that he wasn't going to let her bridge. Oh, why did she have to meet him like this? She found herself wishing feverishly that she could turn the clock back to the time when he still wanted to be revenged on the man they had both thought was her father; when she could go to bed, knowing that he would come to her and take her in his arms.

'I'd better see to your ankle, and then we'll find a bedroom for you.' He seemed to take it for granted that she would stay, and she no longer wanted to argue. Being so close to him and yet held at such a distance was painful, but it was better than nothing at all.

'Could I make another call?' she asked huskily. She wanted to ring Bianca to see if Niko was all right.

'Of course.' He handed her the phone, but made no move to leave the room. Nervously she punched out Bianca's number. Bianca herself answered the phone.

'Honey, is everything all right, I expected to hear from you much earlier.'

'I got lost and ran out of petrol,' Hope told her, 'but everything's fine. How's Niko...' Her voice softened unconsciously as she spoke her son's name, a smile touching her mouth.

She heard Bianca laugh. 'He's fine. I'm thoroughly enjoying myself playing with him. We've just given him his bath—want to hear?' Hope heard her call something to someone in the room. There were a few seconds' silence and then she heard the familiar gurgling of her son.

'Happy now,' Bianca teased, seconds later. Tears filled her eyes, a foolish emotional lump lodging in her throat, but she fought it down, knowing that Alexei was watching her.

'Who's Niko?' he asked when she had replaced the receiver. He was studying her narrow-eyed, scrutinising her flushed cheeks and over-bright eyes. 'Does your other friend know he's not the only man in your life?'

'Dale knows all about Niko,' she managed huskily at last, watching his facial bones tense and tighten. 'I think I can manage to do my ankle myself.'

'I'll do it.' His voice was terse and brooked no opposition. 'But first we'd better get you upstairs. If I strap it up for you you're not going to be able to manage them.'

By the time she reached the head of the stairs, Hope was forced to concede that Alexei had been right. Her ankle was aching painfully, each step a nerve-stretching agony. At the top of the stairs he turned to wait for her, his expression darkening as he looked down into her face, the smothered expletive that left his lips reaching her only distantly.

It was wrong of her to derive so much sensual pleasure from what was mere necessity, she told herself hazily when his arms came round her, lifting her, holding her against his body. She closed her eyes, the better to savour the brief intimacy of being held by him. The man-smell of his skin was the same, the rough rasp of his towelling robe against her cheek, and Hope wished she had the courage to push it aside and lay her head against his skin. A door was pushed open and she was distantly aware of her surroundings; of the bedroom furniture, heavy and old-fashioned and yet exuding an air of comfort and serenity.

Alexei dropped her gently on the large wooden-framed bed, the down quilt giving beneath her weight as she sank into it.

'Stay there.' She could not have ignored the command even if she had wanted to. Her muscles had gone strangely weak, leaving her tremulous and shaking. She guessed that the door Alexei had opened led into a bathroom, and her suspicion was confirmed when he returned carrying a bowl of water, cotton wool and some sort of elastic bandage.

'Dave, who runs the winery for me, is a tennis fan—luckily for you,' Alexei told her as he unwrapped the sterile dressing. 'Now...keep still while I bathe it.'

Thanking her lucky stars that her tan meant that she could go without tights or stockings, Hope endured the clinical movement of his fingers against her skin, forcing down memories of other times when his touch had been arousing instead of clinical and it had been kisses and not antiseptic lotion he had placed against her flesh.

'Right...that should give your ankle some support.' The bandage was in place, and there was no reason for her to remain any longer in what was obviously his bedroom. Of all the places to choose to break down, why on earth had fate decreed that it must be this winery? And even worse, when Alexei was in residence!

'I'll leave you to try and get some sleep now.' He got up and was walking towards the door.

'I...I can sleep somewhere else, Alexei,' she began huskily. 'There's no need to give up your bed for me.'

'I'm not doing. This is Dave and Mandy's room. Goodnight, Hope.' She watched him go in an anguished silence, appalled by the agony of seeing him disappear. What had she expected? That he would suggest they spent the night together? Why should he? She had fulfilled his purpose and there was now no place in his life for her.

Sleep was impossible. Her ankle still throbbed and she lay wide awake wondering if Alexei was awake too, aching for Élise. She forced herself to think instead about Niko, and eventually found herself drifting into sleep. As she slept she dreamed, a confused, tortured dream where Sir Henry tried to take Niko from her, claiming that the little boy was his heir and that she should not be allowed to bring him up. Alexei was somewhere in the dream and she appealed to him wildly, begging him to make Sir Henry give her son back to her, but he simply stood on the sidelines saying that Niko's father was the man she should appeal to, not him.

She woke up abruptly, with tears on her face, and her pillow soaked with them. The bed covers were tangled untidily, evidence of her restlessness, and her mind was still tortured by the fears conjured up by her dreams.

When the light was suddenly snapped on, its brilliance blinded her.

'I heard you crying out,' she heard Alexei saying from the door. 'What's the matter? Are you in pain? Your ankle...'

How could she tell him that the pain she was suffering from had nothing to do with mere physical anguish?

'I...'

'I'd better have another look at it,' Alexei cut in curtly. 'Perhaps the bandage is too tight.'

He was advancing towards the bed, and Hope gripped the sheet tensely, watching him. Her bag and change of clothes were still in the Mercedes, and rather than go to bed in the underwear she had been wearing all day she had rinsed them out in the bathroom, knowing they would be dry by morning.

'My ankle's fine,' she protested huskily when Alexei reached the bed. 'I was having a nightmare...' She shuddered, remembering the full horror of what she had dreamed.

'You still get them?' Unfathomable green eyes probed the shadows of her face noting the tear stains and pallor.

'Just occasionally, but I'm all right now. I'm sorry I disturbed you.'

For a moment an expression she couldn't interpret crossed his face, swiftly replaced by cynical mockery. 'Are you, Hope? I should have thought you would have derived a considerable amount of satisfaction from "disturbing" me. A form of retaliation perhaps for...'

'I don't want to be revenged on you the way you did on Sir Henry, if that's what you're implying,' Hope broke in before he could continue. 'What happened, happened. There's no going back. You see, I did listen to what you told me, Alexei. I have learned to build on the past and go forward from it. To learn from my experience.'

'I never damned well intended you to use that experience as a basis for life,' Alexei ground out, shocking her with the fury she could see leaping to life in his eyes. 'To use it to find yourself a rich lover.'

'No?' She had to stop him before he hurt her any more—before he destroyed what little shreds of pride she had left. 'But that was what you equipped me for,' she reminded him, hating the way he now looked at her, his eyes stripping away the protection of the duvet and sheet, searing her body with a scrutiny that was a world apart from the tenderness he had shown her in the past.

'Then perhaps I ought to check up for myself just how skilled you've become; just how much progress you've made with the man you took to your bed after you left mine.'

She knew before he moved what he was going to do, but still it came as a shock when his fingers grasped the sheet, wrenching it away from her body.

She closed her eyes automatically, telling herself it wasn't just her he was angry with. He was also having to contend with losing Élise. She daren't open her eyes. Would he notice the small changes in her body since Niko's birth; the full ripeness of her breasts; the more accentuated curves?

'Open your eyes, Hope. You can't expect me to believe you keep them closed when your new lover touches you. Are you as responsive for him as you were for me, or have you learned to tease and tantalise a man until he can't rest until he possesses you?'

'I haven't learned anything that you didn't teach me,' she wanted to protest, but the words stuck in her throat, a painful lump obliterating her voice.

'I see you still don't sunbathe in the nude?' Her eyes shot open as his hand rested against her hip, her pupils dilating as she found herself looking right into his eyes. His robe, loosely belted round the waist, fell open, the dark contours of his chest so achingly familiar that it took all her powers of concentration not to reach out and touch him.

'It's strange,' Alexei mused softly, watching her like a hawk with a mouse, 'even your expression seems to have changed. You've matured, Hope, far faster than I expected you to. You ran away from me a girl, and now you're a woman.'

No, she wanted to correct him. I left you as a woman; a woman carrying your child; a woman who loved you, but you were too blind to see the truth. 'You're trembling,' he murmured throatily, watching the shivering tremors ripple under her sensitized skin where his fingers drifted, exploring the contours of her belly—now flat again—the narrow indentations of her waist, and upwards to rest against her heart as it thudded out its betraying message. 'Strange...' He spoke almost musingly as she held her breath and tried to regain control of her rioting emotions. It had been so long since he had touched her, and her senses were on fire for him with a primitive yearning. 'I would have thought you were far too sophisticated now to be affected by such a trivial caress.'

'Alexei, please...' she began hoarsely, intending to beg him to release her and stop tormenting her, but the husky words were her undoing because he bent his head closer to catch them, and her senses were full of the sight and scent of him, her gaze drawn hypnotically to the shape of his mouth, her heart thumping beneath his palm as she stared up at him.

'You say my name so sweetly, little one,' she heard him murmur above her. His thumb probed the softness of her lips, rubbing sensuously along the full bottom curve until she was lost in a whirlpool of sensation, drowning in the jade seas of his eyes. Her lips parted as her tongue stroked wantonly over the fleshy pad of his thumb, her teeth nibbling gently at the hard flesh, her response becoming more fevered as Alexei's free hand cupped her breast, stroking the soft flesh with rhythmic, arousing fingers that drove the last shreds of common sense and caution from her brain.

Her fingers interlinked with Alexei's drawing his thumb away from her mouth, her lips exploring his hard palm, her body trembling when he pulled free to slide his hand into her hair, twining it in his fingers as his mouth closed over hers, devastating her with its sensual demand. His tongue probed the moist sweetness she made no attempt to deny to him, her hands locking behind his neck as she abandoned herself completely to the surging wave of pleasure he aroused. His teeth nipped urgently at her lip, his thumb enjoying the hardened thrust of her nipple. Her hands, of their own volition, unlocking to find the hard muscles of his shoulders.

Her body had started to tremble, weak from reaction and need, the murmured words of pleasure that fell from Alexei's lips music to her ears as his mouth touched all the remembered pleasure-spots of her body, his thumb pressed to the erratic pulse, throbbing in her throat as his lips teased and caressed her soft skin.

There wasn't a part of her body that didn't respond to him. Her lips found the opening of his robe, exploring and tasting the texture of his skin, everything else forgotten as she slid her hands inside it. She stroked over the familiar contours of his chest, and down to the hard flatness of his belly, her lips following her questing fingers, her senses drinking in the feel and scent of him, while still relaying to her the pleasure her own body enjoyed as he continued to caress and kiss her.

She wanted to speak, to tell him how much she loved him, but she was afraid of doing so in case she broke the spell that bound them together.

His hand stroked along her inner thigh making her body quiver with remembered pleasure.

'Does *he* touch you like this, the man you left me for?' The words sliced through Hope's protective bubble, forcing her to confront the truth. Alexei did not love her, he had never loved her. He loved Élise. The clamouring urgings of her senses faded, sick self-disgust taking their place. How could she have allowed herself to debase herself by permitting Alexei to treat her so callously? The mere fact that he was doing so ought to prove to her how little he cared.

'What's the matter? Have you suddenly realised that your new lover might not approve? I could change your mind for you, Hope. I could make you respond to me.'

'I know.' There was no point in prevaricating. 'But if you do I'll despise myself nearly as much...'

'As you despise me?' Alexei interrupted harshly, withdrawing completely from her. It hadn't been what she was going to say, but she could only compress her lips and force back the tears scalding the back of her throat. If he had allowed her to complete her sentence, what she would have said was that she didn't want to despise herself as much as *he* obviously did, but Alexei was already leaving the bed, heading for the door, and she didn't think she had the self-control to endure another moment of his company by correcting him. Her emotions cried out for him, her body ached feverishly for his possession. Nothing had changed; not leaving him, not having Niko, nothing... Niko... A sob blocked her throat.

What would Alexei say if she told him she had borne his child? For one wild moment she was tempted to tell him. To see the expression of sardonic mockery so clearly visible in his eyes change to one of... Of what? she silently taunted herself. Love? Reverence? Giving her his child had been no part of Alexei's plan, and to tell him now about Niko could serve no useful purpose.

Long after he had gone Hope remained awake, tormented by the images of the past; of his body sleek and supple against hers; of his hands as they touched and caressed her, tutoring her inexperienced flesh to melt and yield... Perhaps she had made the wrong decision. Perhaps she ought to have taken what he was offering, even knowing that she was merely a body he was using to blunt his hunger for Élise.

Morning came, the sky a blue-grey arc over the rain-sodden countryside. The storm had died out during the night, but had left behind a distinct chill. Hope shivered as she hobbled to the bathroom to shower, dismayed to discover how painful her ankle still was. How on earth was she going to manage to drive to Dale's with her foot virtually out of use? She would have to phone Dale and call off the weekend. Disappointment pleated a frown across her forehead. She had been looking forward to house-hunting, to making a start towards finding a home for herself and Niko.

Apprehension feathered along her spine as she recognised that coming to live in the Valley meant that she might also run the risk of meeting Alexei again, although she knew his visits to the area were fairly infrequent. Her chin firmed as she decided that finding the right home for Niko was more important than trying to run away from Alexei.

When she left her room she could smell the appetising odour of freshly brewed coffee. The stairs proved more problematical than she had anticipated, but by clinging on to the banister and bracing herself against it she was managing to make some progress until Alexei, no doubt alerted by the noise she was making, emerged into the hall, studying her in frowning disapproval.

'Ankle no better?'

'Oh, sure, I'm just playing hop-a-long for the sheer hell of it,' Hope snapped at him. The sight of him had given her shaky composure a dangerous dent. Dressed in a checked work-shirt and faded, snug-fitting jeans, he presented an intensely virile appearance and she had to fight hard against remembering how his body felt against hers.

'Wait there.' The curt command panicked her into unwise action. Desperate to avoid him, she tried to come downstairs faster, crying out in fear as her good foot slid away under her, and she fell headlong towards him.

Someone's heart was racing, thudding into her body, she reflected hazily, seconds later, touching her fingers to the offending organ, only to discover that it wasn't *her* heart that was thudding so urgently but Alexei's, and that the bands of iron constricting her were, in actual fact, his arms.

'A little bit theatrical wasn't it?' he drawled above her, 'risking life and limb rather than accepting a helping hand? I'd already got the message last night, Hope. You don't want me near you at any price. There was no need to reinforce it.'

If only he knew, she thought numbly as he lowered her on to the settee. 'You're lucky you didn't break the other ankle. Stay there, I'll get you some coffee.'

'I need to phone D—my friend...' Hope protested. 'I'll have to warn him that I can't drive.'

Alexei paused in the doorway, surveying her with an unfamiliar, brooding expression. 'Where does he live?'

When Hope told him he shrugged powerful shoulders. 'I have to go out that way this morning to see someone. I'll drop you off, if you like. After last night you must be desperate to see him.' He saw her face and laughed, a harsh, almost ugly sound in the silence of the room. 'Come on, Hope. I'm not that easy to fool,' he said softly. 'You aren't going to try to tell me you felt *nothing* last night, are you? You were as aroused as hell. I could have taken you, if I'd wanted to. Right now you must have an ache in your body that demands only one kind of appeasement.'

He had never spoken so frankly or sensually to her and Hope felt the heat-induced colour wash up under her skin. 'Alexei!' His name was a choked protest from trembling lips, but he ignored it to say savagely:

'Leave it, Hope. I've been there. I know what it's all about. Now, do you want this cup of coffee or not, before I restore you to the arms of your lover?

'I know all about him, Hope,' he added. 'I saw you with him the last time I came to California. You were walking down a street in Hollywood with him—I'd been visiting friends.'

'You saw me and said nothing?' Pain tore at her insides as she watched Alexei shrug carelessly.

'What was there to say?' he asked, reminding her brutally that he loved Élise and not her.

CHAPTER TWELVE

'HE DOES THINK a lot of you, doesn't he.' Hope was sitting beside Alexei in his powerful car, her face colouring again, this time with anger, as Alexei studied the sleek lines of the Mercedes.

'It's a hire-car,' Hope told him curtly, 'and besides...'

'Besides what?' Alexei taunted.

'Besides, I don't have the kind of relationship with Dale that necessitates him giving me expensive bribes,' she told him proudly, her eyes flashing warning sparks as Alexei turned to study her.

'You do it all for love, is that what you're trying to tell me? Then you're a fool, Hope. He obviously doesn't care enough to make your relationship legal. One day you're going to lose him.'

'And that means that I should take everything from him that I can before I do?' Hope flung at him, stunned by the intensity of her own anger. 'What makes you think I want our relationship legalised, Alexei? What makes you think I'm not content with what we have?'

'I know you, *mon petit*. Love to you means a wedding ring and a promise of fidelity—that much hasn't changed.'

'Is that so wrong?' Her voice was unexpectedly husky as she turned to look at him.

'No.' He shook his head. 'Not wrong at all. I just wish you'd given your love to someone more worthy of it.

Someone who could feel about you the way you feel about him...'

'So do I.' Her voice was brittle, aching with barely suppressed pain. 'I don't want to talk about it any more, Alexei,' she managed huskily. She felt him looking at her, and there seemed no point in trying to conceal her pale face and bruised eyes.

'Dear God, Hope, what manner of man is he to...'

'Just a man like any other. Do you expect him to revere what you so obviously didn't, Alexei?' she taunted, driven to lash out and hurt him as he was hurting her by his very presence within the enclosed intimacy of his car. 'Do you expect him to cherish and protect your discarded mistress?'

Alexei's face had gone grey, the knuckles showing white through his skin where he gripped the steering wheel. 'He has dared to throw that in your face, to...'

'No.' Hope told him shortly, unnerved by the anger she could see leaping to ferocious life in his eyes and at a loss to know the cause of it. 'No... No. Dale hasn't mentioned our...my...what happened between us, but how can I expect him to honour and respect me when I can't respect myself.'

'*Dieu!*' The car came to a teeth-shattering stop as Alexei swore under his breath. 'You are not to say that!' He had half turned in his seat and was facing her and Hope was alarmed by the pallor of his skin. 'Hope, I... Christ, what's the use,' he swore savagely, restarting the engine as quickly as he had stopped it. 'You persist in seeing yourself as a martyr doomed to suffer eternal damnation. I can't go back and alter the past, Hope, and you must accept that if you are to cease tormenting yourself.'

'And if you could, would you?' She already knew the answer and yet still waited for him to confirm it, holding at bay the pain she knew would be hers when he did. He made a small explosive sound, his fingers curling round the steering wheel, gripping it painfully. 'Dear God. Yes! If I had my time over again I...'

'Would never take me to your bed? Never...'

'Enough!' He ground the word out between bloodless lips. 'Enough, Hope. We can continue to maim and wound one another until we are both bleeding to death, but what good will it serve? I cannot eradicate the past. Do you think you are the only one who has suffered?' he bit out, as though unable to repress the words. He wasn't looking at her, but staring unseeingly through the windscreen so that she had to glance at him to assure herself that she hadn't misheard. 'When I found you gone...' She saw him swallow, beads of perspiration breaking out on his skin. 'After what had happened between us I thought...I...'

'You thought I had taken my own life?' Hope guessed incredulously, her voice betraying her emotions.

'Is it so hard to imagine?' He had turned to face her now, his eyes dark with something approaching pain. 'Would it be the first time a foolish young innocent has taken her life because she imagines herself dishonoured and discarded?'

'You thought...'

'I damned nearly went out of my mind,' Alexei told her harshly. 'I thought the shock of being rejected by your...by Sir Henry, the discovery that he wasn't your father, my own unforgivable behaviour...' She saw his jaw clench, and heard his breath expelled on a harsh sigh. 'I was going to marry you. It seemed...'

'A way of making reparation?' Hope suggested, marvelling at how steady she managed to keep her voice. 'A noble sacrifice, Alexei, but an unnecessary one. Think how your ancestors would turn in their graves to see a woman of easy virtue sharing your name.'

'How long had it been going on before... before you left me? How long had you known the... ?'

'The person I left with?' Hope added softly, suddenly furiously angry that he could be so blind; that he could talk about marrying her with one breath and then discuss her supposed lover with the next. 'Longer than I've known you, Alexei. Much, much longer.'

Well, it was true, she told herself. Alexei wasn't to know that she had left the Caribbean with Bianca and not Dale.

'So that was what it was all about.' His lips twisted bitterly. 'I suppose I should have guessed, all the signs were there, only I thought...'

'That I was falling in love with you, Alexei?' Hope challenged. Dear God, could he hear her heart thudding? How had she managed to get into such dangerous water?

'I think we've savaged one another enough for one session, Hope.' He looked pale and tired, and conscience stabbed her as she remembered Élise. No doubt it was the loss of the woman he loved that was making him savage her so unmercifully. In all honesty, she did not believe that if he knew how she felt about him he would have treated her so cruelly. Alexei was many things, but not deliberately cruel.

It wasn't as far as she had thought to Dale's family's winery. Set back from the road, the main house was similar to Alexei's, and it was Alexei who explained to her that many of the wineries had originally belonged to immigrant Italians and that that was why they were very similar in design.

'A nostalgia for their homeland,' Hope murmured softly, suddenly filled with the aching knowledge that there was nowhere she could really call home. It would be different for Niko, she decided stalwartly; she would give her son all the security she had never had. He would grow up tall and strong in his wine-growing valley; sure of himself and his place in life. Later, when he was older, she would tell him about his father... She glanced at Alexei's autocratic profile, worried about Niko's reactions when he would eventually learn the truth. Perhaps, it was better to tell him when he was still young enough to accept it without questioning her too deeply, then later, if he wanted to talk about his father...

What was she thinking? *If* Niko wanted to ask her about Alexei? Of course he would, and probably he would want to do more than merely talk. How on earth was she going to protect her son from the pain of Alexei's rejection? How could she explain without causing him pain? She sighed without being aware of it, deeply concerned about the future.

'Why the long face when you're just about to be reunited with your lover?'

Alexei's voice sounded unusually harsh, but as she looked at him Hope was aware of a door opening and of Dale's familiar figure loping towards the car. Hastily she got out, just in time to be caught up in a warm, brotherly hug. 'Honey, let me look at you. Are you all right?'

'Dale!' Oh no, surely she wasn't going to dissolve in tears now? She felt them blur her vision and she was back in Dale's reassuring embrace being petted and soothed in the same way that he petted Niko when he cried.

'Come on, honey,' Hope heard him murmur fondly against her hair, 'everything's fine. Aren't you going to introduce me?' he added, gently releasing her and proffering a handkerchief so that she could dry her face.

By the time she turned to Alexei all the betraying evidence of her tears were gone. She introduced the two men briefly, watching them measure one another, seeing the alert, questioning look Dale threw her when Alexei said curtly, 'I thought it best to drive Hope here myself. Her ankle is still giving her trouble. The Mercedes...'

'Don't worry about that,' Dale assured him easily, 'I'll
have the hire company pick it up. I thought you'd enjoy
driving it, honey,' he told Hope. 'Looks like it was a good
idea that went badly wrong. The family's all waiting to
meet you in the house. Mama will be fussing around you
the moment I get you inside. Are you sure the weekend
is still on, with the ankle?'

'As long as you don't mind lending me an arm,' Hope
joked weakly. Dale invited Alexei to join them in the
house but he refused, walking back to his car.

'Thank you ... for ... for everything, Alexei,' Hope
managed as he slid in behind the steering wheel. The look
he gave her was hostile; hard and underlined with some
emotion she couldn't name.

Dust and gravel spurted under his car's wheels as it
disappeared down the drive, and Hope was unaware of
the pain and anguish in her eyes as she watched it go.
Dale touched her lightly on the arm, sympathy and comprehension in the look he gave her. 'That's him, isn't it?'
he said quietly. 'Niko's father, the man you love.'

She wanted to deny it, but there seemed no point.
'Yes.' Hope agreed dully. She forced a small bitter smile
as she turned to accompany Dale to the house. 'He thinks
you and I are lovers, and that I left the Caribbean with
you and not Bianca.'

'Ah, so that's it. You didn't correct his misapprehen-
sion?'

'There didn't seem much point.' Hope licked her lip
nervously. 'I was frightened that he might guess how I
feel about him.'

'Would that be such a bad thing? He seemed pretty
reluctant to leave you here with me.'

'Because he feels a certain amount of responsibility. He
doesn't love me though, Dale, not the way I want him to
love me. He loves someone else.'

'And you don't want to talk about it any more, right? Does he know about Niko?'

Hope shook her head. 'No.' Her voice sounded raw and hoarse. 'And I don't want him to know. If he did I think he might very well insist that we marry.' She didn't know where that thought had come from. Perhaps it had been borne of their conversation; perhaps it had come from her intuitive knowledge that Alexei would feel a paternal responsibility for Niko, and with Élise married to someone else, what better way to fulfil it than to insist that they marry.

'And that would be such a bad thing?' Dale's expression was sympathetic. 'Look, honey, I know there are plenty of girls who think nothing of bringing up their kids single-handed, but you're not one of them. I've seen the look in your eyes when you see families together. Love can grow, Hope. I know, I've seen it. My own parents... Theirs was an arranged marriage. My mother came out from Sicily to marry her second cousin, my father, never having seen him before. They've got a good marriage, and they're devoted to one another.'

'It's not because I don't want to marry Alexei that I don't want him to know about Niko,' Hope managed when she had got control of her emotions, 'it's because I'm so desperately afraid that I'll give in and marry him, and I couldn't endure a lifetime of being his wife, but not the woman he loves. I just couldn't, Dale.'

'I think I can understand that.' Suddenly his own expression was brooding, and Hope knew instinctively he was thinking about Bianca.

'It's not because Bianca doesn't care that she refused to come this weekend,' she told him without preamble.

'No?' His eyes glittered, dark with anger. 'Sure, she cares about me. I'm public enemy No. 1 as far as she's concerned. We're even quarrelling on the set these days.'

'Because you want her to do explicit sex-scenes,' Hope told him quietly. Dale and Bianca were the two people who meant most to her in the world after Alexei and Niko and she couldn't bear to see them at loggerheads any longer. Both of them were too proud to tell the other the truth. She, Hope realised, would have to do it for them and just hope that her meddling was justified.

'So?' Dale threw out the word, turning to glare at her.

'Dale, do you care at all about her? Not just as an actress or another woman you want to take to your bed? Please be honest with me now, because if the answer is "no", there are some things I just cannot tell you.'

'What do you think?' He was still watching her with that same keen scrutiny that hid his own expression. Taking a deep breath Hope childishly crossed her fingers behind her back.

'I think you love her,' she said quietly. 'I think you love her very much indeed.'

'And she knows it, damn her!' Dale ripped out explosively. 'God, the dance she's been leading me . . .' He turned away and Hope reached out, touching tentative fingers to his arm, feeling the tense bunched muscles beneath the soft fabric of his shirt. Here, at his family winery, Dale was no longer the Hollywood director, but a virile, angry man, very much in love with a woman he thought didn't care about him.

'No.' Hope told him quietly. 'She doesn't know it, Dale. She knows you want her—want being the operative word. She doesn't want to be simply another brief fling; another scalp on your belt . . .'

'No, because she'd rather dangle mine from hers. I know Bianca, Hope. She's had men wild for her ever since she set foot in LA, but I'm not joining any queue. I won't just be another of her lovers . . .'

'No.'

'No?' He looked at her sharply. 'What does that mean?'

'Bianca hasn't had any lovers,' Hope told him levelly, praying that she was doing the right thing. 'She hasn't been leading you on, Dale, she's been trying to run away.'

'Not had any lovers... Oh, come on, Hope...'

'She told me so herself, and I believe her,' Hope insisted firmly. 'She loves you, Dale, and loving someone makes you feel extremely vulnerable. Bianca doesn't want to end up like me...'

A muscle beat violently in his jaw, his voice suddenly thick as he declared, 'Does she really think if she carried my child that I'd let her...' He broke off, as though suddenly realising that his remarks might be hurtful to Hope. 'You're imagining things, Hope,' he told her curtly. 'Bianca would never risk spoiling that perfect figure of hers by carrying my child. My first wife was an actress,' he added obliquely. 'She didn't really want children...'

'Bianca not want your child?' Hope shook her head. 'You haven't been looking at her properly, Dale. Just watch her face the next time you pick Niko up.'

Watching him was a revelation that brought a lump to her throat, a mingling of pain for herself and happiness for her friend, her own pain heightened by the knowledge that Alexei would never look like that for her.

'Are you really telling me that Bianca hasn't known any other man... that she loves me?'

'There's only one way you can find out the answer to both questions, isn't there?' Hope told him softly. 'But Dale, the only reason I've told you any of this is because I think you love Bianca. If you don't I hope that you're kind enough not to use the weapon I've just given you.'

'Every one of my much publicised affairs has been with a woman who knew the score. I've never deliberately hurt anyone in my life, honey. I've been there—I still bear the scars. After the death of my ex-wife and baby I swore I'd never marry again; never invite the pain that loving and marriage brings. I do love Bianca, and have done all along, but I didn't want to admit it. Now...' He suddenly grinned, his eyes full of laughter. 'So our raunchy lady is really a shy virgin, is she? Don't worry,' he assured Hope when he saw her worried expression, 'I'd never do anything to hurt her, but now that I do know the truth I think it's time I handed out a little of the punishment she's been giving me these last few months. Come on, we'd better go inside before Mama comes out and tears a strip off me for keeping you standing out here. We'll have some coffee and then we'll start. I've got half a dozen properties for you to look at. They're all within your price range—the only problem is that one or two are a little remote.'

Dale's family was very Italian and very affectionate. Bianca would fit in well here, Hope thought appreciatively as Dale's mother questioned her about the actress; betraying to Hope that Dale hadn't been as good at keeping his secret as he had thought.

'We were at the convent together,' Hope told Mrs Lawrence. 'Bianca was always the rebel, but in the nicest way. She's been a very good friend to me.'

'Why did she not come with you this weekend? Dale invited her, I know.'

'Would you voluntarily spend the weekend with the man you love knowing he wants to go to bed with you, and fearing that once you give in you'll be discarded?'

It was taking a risk, Hope knew, but she guessed that Dale's mother was well aware of the gossip about Bianca—gossip that accredited her with a string of men.

'So.' The dark Italian eyes were very shrewd, and unlike Dale she did not question that Hope was speaking the truth. 'You must tell her that next time she is to come. No son of mine would dishonour an *innocente*.'

'I'll tell her,' Hope promised, quickly finishing her coffee as Dale walked back into the room waving a sheaf of papers. 'Just leaf through these first and see if there are any you don't fancy, and then when that's done we'll be on our way.'

Before she left, Hope rang Bianca to check on Niko, laughing fondly when she heard the baby's familiar gurgle.

'I hope you are taking proper care of my godson, Bianca,' Dale chided, relieving Hope of the receiver. Bianca must have made some fiery retort because Hope heard Dale laugh. 'Ah, *cara,* you are displaying an unexpectedly maternal streak. Perhaps you would like a little *bambino* of your own, umm?'

It was several seconds before he replaced the receiver and came to join Hope at the table. 'Bianca is very annoyed with me,' he told her with a grin. 'I think she would like to have strangled me with the telephone wire.'

'Very probably,' Hope agreed dryly, accepting the help he proffered as she hopped towards the door.

'PERSONALLY, this one is my favourite, but I must admit it is rather remote.'

'Umm...' They were standing outside an attractive, creeper-clad building, long and low, rising to only two storeys, set in the most attractive garden of any of the properties they had so far seen. Even better, the house was being sold complete with furniture, and Hope had fallen deeply in love with the cherry-wood, French country-style bedroom suite in the main bedroom. This winery, unlike most of the others, had been the property of a French family, but the property had been sold to a larger landowner who wanted the land, but had no use for the house. Hope was particularly drawn to this house, and she couldn't deny that it was partially because of its

French connections. Here Niko would grow up with a little of his French ancestry.

'It's right at the top of your price range,' Dale went on, 'but I think we can get them to come down a little. The road is in a pretty bad state. Will you feel happy living so far out? When the time comes for Niko to go to school...'

The nearest township was half an hour's drive away, but Hope wasn't too concerned. She liked the house and had been drawn to it more than any of the others.

'I can see that whatever I say, this is the one you want,' Dale grinned, 'and it is the pick of the bunch. Do you want to stop by the real estate office and put in a bid?'

The real estate office in Sonoma was, thankfully, quiet when Dale ushered Hope in. He stood to one side while she discussed the bid she was prepared to make for the property, and Hope was pleased to discover that because the place had been on the market for some time, her bid was likely to be accepted. Further details had to be discussed, including her financial situation, and it was then that Dale stepped in to confirm to the agent that Hope would earn enough from her advertising work to pay for the house outright.

Half an hour later they were free to step back out into the bright spring sunshine. Dale's fingers cupped Hope's elbow as they headed for his car. 'You handled that very nicely,' he told her. 'Although I think you gave our friend the realtor a bit of a shock. He isn't used to well-brought-up European ladies, he's more at home with the laid-back go-getting Californian female.'

There was a faint edge of cynicism to Dale's voice and Hope glanced at him curiously. 'Am I so different?' she asked. 'I thought I'd become more...'

'Southern Californian? Not really,' Dale told her with a smile which robbed the words of any unkindness. 'I'm afraid you still have a very evident gentleness, Hope, that betrays your European origins. You're so diffident, for one thing.' He saw her face and smiled. 'No, don't look like that. It's enchanting. Bianca has it, too, I begin to realise, although she does her best to hide it.' They had nearly reached the car when suddenly Hope froze. Emerging from a building on the other side of the road she glimpsed Alexei, her attention riveted on the stunning brunette at his side. This girl was all-American, Hope thought jealously. Tall, long-legged, with a tan that made her olive skin glow. She was clinging to Alexei's arm, his dark head bent towards her, the building from which they had emerged, an apartment block, Hope now realised. Obviously he hadn't wasted much time in finding some solace for losing Élise. On seeing him, she had come to an abrupt halt on the sidewalk, unaware of how pale she looked or how hugely vulnerable her eyes seemed in the small oval of her face.

'Hope, honey, are you all right?' She was distantly aware of Dale's hand on her arm, offering comfort and commiseration, but the majority of her attention was fixed on the couple coming towards them down the street. The brunette was laughing up at Alexei, and any moment they would be drawing level with Hope and Dale. Giant pincers seemed to lock round her heart, squeezing until the pain almost deprived her of breath. How could she be so intensely aware of Alexei—an awareness that invaded every pore and nerve of her body, making every breath she drew a physical pain—when he was completely oblivious to her presence?

'Hope...' She heard Dale exclaim abruptly, and realised that she had started to shake, tears blurring her eyes. The sudden comfort of Dale's arms was a benison to her aching heart, but her comfort was short-lived when she opened her eyes to meet the coldly cynical rake of Alexei's contemptuous ones as they slid over their interlocked figures.

He didn't stop, didn't make any move to introduce his companion, and Hope was too tormented by his presence to be aware of the sudden explosion of a flash bulb near her head, or of Dale's explosive protest as he turned in the direction of the sudden flash of light.

'You've really got it bad, haven't you, honey?' Dale said softly, when Alexei and his companion were safely past. 'And *he* didn't seem exactly enthralled to see you in my arms.'

Hope shivered as she remembered the contemptuous look Alexei had given her. 'If you ask me, that guy isn't as indifferent to you as you seem to think.'

'If he feels anything for me it's only a sense of responsibility,' Hope replied tiredly. 'A feeling of...'

'Guilt?' Dale supplied wryly.

Hope shook her head. She could never imagine Alexei suffering from such a destructive emotion as guilt. 'No... just responsibility.' Suddenly she felt incredibly tired; exhausted to the point of numbness, her ankle throbbing with renewed pain.

'Come on,' Dale instructed solicitously, noticing her pallor. 'Let's get you back to the winery. I'm going to cut short my visit to drive you back to Beverly Hills myself. I don't want you to risk making that ankle any worse. Besides,' he added shrewdly, 'you're in no fit state to go back alone. You really love him, don't you, Hope?'

'Too much,' she acknowledged wryly. 'But don't blame Alexei, Dale,' she cautioned, seeing the look of censure in his eyes. 'He didn't set out to make me fall in love with him. Far from it.'

'He's how old? Well into his thirties?' Dale queried. 'You were a child when you met him, Hope, you must have been, and from what little Bianca has told me, a pretty innocent one at that. Do you honestly expect me to believe he's not to blame?'

'Alexei had his reason,' Hope told him quietly, her mouth firm.

'He did? You leap to his defence like a female lion guarding her cub. What possible reason can there be for a man to desert a young, friendless girl, and one, moreover, who is carrying his child?'

'Alexei doesn't know about Niko, you know that.'

'And you don't intend to tell him? Hope...'

'If I tell him he will probably insist on marrying me,' Hope told him wryly. 'That's the sort of man he is. But he doesn't love me, Dale, and I don't think I could survive if I had to live with his pity and without his love.'

Dale didn't say anything more, but Hope knew he was glancing at her from time to time as they drove back to his parents' home.

'You've got an awful lot of courage, Hope,' was all he said when they eventually arrived, but deep down inside, Hope knew it wasn't true. She had very little courage at all. So little, in fact, that if Dale hadn't been with her she knew she would have run from the sight of Alexei with that tall, tanned Californian girl at his side—run and kept on running until she had found somewhere to hide, to be alone with her pain.

'MISSION ACCOMPLISHED?' Bianca looked up from bathing Niko to glance over her shoulder as Hope walked into the bathroom. 'Did you find somewhere?'

'Mmm, and it's lovely. Right at the top of my price range, but Dale thinks we can bargain them down. Niko behave himself?'

'Like an angel,' Bianca agreed. 'A pity you came back, I was just getting used to having him all to myself.'

'You should have one of your own.'

Bianca tensed. 'Sure...Dale would love that, right in the middle of filming. Who do you suggest I ask to play "daddy"?' She flushed under the old-fashioned look

Hope gave her. 'Dale doesn't want to know, you know that,' Bianca said bitterly. 'I'm not even sure if he still wants to go to bed with me, never mind anything else! No, Niko's going to be the only man in my life from now on.' She bent to lift him out of the bath, noticing Hope's bandaged ankle for the first time. 'What happened to you?'

Briefly Hope explained, for some reason omitting to mention Alexei. Meeting him again was still too raw and painful a wound to discuss with anyone; even Bianca, who was sister, mother and friend all rolled into one.

'I'm going to miss the two of you when you're gone. There's no hope for your changing your mind, I suppose?'

Regretfully, Hope shook her head. 'The Valley will provide a much healthier environment for Niko. The money I'm getting for the ads will buy the house and leave something over to be invested for Niko's schooling.'

'Talking of which, they showed your third advertisement over the weekend. It's very good. You know, Hope, I think you ought to take up modelling. You're very photogenic.'

'As are thousands of other girls,' Hope reminded her dryly, shaking her head. 'No, Bianca, modelling isn't something that appeals to me in the slightest. I'm grateful for the work Roy got me because it gives me financial independence, but I'm afraid I seem to lack that competitive drive that's really needed to succeed in life.'

'It all depends what you term "success",' Bianca told her quietly. 'Personally, I've always rated happiness and contentment higher than financial and career achievements. Oh, I know we're all taught nowadays that we can find the greatest degree of satisfaction from our careers, but is that really true? Aren't we just substituting "careers" for the old-fashioned notion that a woman found

her greatest fulfilment through her husband? No, I think
true satisfaction comes from something else, something
that's buried deep inside us all, something personal, that
only each individual knows whether they reach or not,
and it's different for all of us.'

There was a lot of truth in what Bianca said, and Hope
knew that while it was true that she wasn't career-minded
she had grown tremendously in spirit in the months since
she had left school. Having Niko had taught her so much,
given her so much, even though barely a day went by
without her thinking about his father. She had Alexei to
thank for much of her mental growth, she acknowledged, and who knew—perhaps it was easier to get all
one's growing up over with in one sharp, acutely painful
burst, rather than have it spread over several years.

SOME OF the script Bianca was working on had to be re-
shot and consequently she was out of the house for long
periods at a time. Hope received advice from the realtor
that her offer for the property had been accepted, and
through Dale she had approached a lawyer and asked him
to act for her. A generous cheque for her third advertisement, which Helen had decided to run in New York as
well as California, meant that Hope was able to go out
and study furnishings for her new home. Hope already
knew exactly how she wanted it decorated; it would have
an ambiance which was decidedly French, and she felt
totally unashamed of her sentimentality.

She was waiting excitedly to tell Bianca of her plans
and ask her to go with her on a shopping spree when
Bianca arrived home that evening, but to her surprise her
friend was cool to the point of curtness, pain and something else lurking in the depths of her eyes as she responded brusquely to Hope's questions about her day.

'No, the filming is not going well,' she said tautly, 'but
then I expect Dale has already told you that. He keeps on

and on about this damned sex-scene. I've told him I won't do it. I'll break my contract before I do. Funny, isn't it,' she added bitterly, 'I'm sure if you were the one in my shoes, he wouldn't dream of asking you to play the scene.'

'Bianca—' Hope was at a loss to understand her friend's behaviour—she seemed almost hostile. 'Bianca...'

'Oh, for goodness' sake, let's not play games with one another.' Bianca drew a shaky breath and Hope could have sworn she saw tears glistening in the huge dark eyes. She reached into her bag and withdrew a newspaper which she tossed down in front of Hope. 'It's there on the third page, a photograph of you and Dale, taken when you were in the Valley.'

Mystified, Hope turned the pages, blenching as she saw the photograph and remembered when it must have been taken. Just after she had seen Alexei; just after she and Dale had stepped out of the realtor's office. 'Bianca, I can explain...' she began, but Bianca cut in bitingly:

'Please don't. You don't have to explain anything to me, Hope. I have eyes...' She bit her lip. 'Of course, I should have guessed that Dale would be attracted to you. He dotes on Niko too.'

'Bianca,' gently Hope put her arms around her friend, 'you are quite, quite wrong.' Quickly she told her friend about Alexei, finishing, 'So you see, all Dale was doing was offering a little brotherly comfort. He loves you, Bianca, I'm sure of it, and if the two of you would quit trying to put on such an act of indifference with one another you both might get round to discovering exactly how you do feel.'

Poor Bianca, Hope couldn't begin to understand what kind of game Dale was playing. Hope was nearly sure that he wasn't going to force Bianca to play a graphic sex-scene, but she could find no means of reassuring her friend. 'We're off to Cannes at the end of the month,' Bianca reminded her, 'please come with me, Hope, you can bring Niko with you. Dale's talking about renting a villa, and I don't think I could endure staying there with him alone.'

France! Her heart leapt at the prospect and, although every ounce of common sense she had urged her against agreeing, Hope found herself reassuring Bianca that she would go with her. 'My very last job as your secretary.'

'Mmm. Thank goodness Dale has agreed to suspend shooting for the time being. I feel so drained at the moment, so on edge,' Bianca grimaced wryly. 'Having Dale around doesn't exactly help. He makes me feel so jumpy, I'm terrified all the time that I'm going to slip and he'll see how I feel about him.'

'Would that be so bad?' Hope asked gently. 'You might find that he's been hiding something, too.'

'Like he's fallen madly in love with me?' Bianca scoffed. 'That man doesn't know the meaning of the word. No, it would never work out between us. I want more from a relationship than sex—I want commitment, Hope. Commitment, love and caring, and I'm not going to find those with Dale. Neither of us seem to be lucky in our choice of men, Hope.'

It was a comment with which Hope could not argue.

CHAPTER THIRTEEN

'WHERE THE HELL is she this time?' Dale demanded explosively. He had walked into Bianca's house fifteen minutes before, startling Hope who hadn't been expecting him. 'She's supposed to be filming this afternoon and there's no sign of her.'

'Well, it's only eleven o'clock,' Hope reminded him placidly, glancing at her watch. 'Bianca is always conscientious about her work, Dale. She'll be there.'

'Yes, but where is she now, dammit?' He looked tired and drawn, more threads of silver mingling with the blond. 'I don't know what's eating into her recently.'

'The same thing that's eating into you,' Hope told him dryly. She put down the work she had been doing and walked over to check on Niko who was sleeping at her side in his pram. 'Dale, Bianca is really upset about this sex-scene. Why are you being so hard on her? You know she doesn't want to do it. It isn't even necessary to the script. You could convey the same impression much more subtly by innuendo.'

'The sound of the sea and fading music?' He pushed tense fingers angrily into his hair. 'Damn her, she won't even give me a logical reason, just keeps on saying she won't do it.'

'What do you want from her, Dale?' Hope asked quietly. 'She's very proud. You must see how difficult it would be for her to...'

'To simply tell me the truth.' He bit out the words, the hardness of his face betraying the tension he was under. 'That's all I'm asking for, Hope. I just want her to tell me the truth. Hell, she keeps on coming on with this sexy lady about town bit, and I know it's all a pose.'

'Only because I told you so,' Hope reminded him. 'Before that you were as deceived as everyone else. Can't you see, Dale, she feels she has to protect herself. She's scared, scared of betraying how she feels about you.'

'And how does she feel about me?' He wheeled round to stare moodily out of the window. 'Oh, I know you say she loves me, but I've seen precious little evidence of that love. She seems to take great delight in thwarting me at every turn. Going missing like this is just one example. Time was when I picked up the phone I knew she'd be on the other end of it.'

'And you, of course, have made your feelings for her perfectly plain?' Hope queried with a smile. 'You treat her as though she were a fragile piece of china, you listen to everything she has to say, you understand completely why she doesn't want to take part in explicit sex-scenes? You don't want her to anyway, because you love her.'

'Of course I don't want her to,' Dale agreed forcefully, failing to see the humour of Hope's comments. 'But why can't she tell me why she doesn't want to do them?'

'How? What is she supposed to do? Walk up to you and say, look Dale, I'm still a virgin, all this lady of the world stuff is all an act I assume because I'm madly in love with you and I don't want you to guess the truth, and it would destroy me to have to take part in the sort of scene the new script calls for? Is that really how you expect her to react?'

He grinned sheepishly at her. 'I guess you're right, but I feel so let down. After our talk I came back to town determined to woo her—you know, dates, flowers, the whole bit—but she's been so damned elusive. I can't get near her, and I can tell you it's playing havoc with my concentration. I ache for her, Hope,' he said huskily. 'Just seeing her makes me feel like I can barely breathe. I've never felt like this about anyone before. Never,' he finished purposefully.

'You know she wants me to go to Cannes with her?'

'Yes,' Dale agreed dryly, 'she's already told me. I've rented a villa just outside Cannes for us. I had thought that once there I might get the opportunity to get her alone...'

'Until she told you she was bringing me along as chaperone? Don't worry, I'll do my best to make myself unobtrusive,' Hope told him softly, 'but Dale, go easy on her, will you? She's under such a tremendous strain at the moment. She looks so pale and tense, and I'm really worried for her. She says you've decided to suspend filming for a while after this week.'

'Yes. This next scene coming up is this sexy one. I was hoping we'd have got ourselves sorted out well before we came to it. It won't do any harm to take a break as we're well ahead of schedule.'

'Wouldn't it make life a lot easier if you simply told her how you feel?' Hope asked gently.

'Like just announce "I love you".' He pulled a wry face. 'And risk having her turn round and fling it back in my face?' He shook his head decisively. 'Look, I know you say she loves me, Hope, but so far I haven't seen any evidence of that love.'

He left, giving Hope a few more details about their trip to Cannes, advising her that he had already organised the air tickets, and all the other preliminary details. Both of them were so proud, Hope reflected after he had gone. Both of them too frightened of exposing their vulnerability to risk telling one another of their real feelings. She had meddled enough, she told herself warningly. There was no more she could or should do, and yet as she fed and changed Niko she couldn't help wishing that somehow she could just play fairy godmother for an hour and wave her magic wand to put everything right for them.

As the days flew by, Bianca grew more nervous and on edge. 'I hate this Cannes thing,' she complained fretfully one day when she and Hope were sitting by the pool, Bianca's fair skin carefully shaded from the strong sun. 'The competition is always such a strain.'

'But this year you're tipped very strongly for an award,' Hope reminded her. 'Your portrayal of "Heron" is getting a lot of good press coverage.'

'That's what comes of having a good agent. Which reminds me, has Roy phoned you yet?'

When Hope shook her head, Bianca told her, 'Well, he spoke to me this morning. Your advertising work has been very highly acclaimed. You could be sorry you signed that contract with Helen, precluding you from taking work with anyone else.'

'I don't think so,' Hope argued reasonably. 'Helen wanted to be sure that my face would be coupled with her shop and nothing else, I can understand that, and to be honest, I don't particularly want any more work.'

'Well, Roy says your adverts are being strongly tipped by the agency for an award, and they're going to be seen at Cannes at a separate showing.' Seeing that Bianca was rather disappointed by her lack of reaction, Hope forced a brief smile. It was getting harder all the time to keep Alexei out of her thoughts, to hold back her longing to be with him. Traitorously, her thoughts often turned to what would have happened if she hadn't fled from the island when she did, if she had stayed and he had discovered her pregnancy.

She already knew that he felt a strong, compulsive sense of responsibility towards her—he desired her

physically too—and now that one of the major reasons
for her leaving—Élise—was out of his reach, wasn't it
possible that they might have been able to build a life together? Alexei wanted a son...their tastes were very
similar...she would have loved helping him to restore the
château, working alongside him. Abruptly she thrust
aside the tempting daydream. She was forgetting the most
important reason her dreams were impossible—Alexei
did not love her. She did not want his kind tolerance, his
amused affection, his care and protection of her. She
wanted his love. She wanted him to feel the same tearing
need and hunger for her that she felt for him. She wanted
to see him tremble and shake with desire for her the way
she did inside whenever he came near her. She wanted her
name to be the one he murmured in the dark emptiness
of the night, her body the one his hungered for, her love
his most cherished and prized possession.

'Ah, there you are, ladies.' Her thoughts were jerked
back to the present as Dale strolled towards them. Bianca
went white and Hope felt a flash of sympathy and fel-
low-feeling for her. How well she understood the stom-
ach-clenching agony Bianca was going through, the need
to conceal her feelings from Dale. Hadn't she herself experienced it on far too many occasions with Alexei?

Dale bent, dropping a light kiss on Hope's forehead,
and she marvelled at the skin's ability to register the touch
of a lover, differentiating between it and that of a friend.
Had it been Alexei's lips that touched her skin, she would
have burned and pulsed with searing pleasure, every
nerve ending in her body acutely attuned to him. Dale
smiled at her and moved across to Bianca, leaning down
to repeat the gesture. Hope saw how Bianca tensed and
jerked away, knowing exactly how she was feeling. There
was an agony in merely seeing Bianca and Dale together,
knowing that for them there was the promise that all
would end well, whereas for her... She turned her head

away, not wanting either of them to witness the searing jealousy she knew must be in her eyes.

'Something wrong?' she heard Dale drawl quizzically as he lifted his head.

Bianca's sharp, 'Nothing except that I'm choosy about who kisses me,' was betrayingly jerky and unsteady, and coils of pain tightened through Hope's heart. Dear God, did it never end, this aching longing for Alexei that was like being without a part of herself, a constant ceaseless pain; the ache of an amputated limb that tormented the body from which it had been torn?

'Call that a kiss.' Dale was openly derisive, and Hope forced herself to concentrate on her friends and put her own pain away from her.

'No wonder you like your love-scenes tepid, lady.' He turned on his heels, leaving them abruptly. Bianca went white and then red, and Hope saw in her eyes an echo of her own pain. 'Does time make it any easier to bear?' she asked desperately.

Hope shook her head, her eyes unconsciously shadowed. 'Not in my experience. Why don't you lower your pride and tell him how you feel?' she suggested softly.

Bianca's mouth twisted. 'For the same reason you won't lower yours. We're both crying for the moon, and both reluctant to accept anything less than...'

'Love?' Hope suggested. An inner voice was asking her how she would feel in twenty years' time, alone, Niko grown up, reflecting on what might have been? Why, oh why had Élise not married Alexei. At least then she would have known that he was happy: that he was removed from her reach for ever. With him married to Élise there would be no temptation, no agonising uncertainty, no longing to go to him and show him Niko, to let him take control of her life.

Who was she deceiving? she asked herself sardonically. If Alexei were to appear now and want her, married to Élise or not, she would go to him. And that was what frightened her so terribly, the knowledge that she would happily abandon pride, self-respect, common sense, everything, just to be with him, just to experience again the delicious pleasure of being held in his arms.

'I'm going inside,' Bianca said shortly. 'If Dale comes back you can tell him I've got a headache. Headache!' she grimaced bitterly. 'Heartache would be a more accurate description. What fools women are, Hope. Why can't we be more like men and simply take our physical pleasure where we wish without the complication of emotional ties?'

'Don't you mean, why can't men be more like us?' Hope submitted dryly. 'Why is it they can take their physical pleasure without emotional commitment? I sometimes think the difference between the sexes is a cruel joke on the part of the gods, making life difficult for men and women alike.'

'HAVE YOU BEEN to Cannes before?' They were in a hire-car, travelling towards their villa, Hope, Niko and Bianca in the back, Dale sitting in the front with their driver. Hope shook her head, suddenly and disconcertingly remembering Alexei talking about the villa he owned between Nice and Cannes. What on earth was the matter with her? Just because Alexei owned property in the vicinity, it hardly meant that she was likely to see him, but still her unruly heart kept on clutching at straws, wanting, against all the dictates of pride and common sense, the extraordinary coincidence which would mean that she would see Alexei again, even though she knew that by doing so she would only be inflicting fresh pain upon herself.

'Never,' she replied in response to Bianca's question.

'Well, keep your eyes peeled, we're just about to turn into La Croisette,' Dale told them from the front, cran-

ing round to grin at Hope. 'Reputedly the most elegant
sea promenade in the world,' he informed her porten-
tously, sounding like a guidebook. 'And look out for the
signpost, it's in gold letters.'

As he spoke they turned into an elegant carriageway,
two long rows of palms and other trees stretching out
ahead of them, wafting gracefully, languid and elegant
as lilies in the soft on-shore breeze. To one side of them
lay silver beaches, briefly glimpsed beneath the forest of
beach umbrellas and elegantly bronzed bodies. On the
other side were shops, cafés, blocks of flats, and then
glimpsed between the central reservations with their
banks of trees and gaudily-coloured flowers, was the
wedding-cake-like edifice of the famous Carlton Hotel in
all its *belle-époque* glory.

'A visit to the Carlton bar is a must during Festival
time,' Dale commented to Hope, grimacing faintly as he
did so. 'Frankly, it will be as crowded as hell, but everyone who thinks they're anyone will flock there and I
suppose we'll follow suit, if only so that you can say
you've been there.'

'You'll have to take Hope on her own,' Bianca interrupted languidly. 'It's such a crush. Besides, someone will
have to stay with Niko.'

Hope was just on the point of saying that she would
stay behind with her son, when she caught the bitter look
that flashed between Dale and Bianca. Beyond the town
lay the purple haze of the Alps marking the border with
Italy. Their villa was somewhere on one of those pine-
darkened slopes.

'How much farther, Dale, I'm getting tired,' Bianca
complained with unusual pettishness. 'We really ought to
have booked into the Carlton or the Majestic. It's going
to be murder travelling into Cannes every day.'

'You said you didn't want to stay in the city,' Dale reminded her curtly. 'You said that you wanted to get away

from the crowd, something about wanting peace and quiet.'

'But you're still coming with us,' Bianca remarked acidly. 'So I haven't got much chance of finding any, have I? I'm not going to back down, Dale,' she added firmly. 'I'm not playing that scene, no matter what you say.'

'If you could give me a sensible reason why you shouldn't, instead of being plain mule-stubborn, I might be more amenable.'

'Isn't the fact that I don't want to do it reason enough?' It seemed to Hope that sparks almost flew from Bianca's red hair, so great was her anger. It seemed to vibrate in the air between them, and Hope marvelled that two such intelligent people such as Bianca and Dale could remain unaware of the sexual tension each generated towards the other.

'The villa is just up ahead,' Dale said quietly when they turned off the main road and started to climb through wooded pine-clad slopes, the sea an arc of blue behind them, small sandy beaches glimpsed briefly as the road climbed and then dipped once more into the protection of the pines. 'It shares a beach with half a dozen others, but it does have its own pool.'

It was quite beautiful, Hope thought dazedly when the car eventually came to a halt. Set in a grove of pines, it was washed a soft shade of pink, green shutters closed against the midday heat. Paying off their driver, Dale stacked their cases on the drive, searching for the key while Hope admired the showy oleanders blooming either side of the front door.

'Here we are—after you, ladies.' The hallway was cool and dark, the floor a soft polished wood. Dale flipped on the light, revealing the room's elegant proportions. 'Drawing room through there, dining room, library, kitchen, conservatory, and pool.' Dale indicated various doors, heading for the delicately balustraded staircase.

The villa had six bedrooms, each with private bath.
Hope's was large enough to hold Niko's travelling cot,
and all the other nursery equipment she had brought with
her, with ease. A maid and a gardener went with the villa,
Dale had informed them, and Hope could see from her
small balcony the attractive formal garden extending beyond the house, and then the deep, rich blue of the Med-
iterranean, dying into hazy lavender on the horizon.

A brief tap on her door broke her contemplation of the
attractive scene.

'Did I disturb you?' Bianca asked, walking into her
room. She looked tense and ill at ease, as she had done
for the past few weeks. 'Hope, while we're here; I want
you to stick close by me. I...I don't want to be alone with
Dale. I know you probably think I'm a coward, but...'

'You still love him?'

'More than ever, and I'm afraid that with the way he
keeps pressuring me about this damned scene, I might
just break apart.'

'Why don't you tell him the truth,' Hope suggested.
'You might find him more receptive to it than you expect.' It seemed ironic that she should be advising Bianca.
She must be the least qualified woman in the world to
advise another on matters of the heart.

'The truth? You mean like, "I don't want to play that
scene because there's only one man I want to make love
with whether it's play-acting or reality, and that's you?"
I can just see his face.' She laughed bitterly. 'No, I'll just
have to find some other way of convincing him. I wish I'd
never agreed to this idea of his renting a villa. He's too
close.'

Hope spent the first couple of days exploring her environs, making use of the car and driver Dale had arranged to be placed at her disposal to investigate the
town. Bianca and Dale were tied up in talks about the
film and its submission for an award, and Hope saw very

little of them during the first week of their stay. 'This was supposed to be a holiday as well as business trip,' she reminded Bianca when she saw her friend at breakfast one morning, looking pale and tired.

'Try telling Dale that. He's got meetings organised for the next three days. I hope you're not too lonely?'

'I'm fine,' Hope assured her. Roy had told her that her own advertisement was being considered for an award, at a special ceremony, but its submission did not involve her in any personal appearances or negotiations. She had been taking Niko down on to the beach, carefully exposing his skin to the sun, enjoying his pleasure in its warmth on his skin. He seemed to grow and develop a little more every day. Already he was impatient to be on his feet, trying hard to stand whenever she picked him up. A vigorous and active baby, a day didn't pass without her thinking how much he looked like Alexei. Even more so now that his eyes were starting to turn from blue to green. Dale and Bianca needed time alone, she thought, watching her friend—time to relax and drop their guards with one another. Perhaps if she wasn't there...

Bianca was using her as a shield, she knew, and she also knew that her friend's elusiveness was infuriating Dale. Thoughtfully she went to look for Jeanne, their maid. Plump, and middle-aged, her dark hair secured in a neat bun, she listened placidly while Hope asked if it was possible that she might babysit for her one night.

'But of course,' she assured Hope promptly. '*Le bébé* is good and makes no trouble. I shall enjoy it. It is a long time since my Gérard and Jacob were little and as yet they have not provided me with any grandchildren. You wish to go out on a date?' She said the last word hesitantly but proudly, showing off her knowledge of what she no doubt thought of as the modern vernacular. The villa was owned by an American, Dale had told her, and no doubt

Jeanne was used to transatlantic guests, although Hope always spoke to her in her own language.

'Er... yes... sort of.' In point of fact Hope wasn't yet sure what she was going to do, but only knew that it seemed imperative that she gave Bianca and Dale some breathing-space to sort out the problems which seemed to envelop them both in a powerful emotional force field whenever they were in wounding distance of one another.

Bianca reacted as Hope had anticipated she might when she told her she was going out. Hope had deliberately delayed relaying the information until they were having dinner. She had come down for it dressed casually in a silk top and matching trousers in a soft lavender blue. The top emphasised the slightly more mature curves of her breasts, and she felt acutely conscious of the way the trousers skimmed the narrow bones of her hips. Her body had altered since Niko's birth, becoming finer and yet at the same time more voluptuous.

'Going out, but where, who with?'

'I think Hope's old enough to go out on a date without you fussing round her like a mother hen, Bianca,' Dale chimed in, looking at Hope with something like appreciation in his eyes. 'Or do your fears spring from another source?'

'Meaning what?' Bianca demanded, taking fire immediately, and under the cover of their battle, Hope started to move away from the table, hesitating only when she heard Dale saying smoothly, 'It occurs to me... this scene that's causing all the trouble... why don't we run through it together tonight? I know I'm not the best actor in the world, but it might help for you to confront whatever it is about it that bothers you, and then if you still feel you can't go through with it...'

Hope held her breath, not needing to look at Bianca to fully appreciate what she must be feeling. Clever, clever

Dale, he must know that Bianca would be unable to back down from the challenge, and somehow Hope suspected that what he had in mind was not so much running through the script's sex-scene, but more a means of using it to force Bianca to admit how she felt about him. At the same time this would give him the opportunity to reveal to her his feelings, without having to put them into words. Would it work? She left the dining room while Bianca was still objecting, knowing when she heard Dale drawl, 'Look, what's the big deal? What is there to be afraid of? Surely not me,' that he had won, and with that knowledge came a certain degree of pain. Not jealous of her friend, exactly, but certainly envious, certainly an aching sense of loss that she and Alexei would never share the degree and intensity of love she sensed existed between Dale and Bianca.

Dale seemed to share her belief that he had won. Half an hour later when Hope was just stepping out of the villa, he caught up with her, smiling conspiratorially, 'Thanks for abandoning your role as chaperone. What made you decide to do it?'

'I didn't think any of us could survive the atmosphere around here for much longer if I didn't,' she said lightly. 'Dale...be careful, won't you. Bianca isn't anything like as tough as you think. She's very easily bruised.' As she herself had been, she thought painfully, but bruises fade, and love does not.

'I've got a few bruises of my own,' Dale told her dryly. 'She knows how to hurt. I only hope I'm doing the right thing.' Just for a second, doubt touched his eyes, and Hope lingered, even though she longed to get away, to escape from an atmosphere too receptive to memories to allow her to linger without being hurt by them for very long. 'I'm gambling for high stakes tonight, Hope. If she rejects me now...if she refuses to listen.'

Hope summoned all her strength of will, sacrificing her own need to be alone to help her friends, fighting down the aching pain inside her that demanded solitude, and counselled softly, 'You know what they say...' Dale looked puzzled, and she explained with a small smile, 'Kisses first, words second, but remember to tell her when you've stopped acting, won't you, Dale.'

She left the villa with no clear idea of where she was going, only knowing that she must be alone... that she couldn't stay in the villa knowing that before the evening was over Bianca and Dale would probably have resolved their problems, would probably have acknowledged their love for one another, while she... She bit down hard on her bottom lip, using the pain to quell the tide of memories threatening to sweep over her, trying to ignore the irony of the fact that she, who would never know the love of the man she wanted, had probably played a large part in helping Bianca and Dale to find theirs. Tonight, her senses so acutely attuned to the vibrations tensing the atmosphere which surrounded her friends, she didn't want to be an onlooker on events which could only increase her own feelings of loss and pain.

Alexei! Would her love for him have been less intense if he had not been her first and only love? Did time and experience help to lessen the degree of pain and anguish one felt when one's love was not returned? She had not experienced any adolescent pangs of calf-love; she had nothing to guide her, only this aching, deep void inside her that cried out for fulfilment; that knew neither pride nor shame, only a fierce hunger for the person who had first brought it into being. No, she could not remain in her room tonight, not with the memories crowding into her mind, more vivid it sometimes seemed with every day that passed.

Jeanne, upon enquiry, had suggested to her that she try one of the nightclubs in Nice when Hope asked her where she might spend the evening. 'Le Busby it is called,' she told her. 'All the film people go there.'

It was surely the hottest and noisiest place she had ever been in in her life, Hope thought distastefully an hour later as she sat and contemplated her exotic and rather weak drink. Couples and singles, both, filled the small dance floor and the floor-space beyond. She had already had to fend off several unwanted approaches, and she was beginning to wish she had gone instead to the bar in the Carlton, but had wanted the anonimity of a large, noisy crowd.

'C'mon . . . dance with me . . .' It was the third time she had been approached by a particularly persistent and rather drunk blond youth whom she vaguely recognised as one of the camera crew from Bianca's film set. 'C'mon, honey,' he persisted when she politely refused, 'I know all about you. You've got that kid. Loosen up a bit, why don't you. We could have fun together.'

Realising that while she remained in the club there was no way she was going to be able to escape him, Hope resorted to a subterfuge which would normally have never occurred to her. 'I will dance with you,' she agreed, 'but first I must have another drink.'

''Nother drink?' He stared owlishly from Hope to the fruit-decorated half-empty glass in front of her. 'Stay there then, honey, and I'll go and get you one, easier than waiting for one of the damned waiters.'

Five minutes later, making her escape, Hope told herself that he deserved to pay for the unwanted, expensive drink and that it would probably teach him a valuable lesson. Another time he might not be so persistent.

Outside, she breathed in gulps of the clean fresh air, sauntering along the boulevard, glancing into the elegant shops. One or two passers-by paused to study her, but she was unaware of the faint stir of interest she caused. Cannes was full of stunning, beautiful women and the male population must surely be blasé, suffering from such a surfeit of pulchritude.

A glance at her watch confirmed her inner fear that it was far too early for her to return to the villa as yet. Stifling a yawn and trying not to think too much about Niko and the peace of her own bed, she made her way into a small bar she noticed on the corner of the street. Inside it was packed, she wouldn't even be able to get a seat.

Stifling a sigh, Hope went back outside, not noticing when two shapes detached themselves from the shadows, carefully following her. It was only when some sixth sense alerted her to their presence that she turned, and realised with a spurt of fear that she was alone on a deserted narrow street, and that the two men, now boldly deserting the shadows and advancing on her, must think she was a rich tourist, perhaps an actress, and intended to rob her.

A sign in front of her offered her a haven, but as she stepped into the small bar the two men followed her. Biting her lip, Hope wondered what to do. It obviously wasn't her night. She glanced round and saw that the men were still observing her, and she made up her mind. Advancing to the bar, she waited until she had gained the attention of the patron, and quickly explained her dilemma. He was in his fifties, stout and balding, but very much a Frenchman and responded with immediate gallantry to her plight.

'*Mademoiselle* must stay here,' he informed her genially, '*les couchons* who dare to make unpleasantness for you will be dealt with, and when you are ready to leave, I, Gaston, will summon a taxi for you and see you into it in safety.'

Allowing herself to be persuaded into a Pernod, Hope looked round for an empty table, glimpsing one in a corner, a man, the corner's only other inhabitant, hunched over the adjoining table.

'Ah, you will be quite safe with him,' Gaston assured her, following her gaze. 'All night he has been in here. We see many like him...drinking to forget. He will not bother you, *mademoiselle*, I am sure of it.'

As she sipped her drink and her eyes adjusted to the darkness, her fear receding, Hope turned her head slightly, covertly studying the man in the corner. Who was he? What brought him here, to 'drink to forget' as Gaston put it? An out-of-work actor? A failed film producer? Her heart suddenly lurched as she recognised his features and knew that he was neither. Alexei! His name slipped past her lips before she could stop herself, and his head lifted, alcohol-hazed eyes searching the darkness and eventually finding her.

'Hope!' He expressed no surprise at seeing her. 'You have me at a disadvantage as you will perceive. Ah, it is no use pursing your lips and looking so disapproving. I am only human, and this—' he touched the bottle in front of him with the lean fingers Hope remembered, almost caressing the glass '—offers me an escape from my nightmares...'

Nightmares? He must mean Élise. Hope was flooded with pity, and an almost maternal urge to take him in her arms. Alexei. She would never have thought to see him like this. 'Even Homer nods—occasionally,' he mocked, his voice stronger and more familiar as he studied her. 'Why are you so shocked? Am I not allowed to have human foibles and weaknesses, and surely you, more than anyone else, know what mine are?' He saw her expression and laughed bitterly. 'What a pity we cannot train our memories to forget those things that cause us the most pain. I have many memories of you, *mon petit*.'

Hope's body was responding to the sensual huskiness of his voice, her pulse racing out of control, her mind conjuring up far too vivid pictures of them together. She shuddered and Alexei witnessed the faint betrayal, smiling unpleasantly. 'Ah, I see that you do remember. Do you ever wake up in the dark reaches of the night, your body aching for mine, or does your new lover make you forget what we shared together?'

'Alexei, please don't...'

'Don't what? Remind you of the past? You have changed, Hope, I saw it in California. You have grown up, so much faster than I expected, almost overnight.'

'All that hot-house forcing,' she joked weakly, stunned to see him pale noticeably, and grasp his glass until she thought it must splinter under his bone-crushing grip.

'You still have not forgiven me, have you?' he demanded harshly. He sounded so anguished that she was moved to protest.

'For what Alexei? I understand why you did what you had to do. There's really no forgiveness necessary. It's over. We both have to put the past behind us.'

'How easy you make it sound.' He laughed bitterly. 'But even if you can forgive me, I doubt that I can forgive myself. How many men have there been since me, Hope, and how many more will there be?'

'I could ask you the same about your women-friends,' she hedged, hoping she wasn't flushing.

'You do well to remind me that I no longer have the right to question your private life. Where is he tonight, your lover, the famous producer? Don't you mind sharing him with the actress with whom he is so frequently photographed. She is an extremely beautiful woman.'

'Extremely,' Hope agreed brittly, not realising what interpretation Alexei had put on the faint tinge of jealousy in her voice until he said harshly:

'You are jealous of her, and with good reason according to the gossip columns.'

If she was jealous it was simply because he had said that Bianca was beautiful, which was stupid because there had been many beautiful women in Alexei's life and there would undoubtedly be many more.

'Don't drink any more, Alexei,' she urged when he went to refill his glass. 'It won't alter anything.' She ought to leave him while she could.

'No,' he agreed, 'but it helps to blot it out. However, you are right, escape is only temporary. What would I have done, I wonder, if I had known beforehand the cataclysmic effect you would have on my life?'

What did he mean? Surely he wasn't blaming *her* because he had lost Élise? But then perhaps he needed to blame someone. 'You should go home, Alexei,' she told him quietly.

'Yes, I think you're right. Can I give you a lift? My car is parked outside.'

His car! Did he really intend to drive in his present state? 'Alexei, you can't drive!' she protested.

'And I can't leave my car here all night.'

'Give me your keys, I'll drive you home, if you direct me,' Hope told him, coming to a decision, not allowing herself to dwell on her own weakness, the need to be with him. She simply couldn't walk out on him and leave him like this. She could telephone for a taxi from his villa, wherever it was, and the later she was getting back the more time Bianca and Dale would have to sort out their differences. At least she need not worry about Niko, she thought with relief, as Alexei stared morosely at her—he would be quite safe in Jeanne's capable hands.

It was ironic that she should meet Alexei again tonight, of all nights, when she was feeling so acutely vulnerable; so hungry for his presence, his touch—dangerously hungry, she acknowledged, on a slight shudder, knowing that if she was wise she would leave now before it was too late, and knowing equally that she would not do so.

'Your car keys, Alexei,' she repeated, 'unless of course you want to complete your folly and get yourself killed.' The fine touch of irony in her voice seemed to have the desired effect, but he would never know how difficult it was for Hope to produce it. The cloudiness left his eyes to be replaced by cold hauteur.

'You have become a very managing woman, *mon petit*,' he drawled tauntingly, 'a failing of American women, due chiefly to the fact that American men are such perennial little boys. For a moment then you sounded almost maternal. You will save such feelings for your American lover, or your child, when you have one— I am still very much a man, and you would do well to remember it. Well then,' he murmured when she said nothing, merely paling and suppressing a mute shudder of torment, 'are you still determined to play the Good Samaritan, for I confess that if you are I will be grateful for it. You are quite right, little one, I am really in no condition to drive. Here,' he handed her the keys to the Ferrari, and as they passed the bar, Hope saw the way Gaston looked at them. 'We are old friends, Gaston, *mon ami*,' Alexei drawled, 'so you need not continue to look at me as though I am Bluebeard.'

'Everything is all right, *mademoiselle?*' Gaston asked Hope warily, and she smiled in reassurance to him. 'It is as Monsieur le Comte says, Gaston,' she reaffirmed, 'we are old friends.'

'You are honoured, *mon petit*,' Alexei drawled as they gained the street, 'Gaston is not normally so caring of the women who walk into his bar alone.'

'This is probably because I was followed in there,' Hope told him, briefly describing the events which had brought her to the bar.

'You were walking the streets of Cannes, alone, at night! What manner of man is this new lover of yours?' Alexei demanded tautly. 'Does he not realise...'

'Dale knows that I can look after myself,' Hope told him acidly. 'Where is your car, Alexei?'

Although he was doing a good job of disguising it, Hope could tell that he had by no means recovered from the alcohol he had consumed, a goodly amount if the level of the bottle he had had in front of him had been anything to go by. Cognac fumes filled the interior of the Ferrari as Hope altered the positioning of the seat, and checked to make sure that Alexei's seat-belt was fastened. He smiled at her mockingly.

'Do you remember the first time you sat in this car, *ma belle?* You looked for all the world as though you expected me to pounce upon you at any second.'

'You were someone completely outside my experience,' Hope retorted calmly, carefully negotiating the Ferrari out of its parking bay. 'Which way, Alexei?'

He gave her precise and brief directions, watching the way she handled the powerful car. 'Your ankle is fully recovered?'

'Thank you, yes. I don't know what I would have done if you hadn't been there that evening.' How politely they fenced with one another. How distant he was. It was better so, but her aching heart took some convincing.

'Oh, I'm sure my manager or his wife would have provided a more than adequate substitute. Let's not play games, Hope,' he said, his voice suddenly harsh. 'I have a particularly vivid memory of how you flinched from my touch. Everyone keeps telling me that it is time I married.'

A crushing pain seemed to seize hold of Hope's heart. 'They remind me that I am the last of my line and that I should have a son. What do you think, Hope?' Why on earth was he asking her! She strove for self-control.

'I think you can hardly really want my advice,' Hope responded lightly, praying that he couldn't hear the suffocating thud of her heart. A son! He already had one, but he didn't know it. What would he say if she told him about Niko? Just for a moment she indulged herself in the fantasy of hearing him say that he loved and wanted them both, before cutting off the foolish thought.

'I must confess that at one time the thought of marrying simply for comfort and the continuation of my line did not particularly disturb me but now... Right here,' he guided her, indicating a road that led upwards through the pines. 'Strange how we should continue to bump into one another like this. You are making quite a name for yourself, so I understand, in the world of television advertising.'

'You've seen... you've seen the advert?' Her heart in her mouth, Hope waited for his response. How could he have seen it and not seen himself in Niko?

'Only partially. You are very photogenic.'

'Yes, so Bianca tells me, but it isn't something I want to make a career out of.'

'I suppose not, but there's no need, is there, now that you have a rich lover to keep you. That was never how I intended that you should spend your life, Hope.'

'I am an individual,' Hope reminded him, suddenly angry that he should so easily believe her incapable of making her own way in life. 'I choose for myself.'

'And you chose to live off my sex?'

Hope didn't reply. She was too busy concentrating on the hairpin bends in the road, carefully negotiating the powerful car round them—too busy quelling the pain his taunting caused her.

'Left here,' Alexei instructed. They turned down a narrow cart-track, the Ferrari bumping over the ruts, an old low farmhouse illuminated by the beam of the Ferrari's headlights. 'My father bought this place before the cost of property around here became astronomical. Stop here.' He indicated a cobbled courtyard and Hope obediently brought the car to a halt. As he reached for the door and stepped out, Hope noticed how he swayed, and how gaunt and thin he was looking.

'Thanks for the caretaking.' How formal and distant he sounded, turning away from her as though in dismissal.

'Alexei, I'll have to come in with you to ring for a taxi,' Hope reminded him, seeing him frown in realisation that she spoke the truth.

The door opened straight into a pleasantly decorated sitting room, wall lights giving the rich rugs and gleaming wood a warm glow. Leaving her to follow him, Alexei went straight to one of the wooden cabinets and opened it. Hope caught the reflection of the lights off glass as he removed a bottle.

'Stop looking so disapproving,' he taunted her. 'Without this...' he tapped the bottle, 'I probably won't get any sleep. Why should that be, do you suppose, Hope? Guilt? Too many uncomfortable memories?' He half stumbled as he turned towards her, and Hope reached instinctively for the bottle, taking it off him.

'Let me help you upstairs,' she offered, suspecting that if she just left him he would collapse into one of the sofas and then wake up in the morning cold and stiff. At first he shrugged off the arm she placed round him, but as though realising the good sense of what she was saying, he slumped towards her, allowing her to lead him towards the door.

The stairs went up from a small inner hallway. After fumbling for the light, Hope helped Alexei up, surprised to see how light he seemed for such a tall man. She frowned as she looked into his shadowed, shuttered face, his eyes closed. All the signs of his being very much the worse for drink were there, and yet it seemed as though something wasn't quite right. But why should he pretend to be drunk? It didn't make sense.

'Which room, Alexei?' she asked him when they reached the top of the stairs. He indicated a door and she helped him towards it, pushing it open, and reaching for the light.

The room made her catch her breath in faint disbelief. The furniture was almost an exact replica of that in the main bedroom of her new house, but there was no reason why she should feel so surprised, she argued with herself. French provincial furniture of this kind was fairly common, especially in French farmhouses, and hers had no doubt been shipped to America by the family who had first owned the vineyard.

Carefully, she urged Alexei towards the bed which depressed under his weight as he sank on to it, rolling on to his side and shielding his eyes from the harshness of the light. Something about the way he moved caught at Hope's memory, something elusive she remembered from the past. 'Alexei . . .'

'Get me a drink of water, would you, please,' he asked tautly, 'and Hope, there are some pills in my bathroom cupboard, a small brown bottle.'

'You can't take pills with alcohol,' Hope began when she saw his expression change.

'Sorry to disillusion you,' he drawled softly, 'but you were so keen to do the ministering angel bit and to think the worst of me, I couldn't tell you. I'm not drunk, Hope, at least not to the extent you seem to think. But I am suffering from the most excruciating migraine, so be a good girl and get me my pills, will you.'

Migraine! Of course, she remembered now. One of the Sisters at the convent had suffered from it. No wonder Alexei had flinched away from the light. She got up quickly, dowsing it, hearing the small sound of relief expelled from his throat. She found the pills he had requested in the bathroom and ran the tap until the water was cold.

'Thanks.' He accepted the tablets and the water with very evident relief. 'I don't get these attacks very often. It started just after I went out tonight. I went into Gaston's bar hoping it might fade...'

'But the bottle in front of you was...'

'Someone else's.' He moved in the darkness and winced. 'Hope.'

'Yes—'

'Stay with me.' His voice was slurred with pain. 'Please.' It was the first time he had asked her for anything, and even though she knew she ought to refuse, somehow Hope heard herself saying:

'Of course, if you want me to. I'll go and find myself a room and...'

'No! I mean stay here, with me,' he persisted, his voice thick with pain. 'Remember, when you had your bad dream, how you needed me. Well, I need you like that tonight. Just to be close to. I need you, Hope.'

She wondered if he was totally aware of what he was saying, and could only guess at the crushing pain he must be enduring, pain which he had somehow kept at bay all the time they were talking, but which now seemed to have swept aside his urbanity. '*Mon Dieu,* these damned pills,' he muttered. 'I can't even think straight.' He reached out, entwining his fingers with hers, drawing her down alongside him, and Hope knew she was going to stay— knew nothing would induce her to leave him now, like this.

She waited until he was asleep to pull the heavy eiderdown over him. She could leave him now if she wished, but there was something so vulnerable about him in sleep that she knew she would snatch these few precious hours and stay with him, no matter how much common sense might caution her against so doing.

'MON PETIT.' The soft endearment seemed to float through her subconscious, the familiar weight of the arm thrown over her body vaguely reassuring.

'Alexei.' She murmured his name without opening her eyes, her toes curling as she heard his soft, familiar laughter.

'So you are *not* just a dream.' His arm moved, his fingers investigating the soft silk of her top, brushing it aside to caress her bare midriff. 'Mmm, so soft.' Hope knew that she ought to move, to make some form of protest, but it was all too much of an effort. She opened her eyes cautiously, it was still dark, just light enough for her to make out Alexei's features.

'Ah, Hope.' His voice was muffled as he bent over her, pushing back the silk and caressing her bare skin with his lips, searing it. He was unfastening her bra, but she felt too boneless to protest, silently watching him while he removed her top and the brief piece of silk she wore beneath it. In the moonlight she witnessed the urgent response of her breasts, hardening and swelling in ardent supplication so that she couldn't blame Alexei for responding to their unspoken message. His lips brushed lightly against each darkened areola, his eyes as she looked into them densely dark, the pupils still enlarged from the painkilling drug.

'Hope.' She could feel his heart thudding against her in the darkness, her lips parting eagerly beneath the warmth of his mouth. Wanton, almost delirious surges of pleasure; an intensity of desire she had almost forgotten, seethed through her like sea foaming on the beach as she responded to the probing hunger of Alexei's kiss, feeling it grow in intensity, his mouth moving avidly over hers.

'Mon petit.' He lifted his head, placing his hands either side of her face, smoothing back the tangle of her hair. He soothed her heated skin with the tips of his fingers, exploring familiar contours with his mouth, touching her with a delicate restraint at odds with the intense desire she could read quite plainly in his eyes.

'You're a woman now, Hope,' she heard him murmur, 'and God help me, how I want you.' His admission seemed to spark off something alien and unruly inside her. She reached up to touch his cheekbones with fingers that trembled, her palm tingling from the brief, hard pressure of the kiss he placed upon it, stroking it roughly with his tongue.

'Your headache,' she murmured, not taking her eyes from his face, needing to believe that the desire she saw there was for her.

'Forget it. *You* make me ache,' he muttered, bending to kiss her, taking her hands and placing them against his chest. 'Feel how my heart thuds. I want you, Hope, as a man wants a woman, for no better reason than the need that exists between them. This will be for me,' he told her softly. 'Not for Tanya, not for any other reason than the most basic of all human needs.'

She knew she ought to stop him because he didn't love her, but her body was already trembling finely against him, and beneath her spread fingers she could feel the mat of hairs covering his chest. Her mind played to her a vivid picture of his body as she remembered it, sleek and golden, taut with muscle, hard against her own, and she reached for his shirt buttons, silently answering his questions with the moist kisses she pressed against his exposed skin.

They touched one another without haste or impatience—Hope because she wanted to store each vivid memory away, and Alexei perhaps because he sensed that this was the way she wanted it. That she could be so unashamed, positively delighting in the way he looked at her naked body, was something new, touching off fresh chords of desire. She wanted him to look at her like this, with deep hunger, and need, just as much as she wanted him to touch her, Hope acknowledged, sighing softly beneath the soft stroke of his fingers. His body was leaner than she remembered, and he tensed beneath her touch, muttering huskily in French, words that brought a dark tide of colour to her skin, strung together like a prayer.

'Hope.' Alexei's eyes seemed feverish in the darkness, his body shivering against her, the passion she remembered from the Caribbean somehow much more finely-honed and kept barely under control. And yet Hope sensed a holding back, an inner tension that didn't spring merely from desire, almost a hesitancy, so at odds with the Alexei that she remembered that it puzzled her. Her hand slid from his chest to his thigh, exploring the supple tautness of his skin, her fingertips stroking idly over the bone.

'*Mon Dieu,* Hope, what are you trying to do to me? I don't want it to be like it was that last time, but you aren't helping.' He shuddered helplessly as she touched his flat belly, raking her nails lightly across it. His eyes closed and now she realised with a growing sense of wonder that *she* was the cause of his tension, that she possessed the ability to arouse him to this fine pitch of need.

'We always were good together,' he muttered the words thickly, sliding his palm against her breast and stroking the burgeoning flesh, urging her down towards him so that his lips could graze against the hard-peaked nipples, and then lower, to her softly-rounded stomach, his hand caressing her thigh, taking her backwards in time. How often had she tried to recapture just exactly the sensation he was arousing in her now, trying to recall the intimacy of his touch? But the memory had fallen far short of the reality and her own hands and lips were eager to respond to each caress, the heated urgency of his response feeding her own desire.

Both of them seemed to know exactly when the moment came for Alexei to move over her, stroking at first gently, and then, when he felt her feverish response, far more urgently into the softness of her body, which seemed at that moment to have been designed purely to accommodate him.

There was nothing else in the world but Alexei, Hope thought feverishly, wanting to contain and fulfil his body, to surround him with her love, more than she had ever wanted anything in her life. She arched beneath him, gasping as she felt the tight, coiling spirals of pleasure begin, surrendering herself completely to his possession, hearing his harsh cry of pleasure as she sank down through billowing clouds of peace.

CHAPTER FOURTEEN

'HOPE, THANK GOODNESS, where have you been?' Bianca hurried anxiously towards her, her red hair curling loosely round her face, her green eyes, despite their disturbed glitter, still bearing a tall-tale trace of languor. Could Bianca see the soft shadows of pleasure still lingering in *her* eyes as easily as she could see them in hers, Hope wondered as she calmed her friend's anxieties.

'I met an old friend, we got talking,' she shrugged. 'You know how it is... In the end I decided I might as well stay for what was left of the night.'

Bianca was regarding her in puzzled fascination. 'There's something different about you I...' Hurriedly, before she had time to divine exactly what it was, Hope said teasingly:

'And about you, too. Where's Dale?' As she had anticipated Bianca's pale skin flushed guiltily:

'Oh Hope, just wait until I tell you...'

Thanks goodness Bianca was too wrapped up in her own very evident happiness to question her too closely, Hope thought as she dropped into a nearby chair. On waking this morning and finding herself in bed with Alexei her initial thought had been one of self-disgust for the way she had acted. She had left Alexei's villa without disturbing him, dreading the arrival of her taxi lest it woke him.

What on earth would he think when he woke up? Her mouth twisted bitterly—he at least had the excuse of his drugged state, and the fact that it was perfectly acceptable for a man to appease his desire with whatever woman happened to be available and willing, without losing any of his self-respect. For her it was different. Alexei had wanted her, and she, in her hunger and need, had deliberately refused to listen to any promptings of conscience or good sense.

'Hope, you haven't heard a word I've said,' Bianca complained. 'You arrive back at seven o'clock in the morning...'

'And find you on your way downstairs wearing a very fetching silk peignoir,' Hope chuckled.

'I was just going to get...' She broke off flushing as both of them heard Dale call quite distinctly:

'Bianca, my love, do hurry up, this bed's too cold and empty without you.'

'I, er, we...'

'You're still rehearsing that sex-scene?' Hope queried with mock innocence, laughing when she saw Bianca's indignant expression.

'I'll tell you all about it later,' Bianca agreed with a grin, adding, 'well, not quite all. We were worried sick when you didn't come back last night. At least, I was. Dale seemed to think it might all have been part of a deliberate ploy, and you, my chaperone as well.'

'There comes a time in every girl's life when the last thing she wants is a chaperone,' Hope teased. 'That's something every Victorian mama knew.'

For Dale and Bianca's sake, she tried to put her own unhappiness to one side, not wanting to mar what, for them, must be a very special time, although it was very hard, and she was glad to escape to the privacy of her own room where she could be alone with her pain without the added anguish of having to hide it from them.

They were both full of plans when they eventually joined Hope and Niko on the beach. 'Marriage first,'

Dale said firmly, the look in his eyes when they rested on
Bianca's flushed and happy face making Hope ache with
pain. When had Alexei ever looked at her like that, as
though she was everything he wanted out of life?

'When the series is over I'm going to retire from acting,' Bianca told Hope as they all trekked back to the
villa for lunch. 'Once, I enjoyed it, but just recently, since
Niko's arrival on the scene, I've begun to think there are
more important things in life, things that I'm missing. I
guess those early years do count for a lot, after all, and I
am still what the Sisters intended I would be, for all my
rebellion.'

They were just on the point of finishing lunch when the
doorbell rang. Jeanne went to answer it, returning to announce that there was a gentleman wishing to see Hope.
'Someone to see me? Perhaps it's Roy,' Hope murmured
to Bianca.

'Show him in here, Jeanne,' Dale instructed, his hand
reaching out to touch Bianca's briefly. 'While he's here
we'll give him a heart attack and tell him our good news.'
But it wasn't Roy who followed Jeanne into the sunny
dining room, it was Alexei. Dale, of course, recognised
him, but Bianca, who had never seen him, looked in bewilderment from Dale's shuttered face to Hope's pale
one, until Dale said curtly, 'Comte Alexei.'

Alexei's response was equally brief. 'Hope, I should
like to talk to you.'

What could he possibly want to talk about, Hope
wondered achingly, unless it was to tell her that last night
was just one of those things that happened and she wasn't
to place any undue importance on it.

'I don't think we've anything to say, Alexei,' she managed calmly. 'I hope your headache is gone, although I
still don't believe cognac and those pills you took were a
healthy combination.' There, that should let him off the
hook. She couldn't make it any plainer that she knew

where to lay the blame for his uncharacteristic behaviour. A little to her surprise, his mouth thinned, and he glanced impatiently, almost arrogantly at Dale.

'Dale, I think the Comte wants to talk to Hope alone,' Bianca murmured hesitantly, just catching Hope's brief negating shake of her head too late. Niko, as though sensing the tense atmosphere engulfing the adults, moved in his cot, giving a protesting cry, and stretching out his arms towards Bianca. Hope could see Alexei following the movement, and her blood started to roar in her veins.

'Oh Niko, hush.' Acting quickly, Bianca lifted him out of his chair, settling him in her arms, her prompt action making Hope shiver with reaction for what might have happened if she had obeyed her own instincts and picked up her baby. Surely Alexei could see the resemblance between himself and the child? Nerving herself to look at him, she saw that he was studying Niko, a frown furrowing his forehead.

'Hope.'

'Please, Alexei.' Her voice almost broke over the words. 'Please go... I don't want to talk about it.' Tears stung her eyes. How could he come here like this to humiliate her? Surely he remembered enough about her to know that she wasn't going to embarrass him by making a mistake over what had motivated him last night? He had wanted her, he said, and she knew he had been speaking the truth, but want was all he felt for her, want and a certain amount of guilt.

'Alexei, please go.' She stood up, pushing her chair back shakily, almost running towards the door. 'You and I have nothing to talk about... I...'

'I think you'd better leave.' That was Dale, speaking calmly but purposefully, and Hope was thankful to leave him to deal with the situation as she fled to her bedroom, dashing the stinging tears from her eyes as she closed the door behind her.

As she dropped shakily into a chair, she found that she was holding her breath, waiting to hear the sound of Alexei's car leaving. When it eventually came, she let out a husky sigh of relief.

'Hope.' Bianca was tapping softly on her door, her voice hesitant. 'Hope, honey, are you all right? Can I come in?'

'The door isn't locked, Bianca,' she called out wearily, correctly reading the uncertain expression in her friend's eyes as she walked in, still holding Niko. 'It's all right, I'm not going to burst into tears. It hurts too much for that,' she added with a truthful grimace.

'It was Alexei you were with last night?' Bianca sat down on the edge of her bed, putting Niko on the floor where he started trying to crawl, trying to drag himself upwards by clutching on to the fringe of the bedspread. Deftly separating the small star-shaped hand from the fringe, Hope nodded her head.

'Yes, I bumped into him by accident in a bar. What happened afterwards was inevitable, I suppose, given his physical condition and my love...' Her throat felt raw with pain.

'He seemed very anxious to speak to you.'

'To make sure I hadn't read anything more than I should have done into what had happened last night. No, Bianca.' She shook her head, seeing the words hovering on her friend's lips. 'In the long run it's far kinder to let me face the truth now. Alexei doesn't love me, and he never will love me.'

'But he wants you. He does, Hope,' she insisted. 'Dale and I both saw that. He asked me about Niko,' she added, instantly saying soothingly when she saw Hope's panicky expression. 'No... No, I don't think he's guessed. He just asked me what his name was.'

'What did you tell him?' Hope's mouth was dry as she remembered telling Alexei about the other man in her life—Niko.

'Just Niko,' Bianca reassured her, misunderstanding the reason for her tension. 'He looked at me rather oddly, and then said that he seemed an attractive child. I got the distinct impression that if it hadn't been for Dale, he would have followed you up here and forced you to listen to him. Does he still believe that Dale and you are lovers?'

'I suppose so. Yes, he must do because he warned me about you.' Hope managed a husky laugh, but Bianca was frowning.

'Hope, I don't want to worry you, but Dale and I are planning to marry just as soon as we can. However quiet we keep the ceremony, it's bound to make the papers, and how do you think your Alexei will react then?'

'Oh, he'll probably have left Cannes by then,' Hope told her, refusing to allow herself to think about the consequences of Dale and Bianca's marriage. What did it matter if Alexei guessed that she had lied, anyway? The only reason he had come this morning was to make sure that she fully understood the position.

'He told me that he was thinking of getting married,' she suddenly heard herself saying to her horror, her voice quivering with pain. 'He feels he should have a son—an heir to inherit.' And then, to her consternation, she was crying, ugly wrenching sobs that seemed to tear into her, and Bianca's arms were round her shoulders, her voice murmuring soothing words in her ear.

'HOPE, DO YOU FEEL like any supper?'

Darkness had fallen while she had been asleep. Her head still pounded from the after-effects of her emotional outburst; a storm which had swept through her, leaving her drained and weak, without lifting the burden of her pain.

'What time is it?' Hope glanced at her wrist watch. It was just gone nine. 'Yes... yes... Look, I'll get up. You and Dale ought to be out celebrating—alone.' She pulled on her robe, sliding out of bed. 'Oh Bianca, what must you think of me, spoiling your big day with such a stupid scene.'

'Honey, you didn't spoil it, I just wish there could be a happy ending for you, too. Are you sure you want to get up?'

'Positive,' Hope responded with more firmness than she felt. It would be all too easy to give in to the inertia stealing over her, to lie there in her bed, drifting into a make-believe world where there was no pain, no past and no future. But she had Niko to think of, for his sake she must be strong.

'Now you go and get yourself all dolled up, I'm sure Dale's dying to show you off.' She could tell from Bianca's blush that she had guessed correctly, and although she wouldn't have hurt her friend by saying so, Hope was glad when they left. The special glowing happiness of people in love acted on her raw nerves like acid, burning into her with bitter pain.

It was when they had gone that Jeanne came in from the kitchen carrying a large bouquet of flowers. 'For you,' she told Hope, holding them admiringly, 'they arrived when you were resting. Shall I put them in your room?' There was a card with them, and it seemed to burn her tense fingers as Hope studied Alexei's familiar writing, reluctant to open the small envelope and see what was inside, fearful of releasing a Pandora's box of emotions inside herself.

The note was brief, but it brought the sting of colour to her face, nevertheless. 'Thanks for last night—you were very generous,' Alexei had written. 'My apologies

if my appearance this morning proved embarrassing. You
should remind your lover that sauce for the goose is sauce
for the gander.'

Meaning that as Dale, or so Alexei thought, was involved with both herself and Bianca, he could hardly
object if she also took other lovers. With a shiver of dis-
taste that surprised the waiting maid, Hope thrust the
bouquet away, sickened by Alexei's assumption that she
would behave in such a way, reducing the act of love between two people to a casual game, with points gained for
scoring off one another.

Much to Hope's relief she heard nothing more from
him, although she did glimpse him one night in the Carlton bar, a dazzling brunette on his arm, her luscious
curves openly accentuated by the dress she was wearing.
'That's Carla Pervali, the Italian fashion designer,'
Bianca whispered to her, following the direction of her
glance, 'she's something of a prominent socialite, very
much an advocate of *la dolce vita.*'

Bianca's film had won an award for its screenplay and
Bianca herself was awarded a 'Best Actress' accolade,
which she said mockingly was exactly the right note on
which to end her career. To see Dale and Bianca together was an unending source of pain. Of course she was
glad that they had finally been able to tell one another of
their feelings, but Hope felt an unnecessary third whenever they insisted she accompany them, and had already
suggested that she fly home ahead of schedule as soon as
they were married, allowing them to have the villa to
themselves. How ironic that she should have been in-
strumental in their achieving happiness but totally unable to secure her own.

'It's not necessary,' Dale told her firmly, 'besides, I
already know where we're going to spend our very brief
honeymoon.'

'Where?' Bianca demanded, lifting her eyes from the
wedding dress designs she had been studying. At first she
had demurred when Dale said he wanted her to wear
white, after all they had been lovers ever since the night
Hope had seen Alexei, but Dale was quick to remind her
that he was her first lover, 'and your last,' he added on a
husky breath. 'I want you to wear white, *cara,* just as I
want to take you to the village where my father was born,
for our honeymoon. It is very quiet, very uncivilised . . .'

'Perhaps our first child will be conceived there,' Bianca
murmured back, her eyes glowing softly as she smiled up
at him, 'it will strengthen his Italian heritage.'

'You are so sure we will have a boy, and without asking my views on the subject,' Dale teased. 'Perhaps I
should prefer a girl, like her mama.'

As Bianca had predicted, although they had planned
a quiet wedding, news had leaked out and by the time
Bianca's car reached the church there was quite a crowd.
Dale had got permission for them to be married in France
and not just in a civil ceremony.

'This is where I want to make my vows to you,' Hope
had heard Dale tell Bianca, and she felt a huge lump
practically close up her throat as she followed Bianca inside the ancient church, pain tearing at her body, envy
sharp and acid.

As Bianca's only attendant Hope followed her down
the aisle, seeing the look of adoration Dale gave her as he
turned and saw his bride coming towards him. Roy stood
uneasily at his side, press-ganged into giving Bianca away.

'As her agent, I'm surprised you don't demand your
ten per cent from me,' Dale had joked when they told
Roy the news, but Roy had been too depressed by the fact
that Bianca intended to give up work to pay much attention.

The service was a simple one, but still very beautiful,
the scent of the massed flowers round the altar and

throughout the church hanging on the air like a benison. She would never forget this day, Hope thought achingly as she followed Bianca back outside. All her life it would serve as a reminder of the difference between a man's love and his lust.

A little against Bianca's will, Dale had insisted that their reception be held at the Carlton. 'It will save one hell of a lot of fuss later,' he urged her. 'As it is, the Hollywood press will think we've cheated them. You and I can slip away early, and I bet they won't even notice we're gone, in the crush.'

It was almost predicted—the guests, soothed by the excellent food and wine, responded cheerfully to the toasts. Bianca looked as every bride should look, staying calm and smiling while flash bulbs exploded in front of her. 'This will make the gossip page of every paper from here to LA.' Hope heard one reporter tell another; and then she was going, helping Bianca to slip discreetly away upstairs to the room where she was to change into her going-away outfit.

'Dale has arranged for a car to be waiting for us outside. We're using the back entrance.' She pulled a wry face. 'Sounds very dramatic, doesn't it. Will you be okay?' she asked Hope, embracing her emotionally. 'Oh, honey, I can't thank you enough for all you've done. Dale told me it all. How you told him how I felt...'

Hope was glad that her friend knew what she had done. 'I did have second thoughts,' she admitted, 'but I was sure that Dale loved you too, yet I know that really I ought not to have meddled.'

'But I, for one, am very glad that you did,' Dale announced, strolling into the room. He had a small jeweller's box in his hand, which he handed to Hope. 'For you, Hope,' he smiled, 'from both of us. Are you ready, Mrs Lawrence?' he asked Bianca softly, his arm sliding round her shoulders. 'Because I warn you, if you

aren't...' He broke off when Hope gasped her astonished pleasure at the beautiful sapphire and diamond
earrings inside the box. 'Oh Dale, Bianca,' she protested, 'these are far too much. You shouldn't...'

'Yes, we should,' Bianca argued firmly. 'Please accept them, Hope. There isn't enough money in the world
to show you how much we appreciate all you've done for
us. You're the best friend either of us are likely to have,
and when you take up residence in the Valley, you needn't
think you're going to escape us. Dale's thinking of giving up producing. His father isn't getting any younger,
but he wants to extend the vineyard, buy more land. With
Dale's help he can do it, and like you I don't want my
children brought up in a Hollywood environment. I
wonder if, when we're househunting, I'll find myself
stranded for the night, with a handsome stranger,' she
teased Dale, biting back a small sound of dismay as she
saw Hope's pale face. 'Oh Hope, I'm sorry...I...'

'It doesn't matter. I'm the one who's being silly. I can't
spend the rest of my life pining away like a Victorian
maiden every time something reminds me of Alexei.' She
reached up, kissing first Bianca, then Dale. 'You'd better go,' she warned them, 'before the press get wind of
what you're planning.' She was glad they were leaving. It
was becoming increasingly difficult to witness their
shared happiness, the love that bathed them both, its aura
unmistakable.

The villa felt very empty without Dale and Bianca, and
to make matters worse there was that flat feeling one often has after the fuss and furore of a celebration has died
down. Niko was asleep in bed, and having tried several
times to involve herself in a book she had picked up outside their local *marchand de tabac,* Hope put it down and
wandered aimlessly around the elegant room. The shrill
sound of the doorbell, especially as she hadn't been expecting it, scraped disturbingly across her painful nerves.

She had given Jeanne the night off, and she walked slowly into the hall, half expecting to be faced with a particularly determined reporter, intent on getting an 'exclusive' story.

'Hope, so you *are* here.' Alexei's grim voice, coupled with his unexpected appearance, brought her fumbling movements with the security chain to a halt. Her weak, 'Alexei, what...'

'I saw the pictures and write up of the wedding in the evening papers and thought you might be able to use a little company. Can I come in?'

He *was* in now and there didn't seem to be much she could do about it.

'Am I in any way to blame for this, Hope?' He reached out, curving strong fingers along her jaw, tilting her face upwards so that he could search her expression, and for a moment Hope thought he was asking her if he were to blame for the pallor of her skin and the haunted, aching pain she frequently glimpsed in her own eyes, but she quickly realised her mistake when Alexei said forcefully, 'If I had thought this would be the result, I would never have called that morning. Is that why he married her, Hope, to punish you for staying with me?'

'Alexei!' What on earth was she going to say to him?

'Or did he marry her because she's a star? Because he knows that series of his will collapse without her? Did she pressure him into choosing between you, Hope?'

'Alexei, is was nothing like that.' Her voice sounded shaky and uncertain but she felt compelled to tell him the truth. 'They love one another—Dale loves Bianca, that's why he married her.' And then to her chagrin tears welled painfully in her eyes and started to roll helplessly down her cheeks. She tried to stem the flow, but Alexei beat her to it, extracting an immaculate handkerchief from his pocket and grasping her chin, firmly mopping up the dampness.

'Little one, he isn't worth it. No man is worth such pain.' His fingers caressed her jaw, moving upwards to catch another sparkling drop as it fell from her lashes. 'Hope, please. Please don't. I can't bear to see you cry.' His arms came round her and Hope submitted weakly to her heart's urging to accept the comfort he was offering her, even though he wasn't aware of the cause of her anguish. She could feel his breath against her forehead, his fingers sliding along her jaw, tilting her chin, his eyes looking deeply into hers, his muttered imprecation as he saw her fresh tears making her shiver with the intensity of anger that it implied.

'*Mon Dieu*, I have always thought of myself as a civilised man, but I could quite willingly kill him for this. Does he know what he has thrown away? Does he really, honestly prefer that redheaded witch? Doesn't he realise how unique and very special you are?'

Strange words from a man who had quite easily managed to turn his back on her, Hope reflected dizzily, quivering with emotional reaction as he bent his head. She longed to reach up and stroke her fingers through the familiar darkness of his hair, feel the warmth of his mouth brushing across her skin, touching her damp eyelids, holding her with the same tenderness she remembered from the first time he had made love to her.

'No, don't pull away from me,' she heard him murmur, as she tried to apply brakes of caution to her rioting emotions. 'We are bound together, you and I, in a very special way. Even though you may not realise it, what we have shared unites us in a way that few people know. I have revealed more of my deepest feelings and thoughts to you than anyone else. You sacrificed something of yourself for me when you told Sir Henry that we were lovers, and that is something I can never forget.

'Let me help you now, Hope, as you helped me then. Don't try to push me away from you. I know how much

it hurts—I know all about the agony of unrequited love.'
He raised his head, and for a moment Hope saw such a
look of grim comprehension in his eyes that she could
willingly have tortured Élise for not loving him enough
to put him before wealth. 'Come, there is no shame in
sharing your pain with me. I want to help you, Hope.'

Somehow they were on the sofa, her face buried
against Alexei's shoulder, finding warmth and reassurance in the thud of his heart beneath her palm, although
it seemed to race faster than she remembered—unless of
course it was matching its rhythm to her own unsteady
pulse-beat which was reacting already to his proximity.

'I half expected that you wouldn't be here,' Alexei told
her. One arm was pinning her against his body, the other
stroking gently through her tumbled hair.

'You thought I might have hit the town, trying to
drown my sorrows?' she asked wryly, remembering the
smell of cognac on his breath and the brooding darkness
in his eyes the night she had come across him in the bar.

'Chiding me, little one? I wasn't drunk that night. Oh,
I had had something to drink, but nothing like as much
as I suspect you imagined. Was it because of what happened between us that he married Bianca?'

'Not entirely.' She had to be careful. She so longed to
tell him the truth, let her defences down and tell him how
she loved him, but what good would it do? It would embarrass him and humiliate her. He had come to her as a
friend, and there was some compensation to be found in
the discovery that he thought enough of her to come to
her at this time to comfort her. And after all, it was true
that her absence that fateful night had helped to cement
the new relationship between Dale and Bianca.

'I should never have come here that day, but when I
woke up and found you gone I was concerned for you. I
hadn't intended that that should happen, but I cannot in
all honesty say that I regret it.'

'Dale would have married Bianca whether I had spent the night with you or not,' Hope told him gently. 'There is no need for you to feel any guilt on that score, Alexei.' His fingers had moved through her hair and were caressing her nape, their touch almost hypnotic, inducing a pleasant lethargy and a longing to stretch her body voluptuously against him.

'Hope, do you know what it does to me to have you in my arms?' The timbre of his voice changed, his touch no longer comforting but arousing, the tension she could feel emanating from his body, stirring her senses. 'I must go,' he said thickly. 'I don't know what it is about you, *ma belle*, that undermines my strongest intentions. Hope.' He ground her name against her palm as she raised her hand to place her fingertips against his lips to silence him, the rough probe of his tongue against her skin splintering through her defences, her need for him a wild, turbulent tide inside her. 'Hope, don't look at me like that. I must go, before I forget that I came here as your friend.'

'Alexei, don't go. I want you to stay, please.'

Green eyes looked into dark violet. 'Do you know what you are saying? If I stay . . .'

If he stayed it would be as her lover, Hope knew that, but she no longer cared that it was only desire that motivated him. She would have tomorrow and all the tomorrows after that for regret.

'Never did I think I would sink so low as to allow myself to be used to replace another man,' Alexei muttered huskily, turning to her, releasing her hand to place it against his heart. 'Feel how you make it race. You are dangerous to me, *mon petit,*' he drawled with a brief return of his normal sardonic humour. 'It is not good that you make my heart thud like a drum.'

'Alexei.' His mouth was almost on hers, his tongue stroking deliberate enticement against the tremulous curves of her lips as she said his name. 'Alexei, please love me.' She saw his eyes darken as he moved towards her, crushing her back against the sofa as though her soft plea had awakened something elemental and fiercely hungry inside him. Her silk dress fell away from her body as he slid down the zip, his eyes moving hotly over her exposed skin.

'These,' he touched her breasts lightly, unfastening her bra before cupping them with both hands, 'are fuller, and here—' his hands moved to her hips, moulding the fragile bones '—you are thinner. I thought every inch of your body was ingrained on my mind, but that last time you felt different. Will you think it very foolish of me if I admit that I cannot bear to think of any other man touching you? That was why I was so angry before on the island. I could not endure to think of you giving yourself to that... boy.' He made a brief explosive sound in his throat, opening his eyes wide and looking straight into hers. 'I was jealous,' he said simply.

'But you had no...' No reason to be, she was about to say, but Alexei grimaced wryly and interrupted:

'...no right to be? I know that, Hope, but that was the way I felt about you. I know I didn't have any right to have those feelings; that...' She didn't want to hear him explaining yet again how guilty he felt about her, how responsible for her he was, Hope thought bitterly. If he couldn't tell her that he loved her, then she would prefer his silence, and she reached up towards him, deftly unfastening his shirt, shivering as she placed her palms against the familiar warmth of his chest, her voice low and unsteady as she pleaded, 'Don't talk about it, Alexei, just make love to me, please...'

Just for a moment she thought she glimpsed anguish in his eyes, but it was quickly gone, his mouth hard and sure as it closed over hers, his fingers biting into her shoulders as he deliberately fed their mutual hunger, quickly shedding his clothes and then kneeling beside her, his fingers hard and warm against her instep, the deliberately lingering caress he placed there followed by the rough warmth of his tongue.

'Like this, Hope? Is this how you want me to touch you?' His whispered words shivered across her skin, her body responding overwhelmingly to his touch, to his sure knowledge of how to please her, teasing her sometimes when she tried to touch him. The game turned swiftly to reality when her fingers stroked along his thigh, and Alexei wasn't able to control his fierce reaction to her, cupping her breasts and savouring their firm roundness, his tongue reactivating the burning, throbbing ache she remembered from the past. Unable to stop herself from biting deeply into his skin, Hope barely caught his thick, muttered exclamation of pleasure, his thumb rubbing abrasively against one tautly erect nipple, the other taken deeply inside his mouth, burgeoning into a full hardness which drew another satisfied murmur of pleasure from deep inside his throat.

His hands stroked seductively over her body, setting it on fire wherever they touched, her own hands rejoicing in the surge of his body beneath her touch as he responded to every caress. Hope mutely implored for his possession, touching and kissing him with a rapt absorption which she knew came perilously close to revealing exactly how she felt about him. The very drift of her fingertips against his skin, followed by the lingering caress of her lips, was almost an act of worship; a true adoration of his physical perfection. His response was unmistakable, more overwhelming than she could ever remember it being before, his unhidden shuddering pleasure when she touched him, leading her on to further intimacies. She delighted in his complete physical surrender to his need for her, desire sharpening and tightening in waves inside her body as he cried out in urgent hunger, perspiration springing from his pores.

He was the one who heard Niko first, tensing in her arms, asking sharply, 'What's that?'

Hope listened and then caught the fractious wail of her son. Poor Niko, he would be hungry. How could she have forgotten about him? 'It's Niko, he must be hungry.' She sat up, reaching awkwardly for her clothes, feeling embarrassed and vulnerable now that the spell of mutual passion was broken. 'I . . . I'd better go to him.'

Alexei was dressing too. 'Niko? Do you mean they have left you here with that child? What's happened to you, Hope? I thought you had more pride. Don't you care at all about yourself? Your lover marries someone else and she leaves you to look after her child. Is he the father? Is that why they married?'

'No,' she told him truthfully, shaken by the bitter anger she could see darkening his eyes. It hurt to hear him speak like that about her. 'Unlike you, I don't believe Dale would marry just for the sake of a child.'

She could see her barb had gone home, but somehow the pain rebounded on her and she said sharply, 'That woman I saw you with in the Carlton bar, is she a candidate for the position of your son's mother?'

'And if she is?' The green eyes were guarded now, aloof, warning her not to intrude.

Hope's lips tightened. 'Excuse me, I must go and get Niko. I'm sure you can see yourself out. I'm sorry you didn't get what you came for. What's the matter, Alexei, is Carla holding out for a wedding ring? Is that why you had to come to me?' She was hitting out wildly now, hurting herself more than she was hurting him, impelled by God alone knew what folly to persist until she was torn and broken on the spears of rejection she could see behind the guarded darkness of his eyes.

She fled upstairs without waiting to hear his response, calming Niko who was crying fitfully. His cheek was flushed where a new tooth was coming, and, as always,

overwhelmed with love for her son, Hope picked him up
and carried him back downstairs, holding him soothingly against her.

The sight of Alexei standing in the room, dark trousers moulding the hard length of his legs, his shirt open
at the neck revealing the fine curling hairs, his expression unreadable, stunned her.

'So this is the other man in your life. The Niko you told
me you loved.'

He *had* remembered that!

'Yes,' she said curtly, unaware of the protective way in
which her hands curled round the child in her arms.

'Is this how you intend to live the rest of your life,
Hope?' he demanded harshly. 'Loving another woman's
husband and child? You *do* love him, don't you?'

'Yes,' she admitted, glancing into Niko's flushed face,
touching his cheek with a gentle finger.

'You should have children of your own.' His eyes
seemed to darken explosively and for a moment a tremor
of reaction shivered through her, then he was turning on
his heel, picking up his discarded jacket, heading for the
front door.

She didn't try to stop him. What was the point? They
couldn't go back to that moment before Niko disturbed
them, and it was better this way, she told herself when she
locked the door behind him. For a few moments she had
suffered from a particularly acute brand of madness, but
it was over now; sanity was restored. She had her pride
and her self-respect so why was she crying with pain and
emptiness for all that she didn't have?

'HOPE, YOU'VE GOT everything looking so beautiful. I
can't believe how much you've accomplished in such a
short space of time. Wait until you see how much we've
got to do.' Over her head, Hope saw Bianca and Dale
exchange loving glances. It was three months since she

had left Cannes; three months during which she had concentrated all her energies on her new home, living quietly there with Niko, watching him grow. Already he was adept at crawling, disappearing the moment her back was turned, his body as firm and round as a plump peach.

'At least you've managed to find somewhere, without applying for a divorce,' Hope countered with a grin. Dale and Bianca had had several voluble arguments about the type of house they wanted, but at last they seemed to have settled on the right one.

'Mmm...this is a good photo of the two of you,' Dale commented. He had been glancing through a magazine and opened it to show Bianca and Hope the photograph he meant. She had been asked to feature in an article about people who appeared in advertisements, and with Helen's and Roy's permission had reluctantly agreed. The photograph was a good one, the photographer having caught an unguarded expression of love and tenderness as she looked down at Niko, gazing back at her from her lap.

'Looks like a little angel, doesn't he,' Bianca chuckled, eyeing the 'little angel' cautiously as he made a determined path towards her, grinning mischievously. 'He's growing so much, Hope, and he's very, very like...' she broke off as Dale shot her a warning look, but it was too late.

Hope smiled wanly, 'Like Alexei? More so with every day that passes, I sometimes think, especially now that he's got so much hair.' For a moment pain showed in her eyes and Dale changed the subject quickly.

'Helen's thrilled with the new advert,' he commented. 'Roy was telling me about it the other day. It's due to go out next month, isn't it?'

Deftly steering the conversation into less emotive waters, he began to talk about his own and Bianca's plans for the future. 'The series ends next month. When it starts up again Bianca's part will be written out. I believe she's going to meet a nasty end as befits a scheming beautiful divorcee.' He grinned at his wife. 'And from then on she'll be at my mercy, wholly dependent on me!'

'Huh, that's what you think,' Bianca threatened humorously. 'Dale's father's managed to purchase some more land, and it looks like I'm not going to see an awful lot of my new husband until it's produced its first crop of grapes. Every day he's out among the vines . . .'

'But I come home every night,' Dale reminded her with a fake leer.

'Yes, and fall fast asleep.'

'Have you heard anything more from Alexei?' Bianca questioned Hope when Dale went outside to check on a leaky gutter Hope had discovered during a recent rainstorm. 'Dale would tell me I shouldn't ask, but I'm worried about you, honey. You look so pale and drained. Don't you think you ought to write to him—tell him the truth. I know and understand why you feel you can't. You love the guy, and if, as you say, knowing about Niko will make him want to marry you, I can understand your doubts—but Hope, would it really be so much worse than what you've got now? You're not the sort of woman who'll ever opt for second-best, so that means you'll be depriving Niko of a father-figure; and not just that. He is Alexei's son,' she said gently. 'How will he feel in years to come when he asks you about his father and you have to tell him that Alexei has married someone else so that he can have an heir?'

Did Bianca really think she hadn't thought about all these things, Hope wondered rebelliously when her friends had gone. Didn't she think she had agonised over Niko's future? Was she being selfish? Was she putting herself; her stubborn pride; her fear that Alexei would capitalise on her love to get Niko, once he knew the truth, in the way of Niko's best interests? He lacked for nothing financially, and never would. But she was denying him a very important part of his heritage. He was Alexei's son; so very much like him that Hope suspected he would probably have inherited more of Alexei's turbulent French and Russian ancestry than her own calmer, English one.

She paced tensely in the room she had decorated with such love and care, barely seeing the attractive terracotta and cream décor; the warmth of the patterned sofa and toning curtains, the plain elegant cream carpet, and the large open fireplace she had insisted on keeping, visualising its warmth when the weather turned colder. All she could see was Alexei's face on the last occasion they had been together; all she could feel was the memory of his skin against her fingers; the desire and rage of wanting only he could arouse. He wanted her; she was honest enough to admit that, and he had the grim determination of character, the resoluteness, to marry her and keep her if he thought their marriage was for the greater good. But not without love, her heart protested achingly, surely not without love?

Two days later when she was tidying up she came across the magazine Dale had been studying, and without really knowing why flipped through it looking for the photograph of herself with Niko. The photographer had been so pleased with it he had insisted on providing her with a framed replica. Once the Beverly Hills mothers saw it, he proclaimed, he would have more work than he knew how to handle. The madonna look was what he had termed the look in her eyes as she watched Niko, and she smiled softly, frowning as she saw the jagged edge of paper where the full-page photograph had been, with its caption, 'Hope, and son, Nikolai Alexander, the mother and child who feature in the "Baby World" advertisements.'

Someone had ripped it out, but who? She tried to think who might have had a reason for taking the picture and then shrugged wearily. Did it really matter? Perhaps Emily Landers, who came in occasionally to clean for her and mind Niko, had taken it to show her family. She doted on Niko and had often admired Hope's framed photograph of the two of them. The phone rang and she went to answer it, dismissing the missing piece of paper, listening patiently as Bianca explained the reason for her unexpected call.

'Our first ever dinner party. The house won't be finished, but we feel like a celebration. You will come, won't you? Roy's coming, and a few of the old Hollywood crowd.'

'Yes, I'll be there.' As she hung up Hope fought back a feeling of envy. Bianca was so lucky, married to the man she loved; a man who was deeply, obviously in love with her. Bianca was right, she couldn't accept second-best, however sensible it might be to do so, and anyone other than Alexei would be second-best. With a small sound of pain she tried to concentrate on her chores, reminding herself that it was useless hankering after the past.

CHAPTER FIFTEEN

'WELL, HOW DO YOU think I'm doing in my new role?' The dinner party was over, and Hope was helping Bianca in her kitchen. The other guests had left, but both Bianca and Dale had pressed her to stay.

'I should say it's definitely a starring one,' Hope laughed. 'The food was delicious.'

'Dale's mother has been teaching me. Twelve months ago if you'd told me I'd have all this, I'd never have believed it. Hope,' she asked urgently, 'how are *you?*'

'Oh, you know, getting by.' She forced a quick grin, turning away before Bianca could guess at the effort it cost her to appear relatively light-hearted. Up until Niko's birth, her pregnancy had kept her going—that, and working for Bianca—but now there were long stretches at a time between ads when she had too much time on her hands, time to think, always about Alexei.

'Dr Friedman called the other day. He asked about you. I think he's quite smitten, you don't...'

She broke off when Hope shook her head decisively 'I like him, Bianca, but there's just nothing else there.' She looked up, smiling at Dale as he walked into the kitchen.

'Have you told her yet?' He put his arm round Bianca, pulling her against him, love and pride shining from his eyes as he looked down at her.

'I, er...' Seeing the look they exchanged Hope suddenly felt very excluded, an outsider staring in on a small, exclusive circle—a circle of love. 'Hope, I...we...we're having a baby,' Bianca managed, fighting back a grin. 'That's why I called Dr Friedman. Dale's like a dog with two tails.'

'Oh, Bianca, I'm so thrilled for you—for you both.' She smiled across at them, genuinely pleased by their news and yet unable to stop the feeling of anguished pain stealing through her body; the hurting, 'why couldn't this have been me' sensation that seemed to live alongside her these days. It was terrible to be so envious of Bianca and Dale, and it crossed her mind that it might be sensible to see a little less of them now. They inhabited a world she would never now enter, the world of happy married couples, families. She blinked back stinging tears, feeling angry with herself when she saw the pity and concern in Bianca's eyes.

'Oh, honey,' she murmured, coming across to her and hugging her warmly. 'Please don't. Hope, you can't go on like this, tearing yourself apart over Alexei. You do still love him, don't you.'

'Unfortunately, yes, but that doesn't mean I have to behave like a watering-can every time I see you. I'm thrilled about the baby.'

'We want you to be godmama, you will, won't you?'

'How about another cup of coffee before you go?' Dale called over his shoulder, but Hope shook her head. She wanted to be on her own, that seemed to be the only way she could come to terms with her pain. What was happening to her? Outwardly she had everything she could want; a healthy, lovely baby, a beautiful home, a job, money in the bank, and yet none of it was enough, and she was too wise, too intelligent to deceive herself that there would be someone else with whom she could share her life. Being with Alexei had taught her a good deal of self-knowledge, and even if she hadn't recognised it then, she knew now that she was, and always would be, a one-man woman.

'FRANCE, but Dale, that's impossible!' Hope stared across her kitchen table, her eyes opening wide, trying to come to terms with what Dale had just told her. 'I can't just simply drop everything and fly out there.'

'You're going to have to,' Dale told her calmly. 'That's where Helen wants the new advert shot. In fact, she's on her way over there right now. You know she has this thing about continental nursery furniture, and no wonder, considering the price of it.' He shook his head and grinned. 'Seven hundred dollars for a basinette, would you believe—I told Bianca it ought to be gold-plated at that price.' He bent down, picking up Niko who was grinning gummily up at him, fingers curled round the fabric of his pants. 'And it isn't as though you have to leave Niko behind. Far from it, you'll have to take him with you.'

'But France! And why? Dale, I don't fully understand it. We've never shot any of the ads anywhere but here in LA or at the shop?'

'Don't ask me—Helen's the only one who can supply explanations. I don't know what bee she's got in her bonnet. All I do know is that Roy phoned me and asked me to give you the news. He's flying down to Mexico to-day. One of his stars is holding up production of a movie they're shooting down there, and he could be tied up for some time. Helen spends quite a lot of time in France, doesn't she? Perhaps she wanted to use that farmhouse of hers as the setting for the next ad, the "country look" style of things. All I know is that you've got three days to get your act together and be on that flight.'

'I still don't understand it,' Hope complained to Bianca later in the day. Her friend had come by to pick up Dale, having dropped him off to talk to Hope, en route for Beverly Hills. 'I mean, why France?'

'I don't know, honey.' Bianca seemed slightly ill at ease, and Hope wondered if it was because of their last

meeting. She felt so guilty about breaking down in front
of her friends, and guessed that now Bianca felt embarrassed about enthusing about her coming baby in her
presence. She seemed tense and kept on glancing at Dale.
He, on the other hand, was perfectly relaxed, a glimmer
of something that could almost have been tender amusement in his eyes.

'Never mind understanding it,' he told her firmly. 'You
just be on that plane. Come to think of it, I'll drive you
there. You couldn't manage Niko and all your luggage,
and still concentrate on your driving. Another couple of
months and he'll be walking.'

'Umm, I think you're right,' Hope agreed, pride in the
glance she gave her small son. 'Dr Friedman says he's
quite advanced, very quick on the up-take.'

'All the mums say that,' Dale teased her. 'You ought
to listen to Bianca, she's taken to reading improving ma-
terial, because she's convinced that if she does, junior
here will turn out to be a genius.'

'Don't you dare make fun of me,' Bianca retaliated.
'It's a proven fact that the mental condition of the
mother during pregnancy does have an effect on her
baby.'

As she listened to their loving banter, Hope felt a re-
newal of the envy she always felt when she saw them together, and as though Bianca suddenly realised how she
felt, she broke off, pushing away the hand Dale had
placed against the rounded swell of her stomach. 'You
will go to France, won't you, Hope?'

'She doesn't have much option,' Dale broke in firmly.
'if she doesn't she breaks her contract.'

None of them were putting into words exactly why she
might not want to fly to France, Hope thought tiredly,
but they all knew the real reason. It was stupid to fear
that she might run into Alexei; surely the arm of coincidence couldn't possibly stretch that far, and she couldn't

spend the rest of her life avoiding situations which might cause her pain.

'Dale's right,' she said quietly. 'I don't really have much choice.' Surely the look of relief on Bianca's face was out of all proportion to the occasion? Unless perhaps her friends were anxious to get rid of her; her constant miseries must be casting a blight on their own happiness. Too proud to ask outright if she had guessed the truth, Hope listened to Bianca murmuring about what clothes she ought to take with her. 'It will be coming on for fall in Europe. You must take something warm.'

'Bianca, it's still only September.' The time of the grape harvest, she thought idly. Alexei would be very busy supervising events at his vineyard.

There was a lot to do and very little time in which to accomplish it all. Bianca and Dale helped, Bianca arriving one morning laden down with packages. 'A going-away present for you,' she announced, dumping them on Hope's sofa. 'Go on, have a look?' This morning there was a glowing aura about her friend, coupled with a nervous uncertainty which wasn't like her. Humouring her, Hope started to open the packages, her fingers stilling after she had displayed the contents of no more than the first two, her eyes accusing as she glanced from the expensive cobwebby silk and lace underwear to her friend's faintly flushed face. 'Well, it's ages since you've spent a dollar on yourself, honey. It's time you had something nice. Look on it as a kind of going-away present from Dale and me.'

'A going-away present?' Her eyebrows rose. 'The last time I had one of those was when I first left for the convent, and besides, this looks more like a trousseau.' She caught the deeper flush dyeing Bianca's cheeks as she looked up. 'Look, what's going on? Oh, I get it,' she said angrily. 'I should have guessed, it's a common syndrome among the happily-marrieds. I suppose you're trying to set me up for some sort of romance? You provide all the trimmings, and Mother Nature will do the rest, is that it? Whom am I supposed to dazzle with these, Bianca? Dr Friedman? Roy? Or some as yet unknown and unsuspecting Frenchman?'

'Why not try all three?' Bianca was laughing at her, unconcerned by her anger. 'Look, why get so uptight? Is it so strange that Dale and I want to see you happy? Remember what you did for us? Please take them, Hope. Like I said, you haven't spent a dime on yourself since you had Niko. It was Dale's idea as much as mine. Now, open the other boxes.'

Unwillingly, Hope did so, primming her lips over a sheer silk negligee with a matching nightdress, but totally unable to resist the allure of a soft cashmere sweater-dress in her favourite shade of grey. 'And then there's something else. You just stay there a moment.' Bemused, Hope watched Bianca go out to her parked car, returning with an enormous bag. 'I knew from the moment I bought this that it was a mistake, but it will look stunning on you. If you won't take it as a gift, then just have it on loan. Like I said, it will be fall in Europe and cold, and besides, you're a famous lady now, so you'll have to make an entrance.' She opened the bag and lifted out a full-length silver fox coat. 'Take it, try it on,' she urged a bemused Hope. 'If you don't like it you don't need to have it, but I promise you it's just taking up wardrobe space.'

Like someone in a dream, Hope slid the rich fur on to her shoulders, noticing absently how it emphasised the fairness of her hair and the dense colour of her eyes. 'It suits you.' Bianca spoke no less than the truth, holding her breath lest her friend refuse the gift she was offering. Dale had said... She shut her mind off from the worried conversations she had had with her husband recently. It was done now, there was no going back.

'Bianca, I couldn't possibly accept this,' Hope expostulated.

'Then just borrow it, believe me, if you do, you'll be saving me a fortune in cold storage and insurance fees. Like I said, I don't really know why I bought it, it doesn't suit me at all. Wear it when you travel, then you can make a real entrance in it.'

'Oh, yes, and who's going to see me?' Hope teased. '*I'm* not a famous actress!'

'Maybe not, but your face is very well-known, at least in LA,' Bianca reminded her. 'Oh, and by the way, Dale said to tell you he's organised the hotel and all the arrangements for you and Niko. You'll be met at the airport, and they're going to have a chauffeur-driven car standing by.'

'When will I see Helen?'

'Er...I guess she'll be in touch with you. I'm not quite sure where she is right now. At her farmhouse, I suppose.' With that Hope had to be content. It was unusual for Helen to alter the arrangements for filming the ad at such short notice. Would they use the normal film crew, or a French one? These and many other questions buzzed through Hope's mind as she tried to concentrate on packing hers and Niko's clothes. How long would they be staying in France? Where were they going to stay? It was annoying not knowing any details. To be on the safe side she packed a little of everything, from casual jeans right down to an elegant silk jersey evening dress, just in case she had to attend any formal functions.

As he had promised, Dale came to drive her to the airport. 'Bianca decided not to come with me,' he told Hope as he helped her carry her cases out to the waiting car. 'No, she's feeling fine,' he assured her in response to her anxious questions. 'Blooming, in fact. She just said to tell you that she hates airport goodbyes, and that to remember that we'll be thinking about you, and that we love you very much.'

It seemed a rather cryptic message, but Hope didn't dwell on it, concentrating on preventing Niko from climbing all over the back of Dale's elegant car.

'All ready?' When he set the powerful vehicle in motion Hope turned to glance at her small house. Why did she feel as though her departure was so portentous? She shivered suddenly, despite the warmth of Bianca's borrowed fox fur. Mist lay in soft clouds in the valley bottom, a sign that Bianca had been right when she predicted that fall was on the way, and Hope could see the pickers working in the vineyards as they drove past, the rich scent of the grapes mingling with the sharp tinge of autumn.

'It's going to be a good vintage this year,' Dale predicted.

'You feel it in your bones, do you?' Hope mocked him.

'No, but my father feels it in his,' he grinned back. 'And he's an expert.'

'I'll have to buy some of the new vintage, then,' Hope joked, 'and lay it down for Niko's twenty-first.' She chanced to glimpse Dale's face as he turned to glance at an intersection and was surprised by the grimness she saw there, her voice sharpening with anxiety as she asked, 'Dale, is something wrong?'

'Nothing at all, why should there be?'

'It was the way you looked.' She shivered again, holding Niko close. Why did she feel as though she were suddenly stepping into a strange and alien world? Why this sensation of prescience; of nerve-tingling hesitation?

'Too late for second thoughts now,' Dale told her, expertly swinging his car into the main stream of traffic on the freeway leading to the airport. 'Paris, here you come.'

He waited with her until they started boarding, kissing her quickly and affectionately, ruffling Niko's dark hair before unexpectedly lifting him from her arms and holding him for a moment.

'Courage, Hope,' he murmured softly. 'Remember always how much Bianca and I love you. How much we owe you, how we'd do anything not to hurt you.' He kissed her again briefly, and with tears stinging her eyes, Hope joined the other passengers boarding the large jet, trying not to let Dale's parting words reinforce her intuitive feeling that there was something he and Bianca were not telling her.

The flight was a dull one. Niko had a sky cot in which he promptly and very sophisticatedly went to sleep, thus leaving Hope free in theory to enjoy the expensive magazines Dale had bought for her, but in reality to grow more and more tense as she dwelt on her arrival on French soil. Pray God she didn't bump into Alexei. Why was it her vulnerability and longing for him seemed to increase rather than decrease? She didn't know the answer to that question.

Refusing lunch she ran mentally over Dale's arrangements. She would be met at the airport. A hire-car and chauffeur would be waiting for her, but to take her where? She had assumed she would be staying in Paris, but surely Helen didn't intend the advert to be set there? Feeling frustrated by her lack of information, Hope nibbled at her lower lip, oblivious to the glances of appreciation and curiosity she was getting from the other passengers.

On Bianca's insistence she had worn the new cashmere sweater-dress, its soft pearl-grey tones enhancing the texture and shading of Bianca's fox. Simple gold stud earrings were her only form of decoration, her hair confined to an elegant figure of eight at the nape of her neck. She was nineteen, still a girl, and yet she felt immeasurably older. Suppressing a sigh she tried to concentrate on her magazine and not think about that first flight with

Alexei and her decision to take whatever he could offer without dwelling on the future.

They were coming in to land, the plane rustling with pre-landing anticipation. Hope closed her eyes, not seeing the spread of Parisian rooftops below them. How would she recognise whoever was going to meet her? How would they recognise her? She tried not to panic, not to give in to the feeling that somehow she had been deserted, cast adrift by her friends and left to fend for herself.

The passport formalities were brief, Niko perfectly behaved as she collected her luggage, seating him in the cart with her cases, and trying not to burst with pride as she saw the other travellers admiring him. He really was a very striking little boy, his hair was now blue-black, the same colour as his father's, and his eyes were Alexei's, too. He was bright and alert, curious about everything that went on around him, watching round-eyed.

'Mademoiselle Stanford.' Hope tensed as she felt the hand on her arm, and heard the soft French voice. 'I am directed to meet you and take you to your car. I am Philippe Devereaux,' her companion introduced himself. 'Monsieur Lawrence instructed me to meet you. If you will come this way.'

He was somewhere in his mid-twenties, charming and very, very French. Was he the reason Bianca had insisted on her wearing her new dress and the fur, Hope wondered, feeling her spirits lift suddenly in merriment. Poor Bianca, charming though Philippe was, he was no Alexei!

'And this is your son, Nikolai? Yes?'

'Yes,' Hope agreed, smiling at him, feeling her earlier fears disappear like the mist in the valley under the warmth of the sun. 'Where am I staying, do you know?' She spoke to him in French almost automatically and was rewarded with an admiring smile.

'Ah yes, Monsieur Lawrence told me that you could speak our language. As to your hotel, I am afraid I do not know, but come, we shall find your car, and then your driver will take you there. Here it is.' He led the way to a gleaming, black Daimler, bending to indicate something to the driver, while Hope hesitated on the pavement, talking to Niko.

'You may safely leave anything to your driver,' Philippe assured her, walking to the back of the car to load her luggage. A panel of dark-tinted glass separated the front of the car from the back and all Hope could see through it was the vague outline of the driver's shoulders and the back of his uniform cap.

'So, you are both quite comfortable?' Quickly Philippe inspected the interior of the car, while Hope nodded her head. They had ample room for the two of them, and the car was unexpectedly fitted with a safety harness for Niko. Philippe helped her to secure him in it, and then wished her a warm 'goodbye'. The Daimler pulled swiftly away from the kerb and Hope lay back in her seat, closing her eyes as she massaged the taut muscles at the back of her neck. She still did not really care for flying. She glanced at Niko happily engrossed with the plastic toy she had given him. He tossed it on the floor and she bent to pick it up, knowing from experience that it was a game he could play for hours. When would she see Helen? She glanced at her watch. Not this evening, she hoped. The flight had left her tired and edgy, all she really wanted was a long soak in a warm bath and then the comfort of her hotel bed.

The interior of the car was quite hot, and gradually Hope found herself becoming drowsy. They were in a quarter of Paris she didn't recognise, probably a route their driver had taken to avoid the rush-hour traffic. She found her eyes closing and gave in to the temptation to keep them closed. No doubt her driver would wake her when they reached the hotel.

Hope wasn't sure what jolted her awake. One moment she had been quite deeply asleep, the next she was wide awake, glancing in puzzled alarm at the darkness beyond the Daimler's windows. Where were they? She could see absolutely nothing. She rapped on the darkened panel to attract the attention of their driver, but he either didn't hear her or he didn't want to hear, because he ignored her.

Forcing herself not to give in to panic, Hope tried to analyse the reason for the fear she was experiencing. Dale had arranged her car and driver, and she had been safely seen into it by Dale's representative, a young man who recognised her and knew hers and Niko's names. Besides, who on earth would want to kidnap her? But where was she? She glanced at her watch, blenching when she saw the time. It was four hours since the plane had landed. She rapped on the panel again, quelling her frustration when the driver made no move to turn round or acknowledge her.

Up ahead of them Hope could see the sight of a small town. Thank goodness, at least she might now be able to get a bearing on where they were. At her side Niko grizzled and she searched in the large totebag she had with her for a rusk to give him. Poor little scrap, he must be starving! Could it be that Helen expected her to join her at her farmhouse and that this was the reason for her silent journey through the countryside of France? It seemed the most logical explanation and feeling happier now that it had occurred to her, Hope watched Niko chew on his rusk, suddenly aware that they had reached the town and moreover that it was familiar to her. They swept down a narrow street, past several shops, and she caught the illuminated words, *L'Auberge de Beaune*.

Ice invaded her veins, a giant fist squeezing like a vice round her heart. Beaune! That meant they must be near Alexei's home. She shivered, suddenly cold despite the warmth of the car. What bitter act of fate had made Helen buy a property in this vicinity? They left the main road, and were back in dense, black countryside, only the occasional light from a farmhouse illuminating the stygian dark beyond the car. The road seemed to be climbing, the car picking up speed as though the driver sensed journey's end.

Niko had finished his rusk, and held out his sticky hands, laughing with delight as Hope sponged them, kissing each tiny digit. It was one of his favourite games, and Hope was suddenly overwhelmed with love for him. Niko. Alexei's son! She smiled at him and missed the left turn the car took, only aware of it when she glanced out and saw how the countryside had flattened out, up above them the only illumination in the vast darkness a fairytale castle floating on a sheet of dark water, its exterior warmly floodlit.

'No.' The hoarse protest was wrenched from her throat, her move towards the door instinctive, the catch failing to give way beneath her nerve-stricken fingers. The door was locked, and she had been tricked, trapped, Hope thought bitterly, forcing stinging tears back as she stared again at the *château*—Alexei's *château!* How could Dale and Bianca have done this to her? All too well she could understand now the worried looks she had seen them exchange; Bianca's almost feverish gaiety, alternating between bouts of deep troubled silence. Whose idea had it been to do this to her? She glanced at Niko, and tightened her lips, her body tensing as the car rattled over the familiar drawbridge and she heard the gate come thudding down behind them, imprisoning her once more.

The car had stopped, but Hope was in no hurry to get out. She had no need to question the driver now as to their destination. A door opened into the courtyard and Alexei walked out. He was wearing dark trousers and a white silk shirt, the breeze moulding the fine fabric to his chest. He looked towards the car and then started to walk across the courtyard.

The driver's door of the Daimler opened and her 'chauffeur' got out. Pierre, Hope recognised on a wave of bitterness. But of course, his faithful henchman was the one Alexei would choose for something like this. Any doubts she might have had as to Alexei's knowledge of her arrival vanished as he reached for her door and opened it, every movement saying far more than any words that he knew exactly who he would find in the car's interior.

'Hope.' He greeted her curtly, his eyes cold and hard, his expression withdrawn.

'Niko...' she protested when he helped her out, turning back to the car to get her little boy.

'I'll do it.' Deft fingers unfastened the constraining straps, Niko gazing solemnly up into the face of this man who he didn't yet know was his father. A lump lodged in the back of her throat as she saw the way Alexei studied Niko's features, but the mood was swiftly dispelled when he turned to her and said harshly:

'Come, we have already kept Father Ignacio waiting long enough. It is long past his supper time, and he grows weary.'

Father Ignacio? Hope's mind reeled, but Alexei wasn't giving her time to question him, Niko held in the crook of one arm, the other pinning Hope to his side, forcing her to match his swift, sure pace across the dim courtyard. Trying not to stumble, Hope stifled her worried questions, gasping with relief when they were inside the *château* and she was released from Alexei's punishing grip. 'Pierre will take Niko,' Alexei informed her, handing him over to the waiting manservant. 'Come with me.'

'Alexei . . .'

'I said come with me, Hope, I am not in any mood to be patient. Later, you may ask me as many questions as you like, now there are other matters to attend to. This way.' He led her down a narrow passage into a part of the *château* she had not seen before. Bare and empty their footsteps echoed over the dusty wooden floor, the corridor opening up into a small private chapel where a priest waited, dressed in ceremonial robes. It was like something out of a novel, and Hope glanced disbelieving at Alexei, half expecting him to tell her it was all some sort of macabre joke, but his fingers biting into her arms warned her against voicing her thoughts, his voice low as he paused by the entrance and said curtly:

'In a moment we shall enter the chapel and the good father will marry us. Any attempt to stop him, Hope, and I shall simply tell him that you are suffering from a nervous malady.'

'Alexei, you can't do this,' she protested despairingly, but he was already propelling her into the bare, cold chapel, sliding the fur off her shoulders with what might appear to an onlooker to be rare tenderness. Now she knew exactly why Bianca had insisted on her wearing her new dress. Oh Bianca, how could you do this to me? And you, Dale, how could you? It seemed as though it was another Hope who listened to the age-old words, who spoke and responded in all the right places, who accepted the cold hardness of Alexei's ring, and then proffered an equally cold cheek for his brief kiss. It was over, they were man and wife, in the eyes of the Church and the State.

Alexei was giving her some papers to sign, and the priest was smiling genially at Alexei who murmured his thanks to him. Then he looked at Hope. Was she genu-

inely supposed to add her thanks? She turned her face
away, knowing that she was trapped, remembering what
a fortress the *château* could be, hating Alexei for decid-
ing her future so ruthlessly, and Dale and Bianca for being a party to his plans.

They all returned to the library. There was no sign of
Niko, but Pierre was there, dispensing a pale, fine wine
and biscuits. Father Ignacio drank his appreciatively, and
offered them both a blessing. Pierre went with him to the
door, no doubt to drive him to the station. She heard the
distant rattle of the Daimler over the drawbridge, but
didn't turn away from her contemplation of the fire.

'I expect you want an explanation?' How casual, uncaring, almost, Alexei sounded. Her fingers curled round
the stem of the wineglass.

'Not tonight, Alexei,' she heard herself saying crisply.
'I'm far too angry to listen to it. I take it that Dale and
Bianca know all about this?'

'Just as I know all about them,' Alexei agreed in a hard
voice. 'Indeed, I am much obliged to them, because it
was they who told me of the existence of my son. If it had
been left to his mother no doubt I would have continued
to accept the charade she was playing that he belonged
entirely to someone else.'

The bitter, icy fury in his voice caught her attention
and Hope turned toward him, pride wanting her to explain why she had not told him, but her attention was
caught by a framed photograph on a low table. It was of
her and Niko, and with a sense of unreality she recognised the torn cutting from the magazine.

'Bianca sent it to me,' Alexei told her curtly, watching
her face. 'Nothing else, just her name and address and
that cutting. I flew straight over to see her, and she and
Dale told me the whole story. How could you do this to
me, Hope?' he demanded bitterly. '*Mon Dieu*, I thought
I knew all there was to know about revenge, but this...'

'I didn't do it for that.'

'No?'

'No.' Hope told him firmly.

'Then why? Why keep the existence of my son from me? Why refuse the support you must have known I would give you? Dear God, Hope, do you really prefer to bring him up alone, rather than with me at your side?'

'Yes, if having you at my side means a marriage without love,' Hope said bravely. 'Why do you think I didn't tell you? I knew what would happen if you found out about Niko.'

'Our marriage might be without what you term "love",' Alexei drawled with one of the lightning changes of mood that always surprised her. His eyes had darkened as they always did when his emotions were aroused, his mouth compressed in a hard line of bitterness. 'But there is *something* between us, Hope. Niko need not be a child alone.'

'No!' Her denial of what he was suggesting was sharp and firm. 'No, Alexei, you might have forced this marriage on me, but there will be nothing more. You've got what you wanted. You've got your son, and now in return please allow me my right to choose my own way of life.'

He had his back to her, and in another man she might have taken the bowed shoulders as a gesture of pain and defeat.

'Very well, but if you ever try to leave me, Hope, you will leave without Niko.'

'I should like to go to my room. I'm tired. It's been a very long day.'

'Very well. I told Pierre to prepare a room you could share with Niko for tonight at least.' His mouth twisted with wry self-mockery. 'Although I must admit I had other plans for the future.'

'You surely didn't expect me to fall into your arms with cries of gladness,' Hope demanded brittly. 'I'm not a complete fool, Alexei. Why, if you thought I might welcome this marriage, was it arranged with such secrecy?'

'Not welcome perhaps, *mon petit,* but I must confess I had not expected such bitterness. You know what manner of man I am, you have already admitted that you knew what my reaction would be when I learned about Niko. If I had to take the steps I did to ensure that my son receives his proper birthright, then which of us is the more to blame? In punishing me by denying me my child, you are also punishing Niko, whom you proclaim you love.'

Alexei always had known how to manipulate an argument, and she was in no mood tonight to do battle with him. He had outmanoeuvred her, it was as simple as that, and her mouth compressed in unusual bitterness as she remembered the part Dale and Bianca had played in helping him.

'I have a letter for you from your friends. He never was your lover, was he, Hope?' How frighteningly easily he had followed the direction of her thoughts.

'No,' she responded shortly, taking the sealed envelope.

'I have not opened or read it, if that is what that look is supposed to signify. They are *your* friends, Hope, motivated only by a desire to help you and they seem to think that both you and Niko are better off here with me.'

'I'm tired, Alexei, I'd like to go to bed.'

'Of course. If you will follow me.'

They were as polite and distant as strangers; the same atmosphere between them that Hope had felt between other warring couples, an intimate bitterness which she shrank away from.

'You are in here. Pierre has fed Niko.' Alexei opened a door and switched on the light. The room was large and airy, furnished with the delicate Empire furniture she loved, the door to a small dressing room stood open and she could make out the outline of a cot.

'When you are settled in we shall go shopping and buy whatever Niko needs.'

'Niko already has everything he needs,' Hope told him proudly, unprepared for the sudden tightening of his features, the biting anger glimpsed distantly in his eyes.

'He is my son,' he swore softly, 'and you have denied him to me.'

As though their quarrelling disturbed him, Niko woke up and started to grizzle. Alexei reached the cot first, lifting him out, seating him on his lap as he sat on the bed, studying him intensely. Green eyes looked into green, and Hope found that she was holding her breath, a curious tight pain locking round her heart. Alexei touched Niko's cheek with his finger—reverence, wonder, awe, and a thousand other emotions nakedly betrayed in his face. 'My son . . .'

Suddenly Hope wanted to cry; for the wasteland her life would be, for the poverty of emotional commitment she would find in it, for the uselessness of loving Alexei and the sheer impossibility of stopping doing so. Even now, when she was bitter and angry, he still had the power to move her emotions as no other man ever could.

'He's very like you,' she murmured inanely. 'Dale and Bianca both think so.'

'On the contrary, *mon petit*,' Alexei surprised her by saying, 'he is very like *you*. There is that in his eyes that reminds me that you have much to blame me for and little to praise. Oh Hope, can you really not understand how it feels to know that you left me, bearing my child, seeking refuge with someone who was almost a stranger rather than turning to me for support?'

'Perhaps if we hadn't had that quarrel, I might not have done so.' She moved hesitantly round the room, touching the furniture, unsettled by his references to the past. 'You had made it plain to me, Alexei, that there was no commitment between us. I have my pride too,' she reminded him wryly. 'I knew of course that you would provide for us, I even suspected then that you would insist on marrying me, but can't you see, I didn't want to lean on you, I didn't want to be weak. I wanted to prove to myself that you were right when you told me I had the strength to forge my own fate, and besides there was still a chance then that you could marry Élise.'

She had her back to him, and didn't hear him until he was right behind her, spinning her round with hard hands, his mouth curling tautly. 'Élise?'

'Yes, I knew you were in love with her.'

He frowned and seemed on the point of saying something, and then shrugged. 'You wanted to rest. Go to bed, Hope, let the future take care of itself. It is done now, and for Niko's sake both of us must learn to live with it.'

She woke up with the sun streaming through the curtains she had neglected to close, beautifully warm beneath the duvet, her mind and body still drugged with sleep. Bianca's letter lay on the nightstand by the bed and she reached for it, slitting open the envelope and extracting the close-written sheets.

It was almost like listening to Bianca speak. It had been her idea to send Alexei the photograph, she explained. She had felt justified in doing it because, despite all Hope's arguments to the contrary, Bianca could not see why she shouldn't marry Alexei.

'If he hadn't responded, we would have left the matter there, but he did. He flew over and rang us from LA, asking us to meet him. We told him everything, Hope... everything bar the fact that you love him, honey—we wouldn't do that to you. Try not to be too angry or bitter. Dale and I both acted for the best. You love him, Hope, and without him your life is empty. Forget your pride—take what life offers and try to forgive us.'

She got up, dressing Niko and taking him down to the kitchen for his breakfast. Alexei was already there drinking coffee. He was dressed in jeans and a cotton shirt. 'We're expecting heavy rain,' he told Hope as he stood up to pull out her chair, 'so we're trying to get the rest of the harvest in before it comes.' Pierre mimed breakfast to her, and Hope nodded her head. 'Bianca gave me a long list of the stuff you have for Niko, it's all in that cupboard over there. Pierre has even managed to root out an old high chair Tanya and I must have used.' It was beside the table and Hope fitted Niko into it, smiling as he banged vigorously on the wood with a spoon. While Pierre was preparing her breakfast she made Niko's. He ate it enthusiastically, mouth open, eyes like saucers fixed on Alexei.

'I'll be gone most of the day,' Alexei told her, 'but I should be back in time for dinner. If you leave and take Niko with you, Hope, I'll get him back and I'll keep him.'

She knew he meant what he said, but there was no point in leaving the *château*. They were married now and she was tired of struggling against fate. It was so much simpler to allow herself to be carried on life's tide.

When Alexei had gone she took Niko into the library and let him play on the floor while she phoned California.

'Hope.' Bianca's voice sharpened with anxiety. 'Honey, have you forgiven us?'

'I'm not quite sure, but I thought I'd better let you know I'd arrived. We were married last night. Very dramatic, and extremely effective. I wish you hadn't done it, Bianca, but I think I can understand why you did.'

'He does care about you, Hope, both Dale and I think so.'

'Caring isn't loving,' Hope reminded her, before she hung up. Caring was a whole world away from loving.

Alexei returned as he had promised just before dinner. They ate together in silence, Alexei looking tired and strained, Hope noticed, perhaps because it was the time of the vintage.

That first day set the pattern for their lives together. One month slid into two, and Hope only saw Alexei at breakfast and dinner. Niko was growing fast, already walking, and Christmas was ahead. Alexei had taken her into Beaune twice, shopping, and Bianca had packed and sent on nearly all her clothes. She still hadn't come to a decision about what she should do about her house. She was reluctant to sell it, but when she discussed the subject with Alexei, he was curt and abrupt.

'Why do you want to keep it?' he asked her. 'A refuge to fly to when you leave me? You are not the only one who is making sacrifices for Niko, you know, Hope,' he told her.

He left her shortly after dinner, telling her that he had work to do in his study. He still hadn't left his work at eleven o'clock when Hope was going upstairs to bed. She saw the thin strip of light under the library door as she walked past, and paused, hesitating, wanting to go to him, but knowing there was little point.

But once upstairs she couldn't sleep, tossing uncomfortably in her bed, impatient with her inability to relax. They couldn't go on enduring the tense atmosphere that lay between them. She couldn't go on pretending any longer. She would have to tell Alexei the truth. The decision, once reached, made her feel surprisingly relieved. He had never been deliberately cruel to her—if she explained to him that she loved him, that that was why she hadn't wanted to marry him, he would surely understand. It would also help to clear the air between them, and she was very conscious that he still thought her refusal to tell him about Niko stemmed from some need to hurt him. She wasn't any good at deception, sooner or later she was going to betray how she felt about him anyway, so perhaps it was better to get the whole thing out in the open.

Once her mind was made up she was impatient to put her plans into action. Pulling on her negligee she headed downstairs. The light was still on in the library and she pushed the door open, coming to a dead halt as she saw Alexei. His head was bowed over his hands, weary defeat in every line of his body, and she had a compelling urge to go to him and touch him.

'Alexei?' He stiffened and turned to look at her, and Hope realised in surprise that he was holding her photograph in his hands. 'I couldn't sleep, I wanted to talk to you.'

'You look and sound about fourteen, standing in the door like that with your feet bare and your hair on your shoulders. Come inside and shut the door, Hope. What do you want to talk to me about?'

She walked towards him, tensing when he got up, the bones of his face taut and hard beneath their covering of skin.

'I could have wished you had chosen another occasion for this, little one. Tonight I am feeling acutely, vulnerable, and seeing you like this does not help. I still have a very vivid memory of how it felt to have you in my arms. If ever a man was hoist with his own petard it was me, is that not so? I started off simply intending to use you as an instrument of revenge, and in my arrogance I also thought I could play Svengali. For the first time in my life I believe I deliberately deceived myself.' He smiled and the bitter pain of that smile tore at Hope's vulnerable heart. 'But not for very long. I suspect I knew the

truth even before we left for the Caribbean, even though
I might have tried to hide from it, but when I thought you
had chosen that young boy in preference to me...'

'You were very angry,' Hope admitted wryly. 'I remember it well.'

'I was very *jealous*,' Alexei contradicted. '*I* remember
it very well, too. And it turned my life upside down. All
that I had told you, all the promises I had made, I knew
I could not keep. There was no way I could let you walk
out of my life. All the time I had told myself it was a
game; that you were a child.'

'Alexei, please don't go on, there's something I must
tell you.' If she didn't tell him now she would never find
the courage! 'I know you think I didn't tell you about
Niko as some form of punishment, but it wasn't that.
You see—' She turned to look at him, holding his concentrated gaze. If he had taught her anything it was to be
proud of herself and everything that she was; the standards he had given her were high standards, and she
wasn't going to fall below them. '—I knew before I left
the Caribbean that I loved you. I also knew that you
loved Élise, and I thought it best to simply go. I couldn't
allow you to take responsibility for me, Alexei, you must
see that? If there was anything I had learned from you it
was to cherish my self-respect. How could I have kept
that, knowing that you had married me to protect me?
Out of pity, when what I wanted was your love.'

'And now.' There was a curious tension about his
downbent head, angled sharply away from her so that all
she could see was the strong dark column of his neck
above his open shirt and the thick crispness of his hair.

'Now?' She was genuinely puzzled, wary as a cat in a
taut atmosphere, starkly at odds with the deceptive air of
detachment he seemed to create around him.

'Yes, *now*, Hope. How do you feel now? Am I to understand that you no longer consider yourself "in love"

with me; that like a bout of chicken pox, the infatuation is over, a necessary part of growing up; an adolescent ailment from which you have emerged—a woman?'

There was mockery in his voice, and something else she couldn't define. How could he deliberately hurt her like this, mocking her disclosure, treating it and her as he might a dense child?

'No, you are not,' she retorted explosively, anger rapidly taking the place of pain. 'I'm sorry if it doesn't accord with the way you planned things, Alexei, but the way I feel about you isn't some childish ailment from which I can recover after a couple of days in bed, and...'

'Oh, I don't know...' The suave, almost amused tone of his voice caught her off guard and for a moment she could only stare at him, not comprehending his meaning. 'It sounds to me as though a couple of days in bed— at least—is exactly what should be prescribed for your ailment.' His voice had dropped an octave, and was softly persuasive, feathering unignorable tremors of responsiveness across her nerves. 'Provided, of course, you share them with me.' He saw her face tighten and, anticipating her anger, added with an entirely different note in his voice, 'And if that is the prescribed medicine, I stand in far greater need of it than you, *mon petit*. I doubt if two centuries would be sufficient to stop my heart from pounding every time you're within seeing distance, and as for the ache in my body whenever I think about having you close to me—' He closed his eyes, and Hope saw that he was trembling.

'Oh, Hope.' Raw pain and wry irony mingled in his voice. 'I must have betrayed to you a dozen times how I felt about you. I was as jealous as a teenager over that boy, why else do you think I reacted in the way I did. And then later in the Napa Valley, I wanted to kill Dale, and torture you, preferably until you were begging for my lovemaking.'

'But Élise, you loved *her!*'

'Never.' He shook his head decisively.

'But I overheard her talking about it, telling someone that she couldn't marry you because she would lose her husband's fortune.'

'Talk was all it was. Élise and I enjoyed a mild liaison at one time, but it was nothing more. There is only one woman I have ever wanted to marry. When you stood up in that dining room and faced Sir Henry, told him about our relationship, I didn't give a damn about Tanya, or revenge, all I wanted to do was to protect you. You were right when you said Tanya wouldn't have cared, and equally right when you said the revenge was for me, which meant that I'd sacrificed you to the monument of my own pride. Can you imagine what that did to me? And then you left. I really thought . . .'

He shuddered, the bones of his knuckles white against his tanned skin. 'When I got your note I wanted to kill you myself. I searched everywhere for you, checked up at the airport, everything! I love you, Hope,' he said it quietly, coming to stand beside her, lifting her hands to his lips, watching her trembling beneath the brief salute, the feelings in his eyes mirroring those in her own.

'All these wasted months, when I have hungered for you until I can't sleep for the ache.' Her trembling increased and he looked at her from beneath hooded lids—the Alexei she remembered, laughter lines fanning out from the corners of his eyes.

'Did I say two days in bed might effect a cure?' he murmured. 'I think I was wrong.' He bent and kissed her, moving his lips lightly over her own, teasing her. 'What do you think, Hope, two weeks, two months even?' he mused.

She reached up towards him, linking her fingers behind his head, feathering her own lips against his in imitation of his light caress, as she pretended to consider the question. Laughter lurked in her eyes when she eventually said, 'I think I'd settle for the two days—in the first instance, at any rate.'

'Oh?' Alexei's fingers shaped the curves of her waist, and started to move upwards, her body delighting in the familiarity of his touch, responding with abandon to him.

'Umm. Just to make sure the reality lives up to my imaginings.'

'Oh, it will,' Alexei assured her positively, both of them laughing as he slid his arms round her, lifting her into them. 'But if madam really wants a sample... You realise, of course, that I can't be expected to carry you all the way up those damned stairs simply for two days? In fact I'm very nearly sure I won't be able to carry you even as far as the fire,' Alexei muttered thickly, burying his face in the side of her throat, stroking the soft skin with his lips, making her quiver with pleasure.

'Alexei.'

'I love you, Hope,' he muttered thickly. 'So very, very much. My life has been a desert wasteland without you.'

'With one or two brief oases,' Hope felt moved to point out, remembering the girl in California and the other in Cannes.

'What use are they to a man who is unable to drink?' Alexei asked frankly, understanding her allusion. 'You have forced upon me the ego-shattering discovery that need is impotent without love and desire, in the most literal sense of the word,' he added dryly. 'A very chastening experience, I might tell you! After the second occasion when I had to make my excuses, I vowed there was not going to be a third. I don't deserve you, and in many ways I know I am taking advantage of you, but I love you, Hope, and I can't let you go. Love me,' he begged fiercely, holding her tightly to him. 'Love me, Hope.'

'I do.' The firelight flickered on their faces, Alexei's taut and uncertain, Hope's peaceful and sure.

'Now you have said it, I will never let you go, you realise that?' he asked thickly.

'I shall never want you to. I want you to hold me for ever and so tightly that I'll know this isn't just another dream.'

She opened her arms to him, knowing that now they were meeting as man and woman, profoundly grateful that they had been given this chance to find one another. How Bianca would crow. A brief smile curved her lips before Alexei covered them, and Bianca and everyone else, apart from the man holding her in his arms, was forgotten, Alexei's lips softly framing the words he had once repeated to her from the *Song of Solomon*.

There will be someone for you some day of whom these words are true, he had said, and he hadn't lied. There was. There was him!

NEW YORK BLOCKBUSTER SWEEPSTAKES
OFFICIAL RULES—NO PURCHASE NECESSARY

To enter, complete an Official Entry Form or 3" x 5" card by hand printing the words "New York Blockbuster Sweepstakes" and your name and address thereon and mailing it in the U.S. to: New York Blockbuster Sweepstakes, P.O. Box 9076, Buffalo, NY 14269-9076, or in Canada to: New York Blockbuster Sweepstakes, P.O. Box 637, Fort Erie, Ontario L2A 5X3. Limit: One entry per outer mailing envelope. Entries must be received no later than 1/31/97. No liability is assumed for lost, late, damaged, nondelivered or misdirected mail. Entries are void if they are in whole or in part illegible, incomplete or damaged.

One winner will be selected in a random drawing to be conducted no later than 2/28/97 from among all eligible entries received. Prize consists of a 3 day/2 night weekend for two (Friday-Sunday) including round-trip air transportation from commercial airport nearest winner's home, two nights hotel accommodations (one room double occupancy), at the New York Marriott Marquis Hotel, and a pair of theater tickets to a major Broadway show (approx. prize value: $2,400 U.S.). Travelers must provide their own transportation to and from the commercial airport nearest winner's home; are responsible for taxes, tips and incidentals; must execute and return a Release of Liability prior to travel; and must depart and return prior to 12/31/97.

Sweepstakes offer is open only to residents of the U.S. (except Puerto Rico) and Canada who are 18 years of age or older, except employees and immediate family members of Harlequin Enterprises, Limited, their affiliates, subsidiaries, and all agencies, entities and persons connected with the use, marketing or conduct of this sweepstakes. All federal, state, provincial, municipal and local laws apply. Offer void wherever prohibited by law. Taxes and/or duties are the sole responsibility of the winner. Any litigation within the province of Quebec respecting the conduct and awarding of prize may be submitted to the Régie des alcools des courses et des jeux. Prize is guaranteed to be awarded; winner will be notified by mail. No substitution for prize is permitted. Odds of winning are dependent on the number of eligible entries received.

Potential winner must sign and return an Affidavit of Eligibility within 30 days of notification. In the event of non-compliance within this time period, prize may be awarded to an alternate winner. If prize or prize notification is returned as undelivered, prize may be awarded to an alternate winner. By acceptance of his/her prize, winner consents to use of his/her name, photograph or likeness for the purpose of advertising, trade and promotion on behalf of Harlequin Enterprises, Limited, without further compensation unless prohibited by law. In order to win a prize, a resident of Canada will be required to correctly answer a time-limited arithmetical skill-testing question by mail.

For the name of the winner (available after 3/31/97), send a separate stamped, self-addressed envelope to: New York Blockbuster Sweepstakes 4815 Winner, P.O. Box 4200, Blair, NE 68009-4200 U.S.A.

Win an exciting weekend for two in New York City at the

NEW YORK
Marriott®
MARQUIS

including return airfare and tickets
to a Broadway Show!

You and a guest could be on your way to the
Big Apple, courtesy Harlequin Enterprises
and the New York Marriott Marquis! See
Official Sweepstakes Rules for more details.

NEW YORK BLOCKBUSTER SWEEPSTAKES
OFFICIAL ENTRY FORM

To enter, complete an Official Entry Form or a 3" x 5" card by hand printing "New York
Blockbuster Sweepstakes," your name and address, and mail to: in the U.S.: New York
Blockbuster Sweepstakes, P.O. Box 9076, Buffalo, NY 14269-9076, or in Canada:
New York Blockbuster Sweepstakes, P.O. Box 637, Fort Erie, Ontario, L2A 5X3. Limit one entry
per outer mailing envelope. Entries must be received no later than 1/31/97. No liability is
assumed for lost, late, damaged, nondelivered or misdirected mail.

NEW YORK BLOCKBUSTER SWEEPSTAKES
OFFICIAL ENTRY FORM

Name: _____
Address: _____
City: _____
State/Province: _____
Zip/Postal Code: _____

KNL

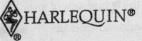

HARLEQUIN®   Silhouette®

NYTentry

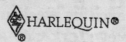 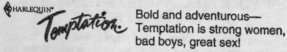
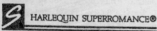

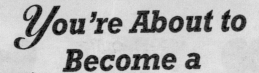

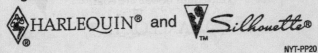

FREE VALENTINE'S BROOCH!
$9.95 U.S. retail value

This Valentine's Day Harlequin brings you all the essentials—romance, chocolate and jewelry—in:

VALENTINE Delights

Matchmaking chocolate-shop owner Papa Valentine dispenses sinful desserts, mouth-watering chocolates...and advice to the lovelorn, in this collection of three delightfully romantic stories by Meryl Sawyer, Kate Hoffmann and Gina Wilkins.

As our special Valentine's Day gift to you, each copy of *Valentine Delights* will have a beautiful, filigreed, heart-shaped brooch attached to the cover.

Make this your most delicious Valentine's Day ever with *Valentine Delights!*

Available in February wherever Harlequin books are sold.

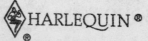

HARLEQUIN ®

VAL97